When a change in collective conscious sends the Outsiders, a group of aliens, to the shadows below the city, humans reason that the demonization of their peers is simply more "humane." There's no question, nor doubt. Just acceptance.

Lydia had embraced that sense of "truth" for as long as she can remember. The daughter of a powerful governor, she has been able to live her life with more comforts than most. Comforts can be suffocating, though, and when the opportunity to teach Outsider children in their private, "humane" community becomes available, she takes it.

What she finds beneath the city is far from the truth she had grown to know. There she meets Alessia, an Outsider with the knowledge and will to shake the foundation of all those who walk above ground. The two find a new and unexpected connection despite a complete disconnect from the technological world. Or perhaps in spite of it.

Still, it takes a lot more than an immutable connection to change the world. Lydia, Alessia, and a small group of Outsiders must navigate a system of corruption, falsehoods, and twists none of them ever saw coming, all while holding on to the hope to come out alive in the end. But it's a risk worth taking, and a future worth fighting for.

A NineStar Press Publication

Published by NineStar Press
P.O. Box 91792,
Albuquerque, New Mexico, 87199 USA.
www.ninestarpress.com

Beneath the Surface

ISBN: 978-1-947904-89-7

Printed in the USA
First Edition
January, 2018

Also available in eBook, ISBN: 978-1-947904-83-5

Warning: This book contains depictions of violence, death, racism/racist ideology, and imprisonment.

Beneath the Surface

Rebecca Langham

For the dreamers of the dreams

Prologue

ALESSIA'S MOTHER ROUSED her from a peaceful sleep. "Darling," Rey whispered. "They're coming for us. We need to move."

Alessia blinked several times, forcing the tiredness from her eyes as she looked about the dimly lit cave. Outside, an owl hooted and tree branches fought back against a gust of wind, but she heard nothing else.

"We've talked about this," her mother said, guiding her up from a nest of blankets and cushions. Alessia had never heard Rey so concerned. "You need to get moving."

"But I want to stay with you," Alessia replied. Her mother, and the reality of the situation, were coming into focus.

"I know, Lessi. But if you do, it's more likely they'll track us all down. Start down the eastern tunnel. Go carefully and try to stay as quiet as possible. You know where to meet us when they've left."

Living in a cave may not have been especially comfortable, but at least they knew their way around in the area closer to the cave mouth. Within minutes of leaving her mother's side, she felt lost, having no experience of navigating this area of the system.

Alessia slid a hand along the smooth, slime-covered rock of the cave wall. Shuffling along at a snail's pace, she played a life-threatening game of hide-and-seek. The edge of her shoe acted as a poor guide, but it was all she had to help her avoid any sudden drop-offs. A depression in the stone could be anything from a small trench to a gaping hole one could fall through for hundreds of metres. Caves were like wild animals. They could protect you, take small bites out of you, or swallow you whole. For a moment, she wasn't sure what was more terrifying: being captured, or trying to find a place to hide.

She inched along the wall as quietly as possible, until the echo of hurried footsteps brought her to a halt. Her legs felt like hollow reeds, liable to snap at any moment. *Be calm. It's just how sound works down here. The humans could be anywhere. You're safe,* she told herself, *it'll be all right.*

The footsteps faded, leaving only the steady dripping of water from stalactites. Alessia put a hand to her chest and willed her heart to slow its exhausting pace. She didn't want to pass out before she had moved deep enough to avoid detection. It took all her strength not to call out for her parents, to see if they had been rounded up, or if they'd managed to find somewhere to hide.

Get moving. She probed forwards with her foot once more.

No matter how many times she blinked, Alessia's eyes would not adjust to such thick darkness. Her family rarely ventured so deep underground, and for good reason. Supplies were scarce, reserved for passages closer to the surface, and not to be wasted in such labyrinthine zones. With no food, water, or even so much as a torch, she had to move far enough into the tunnels to hide, but not far enough to lose all hope of finding a way back out.

The ground gave way, and her leg plunged through the earth, taking her courage with it. Her arms flailed as she fell, seeking something to stop her fall, but they found no purchase. Alessia cried out as her backside hit the wet rock, her leg lodged in the hole she had fallen through.

An icy sense of fear stabbed at her chest. They'd probably heard her. With eyes clenched shut, she forced herself to take slower, deeper breaths. One. Two. Three...she counted to twenty before she let herself believe no one was running towards the sound she'd sent reverberating through the space.

Finding the ground, she pushed herself up. A bolt of pain shot through her thigh. The unpleasant sound of fabric tearing frightened her more than the warm blood gushing over her knee. Alessia bit her lip to hold in another cry.

Damn it to hell! The thought screamed its way through her body. She felt the waxy indignation of it in every muscle. She pictured her mother's face, paler than ever, as she had pulled Alessia to her just before they parted ways; a tight hug goodbye before tossing their wrist-lights to the ground. Alessia shook her head, banishing the image. Rey, her mother, was fighting her own battle somewhere else. She couldn't even hazard a guess as to why her father wasn't there when she'd been roused. She was on her own.

Alessia needed to focus on reality. It was pointless to wish they'd stayed together.

Trying to pull her leg out again might cause more damage, and then she might be unable to walk, which meant death. If she didn't, though, she would be trapped in that spot, left to her own thoughts until her body gave out. There wasn't a choice. She had to free herself and it was going to hurt.

A flash of light swept across the wall in front of her. The sudden severity of it burned her eyes and she clenched them shut. When she opened them again, two more beams of light joined the first. She had been walking towards a dead end draped in sand-coloured sulphurous flowstone. And now they'd cornered her. It was over.

"Boss! I've found one!" came a bombastic voice. "Down there. Looks like a teenager."

Heavy footsteps moved closer, dashing through puddles and navigating uneven ground. They'd found her. The human government had changed its mind about her family's freedom, as they'd been bound to do eventually, and hunted them down. Her fear evaporated with each outward breath, with each jump or sweep of the torchlights. The terrifying darkness that enveloped her had been broken, and for the moment, that was all that mattered.

"It's the daughter," said another voice, more mature than the first. Alessia glanced at the dancing beams of light, two of them growing larger and rounder as the United Earth Alliance's bounty hunters closed in on her.

Alessia's leg throbbed. She bent her elbows, leaning back to rest on her forearms. Tightness had taken hold of her body, and it brought on a manic kind of exhaustion.

Two men approached and stood before her. The older of the two, a sweaty beast of a man, took another step forwards. He bent down and examined what could be seen of her leg before dimming the light and turning it towards her. After the dense darkness, it was too bright, and she turned away.

"Well, then. Premier Abel will be pleased we found you all alive, Alessia." His voice dripped with pleasure at his own achievement. She released a soft sigh. The UEA had gone back on its promise to her family. They'd get nothing from her.

Dropping the light, he leaned forwards and rocked on the balls of his feet. Stale remnants of musky cologne made Alessia's stomach clench, but she kept her face as still as she could. Her discomfort belonged to her alone.

"It's for the best, girl," he told her. "This isn't exactly an ideal way to live, is it? In the dark. Now, let's see about getting you out of this hole." The man stood, removed a handkerchief from his pocket, and then wiped the condensation from his glistening forehead.

"You're not going to kill me?" Alessia asked, her mouth dry.

"Kill you?" he laughed. "Of course not! We're not monsters." He faced the other man. "Spray the wound and get her out of there, Mick. Let's see about taking these people somewhere safe and protected."

Chapter One

QUADRANT FOUR COLONY – FIFTEEN YEARS LATER

The projected silhouette of Lydia's figure cleared within seconds, becoming a near-exact copy of her. Only small errors in the translation of shades, as well as the stagnant nakedness of the image, gave the shape away as being a lifeless facsimile.

Air whipped around her, the cold gusts examining every microscopic detail of her body. Baseline data, they called it. Pearsal insisted on monitoring any changes that occurred during a new employee's stay. Lydia had expected to be profiled upon her arrival, and yet, forewarning didn't make it any easier to have a nude version of herself be the subject of scrutiny for Dr Levi and his technician. Though clothed, she felt as exposed as the naked hologram. It was, unfortunately, a far too familiar feeling.

Lydia knew if the scans showed the onset of any illnesses, the Quadrant Four Colony—Q4C—would put her on the next transport home. The possibility of being sent back to her father's apartment made her nervous. She needed to stay. To work.

A brief click indicated the end of the scan. Lydia pulled the zipper of her gum-leaf-coloured jacket to the top, one more barrier between herself and the medical staff. Dr Levi exchanged a few words with another man and then waved his hand across a control node.

Examining him more closely, Lydia figured Dr Terrance Levi's angular jawline, coupled with his stylish greying hair and hazel eyes, must have endeared him to many. Despite his pleasing exterior, something about the doctor's countenance made Lydia want to keep her distance.

The colony doctor pulled his shoulders back as he walked through to her side of the glass divider. The transparent door closed behind him, leaving the two of them cut off from his technician. Tucking one hand into his coat pocket, he grinned down at her. "Just crunching a few numbers, Mrs. Barrett."

Lydia rolled her eyes. "It's Ms. I'm his daughter. I'm not married to him."

"Right." His grin grew wider. "Nice jacket."

Lydia folded her arms across her stomach and re-directed her gaze to the floor.

The doctor's technician touched a control panel to activate the comm. "No anomalies have developed since the prescreen. You may now proceed. You will be met by another teacher, Jez Blumers, for your employee orientation. Welcome to the Q. Four C., Ms Barrett."

"There you have it, Miz Barrett," Dr Levi said, plainly pleased with his dramatic pronunciation. "You're all set. Come and see me sometime, yes?"

"Hopefully not, Doctor. I'd prefer to stay healthy." She flashed him her best passive-aggressive smile.

"Not all visits to the doctor have to be...curative." He smirked. "Though, there are all sorts of cures to all sorts of deficiencies."

Lydia blinked. There was no point responding. It wasn't the first time she'd met someone like Levi, a person who saw her as some kind of pop-culture toy to be prodded for their own amusement. Being in the public eye gave people a disconcerting sense of entitlement towards her, as though it were acceptable to make comments dripping with innuendo just because they'd seen her face splattered across the media.

Looking past Levi, she asked the technician, "How do I get out?"

Dr Levi smacked his lips lightly, then left the room.

A door, not even noticeable moments earlier, opened to her left, and Lydia stepped through. The air had a mild rusty quality. A Pearsal logo glared at her from the opposite wall—a familiar image—the top section of the P housed a thin slit reminiscent of a serpent's pupil. More prevalent than the United Earth Alliance flag, the logo and its associated corporation had existed long before the eradication of national borders, extending garish tentacles into almost all areas of life. Babies were given a Pearsal Rattle the day they were born. Lydia's mother had once told her Lydia had never really taken to hers.

"Are you Lydia Barrett? The new teacher?" a woman called out as she walked towards her.

She assumed her to be Jez Blumers. Lydia held out her hand and smiled. "Yes, that's me."

Jez kept her hands behind her back, though she did return Lydia's smile. "It's good to finally have a replacement for Max; he's been gone for weeks and teaching all the Outsider children on my own has become jazzin' exhausting. Oh, shit. Sorry. I didn't even introduce myself. I'm Jez."

She kept speaking, but Lydia didn't hear. At first, she couldn't pin down exactly what made Jez so unusual. The woman looked to be about twenty-seven; she and Lydia could've been born in the same year. Maybe it was her stature, her shoulders so much leaner and squarer than her own. Lydia felt she could never match the woman's confident air. It came through in the way she held herself and was emphasised by long blonde hair curling down her back and shoulders in a sophisticated sweep.

No, she thought. It was Jez's bright, golden eyes that captured and kept her attention. Lydia had known it was a common trait in Outsiders, but she'd never actually seen it before. Lydia decided she liked gold-coloured eyes, which were all at once unique and beautiful.

Outsiders, when standing next to humans, always seemed so pale, their skin ghostly white yet nuanced like alabaster. From what Lydia had seen in videos, their ears were also ever-so-slightly pointed at the top where a humans were rounded. Jez's appearance lay somewhere in between. At first glance, she seemed like a Caucasian who'd not seen the sun in quite some time, someone whose ears were simply on the angular side. Jez's expression hardened for a moment, and Lydia realised, with a pang of guilt, she had been staring.

"I gave up wearing false lenses years ago," Jez told her, as though trying to read her thoughts. "I'm half human. The important half, anyway."

An alien half-caste. Lydia hadn't realised such a thing was possible. Her father had always described the Outsiders as 'fundamentally different,' but for Jez to exist the aliens must have a great deal in common with humanity, genetically. A common ancestor? None of the histories had ever mentioned that, though.

"Well, wherever you come from, I'm glad to meet you," Lydia said, making every effort to mask her own social ineptitudes. Making new friends had always been a cumbersome task in her opinion. Doing so whilst trying to politely acknowledge the person in front of her was part-alien was a whole new level of awkward. She had a talent for saying the wrong things, so it was best to keep things simple.

Jez once again adopted the benign tone she had used earlier. "Now that's out of the way, can I show you around? I wanna finish this up before it hits six so I can make it to the card game."

"Sorry. I didn't mean to... Yes. Lead the way." Lydia was relieved her awkward staring hadn't seemed to cause irreparable offence.

Jez led Lydia down a passageway that took them to the secured doorway between the administration areas and the restricted human zone, or H-Zone, where those who worked in the colony lived. As they boarded the elevator, Lydia struggled to focus her thoughts. She was being led through an underground government colony by someone who was half-alien. Which of Jez's parents was human? What sort of situation could facilitate a human and an Outsider having sex? There were ways to conceive children artificially, but Lydia couldn't imagine anyone toying with that kind of thing. Ignoring the UEA charter regarding *Responsible Application of Science and Technology* would be a dangerous practice for anyone, government contracted or not.

As the governor of this quadrant of the planet, her father had much to say about Outsiders. It was one of the few topics the two of them discussed in recent months as she waited for her contract to begin, though it appeared he had distorted certain details. She was not surprised. He had been democratically elected to oversee a quarter of the planet, a collection of what used to be countries and states before the Fall of Nations. Though Quadrant Four couldn't be considered as wealthy or influential as Quadrant One, Damon still had more authority than most, and somewhere along the way, that authority had become more important to him than simple things like being truthful with his family.

"They weren't exactly using their imagination when they designed this place. It's cleaner than a government toilet though. I hope you like eucalyptus-scented antiseptic."

Listening to Jez as they made their way through the complex, Lydia didn't know what to make of her. Jez's drawl was unusual for someone living this far south of the equator. At times, she spoke with the same abruptness you'd expect from a SinTral Hooker. At other times, she seemed as polite as a teenager meeting their girlfriend's parents for the first time.

Jez explained that the four different sections within the H-Zone were each on a different floor. With only the top quarter of the building above ground, the whole place felt restrictive in the way that only a sterile, government-owned complex could.

Section A, found on the lowest level, was divided into cafeterias, game rooms, and an expansive gym. The vastness of the space amazed Lydia, as did the stench of stale sweat wafting from a virtual-reality leisure zone. Jez informed her that VR contact lenses didn't work down there. People had to resort to old-fashioned pod-consoles, the kind that required masks. It was a primitive system.

Jez also told her the gym was usually close to empty, not uncommon since the development of *Dietex*, Pearsal's weight control drug. Lydia was pleased because she planned on spending a lot of time in that gym. Running cleared her head far more effectively than any drug. Skinny doesn't mean healthy, as her mother always said.

"See him?" Jez directed her gaze towards a Latino man about to enter the gym, a few years older than them but somehow youthful nonetheless. He acknowledged two women walking past him with a bombastic greeting.

Lydia nodded. Why was her guide pointing out some guy?

"That's Rafe." The upper corner of Jez's mouth curled into an uneven smile. When Rafe disappeared into the gym without looking back at them, her smile subsided. "Anyway. He's nice to look at, isn't he?"

"Mmhmm," was all Lydia could manage. The question felt like a trap.

"On we go," Jez said.

On the second level from the bottom, Jez stopped in front of a door labelled *Cube 11*.

"Your very own cell. You're bloody lucky they don't make you share anymore. Two people in here would've been as suffocating as an N-C glitch." Lydia's skin tingled as she thought about the reality of a Neuro-Comm sending wayward signals to her brain, fast and relentless sets of misinformation that could completely debilitate a person. Suffocating was a polite word to describe such a feeling. Jez cocked her head as she continued. "Go on then. The lock should be programmed."

"Okay," Lydia raised her hand. The familiar spark of her subdermal marker tickled beneath Lydia's skin, working its way through her thumb towards the black, glossy pad next to the door as she touched it.

Having confirmed her identity, the opaque glass door slid open. Automated lights flickered to life, as did the climate control system, cooling the room in moments. Like the rest of the building, the walls were as grey as an antiquated revolver. A motel-style landscape painting hung on the left wall.

Regret latched onto the inside of Lydia's gut like a parasite. What a gloomy, claustrophobic place she would live in for the next three months. Moving away and teaching such a unique group of people still appealed to her, but the accommodation was nothing short of depressing. There wasn't even a private lavatory or shower. It was all communal.

Two people used to share these. Lydia found it hard to imagine. Her father may be a large part of the reason she needed to leave New Sydney, but still, she owed him some thanks if he changed the accommodation system down here. It might have been nice if they'd added some artificial windows, though.

The far wall was coated with a clear layer of glass that rested atop a foundation of indium tin oxide. It was Lydia's only means of accessing the Hive. A disc protruded from the top of the glass panel, allowing for the projection of interactive holographic data. Remote access to the Hive, the UEA's worldwide virtual environment, had been cut off the moment she stepped on the transport. The rules of virtual connectivity that existed elsewhere did not apply in a place subjected to such strict security protocols. How sad it was that a wall of circuits was her only connection to the world beyond the complex.

"You can get any information about the Outsiders you'll be working with through the colony network, though it won't let you save or send any of that data, obviously." Jez wandered around the open-plan living space, opening empty drawers and then closing them again. "You'll also find the approved lessons and activities. Double-check those before you do anything with the kids. The 'teacher' title is a bit generous for what you and I do here. Let's consider it more as structured babysitting. Alien babysitting."

Lydia knew as much already. Teaching human children wasn't much more than that either, not now that the Hive, a seemingly limitless virtual world, allowed for a ratio of one teacher to every five hundred public students. Education had been completely streamlined since the Fall of Nations. A devastating pandemic like the one preceding the breakdown of national borders managed to bring with it a whole host of consequences, even the kind that resulted in a complete corporate take-over of education systems. Everything from teacher training and student testing to resource management and funding was managed by Pearsal.

Jez leaned over the bed, pushing her knee into the mattress. "It isn't the most comfortable bed, but I've seen worse in some of the other cubes."

"I'm sure I'll make do. I don't always sleep well, anyway."

The corner of Jez's mouth curled into a half smile. "Not needing much sleep might make your life easier. I think you've got noisy neighbours."

Lydia paused for a moment. Jez was right. Beyond the light, rhythmic buzzing of the ventilation system, voices from the rooms to either side of hers could be heard through the walls. "Maybe I'll hear some good gossip," Lydia quipped.

"I bet. We can't even stream Living Blogs in here. People have to amuse themselves, somehow."

The tips of Lydia's ears burned hot. Was Jez suggesting the H-Zone was basically a hotbed of sexual activity? She hoped not. She wanted to keep herself well and truly away from trouble during her contract term.

They continued their tour of the colony. Long-term employees had larger studio apartments decorated with washed-out pastel colour schemes. Jez pointed out that those rooms included double beds, twice the storage space, a small lounge area and a kitchenette.

"Mine is Studio Seven. If you need anything, just come find me." The lack of enthusiasm in Jez's voice told Lydia the offer was an empty one.

"Do you do much cooking in there?" Lydia searched for a topic that would allow a less one-sided conversation.

Jez responded with a shake of her head. "No, why bother? There's a perfectly good AI chef in the cafeteria."

"Makes sense. I just thought, maybe that man you pointed out, Rafe..." She regretted the comment immediately. Jez's interest in him seemed obvious earlier, but Lydia knew better than to make assumptions about people's relationships. Interactions between two people were so rarely what they seemed to be on the surface.

"You thought what?" Jez raised one eyebrow. "We cook together or something? A little holo-lit dinner?" Jez's eyes flashed, and her pale cheeks darkened.

"I suppose, yes. That is what I was thinking," Lydia said.

Lydia's grandmother would've described the silence that followed as being as awkward as a stain on a toilet seat. Her father would've just described it as awkward.

Jez drew in a long breath. "Listen, that's about all there is to show you. You've already seen the top floor where the transports come and go. There are also a few offices for the management types, as well as a medical centre, canteen…the usual."

Lydia was relieved. She had no talent for recovering from such a *faux pas*. "Thanks for being so helpful." Lydia hoped keeping her responses simple would prevent any further social missteps.

Jez arched her chest and shoulders upwards, drawing in a breath. The tension in her face started to subside, and she spoke again, her tone amiable once more. "There's a bunch of us who play cards sometimes, if you want to come along. You should see Rafe shuffle; he's a pro!"

"Cards? As in, real cards?" She didn't think anyone played games like that except through a holo or a Hive tablet.

Jez came as close to laughing as Lydia had seen so far. The woman's disposition changed faster than the East Australian wind outside the compound.

"Yeah. Real cards," Jez said. "We had a bit of an accident one time with a holo-pro and a bottle of vodka, so we decided it would be safer to just avoid any expensive repair bills in the future. The group changes every now and then, but tonight there's about five of us. We meet in Games Room Three if you wanna tag along."

"Sounds great, but I think I'm better off just unpacking some things and having a look through what I'll need for Sunday morning. I'll find my way back to the elevator. Enjoy the cards!"

"Hey, no probs, Lydia. Get to know your own space a bit. Just. Well, maybe think twice before telling everyone what your last name is, okay?"

Lydia was unable to hold back a soft groan. "Surely no one cares. There are no journalists following me around down here."

"Some folks might think you're flashing the Barrett name about to try and get special treatment or something. Best to keep it quiet if you can. Just trying to be helpful." The statement seemed insincere, but they'd just met, and Lydia had no desire to call the woman on it.

"Yeah. Thanks," Lydia replied. "I don't know that I'll be able to keep it a secret if anyone in here has ever watched a feed. There were always cameras following me in New Sydney. But I can try not to draw attention to it, of course."

"You do that," Jez countered.

Lydia's first thought was to put her hand out again, but then she remembered Jez's reaction the first time and waved instead.

LEADING THE WAY to the O-Zone two mornings later, Jez's thick blonde curls swayed as she walked. She was taller than Lydia had realised on the night of her arrival. Even with muskin ankle boots on, Lydia was still shorter.

Being underground in the cool air helped prevent Lydia from melting into a nervous puddle of buttons and synthetic denim threads. Curiosity had kept her awake all night and, just as she was about to leave the H-Zone, her eyelids wanted nothing more than to close.

When they reached the far end of the umbilical passageway, Jez nodded towards the glossy plate beside the door. Lydia pressed her thumb against it, but rather than the gentle tingle she expected, her thumb burned hot. "Bloody hell!"

Jez shook her head. "Sorry. Those morons didn't extend your security clearance to this end. If we tell one of the protectors inside, they should be able to fix it all up." She reached out and triggered the door.

"Here we go, the Quadrant Four Outsider Colony." Jez spoke as though reading from a well-rehearsed script, her eyes fixed ahead as they entered.

After the near silence of the passageway, the chatter and movement inside the brilliantly lit Outsider district assaulted Lydia's ears. She couldn't see any of the Outsiders, but their voices and footsteps echoed from inside their rooms. She'd been curious about the aliens—the only aliens to have ever appeared on Earth—since childhood, but Lydia hadn't understood the depth of her curiosity until that moment. It swelled inside her chest.

"Are the levels set out much the same as on the human side?" Lydia asked Jez.

"Sort of. There are four levels in the O-Zone, but they are subdivided. You won't need to worry about half of them. The lower level is much larger here than on the human side. For the workstations."

"What kind of workstations?" Lydia said.

"Production floors," Jez said as she nodded at one of the guards. "Anything from nano IDs to solar power cells. The Os can make things about three times faster than human workers and use less equipment. So, having them involved increases the global production rate and lets us save renewable energy for climate control systems. Helps the big men upstairs skirt around the hefty carbon emission taxes. This might all run under government orders, but it sure doesn't hurt Pearsal's bottom line.

I bet they were pretty damned pleased to get the colony operation contracts back in the day."

"Hurry it up!" Lydia couldn't see who the protector ahead of them was yelling at. He stood in a doorway and looked inward. "Come on. Clean it up. You're late for work detail."

The protector's black straight-legged trousers, button-up shirt, and clunky boots made for an unimaginative display of authority. The bright-yellow pulse weapon attached to his belt sent an immutable message. From what she'd seen through VR, even a low-voltage blast from a Pulser would be enough to incapacitate a person.

Lydia hadn't considered the means used to keep the alien population under control. In fact, she hadn't thought about them needing to be monitored at all. Weren't these colonies supposed to be self-determining communities? A safe-haven for a seemingly problematic population? The presence of the guards, protectors, usually near a socialisation table, suggested otherwise.

As they approached another soci-table, Lydia caught her first glimpse of a female Outsider. By human standards, the woman might have been in her early thirties. Outsiders were, overall, like humans, but she wasn't sure if they aged the same way. Come to think of it, Lydia couldn't recall hearing much at all about an Outsider's lifespan. Surely it was something that had been observed and studied. Why weren't the general population aware of such details? Why hadn't she herself ever thought to ask the question before now? She dismissed the thought for the moment, preferring to focus on the Outsider woman.

Her eyes focused on a frayed novel. She seemed to be taking advantage of the fleeting peace offered at that time of morning. At least, that's what Lydia would have been doing.

The woman's deep fascination with whatever she was reading could be seen in the hunch of her shoulders and the deep lean of her chin into her free hand. With the shoulders of a swimmer, the woman seemed athletic despite her small frame. Long, straight hair fell across the Outsider's shoulders and spilled down her back like a velvety yellow cape. Her toned shape and quiet concentration all made Lydia want to stop. To speak to her. To ask her name.

Lydia took a quick hop to catch up to Jez. "The woman back there. She was reading a book. The books are supplied by humans?"

Jez stopped walking and glanced over Lydia's shoulder. "Ah, yes. Alessia's often there before work duty, reading whatever she can get her hands on." Her voice reflected a degree of passive disapproval. The Outsider must have heard her name, because she looked up, her eyes as purple and as fascinating as the Dwarf Irises her grandmother used to grow.

"I'd be careful of that one. She's got this way of getting in your head. One time, I found her sitting outside of my classroom, cross-legged on the floor. She must have been listening to a lesson or something." Jez's gaze was still fixed on Alessia. "I told her to bugger off. She did, eventually, but she just looked at me for a while first. You know? That freaky, alien expression?"

Lydia didn't reply. She struggled to seem disinterested in Alessia, but even across the distance between them, the Outsider's eyes found her own. Lydia couldn't see anything 'freaky' about her. All she saw was a curiosity to match her own. She hoped she wasn't imagining it.

Jez kicked the toe of her shoe against the floor. "I guess you'll see it soon enough," she told Lydia as they continued. "But, yes, reading is fine. If they weren't allowed to do anything, I imagine they would all go mad."

Lydia nodded, though she didn't fully understand. Regardless of small freedoms, the place felt like a prison.

"Most of the books are just old crap. They're left over from before the Hive Archive System went live," Jez said. She held her hand outward to indicate their arrival at the school. They hadn't walked far at all, but Lydia's head felt explosive. There was so much to process already, and she hadn't even taught a class yet.

"The classrooms are pretty close to a lot of the living quarters. Most of the families are on this floor, a few single inhabitants. Mess hall is downstairs. They eat at set times based on the job they do."

The first thing Lydia noticed about the tiny school was the aroma. She'd never experienced a combination of scents quite like it before: aged paper, wood, and a sweet floral odour.

The school's two classrooms captured characteristics of the past that made Lydia feel at home. Watching sensory films set in years gone by, she'd often mused she might have been born in the wrong era. The nostalgic mysticism of the quaint school transported her to another realm.

"Good morning, Mistress Jez." An androgynous voice rang out from the back corner of one of the classrooms. Lydia hadn't noticed the Outsider at first; he'd been kneeling on the floor. She didn't know where to turn her attention first. Like Jez, his irises were molten gold. His hair was a tawny orange-brown and fell messily over the tops of his ears. The man's face was the colour of the moon and was smooth and hairless aside from his neat, narrow eyebrows. Lydia was tempted to reach out and run her fingertips along his cheek, just to find out what it felt like.

It just wasn't the same as seeing them—the aliens—in videos or images.

Jez squared her shoulders and one hand moved to her waist. "Peleus. This is Lydia Barrett. She'll be working in the other room as of this morning. You fixed the broken desk?" Lydia was taken aback by her tone. Jez wasn't quite rude, but she'd ignored Peleus's greeting and avoided looking him in the eyes.

Peleus turned his attention to Lydia and nodded, a smile revealing brilliant white teeth. "Mistress Lydia. Welcome. Please let me know if you find anything in this area that is out of order. It's my job to fix things," he said.

The sweetness that filled the air had grown stronger when he moved closer. It was him, Lydia realised. Was that a natural odour? Some sort of pheromone perhaps? Surely they didn't bother with perfumes in this sort of an environment.

She tried to smile back, though she could feel Jez's disapproval passing over her like a cold fog. "Thank you, Peleus."

Her colleague had started to sway ever-so-slightly from side to side as her eyes glazed over, a clear sign of impatience. Peleus dropped his chin and slipped past them, through the entrance, and out of sight.

Jez took a deep breath and seemed to return to herself. "You'll work in the left room. Did you take the course in twentieth-century teaching methods at the Pearsal College?"

"I did. I really enjoyed—"

"Okay, good. I know it's a history elective, but you'll need it. There's absolutely no Hive access and minimal use of projectors or screens. No implants. As far as the Outsider kids are concerned, we all use offline tablets, some paperbacks, two-D video and...well, I suppose you were told all this before you got here?"

"No, no, it's good to hear it again. I appreciate it," Lydia replied. Feeling brave, she spoke again. "Peleus seems friendly. He is so much more—" Her hands drew circles in the air, looking for a way to finish the sentence.

Jez interjected. "Human than you expected?"

"Sorry. I didn't mean...yes. I'm not sure what I expected, though. It's not as if I didn't know they're shaped the same as us. But his whole demeanour..."

"As long as you remember we've got a job to do and that is to keep the children calm, sensible, and busy while their parents are working on the bottom floor, then it won't really matter what expectations you had. Looks like we've got about thirty minutes before everything kicks off for the morning. Do you know what you're covering?"

Lydia nodded.

"You'll do great," Jez said. "It's good to have you here, Lydia. I know I might be a little intense sometimes, but I just say what I mean." She smiled, touching her hand to Lydia's shoulder. "You're about to teach Outsiders. Don't start to feel like one yourself."

With one last nod, Jez entered her classroom. Lydia remained in the doorway of the other room. *Shit.* In a few minutes, the place would be full of children from another planet. What had she gotten herself into?

Chapter Two

FERMI SIDESTEPPED A youngling as he walked towards the entrance of Corridor B. Eventually, the ten hours he spent fusing and testing circuits would turn his mind to pulp, but visiting Alessia gave him something to focus on during the longest part of the day.

The main artery through the floor pulsed with life. Most Outsiders had been released from work and were preparing to flood the mess hall. People Fermi knew waved to him as he passed. He returned the gesture, though he'd never felt particularly comfortable with the lumbering of his hand back and forth through empty air. It was a weird practice.

The first ten rooms along Corridor B accommodated individual occupants, with the remainder being large enough for a family of three. Alessia lived in cube zero-five.

She had been on her own since Fermi first arrived in the Quadrant Four Colony, eleven or twelve years ago. Alessia was only a teenager then, but already a pillar of arduous autonomy. The day he first met her, she was tinkering with some machine that had forgotten its purpose. Even wearing a standard-issue powder-blue uniform, she still managed to shine brighter than anyone around her.

Fermi tapped on the thick red door to Alessia's living quarters. Red indicated a single occupant lived inside, one of many visual cues that made it easier to keep track of who was meant to be where. Protectors didn't often call on anybody after curfew, but they could.

Fermi had never asked what the consequences were for breaking the rules. It didn't concern him because he had no intention of ever doing so. The humans treated his people fairly, despite what his ancestors had done. The UEA gave them life. It may have been a life underground—a life of confinement—but it was one where people could still laugh, love, learn, and most of all, be useful to the planet that provided them amnesty.

Alessia's breezy voice came from within. "Come in, Fer."

Hesitating, he grinned as he glanced at the deck of cards in his left hand. He'd had to trade fifteen meal tokens for it, but a few days without breakfast was well worth the relief from boredom. He could always trade them again when the novelty wore off. With an enthusiastic step, he pushed against the door and entered.

"Ali, look what I—" Fermi stopped talking as soon as he noticed the peculiar way Alessia was sitting. She was upright on her bed, her back leaning into the corner of the room. Ordinarily, he would expect to see her drawing in a sketchbook, reading something, perhaps meditating or stretching. Tonight, she sat with her arms wrapped around her knees, an inattentive, itinerant quality floating within her lavender eyes. The smile she gave him looked forced. After all this time, he knew if her lips did not part, there was no real emotion behind the expression.

He shut the door behind him, lay his card box on the small desk between the door and the wall, and then sat next to her. "What's wrong, Alessia?"

She blinked for what seemed like the first time since he had entered. Her vagueness faded. "I'm fine, Fermi. Just exhausted."

Her words were insincere, but he decided not to push the issue further. He never liked arguing with her. Aside from the fact he did not enjoy confrontations as a general rule, there was no winning when it came to contradicting Alessia. Even when she explicitly conceded a point, she still somehow managed to be right all the same.

"What have you got there?" Alessia asked, directing her chin towards the table.

Fermi grinned, jumping to his feet to collect the box. "This is the absolute finest deck of playing cards in the colony. With only six missing, it's going to offer an intense entertainment experience."

Alessia tilted her head pensively. This time, when she smiled, her lips parted. Fermi's back muscles stiffened and his chest expanded. Every time he thought she couldn't be more stunning, she found a way to prove him wrong. He caught himself looking at her for a moment too long, and knowing she would never look back at him the way he wanted, opened the box and started dealing the cards. It did not take long for their conversation to melt away into a comfortable silence, broken on occasion by a wild thrashing of hands towards the pile and childlike torrents of laughter.

"Fer, did you happen to see that new teacher? The human with the brown hair?" She reached forwards to claim another pile of cards.

Damn. She was kicking his arse.

"So that's your tactic, Ali? Distract me for a sec with idle chit-chat and then swoop in to claim victory?"

"Effective, isn't it?"

Determined not to let her get the best of him, he turned another card. It was a dud. Luck was against him. "No, I don't think I've seen her. Someone at work did mention her, though. Mistress Lydia's her name, apparently. Guess they had to replace that short guy eventually. The half-caste was going nuts trying to run both rooms by herself."

"Yes, Mistress Jez does seem to find it challenging to do anything outside of whatever image of normalcy she has in her head," she replied.

"This is atrocious!" He gave an exasperated sigh as she beat him to yet another pile of cards.

"Oh, come on Fermi." She raised an eyebrow as she appraised her ever-growing mountain of cards. "It isn't that bad. Remember that time you got your hands on a Monopoly board?"

He shivered melodramatically. "We vowed never to mention that again."

The door swung open. An irate teenage girl strode into the room with short, heavy steps. Her Prussian-blue work uniform was torn at the shoulders and knees, loose threads trailing along her white-grey skin. He didn't understand why anyone would do that to their clothes. He'd seen her before. Her name started with a P, that much he could remember.

The girl glared at him before turning her eyes to Alessia, whose visage remained the same, composed and hospitable. It was her neutral facial expression, the one she fell back on because she didn't have it in her to be rude. He'd been on the receiving end of that face himself once or twice.

Petra! He remembered the kid's name.

Petra crossed her arms, shifting her weight onto her left hip.

"Alessia, can I talk to you? Alone?" The girl's tone was sharper than a blade. Her manner possessed an inexplicable quality that contrasted the youthful femininity of her features. Her voice sounded as though it belonged to someone more mature, someone who had stood by and watched as the universe had grown older.

"There's nothing for us to talk about," Alessia said, her tone understanding and modulated. "I think you've probably seen Fermi before. He's a friend, and I'd prefer he stay."

Fermi kept his eyes on the teenager as his friend spoke. Petra must have been holding her breath because when she exhaled a redness that had been climbing up her neck receded.

"Please," Petra replied, her voice calmer but still firm. She seemed to be working hard to keep it that way. "You know what this is about."

"I do," Alessia said. "But this isn't the time or place."

"No. That bullshit's not good enough." Petra pointed at Alessia with two fingers. "You can't just keep shutting us up. We don't want to sit around doing nothing forever. You have to listen."

Alessia stood to meet her. Petra's eyes sat at the same level as his friend's collarbone and she had to tilt her head upwards to meet Alessia's stare. Though she never attempted to intimidate anyone, Alessia's power of spirit had a way of being difficult to withstand. She was an opaque vessel with a storm raging inside, and if you listened carefully, you could just make out the sounds of her unease, but no one could hope to truly see and understand the magnitude of that storm. Fermi was impressed by Petra's unwavering stance, her icy gaze. If she felt any inkling of the power Fermi sensed within Alessia, she was hiding her unease very effectively.

Fermi sat up straight. "Hey, if you guys want a minute, I don't mind coming back."

He was met by silence as the two women continued to eye one another. Fermi tried to sink into the wall, to make himself invisible. He would have liked to somersault through the still-open door—anything to escape the laden awkwardness of the situation. Yet, innate curiosity overpowered the instinct to leave.

"Petra, I respect you, but you're wrong," Alessia said. "I have listened. We can't talk about this right now. Go spend time with your brother or your girlfriend or just go home. But whatever you do, try to focus your energy on something other than your frustrations. Something that grounds you."

Alessia remained still, though Petra shifted her weight, leaning into one hip. It seemed her resolve was wavering.

Fermi relaxed as the teenager turned to leave. At the door, she stood for a moment. It appeared she had something else to say, her top teeth rolling over her bottom lip. She kicked at the door with the toe of her boot, opened it, and pushed her way through. It slammed behind her.

A veil of obstinate silence descended on the room. Just as Fermi started to shuffle forwards, towards Alessia, she sat on the bed and picked up her pile of cards. Placing a joker in the middle, she avoided looking at him.

"Ali. Why are you spending time with that girl? She doesn't exactly seem your type."

"Don't be ridiculous, Fermi. It isn't like that." She scratched the back of her hand. He knew she was looking for something to concentrate on. Something that wasn't him.

"Then what is it like?" Fermi asked. "She's not on the same work detail as you. She's too young to have been in the same class as you. I don't get it. That whole thing was, well, really weird actually." He hadn't noticed his last card matched hers until Alessia's hand landed on the bed with a thump. A smile pulled at the corner of her mouth. Seconds passed.

"Hang on a minute. Since when do I have a *type*?" Her frustration had melted away and her intense purple eyes softened.

He didn't want to smile back at her, but couldn't help himself. Perhaps her interests weren't as limited as he thought?

"Oh, I'm pretty sure you have a type." His tongue poked out between his teeth, teasing her. He meant nothing by it; he enjoyed their sillier conversations but, at the same time, he wished his words were not so close to the truth. The fact was, he'd known for a long time she'd never feel the same way he did. Yet he'd grown so accustomed to his longing that it had become a part of him, an unnecessary appendage he'd come to depend upon for familiar comfort.

"Well. I suppose I do have a type," she said in a disconnected tone. Her face became more serious for a moment. She shook her head as though dispelling a thought, perhaps some kind of longing even. She kept so many of those thoughts to herself. On occasion, they seeped out through whatever minute cracks existed along her exterior, but those moments were fleeting and infrequent. Her forehead relaxed, as though she'd taken charge of her own mind once more. "I quite like toned legs." She let out a short laugh.

"Oh, who would mind toned legs!" Fermi realised how easily she had managed to distract him from his questions about Petra. "You could sweet talk your way out of an execution, Alessia." She became quiet again. "Sorry, I said something wrong." He wasn't sure if he'd meant that as a statement, or a question. Given how little he knew about her past, it was easy to put his foot in his mouth.

She shook her head and wiped her forehead with her thumb. "Fermi...do you think it's the nature of intelligent life to destroy itself?"

Fermi had seen her that way before, morbidly pensive, as though she existed in two different worlds at the same time, her feet not firmly rooted in either. He never quite knew the best way to try and navigate those moments. On the one hand, he wanted her to open up to him, but on the other, he was terrified of what exactly he might discover if she truly ever did.

"Things are good, Ali," he told her, trying to drag her away from whatever capricious thoughts had pulled her from their conversation. Perhaps she did want to open up, but something about the moment wasn't right. He wasn't ready for whatever bolt of lightning she'd been about to let him glimpse. "We are alive. The humans show us mercy every single day. There's order. It's calm. We're all safe. There's no violence anymore. Whatever culture or language our ancestors brought with them is probably gone, so we won't repeat their mistakes... Destruction? It's a word we don't ever need to use."

Alessia nodded through a tight-lipped smile. "Not all destruction is violent, Fermi."

He breathed in. "Maybe we should play this again another day?"

She nodded. "Thanks for getting the cards, Fer. Bring them back, yeah?"

"Just try and stop me." He packed the deck back into its frayed cardboard box and then slipped them into his front pocket.

As he left, Fermi gave her a playful two-fingered salute. Alessia returned the gesture, and sadness crawled up his spine. If only he could find some way to bring her out of whatever strange chasm she let herself fall into sometimes. He knew some things simply weren't possible.

Chapter Three

LYDIA STRUGGLED TO suppress her surprise when she saw the boy's hand rise above his head. Four days here and none of the children had yet wanted to ask a question. They'd listened attentively, attempted each task with diligence, and followed all behavioural instructions. Inquiry, however, had been completely absent from their interactions. Lydia was from a world where most people did whatever they could to be seen and heard. Outsider children, generally, worked to go unnoticed. At least by humans.

"Rosen, you have a question?" Lydia asked.

His arm returned to his lap as the other students' faces fixed upon his.

"Yes, Mistress Lydia. This history lesson is... Well, we know we all live in the colony because our ancestors tried to destroy humanity." He paused, his eyelids blinking faster for a second. "But, why?"

"Why what, Rosen?" Lydia matched the ten-year-old's gaze. His golden eyes glowed beneath a shoulder-length mop of pewter hair.

"Why did our ancestors want to destroy the humans?"

In unison, the eyes of every student in the room moved from Rosen to Lydia. Their scrutiny passed through her in waves. Rarely had anyone considered her with such curiosity. The last person to do so was the Outsider with the book. Alessia.

The scrutiny gnawed like a woodpecker working at her sternum. Even Peleus, who'd been repairing broken floor tiles at the back of the room, stopped. He held a mastic trowel in his hand as he watched on.

Lydia focused on Rosen. "You want to know why?"

The child nodded. It took Lydia a moment to collect the words she needed, to compile the script, to remember her training.

"Your people had lost so much during the Civil War on their planet," Lydia said. Though she was reciting from a corporately designed script, the words were slippery in her mouth, as if she couldn't quite get a handle on their implications. The recount she was about to provide was somewhat exaggerated, she was well aware, but the embellishment had been justified as means to prevent unnecessary defiance amongst the younger generations who may not truly appreciate the social and physical refuge offered by their underground community. It made sense when she'd first read the notes provided to her, but now that she had to say it aloud, Lydia felt nauseous with discomfort. She tightened her core and forced her voice to remain steady as she continued. "They saw Earth as an easy way to get all that back, and they didn't care who they had to kill or enslave to make it happen." She wanted to reel the words back in as soon as they'd broken the silence. *Yes, Rosen, your people had become oppositional, even violent at times, but they never tried to enslave anyone.*

She allowed herself to look at Peleus. He surely understood she'd only given the expected response. He was still as he watched her, his expression difficult to read. She felt as though her face had become nearly as white as his. Peleus's forehead crinkled as he turned away and returned his attention to the floor. The history she knew told her the Outsiders were something of a public menace, but something occurred to her as she pondered Peleus's reaction for a moment. Was history accurate?

Lydia swallowed the dryness in her throat and looked back at the children. "Any other questions?"

A spiritless bell rang to signal the end of lessons for the day, and without a word, the students filed out of the classroom. She watched their quiet, agile movements as they made their way through the corridor, which was separated from the classrooms with a half-height wall.

Jez left her own classroom and followed behind the group, raising her chin towards Lydia as she passed the open door. Jez must have been in one of those don't-talk-to-me moods, as seemed to be the case every second day.

Lydia sank back into her chair. A two-pronged fork stabbed at the inside of her skull, just behind her eyes. Light shuffling pulled her back into reality. Peleus. He was still working on the floor. She sat upright, straightening her collar.

"Hi, Peleus. Good to see you again."

He took a few steps in her direction and then sat down behind a student desk in the front row. As he interlaced his fingers and leaned forwards, she noticed the skin over his knuckles was smoother than hers.

"Good to see you too, Mistress Lydia." He bowed his head.

"Just Lydia works well. We're both adults, after all." The stabbing behind her eyes subsided.

"Thanks...Lydia. I probably shouldn't say that in front of Mistress Jez though."

"Yes, you're right." Her eyes moved from his face to the floor. She wanted to be less formal with him, though she knew such a small gesture couldn't repair the hole forming in her stomach after what she'd said to Rosen, but it wasn't safe to forego the formalities. For either of them. "Maybe you should just stick with Mistress Lydia. Let's not confuse things."

His shoulders sank a little. "I found your lesson really interesting, just then. Do you know if anyone in your family met our ancestors, back when they invaded?" His tone was deceptively casual.

Lydia shifted her weight. She knew all too well he ought not to ask her any questions, let alone anything personal. She thought of the protector waiting at the next junction and wondered if she ought to report Peleus, but before she could think it through, she answered him.

"My father works in the government. My mother was a technologist. I'm sure their grandparents had some knowledge of it all, but if they did meet any of your ancestors, I've never heard about it." She raised her hand to the clip holding her hair in place. Pressing the sides together, she released it. Soft, ash-brown curls fell about her face, sitting unevenly on her shoulders. The relief was immediate and the remainder of her headache retreated.

Peleus watched her. No, he did more than that. He analysed her. His benign curiosity reminded her of Tane, the only friend she was truly missing from her life back home. Tane had been the one to pick her up off the floor when she'd had her heart broken, and he'd also never once judged her for letting herself be dragged into so many of her father's campaign events. Like Tane, Peleus was not looking at her through a lens, her face framed above a scrolling headline about the governor's daughter. He was searching for something.

"One of my fathers was culled." The words spilled from him as though he had to release them or suffer some painful consequence.

Lydia's eyes became foggy. She didn't know what to say. His comment had been both abrupt and chilling. "I'm so sorry," she said weakly. It felt like the most pointless statement to have ever passed her lips.

"The humans probably wouldn't have called it a cull, but that's what I think happened." He sighed before continuing. "It was about five years ago. I was twenty-five. The colony was packed to the brim. Some groups were sleeping in the corridors because the rooms were so full. They had to bring in extra protectors to manage the general traffic around the place and try to coordinate work details. Can you believe it? There weren't enough jobs for us all."

Lydia shook her head. "Jez hasn't mentioned anything about that. No one has." It sounded too maniacal to be true. The UEA was founded on principles of order and collaboration, not systematic killing. Yet, there was no dishonesty in the stoicism of his voice or the glassiness in his eyes. If it was the truth, then what the hell was Pearsal doing down there on the government's behalf?

"Lots of people supposedly got sick. I didn't see anything wrong with my dad. He was getting older, sure, but not sick. Protectors took him off to the med bay for treatment, along with others. None of them came back. They told us it was a virus that couldn't be cured—hit the older ones mostly. We should be happy we didn't all catch it, they said." Peleus's eyes narrowed slightly. "They don't even let us say goodbye when someone goes. I'm not sure how we would go about doing that, but it feels like we should. It feels like you need to do something—say something—when someone you love disappears."

Lydia tried to keep her facial expression calm, her body still. Yes, she believed it too. Saying goodbye was important. For everybody.

She tucked her hair behind her ear and pulled on her earlobe. Such mundane gestures did little to untie the knot in the depths of her stomach.

"Is this something the children would be aware of? The missing Outsiders, I mean," Lydia said.

"The teenagers, of course, they were here. But the younger ones weren't around. Some may know. As is the case with adults, certain children are more perceptive than others."

She nodded. It felt as though he were trying to draw something out of her, but she wasn't sure. "Peleus, I'm exhausted. This week has felt really alien to me." She caught herself too late. "That is, it's been challenging to take in a whole new environment and meet all these kids. I'd appreciate just having some time alone now." She avoided looking at him, though she could sense his eyes still on her. He didn't speak, but she felt he was waiting for her to say something more. When the pause became a lull, he stood.

As he shifted his body towards the door, Peleus broke the silence. "You know, if you do find yourself wanting further insight into the minds of the children, there's an engineer who lives in Corridor B. I think you'd enjoy her company."

Lydia looked up. "Why do you say that?"

"She grew up out there, like all of you, and she gets on quite well with the younglings. She's in zero-five. Her name is Alessia." With that, Peleus left Lydia alone in the classroom, the room now punctuated by hints of his citrus-like scent. An awkward combination of smells, both fruity and stale, made her stomach buzz. Though...she couldn't be sure the disturbance in her core hadn't been caused by Peleus himself and the story he'd just told her.

Lydia leaned forwards in her chair. "Alessia," she repeated. The woman Lydia had struggled to dispel from her thoughts. She'd been above ground? How could that be?

LYDIA SAT ON the edge of her bed, leaning over to remove her running shoes. Muffled voices argued in the next room. The ventilation system blew cool gusts via outlets in the floor and chased the staleness out of the air.

Lydia hadn't realised there were so many variations of the colour grey, but between the brick walls, poorly painted ceiling, and stained carpet, she'd discovered at least six new shades and hues. Jez was right. Every day she came home to the renewed scent of disinfectant.

The chron embedded in Lydia's glass wall brought bad news. Twenty-two hundred hours. She'd missed dinner in the cafeteria. It would be another two hours before the mid-watch meal. "Perfect!" With a groan, she fell back onto the bed.

The residual heat in her body after two hours in the gym seeped into the air. Her limbs stiffened as lactic acid gripped her muscles ever tighter. She lay there, relishing the dull throbs in her back and legs. Every pulsing fibre in her muscles represented the building of strength, a thought that would keep her going when a deeper soreness set in hours later.

Lydia's stomach clenched. She rose to her feet and dug out a protein porridge sachet from the trunk, along with a small bowl and a bottle of water. It was a bland but nutritious meal.

She'd better call Damon. It had been days.

"Activate Hive." A bright Pearsal logo flashed onto the glass wall, her name printed in neat bold letters beneath it. "Open a communication with Damon Barrett." A row of circular icons blinked across the screen as the computer followed her command.

His voice came through after a few seconds. "Lydia, you there?"

She swallowed the food in her mouth. She thought it would take him longer to answer. "Dad, sorry I didn't call earlier."

They chatted politely, as usual. He sounded distracted, but it was his way. She tried to picture the apartment she'd been living in less than a week before, but the feel of the place was already fading from memory. All that came to mind was her mother's face. Her mother's smile was always so full, so energetic and honest. She'd seen that smile less and less in the years before she'd disappeared. Lydia had inherited her soft curls from her mother, and something of Helen's tan Mediterranean skin as well, though her father's genetic influence had left Lydia with a lighter, sun-kissed complexion. She dismissed the image from her mind. She just didn't have the energy for another self-loathing trip down memory lane. It never took her anywhere she wanted to be.

Lydia walked circles around the room as they chatted. On her ninth or tenth lap something caught her attention—a small box wedged between the bed and the wall.

It was a book. Her brow furrowed. Had someone been in her room during the day? The thought bothered her. Should she notify a security officer? There had to be a room entry log.

Lydia slid the novel out. It had a hard cover, the dust jacket missing. Stamps inside the cover and its dog-eared pages reflected its previous life as a loaner. Library stamps reduced a potential collector's item to a piece of recycling. It had no monetary value. Why would anyone leave it for her? The cleaners would have spotted it if the last occupant had left it there, so someone had to have purposely put it there for her to find.

The front page revealed its title. *Fried Green Tomatoes at the Whistle Stop Café*. She'd never heard of it. Heck, she hadn't even held a hard copy book in years and the last time had been in a museum.

Lydia placated her father's fear of losing the next election but kept her gaze on the novel.

As she turned the book over, Lydia dropped it. It bruised her baby toe before thudding against the floor. Without a word, she leapt onto her other foot and hopped rapidly. She exhaled the pain away, put the book down, and refocused her attention to bringing the conversation with her father to an end.

When she was free of the obligatory parental catch-up, Lydia swept her fingertips across the cover of the book, wondering how many people had become enthralled by its pages. It had been well-cared for, but still, this copy must have been at least a century old, probably more. Not even synth-weave paper could resist the yellow fragility of age forever. Frustrated there was no way to solve the mystery of its origin just yet, she placed the novel in a drawer and reactivated the Hive display. It took a moment to remember the correct verbal commands; it'd been years since Lydia had needed to run a search without her Neuro-Comm. Security being the concern it was, it made sense the UEA didn't want staff using that kind of remote access, though.

Damon liked verbal communication with the Hive, which, of course, meant Lydia avoided it. She had to find her own personality, even something as simple as that.

"Computer, run an archive search." A text box opened on the screen in response. "Outsiders arrive, initial alien contact. Search."

An extensive list of articles, video footage, and academic journals filled the wall. They were only the first of a few thousand results. Lydia took slow steps back and forth, deciding what to read or view first. Some of it she'd seen before, some she hadn't.

"Activate holographic projector," she commanded.

The results of her search flew outward into the central space of the room, represented by colour-coded three-dimensional globes. Collecting the orange balls together, she dismissed them in the direction of the wall with a sweeping motion; academia she had no patience to read. Lydia held her forefinger and thumb together, touched a globe, and then opened her fingers wider. The green circle expanded, whilst the others grew smaller.

"Play," she said.

A young olive-skinned woman with braided hair appeared in the room. Her monochromatic eyes drew Lydia in as she spoke. "This is unbelievable, Billy. We're communicating with aliens! If I wasn't standing here myself, I don't think I could believe it."

The journalist was a still mast in a sea of chaos. Business suits and pointed fingers whirled around her as she spoke into a handheld microphone.

Lydia's father once explained those microphones had been unnecessary for years, but they'd become a cultural icon—something for reporters to hold that symbolised the importance of their role in society.

"It's only been two years since our best scientists cracked the theory for sending and receiving neutrino signals. Now I'm told by a reliable source that it was twelve months later when the UEA received its first transmission from these intelligent life forms."

The woman was knocked in the shoulder by an older man with a crewcut as he rushed to find whatever he was looking for in the Thracia Scientific Observatory.

Ever the professional, the woman continued with her segment. "Billy, that source tells me the government chose to keep the signals quiet at first, as there was no real way to be sure who was sending them, where they were from, and why they were being sent. Today, however, whoever these aliens are, they've come closer to Earth, and that, Billy, means video. For those of you just joining us, I am Laurel Elizabeth, and what you're about to see is history in the making."

Lydia tightened her hand into a fist and the news clip crunched back into a bubble the size of a cantaloupe. She'd heard the story already; every human knew about Contact Day.

Everyone on the planet had stopped what they were doing to catch their first glimpse of an Outsider. It had become a conversation starter with people's grandparents. Where were you on Contact Day?

The leader of the Outsiders' youthful, demure visage had appeared on screens across every continent. "Thank you, all of you, for hearing our cries." Tarpeia's first words to humanity were common knowledge. People had responded to the softness of Tarpeia's voice and the intellectual maturity of her face. Politicians celebrated her efforts in learning the UEA's language before making contact. At first, she had been communicating through indecipherable messages using English lettering, all of them less than one hundred and forty characters long.

That was thanks to intercepted signals sent from the old Arecibo observatory.

It wasn't long before the aliens' technology had brought Tarpeia close enough to Earth to find a wider variety of messages humming through the universe in English. The rest of her people took months to adopt the language, but their leader had managed to begin using it with impressive facility very quickly.

Common knowledge. All of it. She dismissed more of the icons.

Lydia's search results flashed for a moment and rearranged themselves. The more she interacted with this Hive access point, the more predictive it would become. Though, she was also conscious that the more she used it, the more of her interests she revealed to the colony security team.

Lydia selected another video from several months later. The same slender reporter sat behind a broadcasting desk next to an older man with thin, greying sideburns. Their tight-fitting, sepia clothes reflected the style of the time. About a century had passed since then. In a technological society, though, a hundred years was a very long time.

The male anchor spoke first.

"Back to the news at hand. Six months to the day after seventy per cent of the UEA population generously voted to grant asylum to the refugees, discord seems to be growing. Yet another brawl has erupted between human and alien. Today, six refugee aliens were verbally abused and spat upon as they entered a solar cell production facility. It seems disappointing, given so many of us saw the arrival of these vulnerable aliens as an excellent opportunity to put into practice the values reflected in our United Earth Charter.

"We are told by a UEA representative the group was reporting for their first day of official employment following negotiations with Discerner Tarpeia. These kinds of reports seem to be increasing in frequency, don't they, Laurel?" He turned to his co-anchor.

"That's right, Billy," she replied. "Citizens were expressing frustration about employment rights being given to the refugees. The incident turned physical when a young man threw his workman's boot, hitting an alien woman in the back."

Lydia found several similar files in the annals. As expected, nothing from the MacNay Network was available for consideration. A facility operated by Pearsal would never source content from its only real competitor.

The Outsiders had arrived as pacifists escaping a civil war, a war instigated by a charismatic but violent despot. Excitement was palpable in the weeks between that first video contact and their arrival. Humans expressed a great deal of empathy at first. Within months, however, words like 'asylum' and 'refugee' were replaced by 'interlopers' and 'intruders.'

Lydia couldn't be sure if the rhetoric reflected, or caused, the political conflict between humans and aliens. It was clear to her there had to be more to the situation—more to explain why people became increasingly frightened of the intergalactic visitors. She'd never thought to question the stories in the past. You hear the words 'overrun' and 'intruders' enough times and you stop questioning the legitimacy of their use.

At first, it was just Outsider employment that was restricted in response to public outcry. They could only work in jobs that couldn't be filled by humans. Lydia was aware low-intel synths weren't being used for as many professions back then; they'd only been around for thirty or forty years and all this had unfolded decades before.

Then alien-only communities were fast established on the fringes of cities. Medical care, education, and access to technology had all been heavily restricted in only a matter of months after the protest involving the thrown boot. Nonetheless, the voice of dissent protesting their presence grew exponentially louder. Yet, she could find no signs of retaliation from the Outsiders. They spoke out; they pleaded but never hurt anyone. That couldn't be right. Could it? There were so many gaps that didn't make sense. Inconsistencies between the news reports and what she'd been taught, as well as inconsistencies between the news reports themselves, like a poorly scripted drama with a revolving-door stream of writers.

As Lydia tumbled down the media rabbit hole, the number of negative commentaries and incidents surrounding the Outsiders increased. She tried to absorb months of fear in the space of two hours. It felt like a weighty cage had replaced her ribs. Much less information had been available to her outside the colony, and some of it seemed familiar, yet different, as though there were more than one version of certain reports.

Humans had accepted the narrative of social unrest caused by the Outsiders, and at some point, it seemed questions around the narrative dissipated completely. Nothing in the videos suggested they'd committed any violence, or even so much as threatened it. Was it simply assumed that they'd become a more serious problem eventually, so it was best to segregate them as a preventative measure?

Did the world just not care whether the establishment of the colonies was a fair response to whatever fuelled the tension between the races? Did the excitement and novelty of their arrival wear off so quickly that it didn't even matter what happened to them?

She wondered if Jez could see all this through her terminal. Or was Lydia's father responsible for the higher level of access? That didn't quite make sense either, though.

The archives thinned. Protests against the restrictions placed upon the fringe dwellers, calls to grant them citizenship, online activism—most of it trickled off.

Lydia selected the most recent Pearsal News report she could find. Maybe it would help her to make sense of it all, of how so much of what she had believed about history could be so wrong. Perhaps the Outsiders had, as she'd been led to believe for her whole life, started a conflict to wrestle resources away from the human population and she just needed to keep looking for the evidence of it. Surely the accepted narrative of history couldn't be totally inaccurate.

Laurel and Billy were like old friends to her now. Laurel's dark-brown eyes revealed nothing as she spoke, yet Lydia sensed the journalist had lost something of herself in the time she'd been covering the failed attempts at alien integration, something entirely personal and altogether irreplaceable. Lydia recognised something of that in herself; it started the moment she met Jez. "Alien refugees have been permanently relocated to remote settlements in regions not considered comfortably habitable for humans. A small asylum-seeker advocacy group has demanded a full report from the UEA government as per the location of the aliens, as well as evidence of their personal well-being. Global Premier, Clay Abel, has provided us with a comment."

Why did he give the order to segregate them all if they'd posed no tangible threat? It wasn't the content of the news reports that bothered her. It's what was *missing* from them, what everyone thought to be the truth: The Outsiders were so great in number, so inherently greedy, they would likely overrun the planet and usurp its resources. It was a plausible narrative, and so Lydia still felt somewhat inclined to believe there was a fair amount of truth in it. It's possible—surely?—that, as had happened so many times in the past, a great deal was covered up at the time, for official documents to be released later. People existing in the very thick of a culturally traumatic time were probably the least capable of objective discussion and reason.

Lydia stepped closer to the image, searching Abel's square face for revelations it refused to give. The joints in her legs groaned under the sudden movement. The Premier had met Tarpeia and other Outsiders. Did he really believe they would purposely try to displace or disparage humans if they'd not actually done so? Lydia shook her head. She barely knew the aliens. The government would have had much greater insight than she'd gained from a few exchanged looks and brief conversations.

Abel's voice was seductively firm as he spoke. "The UEA has successfully negotiated alternative living arrangements for the Earth's refugee population. The protestations of so-called advocacy groups are unfounded and unnecessary. I assure you all that peace and generosity are at the foundation of all conversations between us and the aliens. Humanity has done its part."

Lydia squinted at Abel's face. She recognised the last few words; he was referring to the United Earth Foundation Charter. *When sentient beings, which all share in the same right to dignity and protection, require help or compassion, then our united human race must do its part.* It was a beautiful idea in theory, but like most principles that relied on human altruism, there was bound to be a limitation placed upon its application.

"We are," Abel continued, "finally in a strong position as a society. We have climbed out of the rut created by poor, nationalistic management of human affairs in the past. Our resources are no longer stretched as they were immediately following the outbreak of Pax, and scientific innovation seems to have struck a balance between progress and wisdom. This solution allows us, as well as our celestial visitors, to continue along an undisturbed path."

Billy wrapped up the report; "There you have it. What do you think of it all, Laurel?"

"Well, Billy, I think a huge number of resources have already been dedicated to the preservation of this alien race. How much charity should we be expected to dole out? It sounds to me like they're happy with the outcome and we should be too. They're outsiders, after all."

The anchors signed off and the corners of the holographic image folded in on themselves until the file returned to its spherical representation.

Lydia used both of her hands to wave the icons back into the screen, returning to a two-dimensional display. She sank into her bed. Her temples thundered as her mind raced.

Why was there no real analysis of the machinery used by the aliens to get to Earth? Communities of humans were starting to flourish on other planets in the solar system, but travel beyond the Bernal Spheres near Saturn seemed impossible. The Outsiders had done it. Yet media outlets didn't seem to have demanded transparency from the United Earth Alliance, to have demanded information about what the Outsiders brought with them. *Bloody hell. It's insane.* Those information gaps had always been there, but she'd never noticed. Nobody had.

Something Jez told her a day earlier flashed in her mind, breaking through the fog permeating her thoughts. She'd noticed Lydia smiling at the class as they worked and came to see her later on. "We need to remember they can't be trusted. It's our job to protect the world from the dangers they present. When the UEA told everyone they'd keep our populations separate, no one even batted an eyelid. Everyone was so bloody relieved not to have to think about them anymore.

"We might be cogs in a fucking massive machine we can't even see, but don't let yourself get sucked into thinking they're not dangerous. There are reasons they're in here and not out there."

Without undressing, Lydia crawled under the covers, Jez's words paving a multitude of paths in her mind. Muscle soreness had fully set in and hunger returned, but sleep was the only thing that felt worth doing. She glanced at the drawer where she'd stored the novel. *Later,* she thought, and then she was asleep, dreaming of rhetoric and politics.

...to continue along an undisturbed path.

Chapter Four

BILPIN DOME CONSTRUCTION SITE - QUADRANT FOUR.

Damon Barrett had a genuine love of signing contracts. Both formulaic and complex, they required a certain finesse to ensure a favourable outcome. It was finesse he, the Quadrant Four Governor, possessed.

Arrangements with Pearsal Construction had resulted in the rapid development of the finest habitat to ever be erected on the planet. Quadrant Four was about to become host to the most comfortable living environment on the Earth.

If she hadn't died, Barbara Barrett would have loved the new world her son was helping build. SDC—self-drive car—crashes were rare, but they did happen and no one was immune to bad luck, not even Damon's mother.

"We've screwed the planet, Barb," Damon's father had told his mother. "Better stop screwing each other."

That was years ago; the day the government relocated them to an even smaller, shittier underground dwelling. A bigger family needed their old one and that was just the way things worked when a family relied on government housing, as nearly a third of the world's remaining population did. The ceiling of that dungeon was painted blue, as blue as his mother's face turned when she told his father to stop being 'so bloody crude.' That was the day he decided he would find a way to enact change—he'd enter politics. There was so much promise in a world without the old restrictions of national borders, a world scrambling to reconstitute itself after being so drastically depopulated by the Pax. He'd wanted to be part of realising that promise.

Governor Barrett turned his gaze upwards. The sun had started its retreat for the day as subdued reds and violets pushed their way towards the horizon. He blinked at the sight. The permeable membrane that engulfed the habitat shimmered in the atmosphere.

Humans would soon be living in habitats that not only protected them from extreme weather conditions but rescued them from the constrictive walls of rock and metal they hid behind in the city buildings. Here they could breathe the air and look at the sky for as long as they wanted; no longer subject to the uncomfortable whims of Mother Nature and her erratic storm systems, her fluctuating air quality. He looked back down at the ground. What a relief it was that not *every* possibility within the realm of science was considered dangerous.

If his mother had lived to see the new style of dome, maybe the worry lines that had become permanently matted across her forehead would have ironed themselves out. But she hadn't.

The singsong voice of a young engineer pulled Barrett back to the present.

"As you can see, Governor, once the land-clearing process was completed, things moved quickly. The dome is operating as it should and bore water filtration systems are in place. Now we can begin other underground works. Electricity supply, plumbing, and so forth will be underway within a fortnight."

The boy could be no more than twenty-five. After more than a decade in government, anyone whose name Damon couldn't instantly summon from memory had no more impact upon his interest than an overactive fly buzzing its way through the periphery of his vision.

"Good. It's all going well," Barrett said, scanning the area again. The region was ripe for development, but only because it had been so poorly treated by the men and women who came before him. "A few hundred years ago, no one likely believed this area could be so level, so empty." He spoke more to himself than the young man next to him.

The death of Mother Nature happened so gradually his ancestors barely heard her soft and painful cries for help. The hunt for and use of fossil fuels had intoxicated corporations, but for the natural world, had been nothing but toxic.

"The dome won't be empty for long, sir." The boy fought to match the educated formality of Barrett's speech. His struggle was evident in the awkward pause that preceded his sentences.

Barrett turned to face the young engineer, noticing a bronze name tag on his breast. Kimble! That was his name; the engineer was Sean Kimble. "No, Kimble. I imagine not."

The young man said nothing more. They walked the short distance back to the entrance to the structure. It was so quiet out that it felt as though the entire world was asleep.

Outside the entrance, a grunt—some construction worker—awaited the two men. He looked the Governor up and down, his gaze lingering at Barrett's spotless black business shoes. The grunt held out a transparent tablet. With a swift and confident gesture, Barrett held his hand over the top of it. The device searched out the nano ident-chip within his thumb and an automated voice requested verbal confirmation.

He spoke in flat tones. "Quadrant Four. Habitat construction. Stage three. Damon Barrett. Governor."

The automated voice confirmed recognition of his signature. "Stage Three is now in effect. Thank you, Governor Damon Barrett."

Barrett leaned back on his heels, his hands in his pockets. "And just like that, we can move forwards with this masterpiece. This technological marvel will house thousands of families. No benzene. No photochemical smog. No bloody hurricanes, either. Keep up the good work, boys." *And it'll be my name everyone remembers.*

He headed towards the transport that would take him home.

Midstep, a fiery ball burst to life ahead of them. Its concussive force slammed him to the ground. A piercing shriek reverberated through his bones. It felt as though he'd been hit in the chest by Thor's hammer. Barrett clamped his mouth shut and instinctively raised his arms crosswise over his face to protect from the debris, dirt, and leaves raining down on him.

Kimble threw his body on top of Damon's before the Governor could fully process what had happened. A fragment of steel the size of his palm, propelled by the power of the explosion, embedded in the top of Damon's bicep. The pressure in his arm asserted itself with each pulsing beat of his heart, but there was no pain. He was numb.

Damon opened his eyes but the cloud of dirt made it difficult to see. He peered through the dust that had been violently sucked in towards where the ground transport used to be. A crater had taken its place.

Kimble's shallow breaths hit the Governor's face. He felt like dead weight, making it difficult for Damon to move. At least the kid was alive.

He braced his elbows against the ground and pushed upwards with a moan. The numbness was fading. After a few more tries, he managed to push Kimble off his chest. The engineer hit the ground without a sound. Damon's sense of hearing didn't seem quite right, as though he were trapped inside a soundproof bubble.

He sat up and turned his head from side to side, massaging his neck just behind his ears. The thick silence made way for low, muffled voices as he leaned back on his hands.

"Sir! Sir! Argh. Governor?"

Damon nodded, his neck cracking as he did. It was his first real response to Grunt Number Two, who seemed to have come from nowhere.

"Yes. I hear you," Damon said. "What in fiery hell happened?"

"An explosion, sir. One of the transports went off." The security agent, or Grunt Number Two as he was also known, slipped his hands beneath Damon's armpits and pulled upwards. A ring of electricity shot through Damon's arm, fresh blood oozing down his forearm. Damon groaned but willed himself to push up through the balls of his feet.

"Are you injured anywhere else, Governor Barrett?"

Barrett shook his head. "No."

The agent pulled an oxytocin-med bottle from his satchel. A few sprays later, the bleeding stopped. Damon brushed some of the grit away from his pants and jacket. His hands shook, despite his best efforts to stay collected.

"If you're fine, sir, I'll check on Kimble now." The UEA security agent's voice rang just enough to suggest he may have been asking permission, rather than making a statement.

Barrett looked down at Kimble, who hadn't moved from where he'd hit the ground.

"Yes. Go ahead." His own voice sounded foreign to him, distant. Did they need to check with him about every little thing? *Just get moving, people.*

The governor took the opportunity to inspect the scene now the dust had settled. The obliterated transport had been parked outside of the dome, fortunately, and so the habitat seemed to have escaped injury. Grunt Number One had not been so lucky. The man, who had moments earlier facilitated Barrett's approval of the next development stage, lay on the ground several metres away. Part of him did, anyway. Barrett didn't intend to inspect the body closer, but the missing leg was obvious.

A windmill turned in the bottom of his stomach. He covered his mouth and breathed deeply through his nose to fight off nausea.

His leg twitched. He was grateful it was still attached.

"Agent. Are we clear to leave yet?" Damon asked, still looking towards the employee who would never get to go home again. The sight mortified him, yet he found it difficult to focus on anything else.

"Kimble's definitely unconscious, Governor. I've called in a Medi-Copter. It won't take long, sir." The man's voice sounded as though it came through a foam wall, but Damon could make out the words.

A splintered log rested on the ground nearby. He shuffled over and sat down as slowly as he could manage. The muscle in his arm throbbed as the pain of his injury finally asserted itself.

A sigh escaped from somewhere deep inside Damon's rib cage. *Fantastic. Another incident for the media to sensationalise.* Thinking of the damage control that lay before him, he shook his head.

There were only two likely possibilities. N-C addicts got antsy every now and then. They were always making demands for cheaper broadband access or wider coverage. Somehow people had gotten the idea it was a human right to get online without a console. The Hive was a product, like most things. People paid for it or they didn't use it. The hardcore addicts, who'd all but given away their existence in the real world, didn't seem to understand.

If it wasn't the addicts, it would be those bloody Green Hats. They considered themselves ideologists. Really, they were a bunch of ignorant fools. They had no idea what it took to keep humanity united under the Alliance, what it took to ensure scientific progress was both fruitful and controlled. The group had already made their opposition to Barrett's stance on government regulated bandwidth very clear. Now he thought about it, should his people find any evidence of their involvement, it would finally give him the justification he needed to lock up the GH leaders.

"Governor, the Medi-Copter will be here in three minutes. Are you sorted for travel?"

"Hmm. Yes, I'm ready."

"Do you want to go to the clinic, Governor?"

Damon looked down at his arm. Staring at the wound was, much to his surprise, a good distraction. The crumbs of grit floating in globules of dark-red blood were far less disturbing than the lifeless, torn body of a member of the security team that lay metres away.

He considered pulling the debris out himself, but it looked as if it was deep. "Yes, I should. Let's make it quick, though. I'm dying for a drink. The kind that bites."

DAMON'S HOME WAS twice the size of the one he'd lived in with his parents. Whilst his mother and father had spent their married life sharing a single bed, Damon and his wife, when he still had a wife, had been able to stretch their legs out at night.

Helen and Lydia, his wife and daughter, had shared the space with him for so long he'd thought living alone may become deathly dull. But in the days since his daughter moved on, he felt freer, as though the air were cleaner and more refreshing than before. Though, the memory of his wife lying on her stomach atop their bed with a paperback novel in her hand still made him smile.

"Shh. Not yet. I just need to finish this chapter," she would tell him when he tried to recount some meeting he'd been to. She'd look up at him, a universe floating in her eyes. Helen had to have been one of the few people left alive to actually enjoy the feel of paper beneath her fingers.

Bright pearl lights willed themselves to life as Damon stepped inside the studio apartment. He kicked his muddied black shoes behind the doorway and lifted his pinstripe jacket onto a hook on the back of the door. He rubbed his brow for a moment, pushing away the tiredness that lived there like a parasite.

A holographic projector whirred as it formed the image of a cascading waterfall against the wall behind his king size bed. He saved the Wentworth Falls holo-duplicate for Monday evenings. The constant motion of the water helped quiet his mind, a mind which seemed perpetually trapped in an unforgiving maze labelled 'things to do this week.'

When zipped, his business shirt appeared seamless against his wiry chest and stomach. After unzipping it, he scrunched the shirt into a ball and threw it into the garbage chute. Covered in sweat, blood, and dirt, with one sleeve ripped away, the garment was useless. He felt much the same.

A blinking amber light asserted its presence. "Hello, House. Open food tray."

The voice of his wife spoke back to him. "Hello, Damon. As requested, zucchini pasta accompanied by a creamy white sauce is now ready for you."

Damon's daughter hated hearing her mother's voice recycled by the apartment software, but with Lydia gone, he'd changed it back over from Generic Gina. He may not have been able to touch Helen's face anymore, but he could hear her voice every day. Damon had loved Helen with the same kind of possessive passion with which a florist loves flowers. She would stay his for as long as possible.

Barrett tapped his toe against a black plate low on the wall. A panel sank backwards and off to the left. A retractable table and two stools moved forwards, each one opening outward like a fan. The area he had previously been standing in was now crowded with furniture. He sat down to eat, needing to first take a moment to simply stare at the wall—to make the world stop spinning. The heavy silence of the apartment seemed unsettling after the orchestra of wheels, bells, and alarms at the clinic. When the clanking inside his head quietened, he ate.

Most 'fresh foods' were now cloned from DNA samples collected two or three centuries ago, or from artificially pollinated crops made possible by the Pearsal Agricultural Division. Drastic changes to insect populations around the globe had brought unforeseen consequences. He could access a variety of tastes, making Barrett was one of the privileged few.

As he finished the last of his pasta and took another sip of Drummead, the house computer again mimicked his wife's voice. "Damon, you have an audio-only call. It's Lydia. Would you like to accept?"

He hadn't heard from his daughter since she left for a new job over a thousand kilometres farther inland. It was only a thirty-minute trip via air transport, but the inhospitable space between them was absolute.

Barrett swallowed and tapped the side of the glass with his hand. "Yes. Put her through." A moment passed. "Lydia, are you there?"

"Dad. Sorry I didn't call you earlier." Lydia's voice still surprised him sometimes. He half expected the high, lyrical tones of a ten-year-old to come through the line.

"No concern here. I'm sure you've been busy over the last week. Your first time working in an Outsider Colony... There's much to absorb, no doubt." He took another sip. The sweet liquor spiced with imitation honey warmed his core. He stood, touched his foot to the panel once more, and stepped to his right, allowing the dining area to retreat into its narrow burrow.

"I know that sound. Just finished dinner, did you?" He'd known she was likely to call sometime soon, but wished she'd chosen another day. He was too tired for this.

"Zucchini pasta with white sauce. You?"

"Protein porridge. I have no idea what flavour it was supposed to be. Mucous? Bile? It's hard to be sure." He could hear the smile in her voice. She must have missed the staff meal time to wind up eating something like that.

"Sounds wonderful," he chortled. He had a bandage around his arm and images of a man's dismembered body in his head, but here they were, talking about porridge. "How are you doing in there? The job?" He pulled a nightshirt over his head as he listened to her response. Damon's injured arm felt heavier than usual, but aside from that, the Med-Tech had done a good job as the pain was inconsequential.

"I'm okay. It's strange being surrounded by concrete, brick, and metal every single hour of the day and night, but it doesn't bother me too much...yet. The job is fine. I have zero input into the curriculum, but that's not surprising."

Barrett thought she might be holding back some important detail or other. Open dialogue had never been a characteristic of their relationship, but he could still tell when his daughter was being less than forthright. Though, this was typically the case about fifty per cent of the time.

"Hmm. At least lesson preparation is an easy task. What are the locals like?"

"The Outsiders." She paused for a few seconds before continuing. "They're not what I expected." Her voice wavered. "The children are very quiet, so they barely speak during lessons, but the other teacher says it's not a sign of obedience or respect, but rather apathy. It's only been a few days, so I'll see how everything goes. You doing well enough, Dad? Election preparation under way?"

"Absolutely," Damon said. "We're eight months out, never too early to begin a campaign. In fact, it starts the day after the last time you're elected."

"I know, I know." She laughed for a moment, but the sound lacked genuine sentiment. "You've won the last three elections, so I don't think you'll have much trouble."

"True. The last two were uncontested though. There's a young guy in the running this time; Elijah Grant." Barrett poured another half-glass of Drummead, returned the bottle to its shelf, and sank back on his bed. Three pillows kept him propped up, the glass resting comfortably between his abdominal muscles.

"So long as you keep your corporate sponsors happy, I doubt he'll be able to garner the same publicity you can." A thud in the background rang through from her end of the communication; he considered asking her what it was, but didn't. The answer was unimportant.

"You're right. With me here and you there, they can't doubt our family's dedication to stable governance." When she didn't respond, he continued. "I've got plenty of work to do here, and I'm sure you're still settling in. I'll be out there for an inspection soon, so can I look out for you then?"

There was no reply for a moment. He tried to picture the room she was in, the one he had sent her to, under the ground and miles away. Though he'd been in the colony many times, he just couldn't imagine her there.

"Sorry, Dad. I was nodding at you then. I forgot this was an audio-only line." She laughed. "Absolutely. Come and see me when you're here." The line cut off unceremoniously, as was usually the case when Lydia called. Neither of them possessed a talent for goodbyes.

Barrett rubbed his eyebrows. He lay there for fifteen minutes or so, letting the scotch work its way through his body until his limbs softened and his breath deepened. Tired as he was, sleep seemed ill-advised. There was no telling what he might see should he let his eyelids close. He wasn't ready for flashbacks of the day's carnage, nor was he in the mood for the dream where his mother told him what a disappointment it was he didn't get the dome built sooner.

He swung his legs over the side of the bed. The chron in the upper right-hand corner of the holographic waterfall indicated 22:18. "Switch off the Falls, House. Open a Hive line through the holo."

"Certainly, Damon. Please identify your destination."

"SinTral, House. Open up SinTral Video Chat." As the holographic display flattened to a two-dimensional representation of his search parameters, Barrett started to undress once more.

Chapter Five

"ARE YOU INTERESTED in history?" Rafe asked Lydia as he offered her another drink. She couldn't remember if it would be her fourth or fifth, but as she had no place else to be, she accepted it.

"Yes, I suppose I am." Lydia shouted so she could be heard over the music. There were at least thirty people crammed into the rec room for an informal party. She would rather be in the gym or even alone in her cube watching a movie and doing nothing, but as a new arrival, she ought to make an appearance and try to be social.

Rafe grinned at her. "I'm a disease buff."

"A what?" Lydia must have heard him wrong.

Rafe laughed and dropped his eyes to his glass. "Yeah. A disease buff! I find most history as boring as a silent movie, but diseases? That shit's interesting."

"What do you find so fascinating about diseases?" The music had stopped just as she blurted the word 'diseases.' Half of the room turned to look at her. For a moment, she felt like a rodent caught in a trap, squirming in front of an audience that refused to remove the latch. Having grown up as a Barrett, it was a familiar sensation.

Rafe gave her a sympathetic half-hearted salute. The next song started, the volume, fortunately, a little lower, and the group returned to their drinks and flirtations.

Emerging from the crowd, Jez squeezed onto the lounge between Rafe and Lydia. "You two look way too serious." The glass in Jez's hand was full to the brim and dark brown liquid sploshed out as she moved.

Lydia took a sip of her Drummead. "Rafe was just about to explain to me why the history of diseases is the best kind of history there is."

"Hah! Rafe loves gruesome stories. You know, he can recite all of the..." She sounded like a proud parent more than an infatuated work colleague. Lydia found it hard to concentrate. She was drunk and Jez was talking fast. "Well, I better let him talk," Jez said, her hands falling into her lap, a ring on her middle finger tapping against her hemp-plast cup.

"It's all about cause and effect," Rafe started, his brown eyes flashing with excitement. "What else has had such a jazzin' epic impact on the course of history? Human wars? Sure, people killing each other in their millions has played an important part in bringing us here, to this world, right now." Rafe traced a manicured thumbnail across his eyebrow and took a large gulp of his drink. "But! Think about it. We ended wars with bombs and shit. Nature is a much classier act; she protects herself so much more effectively than we ever did."

"You're talking about the Paxin?" Lydia asked as she moved herself forwards on the seat. Her butt was starting to go numb.

"Well, yeah, the Paxin. Best example, but not the only example. We build all this big, fancy machinery and celebrate our own splendour. Then this tiny, microscopic thing comes along and none of the machines mean a thing. We're still just animals, right? Cause: that disease killed off billions of people. Effect? National borders can't stand up anymore; we've all got to cooperate and get over our shit. Work together. UEA. Boom!"

"He gets so excited talking about this stuff," Jez said. "He knows all of the statistics. He knows the whole sequence of treaty-making right up until the Fall of Nations."

"That kind of history is interesting," Lydia said. "But for me, it's the social side that's more fascinating than the numbers and the surface-level effect of it all."

Jez's head flopped to the side, her mouth gaping. "Well then, the governor's daughter thinks she knows everything. Big surprise."

Lydia tightened and released the muscles in her lower legs, a distraction to keep herself from retorting. Jez seemed to have a lot going on in her life. She was at least fifty percent Outsider and seemed uncomfortable with the fact—always so negative about the alien race she herself belonged to. Jez also seemed completely unaware of how physically stunning she was, putting herself down through comparisons to others, but from what Lydia could see she was also equally unaware of how antagonistic she could be. Something deep inside of Jez seemed to be broken, something personal and profound. Even being aware that there was a sadness within Jez, Lydia still found it increasingly difficult to ignore Jez's pointed remarks about her life. Perhaps from Jez's point of view, her background looked picture perfect. The reality was there were too many pictures and nothing was perfect.

Rafe wagged his finger at Jez and then let his hand fall to the woman's knee. "Now, now, come on, Jez. Let's hear her out. What's this social side of history you're talking about?"

"All right, let's take the Paxin. Disease leads to death and forces political treaties and scientific regulation. But take a few steps back. The disease seemed to start spreading through Africa before anywhere else, right?"

Rafe nodded, and so Lydia continued. "I don't know the numbers, but a lot of people died and the only response came in the form of some ineffective medical teams from the UN. It moved into Syria and Iraq and, still, not a lot of active damage control."

"Right," Rafe said. He gestured for her to resume talking.

"So, *that's* the social side. When people started dying in western Europe, North America, Australia, New Zealand, the richer parts of Asia... It wasn't until it spread to those places that any real attempts were made to try and cure it. Why is that?"

"There could be a hundred answers to that question," Jez slurred. The woman seemed determined to make things more awkward for Lydia. She didn't actually think there was any chance Lydia would make a pass for Rafe? Or Lydia expected special treatment because of her father? Jez must have seen one of the gossip channels go to town on Lydia's love life at some point in the past.

"That's the point," Lydia said, happy to explain her ideas further. "Obvious answers could be that no one saw any dollar signs behind a cure for a disease that was affecting the poor, or that the value of life was still being judged based on skin colour." Lydia spoke in a hurried voice, her words barely keeping up with her thoughts.

"But maybe there's more to it, you know," she said. The warm liquor in her stomach urged her on. "The truth usually lies beneath the surface of things. Could be some government or other wanted to use the disease to deal with the global refugee problem. Or maybe the chaos of it all provided an excuse to bring in big changes to technology usage. A huge chunk of our population dying is a good way to revolutionise a world that's not willing to change. I mean, isn't that what happened after the plague in medieval Europe? It destroyed feudalism and sparked major changes to religious and political systems. The Paxin. Well, that destroyed nationalism and ignited major changes to the application of science. Socially, it's all the same thing. Over and over again."

Lydia realised Jez was staring at her, an eyebrow slightly raised. "Sorry. I'm a talkative drunk," Lydia said.

Rafe laughed, the kind of deep belly laugh that could only have come from a place of genuine amusement. He was older than her, yet somehow, so much more youthful than Lydia could ever remember feeling.

"Don't be sorry!" He leaned back in his chair, the hand he had on Jez's knee moving back with it. She didn't seem to mind. "It's brilliant. I love philosophical drunks. Much more fun than depressive drunks and almost as entertaining as horny drunks!"

Lydia's cheeks flushed. She found respite from her embarrassment in the glass. "I suppose so," she said. "I'm new to this place, though. I shouldn't get so carried away."

"Why are you even working here?" Jez asked, her face steely.

"Same as most people, I imagine," Lydia replied. "It's a job. Good benefits. Good pay."

"But you don't exactly need the good pay and benefits, do you?" Jez crossed one long leg over the top of the other, wedging Rafe's hand between her thighs. "Your father is the leader of the entire damned quadrant. Hasn't he been voted in twice already? I doubt you need anything, except for maybe a good lay."

Rafe's intoxicated smile faded. "Hey, come on, Teach. She's new." He turned away from Jez and focused on Lydia. "Oh, shit! Reminds me. I know I sound like a dick, but if I don't ask, Dualla will murder me."

"Dualla?" Lydia asked, only halfway interested in the answer. The other half of her thoughts were disappointed her glass was empty. She didn't tend to drink very often, but she had to admit, this wasn't the worst party she had ever been to. In fact, it was the first one Lydia had ever attended where she could be fairly confident she wasn't being filmed. It was impossible to know, out there in the real world, who was interested in getting to know her and who was after the next ten-minute headline.

"Carl Dualla. Over there by the speaker." Rafe pointed to a gangly boy, barely into his twenties. Carl Dualla's crewcut hair rested above a narrow, angular face. The boy looked like he had his *Dietex* dosage all wrong; he was so skinny Lydia wondered if he might fall over were it not for the table he leaned against. "Carl asked me to introduce you. Seemed to think you might hit it off."

"Oh!" Jez clapped her hands together and then touched the tips of her fingers to her mouth. "Shit yes! Jazzing brilliant idea. Carl would be perfect for you."

Lydia knew this would come up eventually, though it would have been nice to at least get through the first fortnight. "Sorry, I don't think so." She toyed with the ends of tight brown curls that rested near her collarbone. Why had she put so much effort into her make-up? Lydia imagined it was to try to make a friend or two, though what eyeliner had to do with friendship, she couldn't fathom. It wasn't as though the person she really wanted to notice her would be at a gathering in the H-Zone. No. Alessia, an alien she'd not yet so much as spoken to, may as well have been on the other side of the world. Shaking away the thought, she forced a lopsided smile. "Actually, I think I've had one too many. I should go to bed."

"Oh, come on, Barrett," Jez teased. "Governor's daughter too good to say hello to a Zoner boy?"

Carl was a Zoner? It meant his family had taken up residence in an unprotected zone—the kind of place where buildings weren't climate-proofed. People didn't tend to live as long in those neighbourhoods, so their general approach to life was freer. There had been a few times in her life when Lydia wished she lived in one of those zones. Maybe then she wouldn't so badly need to keep this job. To impress the bosses and get a new contract. To not be the governor's daughter.

"No," Lydia replied as politely as she could. "I didn't even know he was a Zoner."

A blue light flashed throughout the room and Lydia jumped, startled. The music was replaced by a low-pitched siren. She didn't understand the purpose of the alarm and looked from person to person to see if anyone might give her a clue. Was she meant to leave? Were they in danger?

"Damn, I liked that song," Jez said.

The partygoers moved to the edges of the room to make a space in the centre where a woman Lydia recognised from her transport lay on the floor. Her body twitched in all directions. Lydia saw the lower white of the woman's eyes, which were partially closed. She wasn't sure what to do, but nobody else in the room looked surprised or concerned about the convulsing body on the floor.

"Is someone going to help her? Is there a medic around?" Lydia shouted, her heart rate increasing with each moment everybody stood around doing nothing.

Jez shook her head. "Don't bother."

Two protectors arrived. One on each end, they lifted the woman and carried her out to the corridor. As they did, the dull siren stopped, the lights darkened once more and the music started up.

"What just happened?" Lydia asked.

"N-C withdrawal," Rafe said. "There are usually one or two in the new staff crop who start to seize because of the cut-off."

"Yep," Jez added. "Their brain freaks out after not using the Neuro-Comm implant for a couple of days."

It made sense. Lydia had spent days trying to tap into the Hive wirelessly, just for menial things like checking messages or subscriptions, sending commands to her N-C and then taking a moment to remember it couldn't be used in such a secure environment. Lydia's implant was put in when she was quite young and her father's role brought with it unlimited bandwidth; she couldn't even properly remember a time she couldn't just think her way to the online world. She'd had a significant headache from the constant effort of trying to use the Neuro-Comm, but now that she'd been in the Q4C for over a week, she wasn't making so many futile attempts. Perhaps others just couldn't adjust as easily.

"Don't worry," Rafe said as he leaned forwards. "She'll be fine. They wouldn't have let her in here if she was a full-blown N-Cer. An addict. A few injections and a good night's sleep and she'll pull through. Now. Can I take you over to meet Carl? Surely you don't still want to leave after the excitement?"

"Sorry, but I think I will. I've already used up my drunken rant quota for one night. Thanks for the company." She pulled herself up off the lounge, which took more effort than it ought to. Her vision blurred temporarily, then adjusted to the new altitude.

For a second, she thought there were two people stripping naked at one end of the room, but then she realised one of the staff had activated a holo-pro. Someone always had to turn on 3D porn, didn't they? Yes, it was time to go.

As Lydia crossed the length of the rec room towards the exit, Carl Dualla stepped in front of her, blocking her path.

"You're not goin', are ya?"

He had the strongest North Australian accent Lydia had heard in years. These days, it was hard to tell where people were from. Nearly everyone spoke a kind of undecided dialect of English. Part British. Part American. In this quadrant, the Australian accent still prevailed, though often punctuated by slips into something more American.

"I'm a little lightheaded, so I'm off to bed." She realised she was still holding her glass. She leaned past Carl to put it down on the table against the wall, which was covered in other glasses and a few half-eaten food platters.

"Want company?" He moved closer and she tried to move back in the same measure, but knocked into another body. Carl's eyes appeared sunken in his face. There seemed to be nothing between his cheekbones and his skin. Everything about him was sharp and thin.

"Thanks, but no," Lydia replied, forcing a smile.

"You're quite pretty, you know."

"Thanks. That's nice of you to say, but I'm really just not interested." She thought about making her position clearer but decided against it. As a new arrival to her first proper job, she felt it wise to take her time with things.

"S'okay. I'm patient. I can wait." He took a step to the side, his arm stretching outward to clear the beginnings of a path for her.

Lydia's relief was instant. She hadn't realised how tight her chest had become until the tension lodged there uncoiled itself.

Without looking back to Rafe and Jez, she made her way into the corridor and started for her quarters, muffled music and voices gradually fading behind her.

Chapter Six

FERMI'S TOE TAPPED to a rhythmic song in his mind. It was some tune he had heard playing in the game room last week but hadn't managed to catch the title. His hips swayed from side to side as he gazed down the scope at his workbench.

He used the micro-laser to fuse components on a solar cell. Versatile solar cells could be used to fuel an array of machines, but he'd never seen them in action. The colony would be unable to function without them. Such technology allowed the colony's complex mechanisms to provide safe air, water, and food. The cells came to him partially manufactured; they left him fully operational. The simplistic system had a kind of beauty.

His uncoordinated swaying slowed as he tested the power source on the cell he'd been working on. Energy levels registered as normal. He nodded and picked the part up by its silicone edges. Perhaps this one would replace a burnt-out unit in the air filtration system, or it might join hundreds of others to form the arm of a wind turbine, allowing every Outsider in the colony to enjoy hot water.

Fermi returned the part to its box, scanned the barcode on the side and added it to the collection bay behind him. As he did, he wondered what Alessia was doing. She was higher up in the pecking order than he, so she could be assigned jobs all over the community.

Since Fermi preferred to know exactly what he was doing each day, his job suited him just fine. But he'd seen Alessia's lavender eyes eagerly scan the work list, excited for a new adventure. Her dextrous limbs and toned body made short work of most tactile jobs; he'd seen her contort her body to access even the most unfriendly of service ducts. He adored the intensity of her features when she was fixing something, the world fading away one corner at a time, leaving only the problem that needed to be solved.

As Fermi turned back to his workspace, he bit his lip and swore at himself under his breath. Why did her face invade his thoughts so many times each day? Half of the women he'd met were beautiful, yet the image of the curves of her upper body and the memory of her naturally pouty mouth slowed his wits. *It's been years; it's time to get over this idiotic infatuation.* He wiped the back of his hand across his forehead, nudging the rosewood-coloured braids tightly hugging the top of his head.

"Fer, hey." An affable voice came from behind him. He hadn't heard her approach, but turning to face her, he realised it was Cara, a woman who lived on his floor. She was with a small group of mutual friends, though the others waited a few feet away.

"Did you want to come and play some squash with us tonight?" she asked.

He shook his head. He was a friend of hers, but the kind you approached only if the other people you spent time with were busy, or your team numbers for some game or another were uneven.

"Oh, come on. You aren't scared I'll kick your skinny arse again, are you?"

"No way," he replied, grinning. "I just feel like a quiet one tonight."

Fermi stepped back when Cara moved closer to him. She touched her fingertips to his forearm. "Are you sure you don't want to play?" she said.

Just go! he told himself. Fermi liked Cara; she was fiery and intelligent. But he had a feeling she wanted more than a friendly match. He opened his mouth to speak but opted for another shake of his head. "Another time, yeah?"

"What a shame. Maybe. I'll let you know." Cara stepped back with a frown. As she did so, a deep buzzing from an overhead speaker indicated the end of Fermi's work shift. Cara squared her shoulders and walked away from him, rejoining her friends.

He waited a few moments to let the traffic clear and then made his way to a staircase leading to the upper levels. He passed a protector as he walked through the doorway. Fermi tipped his head at her and climbed the steps two at a time.

The honey-beige walls in the stairwell teemed with graffiti. Protectors marked the space at the end of each of their contract terms, even if they were likely to secure a renewal of those contracts. Most of the humans drew inane caricatures of their friends or simply signed their names.

Others wrote out short passages from books or songs. He didn't recognise most of the references. There were also, of course, multiple penises—each one with thicker veins than the last.

Fermi paused at the exit onto Zone C, where he lived. After a moment, he turned on his heel and continued to Zone D, Corridor B, and then knocked at the fifth door. A small dent glinted at him from the surface of the scarlet door. He tapped his knuckle on the same spot every time.

Alessia opened the door and stepped back to give Fermi room to enter. He was surprised to see Peleus sitting on the sterile metallic seat to the right of the table. It was the only place to sit other than the single bed. Fermi was relieved the unexpected visitor was on the chair. It left Fermi the space next to Alessia on the bed. He felt a familiar flutter in his chest, the same one he experienced every time he got close to her.

"Fermi!" Alessia greeted him. "It's been a few days. I was starting to wonder if you were still alive." She seemed to be in a good mood. He hoped the man at the table—and his kindly face—was not the reason for it. Though he knew such a thought was selfish. He ought not begrudge her a single moment of happiness, not given the difficulty she faced in finding those moments.

"Yep. Still alive. Still doing my thing." Fermi stepped past her to the far end of the room, melting into his usual spot on her bed. He acknowledged Peleus with a nod. "Hey."

"Fermi, have you met Peleus before?" Alessia asked. "He's a caretaker, so you probably have." Alessia closed the door and sat on the other end of the bed, closer to Peleus than to Fermi.

"Not properly." Fermi forced his shoulders to relax and his tone to soften. "I've seen you, though. I think you patched a burn in the top of my workstation a few months ago." In truth, Fermi remembered their initial meeting better than he was letting on. He'd, for a moment, considered asking Peleus to join him for a game of squash back then, unable to ignore the caretaker's easy-going charm. Now, seeing he was in some way connected to Alessia, Fermi was glad he'd decided not to act on his initial attraction that day. What a ridiculous triangle that could have turned into!

"Ah, yes," Peleus replied. "You'd slipped with a fuser?" A thick strand of layered, feathery hair had fallen over his left eye. Peleus tossed his head to the side, forcing the messy lock back towards his ear.

"That's the one," Fermi replied.

"Yes. I remember you. Good to see you again. I didn't know you were friends with Ali?"

Fermi's fingers clenched. *Ali?* Peleus looked to be on quite familiar terms with her.

"I'm friends with everyone," Alessia said. A soft smile spread across her face, teasing him. They both knew she didn't have many friends, not truly. Alessia was respected by everyone she knew, but rarely did she build deeply connected relationships. He considered her to be one of the most compassionate people he knew. She'd never walk past someone she could help—even in the smallest of ways—without stopping to do so. But friendships required something more; they required a person to let others know of their fragility, their sadness. Even Fermi, who was gifted with brief glimpses into her psyche, was always at arm's length. As someone who seemed to want others to only ever see her strength and her sense of self-control, Alessia's immediate circle was quite small. At least, that's what he'd always thought.

"Of course you're friends with everyone. A regular Miss Amiability." Peleus returned the smile. It seemed they'd known each other for a while. As Peleus held Alessia's eyes with his, Fermi's face flushed. As much as he wanted to, he couldn't ignore the gentleness of Peleus's presence, the effortless charm draped over each word. "Well, you've got a better offer, Ali, so I'll head off now."

"Oh, no, must you?" Alessia leaned forwards.

"Yes. That little sister of mine is probably breaking hearts as we speak. I better hunt her down for a catch-up. Now that she's allocated to the later mess hall time, I don't see her as much."

"Still breaking hearts? I thought she'd finally made a choice between those two that were both interested in her."

Peleus positioned himself in the doorway, leaning against the frame. "Yes. Yes, she has."

"You don't approve?" Alessia asked.

"Time will tell. Oshana is very spirited. Petra made me promise to at least give the girl a chance before embarrassing her with the don't-hurt-my-sister speech."

"Fair enough. Tell Petra I'll come see her soon." Alessia's voice deepened. Fermi wondered if she was trying to tell Peleus something other than what she'd actually said.

Fermi's hand unclenched as he finally noticed the resemblance between Peleus and Petra. Peleus was at least ten years older than the rugged teenage girl, but now he was truly looking, it was impossible to miss the similarity of their skin tone and feminine facial features. Peleus stood, hugged Alessia, and left the room with a polite goodbye.

"Ali, did I...interrupt something there?" He unrolled the end of his shirt sleeve without looking at her.

"Sweet Earth, Fer, do you think I'm sleeping with the entire colony?" She slapped his knee with the back of her hand.

He couldn't decide if she was joking with him, or accusing him. "Are you?" Now he wasn't sure if he'd meant that as a joke or not.

Alessia rolled her eyes at him and stood, moving to the chair Peleus had just been using before sitting down again. "No. I'm not. I am not having sex with Peleus, or his younger sister, to fill my time. Not only am I not interested in either of them, there's simply not enough space in my head for that sort of thing." She sighed. "Fermi, you've been my friend forever, but there are some things we are never going to discuss. Things we don't agree on. I need to have some other friends in my life. You're still my Fer, though!"

"Like what?" Fermi said.

"Hmm?"

"You said there are some things we don't agree on. Like what?"

"I tried to talk to you about all this years ago, but you didn't want to know. I've respected that. I'll keep you out of it, and I won't expect anything from you. But you need to stop expecting so much from me."

He knew what she was talking about now. The stories. It was all about the stories she'd told him about the world outside of the colonies. Promises broken by humanity. A need for some sort of Outsider cultural revolution, a reimagining of their own sense of worth and identity.

"I can't give you what you want, Fermi," she said. "There are some parts of who I am reserved just for you, and there are other parts that aren't."

Alessia's words burned him worse than a fuser. None of what she'd said surprised him. He'd known it all for a long time, but now she'd said the words—now she'd broken the silence, and his nerves felt as exposed as the circuitry of a damaged engine. He wondered what had changed, what had made her be so abrupt with him all of a sudden.

"Right." He stood to leave. As he neared the door, Alessia reached across the top of the table and held his hand for a moment. He wasn't looking at her, but he knew she was smiling. That gentle half-smile could always melt him. It emphasised how beautiful she was and highlighted that unassailable need for forgiveness she possessed. She hated turning the lights out, hated going to bed when there was an argument left unresolved. As difficult as it could be to break through Alessia's walls, she never wanted to hurt anyone, to be the cause of someone else's discord.

"All these years, Ali. You still haven't worked out this is the best place for us. I might be wrong about you and me, but I'm not wrong about that. This is where you are. This is where you'll live your life." Without waiting for a response, he left.

The stillness of Corridor B wrapped around him tightly like a restraint jacket. The stairs leading back to his quarters offered respite from the pressure as it took him closer to his own room and farther from Alessia's. When he reached door eighteen, he considered the lifeless red paint for a moment. His fingertips slid down the grainy surface as he rested his forehead against the lacklustre door. Fermi's chest expanded when he sucked in the air. He lacked the drive to push his way into the room. It would be so quiet in there. He'd be alone with his thoughts. He was sick of listening to his own voice, trapped in a repetitive loop of unrequited admiration.

Fermi lifted his hand and started walking. Perhaps he could still join Cara's game.

Chapter Seven

SILENCE ENVELOPED THE empty classroom like an all too tight hug. Lydia had never experienced that kind of quiet before and she wanted to take a moment to process it. With noisy neighbours in the human district and overcrowding in the Outsider district, it could be some time before she found herself alone in a quiet space once more.

She rubbed the back of her neck and thought of the Neuro-Comm clasping the top of her spinal cord. Lydia never realised how much noise the N-C transmitted. The constant low hum of incoming notifications in her head wasn't noticeable until it was gone. She couldn't remember living without a wireless connection to the virtual world. Thanks to the wealth of her parents, Lydia's N-C had been embedded at age three. Some people never got one at all. Her mother had always warned her not to become too dependent on the 'damned thing', which was a little funny coming from a technologist. Helen may've developed and improved tech for a living, but that only made her more aware of its potential effects. One could spend so much time focused on the virtual world only they could see, that they might forget to look at the actual world.

In the colony, however, the connection was severed. She couldn't activate local systems with a thought, couldn't be notified of an incoming voice mail or new upload on one of her favourite channels. Her eyes saw only what was in front of her, and she'd discovered the curative power of silence.

Lydia had never been an N-Cer—a full-blown addict of the mobile Hive connection who'd gradually lost their sense of belonging in the physical world—but still, being disconnected from the sea of signals had been jarring at first. No wonder such a small percentage of potential workers passed the psych exam.

Lydia scanned the room yet again, trying to remember the seating arrangement. Most of her students were amiable, but no matter how nice a group of children were, the act of teaching brought with it a sense of suffocation by the end of a week. Kids were a special variety of energy suckers. It wasn't until they were gone that she could relax.

If she'd been teaching human children, Lydia would have spent most of her working time at home, talking at a Hive receiver, and assuming the five hundred or so students assigned to her were listening. Even then, only one to two hours each day would be scheduled for live instruction. A great deal of learning would be delivered by prerecorded lectures accompanied by self-marking quizzes. Lydia's job would have mostly been to answer a small handful of questions in what seemed to be a brief live session. The parents had to get their money's worth. Perhaps, there was some connection between the production-line style of schooling prevalent in contemporary society, and her own failure to ask questions. It was even possible she'd felt that lack of curiosity and criticism within herself, choosing to teach as a way to answer a question she'd not even realised she wanted to ask.

"Teaching? Really?" her father had asked when Lydia mentioned it a year ago.

"Well, why not?" she'd replied. Having already completed training in political advertising, she wanted to do something else. Anything else, really.

"It's not exactly an exciting job, Lydia. You realise ninety per cent of it is administration? Compliance paperwork?"

Lydia had rolled her eyes at him.

"Yes, Dad, I am aware. But at least there's something a little...real about it. Something meaningful."

"There's more reality in an N-Cer's dreamscape than there is in education."

She changed career paths anyway. Though, to an extent, the old bastard had been right. Out there, back in the human world, students were grouped together based on the results they achieved on standardised tests. Teacher pay scales aligned with student success, so they worked on test preparation above all else. More resources and teaching hours were awarded to high achievers. It was a problematic system Lydia was grateful to avoid for a while longer. The colony's out-dated system of classroom instruction sapped her energy each day, but it was preferable to the alternative.

Lydia knew the faces of her students. She recognised their voices when her back was turned. It was worth the exhaustion and the headaches. Being there, in a classroom that smelled of feet and paper, was worth it all.

Bringing her focus to the present, Lydia became aware of Jez shuffling about her own classroom. She called out to Lydia across the hallway.

"Alive in there, Barrett?"

Lydia rested her head against the wall. "Yeah. I'm here."

Jez sauntered into Lydia's classroom, looked at Lydia sitting on the floor, and frowned.

"What did the little demons do?" Jez asked. For once, she sounded genuinely concerned.

"They're fine. I'm just exhausted."

"Tell me about it. They've got a talent for tiring us out." She leaned against the door frame behind her. "One of mine kept looking at me today. You know that weird alien look they do?"

Lydia shook her head.

"Anyway... I want a scalding hot shower before I get some food." Jez sighed. "Well, catch ya." With that, she left Lydia alone once more.

What a sad state of affairs that Jez was the only friend she'd made so far. Jez was as unpredictable as the weather, and these days, that was really saying something. Inside the colony, it was easy to forget about the war raging between Mother Nature and those who lived on this planet. With the exception of the poles, where small communities of people had built themselves homes beyond the economic reach of the UEA, it was impossible to characterise parts of the globe according to their climate. Chaos was Earth's new neutral position. Sydney—or what was left of the once temperate, sprawling city—might find herself drowning one week and dying of thirst in the next.

Occupants of her father's apartment complex, closer to the continental coast than the Quadrant Four Colony, enjoyed the luxury of a reliable climate control system. Temperature, humidity, and oxygen levels were all customisable. The bottom two floors were designed to accept and filter flood water. That system had been needed only twice during Lydia's childhood, but she remembered both occasions distinctly. Though unable to leave the building for days, Lydia was luckier than many. The poor had inherited the Earth. They were the ones who lived closest to the soil that had turned against them.

Lydia's train of thought came to a crashing halt when a yell came from the corridor just beyond the school. "Get your fucking hands off me!"

Her exhaustion melted away as she bounded in the direction of the voice.

"Your allocated work shift isn't over for another hour, alien." The protector was no more than five feet tall, but authority oozed from every syllable. Lydia had met him a few times but had learned nothing more than his name: Liam Tyson. "Get back to the bottom floor," Tyson ordered.

"I've processed enough of those shitty N-Cs for one day. More than anyone else this week. You give me the same mundane crap to do every single day. One hour won't destroy your precious work roster." Lydia guessed the Outsider was about twenty, but she still hadn't worked out if Outsider maturity expressed itself the same way it did amongst humans. Her hair was a mix of pink and silver, roughly cut.

"I'm warning you, girl. Back downstairs. Now."

The young woman squared her shoulders and refused to respond. He grabbed hold of her arm and pulled her towards him.

"Don't touch me." She turned her body away from him, attempting to break free.

"We make the rules here, Petra," he replied, his face morbid.

Petra's skin reddened as Tyson tightened his grip. It must have hurt because she grimaced. Lydia got the impression this girl would have done her best not to let him see as much if she'd been able to control the response.

"Aren't you meant to be keeping us safe?" Petra asked. Her voice stayed strong, but the spark in her eyes had dimmed a little.

"Exactly. Following rules keeps everyone safe, so do what you're told and get back to work." Tyson grabbed hold of her other arm, her petite frame engulfed by his broad chest and shoulders.

Lydia's pulse thundered as the young Outsider launched herself off the floor to kick Tyson in the chest with both feet.

As they both fell backwards, Tyson lost his grip on her and they hit the floor with a *thud*. Several Outsiders appeared in the hallway. Lydia hadn't seen them arrive, but in the dazed quietude after the two figures went down, she became aware of their presence.

Lydia fought the urge to lunge forwards and check the young woman for injuries.

She ought to have been hitting the alarm plate behind her. Instead, she stepped backwards, allowing the crowd to form a line between herself and Tyson.

"Petra? Damn it."

The new voice belonged to the woman Lydia had seen reading at a socialisation table on her first day. Her intensity and stature were unmistakable. They'd burned themselves into Lydia's memory.

"Come on. You need to get out of here," Alessia said. Her movements were gentle as she helped the young one, Petra, to her feet.

"This has nothing to do with you. I've got this." Petra shook away her would-be helper.

Alessia. The same person Lydia kept telling herself she wasn't looking for around every corner since the first time she'd seen her. Finally back in the same room as her, Lydia studied Alessia as much as she could given the circumstances, but the only thing she could really see were those eyes. Jez's eyes had astounded her at first, but now gold was a colour she was accustomed to. Alessia's lavender eyes weren't merely astounding; they were uncompromising.

Tyson had sucked in enough air to call for support via his Wrist-Comm. He clumsily pulled himself into a catlike position on all fours but could drag his body up no further. That kick to the chest must have knocked more than just the wind out of him.

Alessia shook her head at Petra but did as the girl asked and stopped trying to drag her away. The lights in the ceiling started to flash, alternating between a pearly white and dark blue.

Three protectors arrived from different directions. Alessia's face hardened as she moved backwards, absorbed into the humming crowd. Strips of refulgent light reached towards her between the bodies, but Lydia soon lost sight of her.

"Get on your knees, Outsider!"

"Fuck you." The girl's head flew forwards as a protector thrust a cudgel into her stomach. All the air in Petra's body seemed to burst out her mouth in one violent blast. Lydia bit her lip to stop from screaming. The people standing around her, all of them permanent residents of the colony, turned away. A few gasps escaped, but no one spoke. No one stepped forwards. They wore their fear like an old coat.

The three protectors watched as Petra coughed, bloody spittle trickling from the side of her mouth. As she tried to return to an upright position, the protector with the cudgel delivered a powerful slap to her face with his free hand.

Lydia's fingernails sank deep into her palms. Why didn't the other protectors say anything? Surely they knew the slap was at *least* one step too far.

Her gaze dropped to the floor. Why didn't *she* say anything? The colony was not the free and protected community she had anticipated. What was happening was wrong and she knew it. But she felt frozen, incapacitated by her own expectations and the lies her father told her. Lydia was ashamed of her own privilege, her cowardice, her unwillingness to truly let the reality of that moment override everything she thought she knew about these colonies. It was a shame that reached so deep she could feel the gravity of it clawing at her, trying to pull her whole body into the floor.

Lydia couldn't drown out the sound of boots and fists striking flesh, nor the smell of human sweat as the man worked through a frenzy. Why didn't Tyson or one of the others, who stood there like dumb open-mouthed carnival clowns with their heads shifting from side to side, do something to stop it? Why didn't he just knock her out with a Pulser? She realised she hadn't really paid much attention to how the protectors kept order. No. That wasn't true. She was lying to herself. Again. There were no internal locks on the doors. Outsiders had no access to information, no right to choose their own occupation, no ability to shape the order of their days. She knew exactly how the protectors kept order. They did it with quiet intimidation, with a watchful eye that never slept, with fear.

Lydia choked back tears as a Senior Protector pushed her way into the fray. Her uniform was much the same as what the others wore, but the Pearsal logo over her heart was noticeably larger and a white strip ran down the centre of her sleeve. Lydia's stomach lurched and she swallowed hard to fight back against the nausea threatening to overcome her.

"All right, all right. Enough."

The maniac stopped as soon as he heard the voice of the shift supervisor. Lydia was surprised by the ease with which he reined in his behaviour. He was red-faced and out of breath, yet suddenly quite calm.

Lydia guessed the girl had been beaten for no more than twenty or thirty seconds, though it took much longer for Lydia's heart to slow. The knots inside her stomach started to untie themselves when the young Outsider's arms moved to hug her stomach. She was conscious.

"Pick 'er up, boys."

Tyson and another protector grabbed hold of Petra's arms and dragged her to her feet. Blood oozed above one eye. Her pale skin was soiled by dark welts forming fast across the backs of her arms. Lydia could only imagine what injuries lay beneath the ripped clothes. The two female protectors ordered the onlookers away and people started to move towards the staircases and doorways, silent as ghosts.

One of the guards pulled a small black case from her belt. When she pushed her finger into it, the case flew outward in all directions, quickly forming a personal shield. It was more for intimidation than for defence. No one was ignoring the instruction to leave.

Petra's toes dragged as she was taken away. They showed no care for her physical state, despite the fact she was barely conscious, one eye bruised shut, the pupil of the other eye rolling back and forth lazily.

"Idiot. Got what she deserved." Jez's voice cut the air. Lydia turned to see her standing a few feet away. They must have been near each other during the entire incident, but bodies in between had blocked Lydia's peripheral vision.

"Excuse me?" Lydia asked flatly.

"Petra's always been a hothead. No one else has been stupid enough to ignore directions in the time I've been here. The second an Outsider lays a hand on a human, they're asking for it."

She wanted to defend Petra, a girl she didn't even know, from Jez's admonishments. She'd just been beaten so badly it would probably take her weeks to recover, and all Jez could say what that she deserved it. *Asking for it? Really, Jez? She was mouthing off, but she didn't deserve to be assaulted!*

Jez moved closer to Lydia, who continued to stare at the red smudges across the floor. "Hey, what's wrong, Barrett?"

Lydia shook her head. "Nothing. I've just—ah, I've never seen anyone get beaten up before. Not in real life, I mean."

"Oh. Of course. Fair enough. It's okay, though. She's just an alien. They'll stick her in a cell for a couple of days, and then she'll be back again, making out with that girlfriend of hers in every public place they can find or giving attitude to the guards."

Just an alien. What did that even mean? Lydia was horrified that people could be so casual about violence, about brutality. Jez was so unbelievably disconnected from her own identity that Lydia wasn't sure whether to be disgusted by her flippant remarks, or to feel sympathetic for the self-loathing deeply rooted inside Jez's psyche.

Lydia had heard of cognitive dissonance, but for the first time, she understood what it meant. If people thought locking up Outsiders in underground communities where they had next to no decision-making power over their own lives was a display of human altruism, then the whole damned world was completely blind. Given she thought this place would be a safe-haven, a place where everything was driven by a desire to provide refuge, Lydia certainly had been. No amount of VR games, as graphic and as confronting as they usually are, could have prepared her for the reality of watching someone so vulnerable be hurt in the way Petra had just been.

Shaking off the line of thought, Lydia looked at Jez. "Will they treat the injuries?"

Jez sighed. "Yes, yes. They have to, I suppose. We may be managing aliens, but the powers that be aren't about to forget their own humanity. There is a duty of care to meet." Jez checked the chron embedded in the wall behind her. "Well, I'm going for a drink before that shower, I think. My throat's as dry as chopped wood. Catch ya."

Lydia needed to hide again, just for a few moments. She crouched in the corner of her classroom, underneath the half-height wall. Her chest felt heavy with an onslaught of emotion as she replayed the incident in her mind. Just like everyone else, she'd hidden behind that coat of fear; she'd done nothing but stare. Lydia longed to be rid of her inadequacy, her indecision, her ignorance.

As she let her head fall, the tears she'd been holding back all week burned channels into her cheeks. She sat there, alone, in the glaring artificial light, and cried.

Chapter Eight

Damon Barrett rubbed at the five o'clock shadow that spread across his cheeks. It had taken longer to pass through colony security than he'd expected, the nonresidential staff not taking their jobs as seriously as they ought to. He'd have to do something about that.

Stepping into Sara Taylor's office, he was met by the herbal notes of her perfume. In a space characterised by metal and circuitry, the familiar sillage was a delicious welcome mat. One of the guards nodded and pulled the door closed, leaving Damon alone in the space with the Q4C overseeing manager.

Sara sat behind an impressive oak desk. Given the use of genuine wood products had been taboo since unification, the presence of such an edifice seemed too bold of a statement for someone like her. Sometimes there were things about Sara Taylor that just didn't sit right with Damon.

Sara looked up from the touchscreen embedded into the desk, her dark brown eyes meeting his. "Ah, Governor Barrett. You're here."

He did enjoy the way she spoke. Those strong consonants and abbreviated vowels were less common in Q4; reminiscent of the American Age, they belonged to the wealthy elite of Quadrant One.

She rose and crossed the room to shake his hand. Barrett waited for her to come to him, appreciating the opportunity to watch her movements. Each step was mechanically perfect. A black skirt rested comfortably on her hips, its diagonal hem emphasizing her graceful knees, a pristine white blouse hugging her breasts and toned stomach.

"Good to see you, Sara. You're looking well." He leaned in, pressing his cheek against hers.

"Thank you, sir. I was expecting you an hour ago. Is everything okay?" She stepped back and perched on the edge of her desk, drawing attention to the high-heeled shoes and opaque stockings that accentuated her legs. Overhead lights highlighted the orange undertones in her face, complementing the russet brown skin. She wore her mocha hair in a flawless knot, as she always did.

"Oh absolutely. Everything is fine." Damon settled into a lounge chair and crossed his legs. "The security lackeys took their time clearing me. It's all fine now."

"Excellent. What were you after this month? I take it you've already looked over my video reports. Do you want to see the doctor? Perhaps a verbal report from the supply officer?" As she spoke, Barrett couldn't help but admire Sara's firm calves as they thinned downwards to her ankles.

"Yes, the reports were thorough, as ever. Thank you, Sara. You always keep me well informed. It's been quite a while since I've had a walk-through of the colony. I thought we could do a visual inspection, and since I'm here, I could stop by to see my daughter. How is she settling in?"

Sara looked to the chron above the door. Damon followed her gaze to see it was just after three o'clock. "Lydia's been doing well. I haven't actually had a chance to meet her, but I haven't heard any bad reports."

Barrett had expected as much. She'd managed to avoid meeting Lydia for two weeks. Impressive, he thought, given the enclosed nature of Sara's world.

The overseer hadn't seemed especially happy when he had told her of his daughter joining the Q4C staff. He had been clear Lydia would be afforded no special conditions, but that had little impact upon Sara's reception of the idea.

"The children are calm," Sara said. "Their parents seem happy enough. Silence is golden, and so forth."

"Yes. Indeed." Nobody knew better than an elected official no news was good news. His talent for avoiding media scandals more effectively than his competitors had kept him in the good graces of both the UEA and Pearsal. Politics was not about living without sin. It was merely the art of not getting caught.

"Okay, well, let's head down to the lower levels," Sara said.

BARRETT'S PRESENCE IN the east wing of the complex where Outsiders lived and worked was unusual. Each protector watched him. Being quite accustomed to eyes on him, Damon took it in his stride; their curiosity rejuvenated him.

The governor shook hands with a few of the staff along the way, thanking them for their service to the UEA.

When they came to a T-intersection, Sara indicated a passage marked as *Zone D, Corridor E.* Barrett walked ahead of her. At a socialisation table, six Outsiders chatted quietly. He couldn't discern what they were saying, but their hunched shoulders and heavy eyelids piqued his curiosity. "What's that all about, Taylor?"

She followed his gaze towards the whispering group.

"There was an incident yesterday—the kind we don't have very often. It will be in my weekly video report."

"You can just tell me now, yes?" They came to a stop, hovering in the corridor outside the entrance to the school.

"An Outsider was involved in an altercation with a guard. The girl was antagonistic and kicked Protector Tyson. Backup arrived and subdued her. That's all there is. It's been handled."

"I'm glad to hear it's under control. They haven't attacked one of you like this in recent years, to my knowledge?"

Sara's eyes travelled from his face to his chest. "No. No, they haven't. It was just the one isolated incident. The other residents were sensible enough to stay out of the way, but I imagine they're going to talk about it for a few more days." Sara raised her hand, indicating a direction. "Shall we?"

"Let's. After you."

Barrett hadn't expected such a drastic change of atmosphere. While the previous corridor had inundated him with steel and concrete, the schooling area possessed a sense of organic warmth.

The outer walls and ceiling were carved directly into the red rock of the earth, coated with a glossy transparent sealant. This section must have been added sometime after completion of the initial project. It was too different to the rest of the compound to have been part of the original plans.

The floor was tiled. Wiring from beneath the tiles led to traditional schoolhouse pendant lights in the ceiling. Each globe was encased in an identical, wide, spinning-top-shaped enclosure. Pearsal had installed more of them than was needed, drowning the room within broad, pearly beams.

A straight pathway lay ahead, with one classroom on either side. He could see directly into both, given the inner walls only came up to the height of his waist, with the top half made of glass.

What a ridiculous set-up, Damon thought. *How does anyone concentrate?* Nevertheless, the blonde woman's class was near-silent. Lydia's class, on the other hand, engaged in energetic chatter as they completed a task.

His daughter knelt on the hard floor, bringing her to the same level as the students at their desks. Damon took a few steps closer so he stood within earshot.

"Finished, Rosen? You've put your pencils away." The child avoided looking at her. "Come on, you're not usually a quiet boy. Can I see your picture?" Lydia held her hand, palm facing up, towards Rosen. He was barely old enough to have nominated a gender, his facial features still largely androgynous. He breathed out his trepidation and handed Lydia the drawing. After a brief inspection of the sheet of paper, Lydia folded the drawing, and, as she stood slid it into the back pocket of her jeans. *How strange*. Her face was angled away from Damon so he could not gauge her thoughts.

"Lydia!" Damon's voice boomed from the school's vestibule.

Looking up, she smiled. It was fake, though. Just like every other smile Lydia had given him since he lost his wife.

"Dad. What a surprise. I didn't know you had a visit scheduled today." She walked over to meet him. The students' eyes followed her.

"How are you?" Lydia stepped in for a half-hug with her father.

"Good, good. I don't think you've met Sara Taylor. She's the administrator of this facility." Barrett's arms crossed his chest as though the introduction were an achievement.

"No, I haven't. Nice to see the face that matches the name, Ms Taylor," Lydia replied as she held out her hand.

"Good to meet you, too." Sara shook Lydia's hand firmly. "Mind if I see what the children are doing while you and your father catch up?"

"Of course not. They're just having some downtime, playing with a bit of art." Rosen had started a new piece, the child was keeping his head down.

Sara's heels clicked against the tiles as she walked about the classroom, a soft echo bouncing between the walls. Lydia and Damon watched her interactions with the children for a few moments. Sara bent down to inspect their drawings, smiling at each child with such genuine interest that Damon found himself wanting Sara to come back and join them—for Sara to smile at him like that, too. She continued to show no interest in him whatsoever, as though it were against her wiring.

"Taylor's good at this sort of thing, isn't she?" Barrett rocked back on his heels for a moment. He continued before Lydia could reply. "You look pale, Lydia. I suppose living underground for a few weeks will do that? Not interested in the solarium?"

Lydia turned her attention back to her father and examined him from head to toe.

"Oh, well. You look like you've gained some weight, Dad. I suppose living alone for a few weeks will do that? Not interested in the gym?" she replied.

"Ah. Touché."

He looked to Sara. One of the younger children had pointed to Sara's necklace. She invited the child to touch the gold cross resting atop her collarbone. The girl beamed at the overseer, clearly pleased at the opportunity to inspect the jewellery.

"It isn't hard to garner trust from children, is it?" he said to Lydia. The colony was such a strangely isolated piece of the world; he couldn't help but fall into a pit of pensiveness while observing its inner workings. "You just have to convince them they're safe and you care about who they are. She knows it, too. A good relationship between us and them keeps this place going. I understand why they were all kept alive. We aren't barbarians.

"Still, I didn't quite understand why they had this school system in here. It's starting to make sense now, though. Strong relationships with humans from a young age results in compliance—a compliance based on the wholehearted belief we know what's best for them." His hands moved to his hips, his chest opening as he pulled his elbows back. "And we do, Lydia. We do know what's best for them."

"I'm sure you do, Dad." Lydia seemed more aloof, as though she were speaking to him through a Vid-Call rather than standing right next to him. Her mind was elsewhere.

They watched in silence as Sara finished her lap of the classroom. Damon could feel Jez, the other teacher on the payroll, looking at them with deep interest. Perhaps he ought to have introduced himself. By the time Sara returned, the moment had passed.

"They've drawn some charming portraits in there, Lydia." Sara's demeanour had changed as soon as she stepped away from the classroom. Still polite, but the allure she'd exuded with the children had been replaced by upright formality. "Are you finished here, Governor?"

"Indeed I am. My daughter seems just fine under your leadership, Sara."

"Fabulous. I'll lead you back to the western side, then?"

Barrett agreed, and with a quick goodbye, Lydia returned to her students for the last few minutes of the school day. As soon as she entered the classroom, his daughter seemed to return from whatever alternate space her mind had slipped into earlier. He hated to admit it, but teaching suited her.

The central corridor was busier than it had been before the school visit. Protectors had moved in, anticipating the four o'clock finishers making their way to the living quarters and social sectors. Each floor had an umbilical like this one, twice the width of all other passageways to allow for the flow of traffic.

Two children, not yet old enough for school, had used their sheets to turn a table and benches into a cubby house. A few metres beyond them, a man with shaggy hair was working at a junction panel, a multi-tool in his hand. Outsiders tended to be a couple of centimetres taller than the average human, but this young man was tall even by the standards of his own race.

"You!" Governor Barrett's voice caught the Outsider's attention. The alien turned towards him and lowered his eyes.

Barrett had to remind himself they were from a different planet. The physical similarities between humans and Outsiders were immense.

"Replacing burnt-out cabling?" he said. The Outsider nodded. "I would be willing to bet that with your hands, you could complete the task at twice that speed."

The Outsider kept his chin close to the base of his neck. Looking off to the corner of his eyes, Damon could see Taylor's silhouette. She stood as still as the Outsider.

"Well, do you speak?" Barrett asked. It frustrated him when someone—anyone—didn't seem to realise how privileged they were to be on the receiving end of the UEA's mercy. The Outsider needed to pull his weight, to adequately support the hand that fed him.

"Yes, sir," he replied.

"Name?"

"Peleus, sir."

"Taylor, arrange to have this one's food tokens reduced by thirty per cent for the month. An adjustment to his energy intake might remind him how lucky he is to have our protection. All we ask in return is for efficient help in keeping the facility operational." Barrett pushed past the Outsider, their shoulders colliding.

"Absolutely, Governor." Sara waved her hand at a nearby protector and relayed the instruction. Sara started back for her office, not waiting for Barrett. He caught up to her within two steps.

"You said something in the last report about rumblings. Tell me more."

"They're just rumours, but I thought it best to report them. A few of the guards say they've heard small groups talking about resistance. Resistance to what, they have no idea. The groups they hear chatting are always lurking around a corner, gone when the guard tries to investigate."

Sara held her thumb to a scanner. With a click, the door leading back to the human zone slid open. "It's hard to place, really. But it does seem like there may be a minority attempting to undermine the status quo. Perhaps that girl losing it yesterday was connected, or maybe she was angry about something totally unrelated and lashed out. We aren't sure."

"It seems an obvious conclusion she's part of the...rumblings, as you call them?"

"Petra. Well, the security crew will have words with her when she is more lucid. Right now, though, I wouldn't say there's an obvious link."

"I see. There's not much any of you really know, is there?" He overtook her at the other end as he stepped into the crisp, purified air of the western zone. He despised being out of fully climate-controlled areas any longer than necessary. "Aren't you picking up anything through the surveillance system? Isn't every corridor monitored?"

"They are."

"Then what the hell is going on? Why don't you know what they're saying around this place?"

The tap of her shoes echoed as she searched for an answer. "There are holes in the security logs. Some kind of glitch in the memory stores. Rafe Garland has some members of his security team hard at work to identify the problem. So far, they've found no evidence of external interference."

"Sara, you do realise our employer would gladly replace both of us if it seemed we weren't meeting management expectations? MacNay would love any excuse to pull this contract out from under Pearsal."

"Yes, I realise, sir."

"Good. Because I would imagine you would go first, given I'm the elected governor of one quarter of the planet."

"We will keep an eye on it. That's not lip service. If we need to, a random population transfer would weaken any colluding groups."

Barrett stopped walking. A flirtatious pair making eyes at one another nearly knocked into them, but one noticed just in time and dragged the other out of the way. Sara nodded at the two. The governor did not.

"Excellent. I appreciate the walk-though, Sara. You always brighten up these visits."

She seemed to want to say something, and swallowed. "You didn't have to spe—" She shook her head, hands on her hips, and then smiled the thought away. "You're welcome. Did you want to discuss anything else back in the office?"

"As tempting as some time with you in your office sounds, no. I don't really have anything else that warrants attention this time around. I'll take myself back to the transport, thanks." He leaned in, repeating the cheek-to-cheek greeting he had offered upon arrival. "See you in a few weeks." His farewell came through an asymmetrical smile.

Damon returned to the elevators alone as Sara walked in the opposite direction towards her office.

She'd said there was a glitch that somehow resulted in deletions from the memory stores. By the sound of it, the deletions were conveniently selective. He'd need to keep a closer eye on the colony.

Chapter Nine

ALESSIA TURNED ON her heel and then turned back again. The size of her room rarely jazzed her off, but today, it did. She disliked situations when she displayed any kind of agitation. She prided herself on presenting as calm, measuring her words and her steps no matter the circumstance, no matter the hurricane swelling inside. Since Petra was beaten, however, she'd found it more difficult to maintain her usual outward composure. "I don't think it's a good idea, Peleus."

"Won't you just go and see her for one minute? That's all I'm asking. We all know she's got a temper on her, but my sister loves you. You've been her inspiration since she was a youngling."

"You know how much I love Petra. I don't know how many hours we sat in the back of the library telling her stories. But if I'm her inspiration for acting this way, then I'm failing at everything. All of it. I'm failing." Disappointment—aimed only at herself—stabbed at her gut like a blunt fork. She'd wanted so badly to show Petra a peaceful path in life. It was her responsibility. But from the first moment Alessia had started teaching Petra what she knew of their past, of the things that conflicted with what the humans had been teaching their people, Petra's reactions had been abnormally hostile. She possessed an anger, a fire that Alessia hadn't seen in any other Outsider. Alessia had hoped to quell that fire, to temper its blaze with her own cooling logic, but the opposite had happened.

Peleus sat cross-legged on the end of the bed, shadows across his face revealing a lack of sleep. "You're not failing. She's just frustrated." He fell into silence for a few seconds before continuing, rubbing his chin as he looked about the room before returning his gaze to Alessia. "She wants to fight the battle you put her in the middle of, and she wants to fight it now."

"I didn't put her in the middle of anything. Nobody did." She was trying to convince herself more than anyone else. Each individual was responsible for their own actions, in the end. Though she knew all too well that beliefs and actions were shaped by circumstance, by experience. Alessia had changed Petra's understanding of her own experience, and so, in truth, she was more to blame than she was—as yet—willing to admit to anyone other than herself.

"Dammit, Alessia!" He leaned forwards, his forehead dropping to his fingertips, elbows buried in his quads. She stopped moving about the room. "You're right. You didn't force her into anything. I'm sorry, I didn't mean to snap at you."

"Yes. You did." Alessia sat down next to him and let out a sigh. "But I understand why. *You're* right; she's a good person. I don't know if now is the right time to be seen with her. The children are starting to believe us about what exists out there. What I remember of it. This process must be a slow one. Too many don't even realise how much we're missing out on. Out there." She waved her arm to indicate the world beyond the wall. A world that had become only a half-lived dream to her. "We can't rush into a world we don't understand as much as absolutely possible. Nor can we expect to succeed as an autonomous community if we see ourselves as unworthy of such freedoms. And if there is a suspicion we are connected to someone making such public displays of defiance, our ability to engage in those conversations may be restricted."

"But that's just it. Petra doesn't understand *why* it needs to be slow." He turned his body to face her more directly. "She needs to see you forgive her for making a mistake."

"It was a very public mistake, Pel." Alessia pinched the bridge of her nose. She shifted her weight and then the room became stagnant for a time as they sat in a pensive silence. Alessia wanted so badly to support them: Peleus, Petra, and anybody else who needed to feel validated. She wanted to be the friend they needed, the friend who could just be in the moment, hold their hands, and alleviate their pain, their frustrations. But there were times when such individual concerns were at odds with one of her most intrinsic beliefs: Cooperation will bring change. Yes, many revolutions in human history were instigated by brutal dissonance, by chaotic upheaval. But Alessia and her community weren't human. They were not afforded the luxury of such a distinction, one that often justified even the most heinous of crimes. If her people were ever going to be masters of their own fates, they had to set a standard much higher than the one humans had set for themselves. They had to rise above in order to live above.

Perhaps it was an impossible task. Or perhaps one that could not be achieved without great cost, as the divide between herself and those she loved grew ever wider, a gap becoming a chasm. Alessia forced herself to release a slow and measured breath. She couldn't help but replay the scene in her mind. Petra, on the floor, battered and bruised, with no way make it stop. "I don't know how to help her calm down. She wants to know where all our stories and rumours lead. The fact is, I don't know. I don't know how we can finally bring it all together and find a way out of here, find a life where we aren't confined by tonnes of rock and fear."

"Maybe Petra can help us work it out. She's smart. Really smart. We need to bring her closer, not push her farther away. She's already got a little band of followers developing. Her new girlfriend, Oshana—she's a tough one; she probably taught Petra that little move that knocked the guard down in the hallway. They could channel their frustration into something constructive."

"Perhaps. All things are possible," she replied. "I don't think she's in a place to think logically just yet." She shook her head, more to herself than to Peleus. "The narratives of history have power. Perceptions of the past can be a poison that turns people against their own ancestors and gives birth to shame. By fighting their history with our own, we can, at the very least, stop hating ourselves and begin to see our own worth. If the other young ones start behaving like Petra, then what worth do we have?"

"What worth do we have if we don't love our own people, even when they lose their way?"

The question hung in the air. Alessia could feel the soft, cool purity of it. He was right. That's what made him so important: his innate ability to remind her of her own convictions. All of them.

Without another word, Alessia made for the door, leading Peleus in the direction of Petra's living space. They walked in silence, for which Alessia was grateful. Peleus was never one to push points further than was necessary.

"Hey! Where are you two off to?" Fermi's voice drew Alessia from her thoughts. A light jog allowed him to catch up quickly. "What's happening?"

"My sister came back from an iso-cell this morning," said Peleus. "Seems fitting to make sure she's all right."

"Petra?" Fermi asked. "You're going to see her now? Is that a good idea?"

Peleus stopped walking. "Why wouldn't it be?"

Alessia, a few steps ahead, stopped and faced them. She considered diffusing the situation, but her instincts told her the conversation about to take place needed to run its own course.

"Well," Fermi replied hesitantly. "I just thought open association with a dissenter—"

Peleus pressed Fermi into the wall behind them, his forearm bearing down on Fermi's chest as Fermi grunted in protest. Alessia grabbed at Peleus to try and pull him away. She'd never seen her friend so worked up before. She knew his nerves were raw after his sister had been hurt, but laying his hands on Fermi was completely unwarranted.

"Alessia," Peleus said flatly, his eyes fixed on Fermi as he squirmed. "I won't hurt him."

"What the hell are you doing?" Alessia said as quietly as she could manage. Her heart raced as she tried to simultaneously scan the area for protectors and keep watch over Peleus. The last thing she wanted to see was another person end up on the receiving end of human *protection*. "This isn't like you. I know you're going through a lot, but one of the guards—"

He leaned forwards, locking eyes with his captive. Fermi melted under the scrutiny, and his haphazard attempts to break free ceased. "Fermi, you're a good person," Peleus said. She could tell from the timbre of his voice he truly meant it. "I can tell you are. But don't you ever speak that way about my sister."

Fermi flushed crimson and nodded.

Peleus stepped back, freeing Fermi. "If even one per cent of our population had the courage and strength my sister has, our confinement would have been over long ago." His voice deepened with each word. "You can either come to wish a fellow Outsider well, given she is injured, or you can return to whatever shaded universe you seem to exist in."

Alessia looked from Fermi to Peleus. Peleus's lips glistened with saliva and Fermi's skin pulsed with visible heat. Both men had been her friends for years. Both were people she considered safely predictable. Now, she had no idea what either of them would do.

"Okay. I'll come with you." Fermi spoke with more clarity and certainty than Alessia had ever heard from him. Peleus's prismatic view of the world had inspired her many times, but now it seemed Fermi had been entranced by the vivid beauty of Peleus's honesty. She'd never been able to bare her soul the way Peleus had just done. Alessia's cage, the one that isolated her from other people, wrapped around her tighter than ever, just as Fermi's seemed to unshackle itself.

"Come on then," Fermi said. "The one time I met her she was pissed I was even in the room. Introduce me to your sister, Peleus." Fermi looked in the direction they had been walking. He avoided Alessia's gaze.

Peleus relaxed as he once again wandered down the hallway. Alessia knew people had been watching them, wondering what he might do next. Fermi had surprised her. Anyone else would have kicked, punched, or pushed their way free of Peleus's grip. Their eyes would have sizzled with anger or revenge. Fermi's mustard-gold eyes had not. Instead, somehow, his face had become more peaceful. She'd also been able to see the exact moment Peleus softened, the moment he'd decided Fermi might be an ally after all.

The unusual silence of the corridor was broken only by intermittent sighs from the air vents in the ceiling. She was surprised to find Petra's door open. Usually an invitation for socialisation or a purposeful attempt to get the attention of someone living across the hall, such a gesture seemed unlikely in this situation. If Alessia had been in Petra's position, she imagined she would have the urge to barricade herself in, to use every item she owned as another means to keep the world at bay. As they got closer, the reason Petra's door was open became clear. Each door had a latch allowing the door to remain closed. The protectors had removed hers.

"Petra, it's me, with Alessia and...and our friend Fermi," Peleus called out before they reached the door.

Alessia listened for a response—a shuffle, a word. Anything. When no reply came, they moved through the doorway, Peleus first and Alessia second. She saw the subtle hues of Peleus's skin darken as he caught sight of his younger sister. Alessia took another step.

Normally, Petra had cropped silver-pink hair, with longer strands that acted as a soft curtain to one side of her forehead. A smooth chin and voluminous coral pink lips rested below a delicate, straight nose.

Now, though, Petra's head was shaved unevenly. Her lips were more purple than pink, her nose swollen. The girl's eyes were hard. She sat on the floor, her back against the side of her bed and her knees drawn to her chest.

"Petra, can we come in?" Peleus asked.

"Do what you like." Her voice was still the same, of course, but something about it vexed Alessia. This girl, her friend, always had a certain sharp attitude about her. But this wasn't merely attitude; this wasn't even anger. Petra was calm. Such a stillness was eerily uncharacteristic and totally unexpected. Given the propensity of Alessia's mind to project and to analyse, it was rare for her to be faced with scenarios that were truly surprising. The sensation always brought with it a small but assertive discomfort at the base of her skull, a kind of rodent-like gnawing as she tried to re-evaluate.

Fermi hovered near the doorway as Peleus and Alessia stepped into the room. Alessia knew Fermi well enough to know he was questioning his presence; he didn't know what to do or say. Looking at Petra again, Alessia was starting to think the same thing.

"Are you feeling any better?" Peleus asked as he sat on the end of the bed, the side of his shoe resting near her feet. The soles of those feet were as raw as Alessia's nerves. Scanning the girl's body, she could see multiple bruises on Petra's arms and neck. Various shades of yellow and green, most of the bruises were a similar size and shape of a person's hand.

"Can we do anything?" Alessia asked, though she knew the answer. "I can try to locate some ice packs for those bruises."

"I don't need anything from any of you," Petra said, resignation in her voice.

"I'm really sorry this happened to you," Alessia said. "How badly did they hurt you?" She held her breath, terrified of the answer.

Petra's face distorted. It was hard to know whether it was a frustrated grin or an angry grimace. Fermi's hand touched the back of Alessia's shoulder. She leaned into him a little, grateful for his support.

"How badly did they hurt me? They're humans. They're evil."

Alessia said nothing. She was irritated at her first instinct: to defend the humans. She thought of the teacher Peleus had discussed, the one she'd watched a few times from her workstation. Lydia. The welcoming softness of her green eyes, the intelligence hidden within them. She didn't want to defend them in the same way Fermi had done so many times, as though they ought to be grateful to their captors, but rather to suggest not all people of a kind could be fairly considered the same. Alessia knew the native species of this planet hadn't jailed them down here to keep her people safe. She had no delusions about charity or protection. Evil, though? Alessia didn't believe there was any such thing as an evil person, human or otherwise. No. Humans weren't evil. Rather, they were lost in an obsession with their own power, their own capacity for planetary dominance.

If she said anything of this to the young woman in front of her, the woman with the bruised soul, she'd lose Petra forever. So, Alessia said nothing. Given the part she had played in planting the seeds of dissent that led to Petra's defiance and subsequent injuries, it was the least she could do.

"Pet, we didn't come here to upset you." Peleus reached his hand towards his sister's knee, but she pulled her legs closer to her chest.

"I know, Peleus." She looked at nothing but the wall ahead.

"I want you to be safe," her brother said. "I love you."

"You drive me crazy," Petra told him. The hardness of her eyes eased somewhat. "I know you love me. But the anger I've got in me right now...this anger. I don't know what to do with it." There it was. Alessia recognised that tone, that voice, at last. Petra was softening, not by much, but it was better than nothing.

After a moment of quietude, Petra let loose a short, horrible chuckle. She winced, her hand moving across her ribs as though to brace them. A ghostly shiver passed down Alessia's spine, an ache spreading across her own ribs as she saw the depth of Petra's anguish. She knew Petra and a couple of her young friends were becoming antsy for an active showing of defiance, a public statement, but Alessia hadn't realised that Petra didn't only want that because she needed a sense of power. She wanted to prove her *worth* to the humans, even if that worth came in the form of dissent that sparked debate. The episode in the corridor hadn't been the open rebellion Petra had wanted, it was a snap, a moment of tension released inappropriately, and Liam Tyson had treated her as though she were nothing but another stain on the floor. She and Alessia agreed that Outsiders were not, as humans believed, second-class citizens. Yet, they could not agree on an appropriate way to correct that gross injustice.

"When those bastards just kept kicking me, I was thinking some weird shit. I kept thinking: why do we have to look so much like our captors? Why can't they have reptilian skin? Or even just a damned tail or something. Something. *Anything* that would make us more different to those monsters."

Alessia knelt before the girl and held her hand against her own heart. "Your soul is...it's screaming at you, Petra. It's screaming at all of us. I can hear it. It'll take some time to soothe it. But we can help you. Let us help you, and then we can all work together to find a way out of this." On this last note, Fermi crossed his arms across his chest.

Petra's hands were around Alessia's neck, dragging her to her feet, before any of them had realised the girl had even moved. Her nails dug into the skin and Alessia bit her lip to suppress a pained cry. Peleus and Fermi both pushed forwards to separate them. Alessia held her hand up, indicating to both men to keep out of it. She would handle this herself.

"Soothe my soul?" the young woman screamed. "Is that meant to be a joke? You stood there and watched them kick the bleedin' piss out of me, and you did nothing!"

Petra's hands were not tight enough to cut off her oxygen supply, but Alessia had let this go on for long enough. Her hot-headed friend had made her point. With a swift movement, Alessia pushed her hands up between Petra's arms and drove them outward, breaking her grip.

Alessia stood upright and shoved Petra onto the bed. She sat on top of the young woman and pinned Petra's hands with her knees, trying her best not to exacerbate any injuries the teenager had already suffered. Petra bucked her body in a futile attempt to extricate herself. Petra could out-gun a human, perhaps even most Outsiders, but she could never hope to match Alessia in a physical confrontation. Though she'd yet to reveal her genetic heritage to her friends, she possessed certain traits that made her formidable when required. Thankfully, it was rarely necessary.

Alessia pinched her thighs on either side of Petra's body. It wasn't enough pressure to hurt her friend, but it was enough to stop her from getting back up. Alessia heard Peleus's breathing become faster. She knew he would have been struggling to let his sister and his best friend sort this out for themselves. She glanced at him. Fermi had his hand on Peleus's bicep as though to calm him, but Peleus's strained facial expression made it clear he was only moments away from becoming involved.

Gradually, Petra's movements slowed and Alessia released the vice grip of her legs. The girl's chest heaved, and with the indignant passing of time, her breathing became less laboured.

Petra sat up and brushed away a tear that had been clinging to her chin. "Don't we want the same thing, Ali?" Her voice wavered. She took a moment to collect herself. "After all those meetings we had, after all those ideas you put in my head, why aren't we on the same side?"

"I want us to be." Alessia shook her head. "But we can't just provoke a fight."

"Why? Why the hell not?"

"We are in the middle of a web entangling humans as well. If we alienate those who control this planet, there will be nowhere to go when we finally win the opportunity to decide our own fates."

"Petra..." started Peleus.

Alessia reached her hand towards Petra's face, but she turned her cheek towards the wall and used the outer edge of her forearm to force Alessia's hand away. Alessia had expected that reaction, but she'd had to try just one more time, to express her regret and her desire to try and fix things as best as she knew how. As much as she understood Petra's feelings, the rejection stung.

Moments passed. There was nothing left for any of them to say.

Alessia left the room first, glancing at Fermi as she passed him. His face seemed vacant, giving no indication he planned to walk back the same way they had come. He was clearly lost in thoughts of his own as he wandered in another direction.

She considered following him and decided against it. Alessia would talk to Fermi about all of this later. She couldn't deal with that just yet. She needed time to consider what to do, how to best salvage her relationships with all three of them. So much space in her head was taken up by thoughts of the past and the future that Alessia could so often feel utterly lost in the present, the place where all relationships exist. The burden of her mind's hyperactivity was hers to bear though, and the fact her distracted nature often left those friends she did have feeling like they were stumbling in the dark—a sensation she understood all too well—pulsated deep in her gut.

Peleus sat on the bed by his sister, apparently choosing to stay behind.

Back on her own floor, Alessia saw the overseeing manager of the colony: Sara Taylor. Taylor hadn't been seen wandering the halls very much in the last few weeks. It was unusual, given she made it a habit to personally interact with the Outsiders. It helped foster a sense of calm in the community, something she knew the humans worked very hard to cultivate for reasons she'd not yet fully discerned. It was deeper than a desire for smooth daily operations.

The two women made eye contact as they approached one another.

Sara's eyes didn't tell her anything specific, but Alessia knew: Something was going on. In a place where, until recently, nothing much ever seemed to happen, all of this, whatever *this* was, felt too fast. Her world was like a spinning coin frozen on its outer edge, liable to drop at any moment.

Chapter Ten

UNCURLING FROM A lotus position, Lydia wiggled her toes. She closed the cover of *Fried Green Tomatoes at the Whistle Stop Café*, the novel she'd found a few weeks earlier.

It took a while to stop feeling as though the mysterious book had invaded her space, but now she'd started reading it, and the historic landscape of the twentieth century Depression era had pulled her in. She was fascinated by not only the hard copy itself, but also a time in human history where people had to hide the nature of their relationships. Black or white. Gay or straight. Everything a dichotomy. It didn't make any sense to her yet, at the same time, it felt uncomfortably familiar.

Today, the UEA's laws saw no distinction between one form of relationship and another. Why would they? Such distinctions would be as ridiculous as seeing a human driving a car. It wasn't necessary.

"Your clothes are ready, Ms. Barrett." The synthesised voice of Generic Gina, the default vocal setting for all interactive systems, spoke to Lydia through a speaker embedded in the holo-pro.

"Thank you. Send them in." A popping sound, followed by a click, indicated the arrival of her clothes in the trunk at the end of her bed. They'd been removed from the room, cleaned, and returned by automated machinery using a subfloor system of vents. She was grateful the company had installed a full-maintenance system when they built the human quarters.

Rosen's drawing sat on the small table next to the bed. Lydia leaned over and picked it up.

The face at the centre of the page had rebe same silver eyes as the artist. Rosen's rounded chin and tapered nose were skilfully represented. He'd coloured his hair orange, the closest he could find to the rusty colour it was. The boy's figure stood against a purple background that reminded Lydia of a darkened, cloudy sky when lit by lightning. A group of winged animals flew high above him in a circular pattern, as though watching over him. Or perhaps taunting him.

Lydia would have been impressed by Rosen's effective use of art forms, were the image itself not haunting. The character at the centre, his self-portrait, stood trapped within a cell. His arms reached out between the bars, but he could go nowhere. The figure's head butted against the top of the cage.

She didn't know what to do with the picture, nor the feelings it evoked. Rosen had somehow managed to reach inside her and put a string of burning lights around her heart.

Wiping a tear from her cheek, she drew her shoulder blades together and stretched the tight muscles in her chest. Lydia bounced to her feet. "Activate hive projector. Open up Outsider profiles."

The holo-pro whirred to life. Hundreds of small three-dimensional circles, each one with an Outsider's face, flew out from the wall and surrounded Lydia. The gender of each person was indicated by the colour of the circle. From what Lydia could tell, the fifty or so red icons signified adults who had chosen to remain without gender, regardless of the sexual traits their bodies may have expressed. It was an aspect of their culture she'd always found quite beautiful, and one that—unlike so many other things—had been discussed above ground. Humans had come so far when it came to the acknowledgement and respect of a range of gender identities, or lack thereof should that be the case for some, but for the Outsiders, such respect seemed ingrained, organic. They responded to the emotional and physical well-being of one another without question. Humans, on the other hand, had to be shown the way step-by-step, led to tolerance and understanding by a pioneering few who'd possessed the compassion, the tenacity, and the intelligence to break down the walls of gender and sexual segregation.

The faces of pre-ceremonial, androgynous children were attached to the white icons. A symbol in the lower left corner indicated their physical sex. Most Outsiders, as with humans, were born with the physical traits that established one aspect of their identity. Unlike humans, Outsider parents allowed children to develop without a strictly enforced gendering program.

The whole concept fascinated Lydia. Humans who changed sex or gender were, of course, widely accepted and supported in the world. Growing up without the assumption their gender would be in alignment with their physical sex, however? Rare indeed. For the aliens, it was their way of life. Somehow that aspect of their culture had survived despite the years of human 'education.'

"Remove yellow and white," Lydia told the Hive.

The remaining icons grew larger, expanding into the space vacated by the files Lydia had sent back into the access wall. She selected a few profiles, one at a time, leaving each open for a short time. Lydia skimmed them to ensure the security logs would show she had been trawling through a variety of Outsider files. She hoped they'd think she was just bored or curious. Otherwise she'd be hard-pressed to explain, even to herself, why she wanted to know more about one person. Most of the women whose profiles she read lived innocuous lives. Nearly all the Os seemed to be pansexual, each one having had relationships with a variety of people, not confined by sex nor gender. Though humans saw all types of relationships as valid and equally dignified, the fact was that most people still tended to identify as heterosexual. It was just the way of things. The Outsiders, though, they apparently had no such statistical majority of sexuality.

Satisfied that she'd left a meandering trail through the system, Lydia selected the profile she'd wanted to read in the first place. As she did, she was struck by a niggling sense of guilt. The profiles felt far too similar to systems she'd seen used to catalogue animals or buildings or any other number of corporate assets. As intrusive as she felt looking through them, she chose to continue. She'd gone this far, she may as well learn more.

Alessia's photograph must have been taken a few years earlier. She seemed lighter, somehow, in the image. As though life's pains had not yet taken their toll on her ingenious face. The details provided within the profile were basic. It seemed Alessia had not drawn much attention to herself in fifteen years. There were only two protector reports written about her; both suggested Alessia had failed to arrive at her work shift on time. The woman had apologised profusely both times and made up the hours without a fuss.

Lydia swiped her hand sidewards, scrolling to a new page. Alessia's work detail arrangements. It seemed, without being labelled as such, Alessia was a sort of mechanical engineer. Anything that needed problem-solving, whether it was fixing a piece of machinery or repairing code that interfered with the effective operation of an AI chef, Alessia would be assigned to it. Job designation: critical. She had the most authority, the most colony access, and the most professional respect an Outsider could achieve. *Impressive,* Lydia thought. This woman was smart. Really smart.

One page of the Outsider's file was noticeably bare though—the one concerning relationships. Every other profile listed significant people, those an Outsider was connected to through blood, through ongoing sexual relationships, through love. There was no one listed on Alessia's profile, just a brief comment from one of the protectors: *suspect same-sex attracted only*. Lydia was more pleased by the single line of text than she knew she ought to be. Connections keep you sane, she thought. What kept Alessia grounded? A deep sense of unease replaced her initial pleasure at reading the data. The existence of such indecorously personal profiles, akin to a catalogue of animals being offered up for sale, made her mouth go dry. Yet wasn't she part of the problem, given she was looking at all of this, simply because she could?

Lydia sighed. Peleus had told her Alessia was worth knowing. She'd been on the outside. The file said nothing about any of those experiences.

"Oh! Oh!" A feminine screech came from the other side of the wall. "To the left. Yes! Good Earth, right there!"

Lydia rolled her eyes. Her neighbour was at it again. She wondered how some people had the energy to have sex so often. Her face warmed when a second voice came through the wall. It was another woman; a change from the string of men her neighbour spent time with. It was so long since Lydia had been with anyone she could barely remember what it felt like to be touched.

Alessia's profile still occupied the space in front of her. The woman's picture was static, yet the purple eyes, the first wholly Outsider eyes Lydia had ever seen, felt as though they were watching her. Having her photograph there, in such a large projection, while two people on the other side of the wall clawed at each other...it felt wrong. Lydia may have been fascinated by the engineer, but it was a fascination based on so much more than physicality. The sense she was intruding reignited in her chest. If Lydia wanted to connect with Alessia, she needed to do it properly, but the thought of approaching her was terrifying.

Lydia deactivated the projector. She slipped off her jeans and, leaving them on the floor where they fell, crawled into bed. Sleep never truly came to her, only a small measure of shallow rest.

CLASSES WEREN'T DUE to start for a good two hours, but there wasn't quite enough time to fit in a gym session before eating. In the near-empty cafeteria, Lydia had a breakfast of steamed spinach and cultured bacon or, as some liked to call it, 'test tube meat.'

The Artificial Chef who prepared their meals looked much like a human in many respects, but its skin was a greenish colour, its hair straw-like. His—*its*—thinking and communication capacity was designed only to allow for relevant job performance and simplistic discussions with humans. Artificial humanoids, by UEA law, had to have clear indications of their synthetic nature, as stipulated in the *Responsible Application of Science and Technology* charter. A major public and political concern after the Paxin was how the newly formed global government would protect people from the dangers presented by unchecked science. One of those dangers, and many were identified, related to the moral and economic dangers of producing synthetic beings that were too intelligent, too capable. People needed to know exactly who was who and what was what. They also needed to know their jobs and their families were unlikely to ever be truly touched by an artificial being. The charter and its harsh penalties were some ways of ensuring it.

Watching the nimble movements of the synthetic worker, Lydia replayed a long-dormant memory in her head. Uncle Tobin. Not really an uncle, he was just an eccentric friend of her mother's who'd spent a lot of time with the family. Like Helen Barrett, Uncle Tobin was a technologist, a researcher. One day he'd just stopped visiting. The long, indecipherable conversations he'd had with Helen always came with some sort of sugary treat for Lydia, so as a child, she'd noticed his absence. When she asked her mother where he'd gone, Helen's face had turned ashen. "He couldn't leave well enough alone," her mother had said. When Lydia pressed her further, Helen had added, "Some sciences shouldn't be toyed with, beautiful girl. The implications for our species are too great. We are not gods."

Her vision sharpened on the rim of her cup, the tea inside gone cold with the time spent visiting an old memory. *Just go*, she thought. *It'll happen eventually, anyway.*

Alessia's profile had listed the location of her living quarters. The room was easy enough to find. Each intersection of corridors was marked by large printed signs. None of the protectors asked her why she was entering the Outsider Zone so early in the morning. Early mornings came with the job no matter how prescribed the curriculum, no one would likely question a teacher being up and about long before classes begin.

The door to cube zero-five was shut. Lydia stood in front of it and rocked slowly back and forth between her heels and the balls of her feet, wondering what the hell she was doing there. She didn't know this woman. She'd only seen her a few times in passing. What would she say when the door opened? Lydia started to regret her decision to come. Before she could turn to leave, Alessia opened the door.

"The school teacher," Alessia said in a matter-of-fact tone. She was a few centimetres taller than Lydia and wore a long blue dress that was tight from the waist up. There was a gap near the bottom of the sleeves allowing her thumbs to poke through, creating a half-glove. Lydia had only seen her wearing shorts or pants before. The change was all at once welcome and disconcerting. "Mistress Lydia, right? Can I help you with something? Are you lost?"

"No. I'm not lost," Lydia said, surprised at her own abruptness. "Peleus sent me."

Without a word, Alessia moved to the side to invite Lydia into the room. The woman's movements were agile, somehow seamless, as though her joints were more flexible than was normal...for a human. The engineer's room was even smaller than Lydia's cube. The Outsiders had to rely on storage space under the bed, for there were no cupboards or drawers and only two shelves fixed to the wall. The upper shelf on the far side of the room was covered in books. On the end of it sat two small statues. One was a cat arching its back and the other a dog sitting on its hind legs. In a world like this one, such decorations must have been worth a lot of food rations. Either Alessia skipped a lot of meals or she had more influence than Lydia realised.

"I don't really know why I'm here," Lydia admitted as the door closed behind her.

"None of the protectors saw you come in?" The Outsider seemed concerned more than anything, which surprised Lydia. She'd expected her to be annoyed or angry her private space had been invaded by an uninvited visitor. "Well, all I can offer you is the chair behind the door there or...or the end of the bed if that's more comfortable." Alessia's hand moved to the side of her own neck, fingers toying with a studded earring. Lydia wondered if her hands were as gentle as they appeared.

"Thank you. It looks like a great chair," Lydia said, trying to sound more relaxed than she was. She sat down and crossed her ankles. Her red, heeled oxfords tapped against a chair leg.

A few moments passed in silence. Alessia remained standing as her eyes passed over Lydia. The Outsider—this woman—didn't look at her with anything but amiable interest. Lydia knew she ought to feel nervous or uncomfortable, having someone just stare at her without speaking, but Alessia's half-smile provoked an unexpected sense of tranquillity. The mechanical engineer's relaxed stance and mature eyes didn't make Lydia feel anything but grateful—grateful she'd opened the door.

"I've seen you before. A few times. You were in the corridor when Petra was sent to the iso-cells," Alessia said as she sank down onto her single-sized bed.

Lydia nodded. "Yes, I was there. You tried to help her."

"Tried, yes." Alessia's gazed moved towards the ceiling. There was a sadness within her stare. *What is it about you?* Lydia thought. Everyone bore sadness within them, so what made Alessia's mixture of cheer and melancholy so special? Ever since she'd seen her reading, Lydia had wanted to know what weighed on Alessia's soul. Maybe she even wanted to repair it, to make this woman smile in a way no one else had. She told herself she'd come to the engineer's room because Peleus believed they would enjoy conversing, sharing ideas. In truth, Lydia knew she was interested in sharing so much more.

She leaned forwards and rested her elbows on the small, rounded table in front of her. "I'm sorry she was hurt," Lydia said. She hoped such a comment, coming from a human, didn't come across as patronising. "She's important to you, isn't she?"

A mirthless smile moved across Alessia's face and then disappeared again. "Thank you, Miss Lydia. Your words mean a lot, really."

"You don't have to call me Miss," she replied. "At least, not in private anyway." She felt embarrassed for some reason. Cocking her head, she searched for a way to move ahead with the conversation. "I don't think you could have done anything else for that girl. Not without getting dragged into it yourself."

Alessia shuffled down the bed, bringing herself closer. Her eyes passed over Lydia's face and neck. Lydia wanted Alessia to move back, to stop looking at her with such attentiveness. Alessia's wandering gaze felt like a dangerous gift, something precious that didn't belong to her.

"Why didn't you hit the alarm?" Alessia asked.

"I don't...I don't know."

Alessia met her gaze and held it as she spoke. "I think I do."

Lydia had to look away, back to her hands and her lap. Anywhere but at those intense, discerning eyes. She shifted uncomfortably in the chair, the sound of paper being creased accompanying the movement. She remembered what was in her back pocket. She leaned forwards and slipped it out of her cut-off black jeans and passed it across the room.

"Rosen drew it yesterday," she said as Alessia unfolded and inspected the drawing. "I wonder what compelled him to see his life this way. He's never known anything else, has he? His parents wouldn't even have known anything else either. No Outsiders have. Except for you."

Alessia nodded. "No, you're right. This colony has been their whole world. Rosen is a special boy, though. As soon as I told him about the sky, about the stars and the moon, he knew it was true—as if he'd seen it with his own eyes. He just understood in a way that takes most of the children a long time." She handed the sheet back to Lydia.

"You've got a tattoo?" Alessia asked, nodding towards Lydia's ankle. "The owl of Athena."

Lydia turned her ankle to get a better look at the tattoo herself. "Yes, that's exactly what it is. How did you know?"

"Books. There are a few of them in the library, and more than you'd expect written on the ancient societies of humanity. There's nothing much to read about beyond the early stages of the Industrial Revolution, but most of us have read the *Iliad* at least twice."

That explained why so many of them had classical names. Like humans, the Outsiders had just absorbed and adopted the history and culture they were given access to. "I haven't been to the library," Lydia said. "Is there much in there?"

"Yes. Not a great deal of contemporary fiction, though. Much of it was smuggled out into the corridors. Valuable currency."

Alessia's face changed when she spoke of the books. Her eyelashes flittered just a little faster. It made Lydia like her more than she knew she ought to. Lydia scratched the back of her hand. It didn't quiet her nerves.

"I should go." The statement carried less authority than Lydia had intended. She didn't want to go. This was the closest she'd ever been to her. She wanted to step across the room, sit down on Alessia's bed, reach out, and stroke her forefinger across the pearly skin atop the woman's collarbone.

"Yes. You're probably right," Alessia said, uncertainty passing over her face. "If you want to come back another time...you can. I wouldn't mind, Lydia."

Hearing her own name pass through the Outsider's lips felt like the first taste of a warm alcoholic cider. It tingled inside Lydia's mouth before settling in her stomach, thick and sweet.

Alessia stood, gazing down at Lydia, her expression soft. "Do you have to go?"

Lydia rose from her seat, bringing her closer to Alessia. One more step and they would have been touching. The woman's warm breath struck her in sweet, gentle waves, while Lydia's breathing became shallower. It felt as though a fuser were slowly working its way along her sternum, burning holes into her chest.

"I—I wouldn't mind talking to you some more," Lydia said, her chin dropping. "But I have classes soon. Jez will notice if I'm late. They'll all notice."

Alessia's face relaxed as though defeated and she pushed the door open. "Good to talk to you. Up close, I mean."

"Yes, you too." She tapped her fingernails against the doorframe, hovering a moment before speaking over her shoulder. "Can I ask you something?"

"Anything." Alessia stepped closer to Lydia, who continued to face the corridor. She wanted to turn around and look at the Outsider properly, to establish and hold some sort of connection, even for a moment. But she couldn't. What if there was no connection to be found? Or what if there was? Both possibilities were equally terrifying.

"Peleus suggested I should meet you," Lydia said quietly. "That I should speak to you. Do you know why he would've said that?"

Alessia replied without hesitation, her voice confident and crisp. "Because I asked him to."

It was ridiculous. They'd only just met. Why did Lydia want so badly to stay? To learn more about the Outsider? Lydia drew in a deep breath, slowly. As she exhaled, she stepped out of the doorway, knowing if she didn't leave that moment, she might very well end up leading herself into an awful lot of trouble.

As Lydia started down the hallway, Alessia murmured after her. "Look after Rosen for me, won't you, Lydia?"

"I'll do my best."

Chapter Eleven

IT HAD BEEN some time since a youngling had sought to undertake Ceremony. Alessia felt an enormous sense of pride that Imogen, a child living three doors down from her, would be doing so that day.

As someone who worked at fixing things, Alessia's height was rarely an advantage, but when it came time to attend a Ceremony, her stature was an asset. It allowed her to settle against the back wall and view the goings on from a comfortable distance.

Everyone who knew the child of the hour filed into the room. Their conversational buzz became louder by the minute. Several people traded greetings with Alessia before elbowing their way to the front. She refused several offers to join her friends as they moved through—being swallowed up by eager observers closer to the open, circular space in the middle of Rec Room One was not appealing.

"I see you've come to experience the festivities," a voice directed at someone nearby sliced through the hum.

Alessia turned her head, gazing through the crowd to the other end of the doorway, where Protector Dualla sidled up to Lydia.

She hadn't noticed her enter the room, having been lost in her own thoughts until Dualla's jocosity dragged her back.

The protector was almost yelling to ensure Lydia could hear him. Alessia shuffled herself as close to her side of the door as she could without being overly conspicuous.

"Yes," Lydia said in response to the off-duty protector. "My class isn't operating while it's taking place anyway, and I've been curious to know more about this whole declaration thing." Her tone was polite yet aloof. She did not look directly at Dualla, instead keeping her gaze fixed towards the middle of the room. Alessia wondered how much she could see though given the human was half-a-head shorter than she.

The chatter of the assembled group started to fade as Imogen's parents emerged, paving a path through the Rec Room from the door to the centre. A sense of pride radiated throughout Alessia's rib cage. This was the only remnant of Outsider cultural practices to have survived decades of underground detention, and for reasons unknown to most of them, humans facilitated its continuation by letting students and workers cease duties for the time needed to participate. They might not know the name of their home planet, or even what people originally called their species, but they still had *this*.

"Carl," Lydia said. "Do you know why they do this? What it's for? Jez just called it the Ceremony, said something about a good chance for a VR cube and kind of huffed off."

"Not really," he replied. "I just know it's some weird sex thing. A rite of passage or whatever."

It seemed to Alessia the man was trying to downplay his own ignorance, to make it sound desirable not to have an answer. His characterisation—some weird sex thing—was wildly inappropriate, and had things been different, she would have interjected with a warranted conveyance of fact. As it was, doing so would achieve nothing, except perhaps garner a command to return to her living space and miss the event.

"Oh," Lydia said. Her disappointment hung in the area long after the syllable was spoken. Alessia wished she could put a hand on Lydia's shoulder and stamp out her sadness with a gentle smile. The inclination surprised Alessia. Drawing people closer, inviting them to her, was not something she ordinarily felt comfortable with. The connections she made were always carefully considered and, often, conducted from a safe distance. With Lydia, however, Alessia felt something inside herself shift, something that had been asleep for a very long time.

"Hey, you!" Dualla said, looking at Alessia. Sweet Earth. He'd seen her watching them.

"Yes, sir?" Alessia replied, straightening to full height. She looked blankly across the empty space left by Imogen's parents. Lydia turned, noticing Alessia's presence. She thought there was a hint of a smile on the brunette's face, but couldn't be sure it wasn't just wishful thinking.

"Come over here, wouldya?" Dualla said. "Explain this whole thing to the teacher." He beckoned her like someone might make demands of a noncompliant child.

She nodded, waited for a late-comer to jostle their way past, and then stepped across the threshold to stand closer to the pair. She bent her knees a little, bringing her closer to the protector's height.

"How can I help, Protector?" Alessia's question was purposely melodious with just a touch of obsequiousness. She understood the protectors did their job as they were instructed, and she'd had no past grievances with Carl Dualla, aside from his ridiculous generalisations about their ritual practice. As such, her annoyance at his closeness to Lydia represented a definite lack of clarity on her part. It was a sensation she neither recognised nor enjoyed.

He clicked his tongue, eying her intently. "As I said, Mistress Lydia would like some insight into the Ceremony. Talk her through it."

"It's all right, Carl," Lydia said avoiding Alessia's gaze as she tucked a wayward curl behind her ear. "She doesn't need to."

"I'd be glad to." Alessia hoped in vain Lydia would look up. "It'll start any moment."

As though on cue, a polyphonic hum rose as a small choir started to perform a wordless song. Even the weedy protector fell quiet, drawn towards the expressive voices, though they were spread around the circle and could not be seen. The deep, rich sounds were effectuated by the child's nearest relatives and any others nominated to cleanse the space of negativity.

"This is an individual's introduction," Alessia whispered. "Imogen will enter the room as they finish their song. It's a way of preparing the observers—to make sure we are all able to witness and accept her as she chooses to present herself." Alessia relished having a legitimate reason to speak to Lydia, even if they weren't alone.

Dualla's eyes rolled as he huffed, though he did so quietly, exposing an unspoken need to allow the performance to continue unhindered. It seemed the a cappella group achieved its purpose.

Alessia watched Lydia's face as she peered towards the source of the music, her features tightening as she concentrated. The teacher's fascination somehow reminded Alessia of the way a seemingly flimsy tree might sway and bend in the wind, moved by the power of an unseen force, but never broken. Her eyes glazed over, as though she looked but could not see. The liturgical chanting had taken the human outside herself for a brief, special moment in time. Alessia was sure of it.

Imogen, a petite youngling with shoulder-length, blue-grey hair, shuffled past them, the eyes of everyone in the room upon her. She wore a simplistic green chemise pulled tight by a white belt at her waist. As she moved closer to the clearing, the celestial singing faded, replaced by a silence that mourned the choir's dissolution.

"This is all about gender, then?" Lydia asked in a hushed voice, continuing to look away from Alessia.

"Yes." Alessia nodded. She wished Lydia would turn her head. She wanted so much to make eye-contact with her; it was the best way to gauge her thoughts. "Gender is a cultural acquisition. If someone wants to proclaim their identification with a particular identity, this is how they share that choice with us. It can happen at any age, and it can happen more than once for the same person."

"Is the ritual the same for everyone?" Dualla said, shifting his weight.

She held back a satisfied smile. He was as curious as Lydia.

"It is," she replied, leaning a shoulder into the wall. "Male. Female. A combination of both. Regardless of the sex you were assigned at birth, the Ceremony is the same."

"You say she. You don't all use gender-neutral pronouns before this ritual happens?"

Alessia shook her head softly. "Not in all cases, but it can vary. I suppose a child's sense of self becomes clear very young, and we don't assume that a person can't be both female, yet masculine, either. Imogen was born female and as a youngling referred to herself with feminine pronouns, so we use them also. If she'd used other pronouns growing up, we'd use those."

"Why the ritual at all, then?"

"It's Imogen's opportunity to assert and celebrate how she feels about herself. Or perhaps to correct us if she's now come to realise that how she felt as a younger child has evolved, something that isn't altogether uncommon. It's important to us that we have this space to openly acknowledge and respect one another's spirits."

Imogen stood in the middle of the room. Thanks to the path paved by her parents, the trio had an excellent view. No one seemed willing to spill back into the space, though many crane-necked and tiptoed dance moves suggested they wanted to do so.

Four children around the same age as the girl stepped forwards. They bowed their heads gently.

This was Alessia's favourite part of the ritual. One at a time, Imogen approached each of the other children, touching her hands to their shoulders. None of the four had undergone their own Ceremony. That was the point; Imogen was giving them an unspoken blessing, reassuring them that however each would develop, she would accept them.

Lydia focused on what was happening, whilst Dualla's face silently willed an explanation from Alessia. She gave none. This was an important moment, and she had no intention of speaking, however quietly, as the child exchanged sentiments with her friends. When the last of the younglings had been acknowledged, they moved forwards to hug Imogen all at once. Their faces were bright, characterised by a veritable happiness only a child could express.

"I don't get it," the protector said as the crowd started to mutter again, watching the children move off. "She's already a girl, ain't she?"

Alessia regarded his question for a moment, trying to identify the heart of what he wanted to know. "People can be conscripted into a gender, of course," she replied.

Lydia refocused her attention on the conversation. The teacher's thick eyelashes distracted Alessia for a second before she could continue. "We're all influenced by what's around us, the company we keep. I believe it would be foolish to think we are free agents in the whole thing, but this is just how it is. You make choices with the information you have."

Dualla's eyes narrowed as he moved a hand to his hip. "But—" He waved his hand through the air. "It doesn't make sense. There's biology, ain't there? What if she gets up there and says she feels like she's a boy?"

"Why assume social and biological identity to be incongruent?" Alessia forgot who she was speaking to. Before anyone could respond, Imogen's confident voice quieted the chatter in the room yet again.

"I wish to thank my parents for giving me life," the youngling said. Her mother and father stepped forwards and took their positions behind their daughter. She turned to face her parents.

"You have given me a body," Imogen continued. "It is a body that allows me to grow. Now, as I become older and learn more of who I am, I wish to share with you the soul that exists within me. It is an identity I have come here to acknowledge and to celebrate."

The eleven-year-old fell silent. Alessia wondered if she'd forgotten the format of her declaration, but after a few breaths, Imogen found her place. "I may change in the future, but at this moment, in the depths of my soul...I feel I am, in most ways, a feminine being."

Feet around the room stomped against the floor, applauding the girl's willingness to reflect upon her own nature.

It was as Alessia suspected. Most Outsiders felt an alignment with their sex, but not all. No one would have reacted any differently had Imogen declared a desire to be acknowledged as mostly masculine or, as a few did at times, neutral. It was no one's place but her own to make such a distinction.

Imogen and her parents knelt, joining hands as they did. With downcast eyes, they began humming. More voices joined in. After a minute or so, the family stood, smiling at one another. The formality of the occasion gradually dissolved and conversations broke out within the space.

"That's it?" Dualla said.

Alessia nodded in reply. He seemed to have expected more, but for those who truly appreciated the event, they'd been provided with more than enough emotional fodder to process.

"May I ask," Lydia said, "if there are any expectations? You know, after they've been through this Ceremony?"

"What do you mean?" Alessia said, her brow furrowed.

"Well, for some human groups, especially in the past, a rite of passage like this comes with new legal or familial responsibilities. Like having children or assuming management of a business passed on through the generations." The human's contralto-like voice had almost lulled Alessia into believing they were alone.

"No, there's nothing like that. I suppose the only expectation is each one be open and honest with themselves. They need to remember nothing stays the same, least of all one's identity. The soul is all at once timeless and transient."

Lydia's eyes flashed momentarily. It was clear that she wanted to understand Alessia's explanation, but struggled to do so. Alessia would have loved nothing more at that moment than to spend hours sitting on the floor of the library with Lydia, discussing how important freedom of gender really was to the Outsiders. Or any other topic she may have wished to explore.

The sliding glass door to the Rec Room opened at the behest of Imogen's papa, who walked towards them as they spoke. Alessia hadn't realised how crowded and stifling the space had become until cool air came in through the opening. People started to move outward, congregating in the hallway as they exchanged hugs and shared good wishes.

"That'll do then," Dualla said to her. "You can go now."

Alessia's heart felt heavy, for Lydia avoided looking at her. The teacher was only a metre away and yet a thick wall existed between them. In such a time and place, she was powerless to climb it.

"Thank you, sir," Alessia replied and swallowed her disappointment. She waited a moment until the teacher felt her stare, Lydia finally shifting her head to meet it.

"You know where I am if you require anything further." Alessia spoke at both of them, but hoped Lydia would understand the statement was meant only for her.

After an indifferent farewell, she left the two humans to look for Imogen so she could offer her best wishes. She felt a growing emptiness as she navigated the crowd of familiar faces. Protector Dualla was getting closer to Lydia at the same moment Alessia was walking away.

Chapter Twelve

LYDIA FORCED HER foot hard against the wall. Lean fibres in the calf muscle screamed in pain as she stretched. She'd learned if she ran until her chest burned and her throat ached, she could improve her chances of finding some measure of rest when it came time to turn out the lights and hoped that would be the case this time around. She had ten minutes before the cafeteria shut down for the night. Food, shower, and then bed. Somewhere in all of that, she hoped to be able to, just for one moment, stop replaying her conversations with Alessia. Nine hours since the Ceremony and all Lydia could think about was Alessia. Mooning over a near stranger? Lydia felt like an infatuated teenager. She was a tensed coil ready to spring into Alessia's arms. For the hundredth time that day, she threw a curtain over the thought. No laws existed to prohibit romantic interactions with an Outsider; there was no point given they were segregated, but still, Lydia knew such ideas were dangerous. Not least of all because she was the Quadrant Governor's daughter and nothing in her life had ever been kept private.

Lydia moved down the corridor towards something that could quiet her grumbling stomach, shaking the strain from her limbs as she went. The sight of Jez, the side of her face flat against a cafeteria table top, was not what Lydia had expected to see. Her colleague was mumbling to herself, the words slurred. The woman drank more than an N-Cer going through bandwidth withdrawals. Lydia toyed with the idea of leaving Jez there to sort out her own drunken stupor. She could just approach the AI chef, order her meal, wait for it to be cooked, and pretend she'd never even noticed Jez. But in the end, she knew her plans for the evening were officially cancelled. With no small measure of trepidation, Lydia crossed the room and sat down next to Jez.

"Hey. Are you awake?" Lydia asked in a hushed tone.

Jez's head snapped back so fast it made Lydia jump. It flopped on top of her neck like a novelty transport ornament.

"Huh? What? Who the fu—Oh, it's you. Yoho Lydia." Jez let her head smack back down against the metallic table. Jez had barely been outside for ten years and it showed. No one said yoho anymore.

"Jez, how 'bout we go for a walk? I can take you to your quarters."

Jez shuffled down the bench, but misjudged the distance and fell to the floor. Lydia leapt to her feet but sat back down as soon as she heard Jez's healthy cackle.

"Go with you?" Jez said. "No bloody way! Hey, look, you're all right, Barrett. But I am not interested in women."

Lydia rolled her eyes as she turned her head. "Jez, you're drunk. Though clearly, you remember the conversation we had the *last* time you drank this much. When I told you about my ex-girlfriend, I was not making a pass at you. I have less than zero interest in you that way." Lydia turned back to Jez, whose expression was now listless. "So, come on. Up you get."

Jez's laughter resumed as she made three attempts to lift herself up off the floor, each time falling back onto her rear end. She succeeded by turning over onto her stomach and then pushing onto her feet. Her giggling finally stopped when she was almost standing upright while leaning against the table for support.

Jez brought her face closer, her breath hot and sticky. She smelled of vodka and toothpaste. They stared at each other for a few moments, long enough for Lydia's bravery to fade. She wanted to replace her verbal sword with a physical shield. She leaned back to try to find some space and escape Jez's scrutiny.

"Hah!" Jez released a torrent of air in one abrupt, putrid blast causing Lydia's eyes to water. Jez stumbled back a few steps.

"Okay. Come on, I'll help you get back." Lydia hooked her arm underneath Jez's elbow and accepted some of her weight. Jez didn't fight her this time, but rather nodded and followed Lydia's lead. *Thank Earth.*

"Hey. Sorry. I know you're not after me." Jez's feet scraped haphazardly along the floor as they shuffled towards the elevator.

"It's okay." Lydia wasn't convinced it was okay, but Jez's attempt to insult her—again—was not worth wasting another breath on. Not while Jez was so trashed, anyway. One thing Lydia had learned from her parents: there was absolutely no point in trying to argue with someone who'd had more than five drinks. They were always right. "Listen, this bizarre transparent elevator probably won't do much good for your stomach. Maybe close your eyes?"

Jez swallowed hard and covered her mouth. *Please don't vomit.* Jez's hand returned to her side.

"Excellent point." Jez seemed to be working hard not to slur her words. "The design probably came out of the head of some wanker, trendy designer-type."

Inside the lift, Jez wrapped an arm around Lydia's waist, leaned against Lydia's shoulder, and closed her eyes, applying herself to the task of keeping vertical.

Lydia had come to enjoy the brief blur of steel, concrete, and wiring that flew past the see-through elevator doors. Something about the combined predictability and disconcerting speed of the haze just made sense to her. The trip to Section C took only a few moments, the rambling walk to Jez's room somewhat longer.

"Okay, here we go." Lydia guided Jez's pale hand to the smooth security plate next to the door. The door skulked off to the left, and they stepped inside just as the lights willed themselves awake. The two women stumbled into the room. Lydia was eager to unload Jez's weight and straighten her spine.

With a graceless plonk, Jez fell onto the bed, pulling Lydia down next to her. It was a double bed and, compared to Lydia's, felt decadent and spacious. The two of them lay there for a time, staring at holo-posters of the night sky fixed between unforgiving tubular lights.

Lydia's stomach made an obnoxious gurgling, reminding her she still needed to eat. The sound made Jez giggle. Luckily, the laugh was short-lived this time around.

"I think you'll be fine now. I'm going back to my place," Lydia announced as she sat up. Her hair had been mottled and sticky after using the gym, but now, after the effort required to guide her colleague back to her quarters, Lydia had started to feel dirty. She wondered if it might be wrong to eat whilst in the shower.

"Did you know I've been living here for eight years?" Jez's words, while still slower than normal, possessed a newfound sense of clarity.

"No. I didn't. You don't ever leave?" Lydia asked. She'd wanted to know more about Jez's past since they first laid unfamiliar eyes upon each other. Jez was all at once infuriating, intelligent, and cryptic.

She could postpone the shower a little longer.

"Not really," Jez replied. "Well, sometimes. Last year I went out for a while. Switched on my N-C. Connected to the Hive. Got fucked up. Then got fucked. You know, the usual."

Lydia looked away. Jez was lying flat on her back beside her. Lydia had meant what she said: she was not in any way attracted to Jez. Not in a sexual way, anyhow. That didn't make her feel any less awkward that a woman lying with her legs sprawled across a bed, directly next to her, made an overt reference to being screwed.

"Of course," Jez said matter-of-factly, "I had to pay a guy to go near what I've got." She rolled over on to her stomach and turned her head towards Lydia. "I can wear lenses, ya know. But they're a temporary fix. One DNA swab and I'd send the 'thorities into a frenzy."

Lydia wanted to ask Jez why she'd had to pay a prostitute. She realised she didn't know very much about an O's body aside from the fact that, at least with clothes on, they were shaped much the same as humans. The accounts of their arrival had never spelled out that sort of intimate detail. She forced the question to the back of her mind, into the same cavernous pit she used to house fantasies about a certain alien.

"If you don't like your eyes...why don't you get a chem-colour?" Yes. A safer question to ask, she decided after speaking the words. Much to the disgust of many punksters, the law stopped anyone from injecting 'unnatural-looking' gels, but brown or black eyes would have served Jez's purpose.

"Because!" Jez blurted. Her hand flew above her head before thwacking back down against the pillow. "Because I already have. I've had three of those damned treatments already. They don't work. These golden globes are stubborn."

Lydia didn't reply. She couldn't. Jez was angry at her golden eyes, her own body too. It seemed she hated every Outsider gene she had. How could a person begin to say sorry for that kind of thing? Especially when it was hard for Lydia to understand why Jez would hate the most fundamental aspects of who she is.

"She didn't want me, you know." Jez said it with such alacrity Lydia wondered if she hadn't written herself off with booze just so she could say that exact sentence.

"Sorry?" Lydia replied. Jez's unsolicited statement hit her with all the force of a back-handed slap. Though she'd asked, Lydia wasn't sure if she wanted Jez to explain.

"My...*mother*, or whatever she is. She was some O slut who seduced the guy who happened to own the sperm that made me. He was a guard, ya know? Not here. It was the Q3 compound. He didn't even tell anyone about it until a kid came out practically tanned and the whole lot of them were interrogated. Must have been humiliated by the whole thing. Screwing an O. I sure as hell wouldn't want everyone to know about it. Anyway, apparently neither of them wanted anything to do with me. She died during one of the sicknesses not long after. No idea where he went, but obviously he wasn't keen on taking his half-breed kid home to meet the grandparents."

"Jez, I'm..." Lydia shook her head, her eyes cast downwards. Earlier she'd possessed a surprising ability to tell Jez exactly what she was thinking. That bravado dissolved like an aspirin in hot water. Being rejected by your own parents for your own nature—the one they'd played a part in shaping—was horrible. She just couldn't think of anything to say. But, shamed as Lydia was by her own thoughts, Jez's story wasn't what muted her. It was Jez's judgment. Her unabashed and scathing dislike for all Outsiders and, just as bad, for those Outsiders that might find humans to their liking.

"What? You're what? *Sorry?*" Jez pushed herself onto her forearms. The glaring overhead lights cast shadows across one side of her scowling face.

Confusion pushed through Lydia's mind with the same force as a pulser blast fired against bare skin. She *was* sorry; she really was. Being the unwanted product of such a taboo act explained a hell of a lot about Jez.

Maybe that's why Pearsal kept Jez down there. Perhaps safety and comfort was some kind of consolation prize for her existence.

"I saw you," Jez said as a twisted grin curled across her face.

Saw what? Lydia started to think faster than she could breathe. "What are you talking about?"

"Yesterday. You. An alien. I followed you in the O-Zone."

Lydia's swirling thoughts fell into a puddle of granulated images, eventually replaced by a single overarching thought: *shit.* The word repeated itself several times over. She couldn't tie down the panicking rat clawing its way through her head. There was no legitimate reason for a teacher to enter the private cell of an Outsider, which is why only protectors had permission to do so. This could end badly. Before Lydia could formulate an excuse, Jez spoke again.

"So, ya don't often see a human going into an O's room on their own. Unless maybe you're a protector and can't get backup for a search." Jez seemed to be, somehow, soberer than she'd been only minutes earlier. "If I were you, Barrett, I'd keep a pole's length between you and any of *them*."

Out of nowhere, Jez slumped onto her stomach, falling asleep almost as soon as her head had hit the pillow. It was a deep, pitch-black sleep that only came about with chemical assistance. Lydia breathed a sigh at not having to try and find a reply to Jez's challenge. Without hesitation, she returned to her own room, working hard to keep herself from running there. She didn't want to draw more attention. Leaving Jez's room in the middle of the night wearing her gym clothes was enough to cause a stir as it was.

Lydia kicked off her shoes, each one landed somewhere near the study desk. Hands on her hips, she pulled her lips together into a thin line. *What the hell am I going to do?* Jez didn't say she would tell anyone about what she'd seen, but Lydia had next to no trust in Jez's ability to keep a secret. At the very least, she'd be fired. She had no real idea what could happen to Alessia for allowing her into the room, but after what she'd seen happen to Petra, Lydia didn't want to linger on the thought for too long.

Searching through a drawer, Lydia found a clean towel and new underwear. Showering was all she could think to do. Maybe the hot water could settle the shaking of her hands. Flinging the towel over her shoulder, she turned to leave in the direction of the communal bathrooms. As she did so, she caught a glimpse of a folded holo-sheet on her pillow.

As was always the case with such printouts, one side was a shiny black. Lydia unfolded it to reveal a moving image of an owl in flight on the printed side. On a repeated loop, the bird launched from a tree limb to take flight against a burnt orange sunset. It was a stunning image and, for some reason, helped her relax. She hadn't realised quite how tightly her muscles were gripping her bones.

Alessia had noticed the owl tattoo on her ankle. Did she manage to get this brought in somehow? Maybe she had been the one to send her the book as well. Lydia, at first, felt an unfamiliar sense of pleasure at the possibility of Alessia taking such effort to send her veiled messages. If the book had been one of them, then she'd been noticed by the

Outsider much earlier than Lydia had thought. The look that passed between them on that first morning was, perhaps, memorable for the both of them.

The feeling of jubilance was a fleeting one, as doubts elbowed their way into her mind. *What if Jez is right? What if the Outsiders are dangerous?* Lydia felt her muscles tense again as she considered the situation. Alessia might very well have been manipulating Lydia and, being too trusting, Lydia may not have even realised when she let it happen.

The answers couldn't be found in staring at the holo-sheet. Clean, hot water and a seaweed bar were all that stood between her and sleep. She tucked the printout under her pillow and headed for the showers, trying her best not to believe the gifts left in her room had, somehow, come from Alessia.

She stepped down the hall as quietly as she could manage and Lydia wondered if, by some chance, Jez might forget their entire conversation by the time she woke up in the morning.

Chapter Thirteen

ALESSIA HAD READ the same paragraph three times, but hadn't absorbed any of it. She'd been sitting on Fermi's worn mattress for two hours, waiting for him to finish work. Ordinarily, she considered herself more patient than most. Not recently, though. Since Petra came back from the iso-cell, her composure had faded faster than the light in Petra's eyes. The changes in her relationships were unnerving, as was the gradual ripple of discontent she could feel spreading throughout the colony. As much as she wanted Outsiders to question the things humans told them, she'd not wanted it to come about in response to an act of violence. She'd hoped thoughtful consideration of their past and their future to come from truth, from history, not fear.

At last, Fermi pushed through the door. He looked straight through her as he slipped out of his shoes and pushed them under the bed with a great deal more force than required. Alessia sat up, crossed her legs beneath her, and allowed the novel to fall into her lap.

"Are you going to keep ignoring I'm here?" she asked as Fermi unbuttoned his shirt. He tucked the shirt into a rusted tin crate at the foot of the bed. The silvery-white of his bare chest enhanced by a long fluorescent globe that clung to the ceiling.

"Fer? Please." Her voice wavered. This was harder than she'd expected. "I know you're angry. I felt the exact moment you gave up on me in Petra's room the other day. Will you talk to me?"

He slipped a black T-shirt over his head. One side of the garment was riddled with holes. The dark fabric against his skin made him appear younger. His left hand rested on his hip, the other picked at the tip of a cornrow. "What do you want?"

Without looking at her, he sat down on the foot of the bed, leaving as much distance as possible between them. The space, though she could have easily reached across it with her arms, felt immeasurable.

Alessia wished there was somewhere else to have this conversation. Her whole life was playing out in confined spaces. The restrictions enforced on her body were starting to feel like limitations on her whole being. She missed being able to move from one place to another and have it look and feel different. She wanted to lay her eyes on something new. She wanted to engage with new topics of conversation, explore new books, meet new people. Over the years, some aspects of life had started to feel like constant re-runs of the same program. Stability was important, but so was variety.

"You're mad I didn't tell you about the meetings. They aren't what you're thinking they were. There wasn't some grand organisation going on. W—"

"We?" he interrupted.

"Peleus and me, most of the time. Petra sometimes as well," she replied.

Fermi nodded.

"We would try and spend some time with the younglings, asking them questions, see how they felt about themselves. A lot of them seemed to think their entire life being dictated is normal. School. Ceremony. Work. Make more Outsiders. Die."

Fermi frowned at her. He seemed to want to stay angry, but he couldn't. His familiar exuberance didn't return, but neither did his frustration remain. "That...that's the saddest thing I've ever heard," he whispered through tight lips.

"Yes." She edged her way closer and rested a hand on his shoulder. "Peleus and I became close after his parents were taken and he realised how small his world was. He didn't want other Outsiders to have so little control over their fates."

"He told me," Fermi said in a stoic voice.

Alessia's hand fell away, it being obvious he didn't appreciate the contact. Peleus and Fermi had been spending time together. She thought that might happen, given the intensity of their interaction a week earlier. She was glad; they'd be good for each other.

"Peleus has been more honest with me in the last few days than you have been in over ten years," said Fermi.

"I deserve that."

Fermi was hurt, and she was the one who had hurt him.

He shifted his weight and turned to face her. He glanced over his shoulder, as though checking nobody was there, even though they were clearly alone.

"Tell me, Ali." Fermi's eyes pleaded with her. "Tell me what you know about the surface."

Alessia was tired of telling her story. Having Peleus and Petra to help spread it amongst the younglings had been a blessing. Fermi was a friend, though, and she owed him her time. She owed him a lot more, really.

"Well, you already know I was fourteen when I came here. I told you about my parents, Rey and Griffin. How we lived in the mouth of a cave system south of the mountains."

"Yeah."

As Fermi's eyes softened, she wondered if he felt guilty about his own role in building the wall between them, having never been willing to listen to this story before. The parameters of their relationship had long been set. He didn't pursue his infatuation for her, and she didn't push him to question their confinement or the accepted narrative of how it had come to be.

"It wasn't perfect. It was always dark there, even though we didn't live very far down. Occasionally, we explored the surrounding hills. We got to stay together, though. That's the main thing." She couldn't repress a smile at the thought of her parents.

Fermi's jaw tightened, however. She knew he had no idea if his parents were still alive, and it could be hard for him to think about that sense of lost connection. They'd been moved to the Quadrant One Colony when he was brought here. Though he rarely mentioned either of them anymore, she knew he missed them.

"How did your family avoid the collection? Tarpeia...didn't she bring us all together for the UEA to herd us off in transports?"

His forthright summation of the events from a century ago was a shock. Fermi had never said a harsh word against the UEA in his life—as far as Alessia knew, anyway. He was right. At the time, Global Premier Abel held a major celebration. Every Outsider on the planet was there, ordered by Tarpeia to attend. Abel and Tarpeia promised it would be a symbolic beginning, an open display of solidarity. In fact, not one Outsider left that building through the front door. Transports had relocated all of them; a colony in each quadrant. Peleus must have told Fermi that part. The teachers delivered a rather different lesson on history and it was only in the last couple of years the younglings had heard Alessia's version of events, handed down to her by her parents.

"We were part of the deal, apparently," she said.

Fermi's face went blank. "What do you mean? The deal between Abel and Tarpeia?"

"Yes. To use my mother's words: it was bullshit. Tarpeia realised Abel's picture of our future was a bit too rosy to be true when the transport doors opened at the celebration in the capital."

"How does that have anything to do with you and your parents living in some cave system for years? Near humans, even?"

"I don't know what tipped Tarpeia off, but she realized the deal wasn't going to go ahead as planned. The first ever group of protectors were herding the refugees onto the flight ramps when Tarpeia confronted Abel. But the underground colonies were already built and her people were already sealed into the transports. She threatened to kill herself. She knew he needed her knowledge of science, of space, heck...her knowledge of her own body. So he made her an offer."

"What was it?" Fermi's face hardened.

"If she went into one of the colonies, lived out her life, and shared her knowledge with the overseer, then her family would be allowed to live in seclusion on the surface."

"Her family?" He blinked, then his lips parted. "*You're* related to Tarpeia? Tarpeia the Discerner?"

Alessia's eyebrows drew closer together. "Yes. She's my grandmother. Long generations in my family."

"Bullshit!" His outburst came as a mixture of surprise and excitement. Fermi scanned her face, as if searching for a sign she was lying. "Good Earth, Ali. Are you a discerner, too?"

She reached her hand behind her neck to pull some of her hair across her shoulders. The top layers were the golden colour common to their kind. Twisting it in her hands, she revealed a second colour hiding beneath the outer layers. It was a luminous orange broken by hues of apple red. After a few moments, she let it go, allowing the thicker blonde curls to swallow the thinner red curtain beneath.

His eyes widened. Clearly, he recognised one of the key physical traits of the discerners, the genetic line traditionally recognised as leaders amongst their community. Tarpeia had been the last one the community had been aware of. Alessia had wanted it to stay that way. "Does Peleus know?"

"No," she shook her head. "He knows I'm related to Tarpeia, but he doesn't know I inherited her D-Strain. There's a lot about myself I don't know. I don't yet feel qualified to assert any sort of genuine authority. The time isn't right."

"Petra—" he started, before being cut off.

"Is a smart kid with a short fuse. She and her crew don't even know what the discerners are. Nor do they need to. It's an antiquated concept of power that only made sense on our home world. That's why people our age are probably the last ones to even know what discerners are. Or were."

Fermi took a few deep breaths. Alessia felt the need to match each one. "What they tell us about why our grandparents and great-grandparents came here. Is any of that true?"

"A little. They were escaping a war, as we are all told. A fringe group managed to garner support from advisors within the council, enough support to secure a weapons supply. The coup happened in just a few days. A lot of people refused to fight. Running away was their best hope of life for their children. They were genuinely frightened their younglings would be killed. Or worse, somehow become an active part of the new regime themselves."

"Pacifist refugees, then?"

"Yes. Pacifists." It sounded more absurd to her every time she retold the story. If their ancestors had fought back it's possible they could have been wiped out. On the other hand Rey, her mother, could be sitting at the head of a healthy, functioning council on a planet that didn't segregate.

"When they got here, the humans promised help," Alessia continued. "Safety was the word of the day back then. As far as I know, no Outsider ever tried to take anything from a human not freely given. But something went wrong along the way. Humans became scared of us after the initial novelty wore off. Relations became shaky, even violent. Tarpeia was frightened our whole race would end up living in shanty towns on the fringe of cities, stuck in social limbo with no way out. For some reason, the discerners live longer than everyone else. She would have known, better than anyone, what they'd already been through before even arriving. Premier Abel offered her a chance for all refugees to live separately but freely in parts of the world too hot or cold for humans to feel comfortable. I guess it sounded like a good deal at the time."

But it was not a good deal. They were separate, but they were sure as hell not free. They'd thought they were accepting a reasonable compromise, but their concession did not bring with it the promised autonomy. Nor had they truly understood the long-term consequences of being hidden away from the dominant species of the planet. Outsiders, over time, had become increasingly robotic in their approach to life. Existing more so than living.

"Why do they keep us here? By the sounds of it, the humans could just kill us all and save themselves a lot of trouble."

"I assume it's so they can maintain the delusion their government is as hospitable and tolerant as they keep telling everyone they are. I don't imagine all the products we make down here hurts their economy, either." Her answer didn't seem to satisfy Fermi any more than it satisfied her. There must be more to it, but she was in no position to find out. Thinking about it often kept her awake at night.

"Good point," Fermi replied. His countenance softened. "We have no idea what kind of workforce they have up there. We don't really know about anything they've got on the surface, do we?"

"No. No, we don't. We will, though. It'll just take some time."

Fermi rubbed both of his temples with his fingers. Alessia still wasn't sure she should have told anybody about her family, but it was too late to take it back. Surely such a weighty truth would help repay her debts to Fermi.

"You never could have been yourself with me, could you, Ali?"

She would have liked to soften the blow for him, to make her rejection less abrupt somehow, but after so long avoiding the issue of his infatuation, being direct seemed the only way to deal with it now. "I'm sorry. But no, I don't think I could." Being this open with him, talking about the things that occupied such a great deal of space in her head, eased her soul. It may have been hard, but it wasn't a mistake.

"And now it's too late for us to be anything but friends. It all works out the way it is supposed to, though, I'm betting."

The human teacher's expressive face flashed behind Alessia's eyes. She blinked the image away and refocussed her attention on Fermi. "I think you're right. You're pretty smart, you know."

"Don't act so surprised. Not all of us are genetically superior leadership types, but it doesn't mean we don't know stuff. And things."

She couldn't help but smile. That was the Fermi she knew and loved. Not in the way he may have wanted her to, but love him she did. "Yes. You definitely know *stuff*," she said.

"Listen, Peleus is coming by soon. But maybe we can hang out later?"

"What, I'm being evicted?"

"Damned straight you are," he replied.

"You two are getting on then? Things seemed a little tense when I last saw you together."

"I think we've found some steady ground to build a friendship, yes." Something in his face told her they'd been spending a lot of time together since the day they'd visited Petra. "Okay. Time's up."

"Can't invade the boys' night?"

Fermi's cheeks flushed. "Something like that. Besides, my brain probably can't handle any more revelations today, and when you two are together, everything is always so freaking serious."

Alessia hugged him tightly. The wall between them crumbled more with each breath they took.

"Ali, I would love to get my arms back now, please."

She laughed and let him go. "Fine. See you soon, yes?"

Fermi nodded as she walked past him and pulled the door open. She knew what she was about to ask might insult him, but it had to be done. "You won't tell anyone, will you?"

"What? That the leader who brought us all to Earth has a living bloodline and the weird genius living on the top floor is her granddaughter and should be leading our entire race?" She raised an eyebrow at him. "No, I won't tell anyone, Discerner Alessia. Now, bugger off so I can hang out with Peleus."

Chapter Fourteen

ALESSIA HAD TO see Lydia. It was that simple. Three long days had passed since their conversation. She had sorted things out with Fermi, diagnosed and fixed a major food processing error, run the length of every level in the colony ten times, and rearranged the books in her room by title. Still, thoughts of Lydia persisted, undampened.

It didn't make any sense. Alessia had felt connected to Lydia since seeing her with Mistress Jez in the main corridor. They didn't even speak to each other that morning, only locked eyes across a near-empty corridor. Yet, ever since, Alessia scanned the halls when she moved between jobs, trying to catch glimpses of her. She may have been human, but Lydia's quiet energy was magnetic. Each time they spoke, that pull was amplified.

The chron above the school entryway read 15:46. Fourteen minutes left. Alessia wished she'd dragged her feet with the ventilation system safety check. Fourteen minutes outside the classrooms without looking like a suspicious maniac? She certainly felt like one. She always thought through her decisions. Analysed potential outcomes. She didn't like to linger on dangerous thoughts.

Unable to chase the confusion away, Alessia gave up trying and sat cross-legged on the floor. Sitting at the edge of the entrance, back against the wall, Alessia heard the soft chatter of children. A few weeks earlier, she would have only been able to hear the teacher barking instructions.

Mistress Jez had a sing-song voice, yet still managed to be terrifying when she told someone what to do. Even if it was a simple 'sit down' or 'finish your quiz.' Lydia was so much calmer. No wonder all the kids in the other class wanted to trade places.

The chatter in Lydia's classroom died away. Perhaps they were writing something.

"Why do you have your hand up?" Mistress Jez's voice cut through the now quiet air. Alessia wanted to stand in the doorway and see what was happening but thought better of it.

"Excuse me, Mistress, but may I ask a question?" She recognised the voice. It was Thea, a beautifully cheeky little creature who lived with her parents in the cell directly below her own.

"Right." The word sounded more like an accusation than affirmation. "Fine. Go on, then."

Interesting, Alessia thought. She was surprised the mistress allowed the question.

"In the history classes, you told us why our great-grandparents came to live here. It's been a long time though, right? Aren't the humans ready to try again? Let us onto the surface, I mean?"

Agonising silence followed. Though she couldn't see Mistress Jez's face, Alessia imagined it probably resembled the rear end of a cat at that moment. It took all Alessia's resolve not to burst into the entryway and put herself between Thea and the teacher.

"Thea. Child. It must be hard for you to understand, I suppose. The fact is..." Alessia turned her face towards the door frame, breathing faster.

"The fact is, Thea," Jez continued, "everyone is better off if we keep the two groups apart." The mistress must have moved closer to the back end of the classroom; her voice had become louder. "Jobs, housing...there's just not enough to go around up there. You're better off down here. That way, no one is disappointed and the Outsiders don't get angry. It is a trait of your species—to get angry, you know."

Alessia's hands balled into fists. The teacher always referred to Outsiders as 'you' and 'they,' even though the eyes she saw the world through were the same as Thea's. Telling a nine-year-old her entire community is better off trapped in cells was horrendous. Or that her people were somehow violent. The child had probably never so much as sworn at another person.

"Oh," was all the youngling said.

Mistress Jez clapped her hands together. "Now, now. Enough. Tidy the room. Spick and span. Get to it."

As chairs and tables scraped against the tiled floors, Alessia wiped the back of her hand across her face and stood to leave. Someone's foot swept behind her ankle, and Alessia grabbed the wall behind her for support. The fast reaction kept her upright, but that did not seem to be what the protector had wanted.

"Watch it, O. You nearly knocked me down," came an acidic male voice.

The voice belonged to Carl Dualla. The last time they spoke she had only felt unease because of his apparent familiarity with Lydia. Aside from that, they'd never had any real problems with each other. It didn't make sense for the man to target her now.

"Protector Dualla. I was sitting, then I stood up. I couldn't have knocked into you," Alessia replied, trying to keep her voice monotonous. It was all she could do to swallow her frustration. When it came to following the rules of engagement with a protector, some days were more challenging than others.

Dualla stepped into Alessia, forcing her back against the wall. The protector's hot breath came in waves against her neck. "You'd be aware purposely hurting one of us, the guards who protect you aliens from each other, means a visit to an iso-cell."

Alessia didn't understand the fierceness flashing within his eyes. Most of the guards avoided talking to an Outsider unless they had to. Only a small handful of them enjoyed stirring up trouble. To her knowledge, Dualla had never been one of them.

"Yes," Alessia replied. "Thank you for reminding me. I apologise."

Dualla already stood as close to Alessia as possible, yet he still leant forwards. The concrete wall scraped against her shoulder blades. He forced his knee between her legs and she suppressed a groan.

"It's important to be reminded of things sometimes, isn't it?" Dualla pulled his lips into a straight, thin line as he examined Alessia's face. "Here's one more thing for you to remember, Outsider. Don't touch things that aren't yours."

A sigh pulsed though Alessia's body when the protector stepped backwards. Utterly confused by what had just happened, she remained silent and still until the man had disappeared down the corridor.

Alessia ran back to her cell, slamming the door behind her and then falling heavily against it. She had no desire to let anyone else see her come undone over something that, ordinarily, she ought to have been able to handle. She replayed the event in her head. The sickly smell of his breath. The pressure of his thigh against her body. Pressure built in her chest, the product of too many thoughts, too many expectations for herself, too many moments of restraint.

Her breathing became heavier and her face grew hotter.

"Fuck!" She pulled off her shoes, throwing one after the other at the ceiling. When they fell, she threw them again. Beads of sweat formed at the base of her neck.

"Damn it!" She grabbed her pillow. Holding it against the wall with one hand, she punched it repeatedly with the other. "Now *this* is bloody violent!" She punched at it until smears of blood from her knuckles stained the tattered rayon fabric, giving in to the mania that had taken over her body.

Two arms wrapped around her waist and pulled her backwards. "Hey! Stop! You'll hurt yourself." The human's voice was like a spotlight shining through a thick fog; she knew exactly what—who—it was, but the finer details were indecipherable.

Lydia pulled her in tighter; Lydia's chest pressed against Alessia's back. She hadn't even heard her open the door, but those arms could belong to no one else. Alessia hadn't wanted anyone to see her like this, completely unhinged, and for reasons she couldn't fully explain even to herself. Something had just snapped.

"Get your hands off me!" Alessia freed herself from Lydia's grasp, the closeness of her body making Alessia feel even more confused about her inner-turmoil. She turned to face her. "Why are you here?"

"Jez," Lydia said before pausing to catch her breath. "She told me you were sitting outside the school. One of the protectors saw you." Lydia shook her head, as though shaking off an unpleasant thought, before continuing. "Jez thinks you're dangerous. She loves gossiping about whatever you get up to. Why were you there?"

"I'd finished my job list and was simply sitting on the floor." Alessia picked up the remnants of the pillow from the floor and replaced it at the head of the bed. She wanted to calm down, she really did, but the hot pit in her stomach wouldn't stop growing.

Alessia kicked at the side of her bed. She spun, hands on her hips. "Bitch!" She kicked the bed again. Hard. The metal joints groaned. She knew she'd come unhinged—a fact that horrified her—yet she couldn't seem to calm down. Nor did she feel that she had to in front of Lydia. Nothing about Lydia's face or body language suggested judgment, she seemed only concerned.

Lydia stepped across the room and grabbed hold of her again. She had only a fraction of Alessia's physical strength, but this time, Alessia didn't fight back. Instead, she allowed Lydia to envelop her body. Lydia's fingers ran through her hair, and with each stroke, Alessia slowed her breath. Characterised by genuine compassion, no one had touched her like that in years.

They stood together, arms wrapped around each other. Alessia let her cheek fall to rest against the side of Lydia's forehead. The heat in her gut dissolved in measured contractions until it had all but faded.

"Want to sit down?" Lydia asked, holding her hand against the back of Alessia's neck. Her touch was warm—it made Alessia feel a physical need she hadn't experienced before. A need for comfort.

"Okay." The two women sat on Alessia's bed, their backs against the wall. "I'm sorry," Alessia whispered. "I don't normally behave this way."

"Don't be sorry. Everyone has their moments."

Lydia slid her hand along the comforter, but stopped short of touching Alessia's fingertips. "I... Well. I don't really know why I came." Lydia rubbed at the back of her hand. "I don't know anything about you."

She studied Lydia's face. She had a small dimple, barely perceptible, at the centre of her chin. Her eyelashes were long and thick. She could barely believe Lydia had come down to check on her. Jez Blumers had said something about Alessia, probably something insulting, and Lydia had raced down to her cell so fast she'd been out of breath. Maybe Alessia wasn't crazy. Maybe Alessia's initial instinct was accurate; Lydia really was special.

All this thinking all the time. Measuring each person to know what was safe to say and what wasn't. Alessia was exhausted.

"I think you're here because you want to help me," Alessia said. "Maybe you want to help all of us."

Lydia's eyelashes fluttered, and she looked at the floor.

Most humans wanted to keep Alessia's entire community locked away, under the ground, miles from anywhere and completely out of sight. But not Lydia. The feeling in the pit in her stomach returned, but it felt different than before. It pushed ripples of sadness through her spine, sapping her energy with each passing moment.

The corners of Alessia's mouth twitched as she tried to hold back the tears that had already started streaming down her face. Lydia gestured, inviting Alessia to her. Her body relaxed as she fell into Lydia's arms, curling into the foetal position and resting her head on Lydia's thigh. Alessia's shoulders shuddered as the tears became more insistent, more overwhelming.

Lydia stroked her cheek, her fingers gentle and soothing. Alessia let herself sink deeper into the moment, neither one of them needing to speak as minutes passed. She ran a finger back and forth across Lydia's leg, just below the knee. Her tears slowed, as did her breathing.

The tears on Alessia's face dried into a thin, sticky membrane. The heaviness of her eyes soon overpowered her desire to stay awake, and she allowed her eyelids to close.

ALESSIA WOKE TO find Lydia lying by her side, legs curled into her chest.

She'd not realised how exhausted both her body and mind were until she awoke after a restful sleep. For the first time in days, Alessia hadn't dreamt of Petra on the floor, beaten.

Lydia stirred, stretched out her limbs, and sat up next to Alessia. Looking down, the teacher ran her thumb over Alessia's cheek. She leaned her head to the side, celebrating and inviting Lydia's soothing touch.

"You stayed. Thank you." Alessia remained lying down, and she repositioned herself so the top of her head nestled into the side of Lydia's thigh. She stayed that way for a few minutes, neither of them speaking.

"I should go soon," Lydia said. "I shouldn't go to my classes in the same clothes I was wearing yesterday."

Alessia sat up and took hold of Lydia's hand. The human did not pull away and she was glad of it. "Of course. I apologise. I don't know why I was behaving that way before."

"You were upset," Lydia replied. "It's normal. We all lose our composure sometimes."

"Normal is a subjective term. I don't think whatever *that* was yesterday is how I am supposed to deal with my emotions."

"It's no one's place to tell you how to express what you feel."

Alessia traced her fingernails along Lydia's forearm. It was the last thing she ought to be doing, but the compulsion to connect with the human was overwhelming and she could see no sign Lydia wanted her to stop. "Do you think you might be able to return. Soon?"

Lydia pulled her arms back towards herself, erecting a wall between them. "No." She shook her head. "I need to be careful. People tend to watch me. It's because of who my father is. I should wait a while, see if anyone noticed I didn't return last night."

Alessia felt a sharp disappointment stab at her spine. She'd forgotten Lydia shared a family name with the governor. While she would never assume anything about someone's motives or personality based on who their parents were, Lydia's connection to the man Peleus had been confronted and insulted by did ignite a small degree of discomfort. His description of that incident had been saddening, to say the least. "Understood."

"It won't be forever. I just need time to...to work out some things."

Lydia unfolded her arms and let them fall to the bed. Just as they started to lean towards one another, a horrendous sound, like tearing metal, reverberated throughout the corridor just outside the room and the lights went out.

Chapter Fifteen

FERMI USED HIS knuckles against the monochrome tabletop to rap out a fast beat. What he wouldn't give for a proper set of drums, the kind he'd seen humans playing in films.

"...security...aware...did you?" The overseer's words to the protector were difficult to hear through chatter and footsteps in the central corridor, but he recognised her distinctive voice.

Fermi sat at a soci-table a few metres from the woman and her protector escort. Sara Taylor had been spending more time in the Outsider Zone of late. They'd all noticed it. She spoke to protectors, checked production reports, and inspected storage areas. It was the sort of thing Taylor had always done, just not so often.

Something felt off, and the rhythmic drumming—which normally settled any uncooperative thoughts—didn't ease the unsettling ache.

He wondered if he ought to tell Alessia about Taylor's presence, as though she were a general and he a soldier. A soft laugh spilled from his mouth. She was a discerner, but she was still Alessia, his friend, the woman he relied on to listen to all his thoughts, no matter how inane they may be. He wasn't one of her subjects, because she wasn't leading the council on their home world. There was no council anymore. And in all likelihood, there was no home world either.

Fermi stopped fidgeting and stood to leave for his work shift, his boots squeaking against the smooth concrete floor. His knees hit the tabletop as he slid off the bench.

"...inform me...too careful." Taylor's voice came from behind him. She sounded concerned. She was close, and the herbal, tea-leaf scent of her ever-present perfume became uncomfortably soothing given her status over him.

A sense of uneasiness gnawed at Fermi's stomach. The walls felt closer together than they used to and there were more protectors on duty than usual. The stairs leading to the production floor were behind him. Peleus's quarters lay ahead. *Work can wait.*

Fermi found Peleus sitting cross-legged on the floor outside his room, braiding the long, charcoal-coloured hair of a teenage girl sitting in front of him. Her eyes were closed and she swayed gently in response to his movements. Peleus looked up and smiled, beaming. It was almost enough to distract Fermi from the uncomfortable sensation in his core. They'd spent time together lately, a lot of time if he was honest with himself, and yet Peleus's infectious smile had not yet lost its effect on him.

"Sorry to interrupt. Can I borrow him for a minute?" Fermi asked the girl. "Pel. I've got a feeling." Fermi's shadow moved across Peleus's angular face.

"Hey, Letha, gorgeous girl, can I have a minute?" Peleus said. "Don't worry, we'll finish up. I won't send you off with only half of it done."

"Sure." She stood and stepped into the next room. Letha must be his neighbour, Fermi realised. Peleus leaped to his feet.

Fermi moved closer to Peleus and rested his back against the wall, hoping the two of them could fuse with the paint and not be noticed for a few moments. People walked past them. A few smiled in their direction; some waved. Peleus nodded a polite response to each.

Peleus turned on his side, shoulder pressing into the wall and arms folded across his chest.

"You seem shaken up." Peleus reached out, gently pressing his hand to Fermi's chest, and Fermi's throat tightened. "How strange, to see you looking so serious. Talk to me," said Peleus, leading him through the doorway into his quarters.

Fermi's gaze dropped to Peleus's feet. The two of them were standing toe-to-toe, Fermi about a head shorter than his friend.

"I just felt like I needed to be here. To see you," he said.

Peleus straightened up, while Fermi's shoulders continued to press into the uneven surface of the door. Fermi remained still as Peleus leant inward, taking a moment to pause, the tip of his nose barely touching Fermi's cheek. "Can I?" Peleus whispered.

Peleus' skin was warm. It made Fermi feel all at once calmer and feverish. Normally, he considered himself something of a talker. At that moment, though, all he could manage was a weak nod.

Peleus shifted the angle of his face, nudging Fermi's lips with his own before pulling Fermi closer and strengthening the kiss. Peleus's chest pressed against his own. He'd been kissed before, but not like this. He wanted to stay wrapped up in it, in Peleus. But he couldn't. Something bad was going on and he needed to tell Peleus. Fermi turned his face to the side and leaned his cheek against Peleus's chest, just above his heart.

Reluctantly, Fermi straightened.

"The overseer," he said. "I heard her having a conversation with a senior protector. I couldn't hear most of it but...I don't know. I just had this flash." He shook his head, a wry smile spreading across his face. "This sounds insane. I just had this feeling she shouldn't be there. That something dangerous was going on." He dropped his head. "Listen to me. I sound like Alessia. Except when she talks about her weird hunches, she actually makes some sense." He tried to smile and breathed in Peleus's sweet scent. It had grown stronger after their kiss.

"Wait," Peleus said as he took a step backwards. "Where did you say you saw her?"

"The Section D Main Corridor. Why?"

Peleus looked to the ceiling as though searching for a thought he had misplaced. Then, his eyes widened so far and so fast Fermi's heart jumped. "I have to go. Stay here!"

The loud *thud* of Peleus's feet crossing a ventilation grate in the floor brought the girl, Letha, back to her doorway and she stared down the hallway after him.

Fermi wondered if he ought to have chased after him, but before he could contemplate taking any action, Peleus was already out of sight. What did Peleus know that he didn't?

The world seemed to fall around Fermi when waves of heat rushed through the hallway. An overpowering gust of air assaulted his body and a deep, relentless ringing in his ears incapacitated him, forcing him into the foetal position on the floor, hugging his head. His temples throbbed. It felt like an age before the sharp noise softened enough for him to rise to his feet. Fermi's limbs felt heavy as he willed himself to get up.

What just happened? The ceiling and walls were intact. Nothing was about to fall, though he took care to avoid a light fixture hanging precariously from the ceiling. The powerful blast of heat and the painful ringing in his ears reminded him of the explosions he'd seen in action films, minus the fire. He sorted through options to explain the phenomena, but nothing fit. A burst pipe shouldn't hold such heat, and a malfunctioning air vent wouldn't bring with it that kind of a cacophony.

He ran his hands along his legs, stomach, and back, looking for injuries. Finding none, he started to check the people around him. Letha crouched in the doorway with her hands over her ears. He stumbled towards her and then gave her a reassuring hug before carefully searching her for injuries as well. Shattered glass, blasted away from the light fixtures, cracked beneath his feet as he moved into Letha's room, his mind somehow both cloudy and clear, as though he were moving at top speed through a scene playing out in slow motion. Most of Letha's personal belongings had been flung off the shelves but both she and her quarters were largely unscathed. His heart thundered in his chest, pushing adrenaline throughout his body, his fingertips tingled with its potency.

He turned to an older couple. The woman struggled to lift her partner from the floor. Fermi helped guide them both to a soci-table where the couple huddled together, arms interlocked and shoulders shaking.

Feeling, to some degree, calmer than he had minutes earlier, Fermi scanned the area again. They had to have been far enough away from whatever blew up that it was only a strong surge of air and heat that passed through. No flames. Lighter objects like cups and books had been strewn across the floor. Most of the Outsiders, having thrown themselves to the floor in search of safety, were now moving about. He could see no one with major injuries, so no real harm had been done. The protectors were nowhere to be seen. Only a few weeks ago, he probably would have been surprised, but now he knew Peleus, and things were different. He was different. He saw things for what they were. The protectors most likely ran away and left them to sort out their own injuries.

Peleus. Alessia. Oh, Earth. Where were they?

Fermi took off in the direction of a growing rumble of noise. The closer he got, the more damage there was—most of it superficial. Swirling clouds of scorched paint were sprayed across the walls, air vent grates dangled from the ceiling, smashed hemp-plast chairs crunched underfoot. Fermi realised he'd been travelling back the same way he had come. The scurrying of feet and echoing voices were all coming from the level's main corridor.

"Where the fuck is Levi?" The panicked voice came from a protector who usually manned the exit, Rafe Garland. "Someone get the goddam medical team down here!" He pushed past Fermi, barking orders at whoever he found. When Fermi got closer, he understood why the young man had been so frantic, his movements disjointed and oafish.

Even through the thick, acrid smoke, he could see the outline of a battered, lifeless body. The skin on one side of her face had been pulled free of the cheek and hung there like a demented, artificial adornment. Small but innumerable pieces of debris poked out of her face, neck, and chest. The flesh along her arms and torso was scorched, and in some places, smoking. Fermi had never smelled burnt flesh before. The severe scent grew so pungent he could taste it, and his stomach turned in a vain attempt to dispel the sensation.

Overseer Taylor's eyes were lifeless, glassy marbles. Protectors and Outsiders rushed about in a frenzied ballet of pirouettes and twirls. A guard bent down and tried to shake the life back into Taylor's body, gripping her by dead shoulders as they screamed into her face. If he'd ever been trained in how to handle a crisis, the young protector seemed to have forgotten it all, as panic swam across his face in waves. "Boss! Wake up! Wake up! Earth. Shitting jazz. Shit. She's not waking up."

Fermi struggled to take a step. His hand searched for the wall, a chair, anything to help him stay upright as he shuffled past her body and the small crowd gathered around it. The surge of energy that powered him fell away suddenly, leaving him exhausted and confused. His world was small, it was simple. Nothing much changed, and yet here he was, struggling to make sense of anything at all.

A woman's scream pierced his soul. It wasn't a manifestation of shock, or fear, but rather the unmistakable expression of pure, unfiltered heartbreak. Reawakened by the sound, Fermi's legs carried him past the scurrying human staff and cowering residents. Pushing his way through a wall of backs and shoulders, he found a woman hunched on the floor, her arms wrapped around a small figure she'd pulled into her lap. Zandra. She worked in the same production line he did. She was always nice to him.

Zandra rocked back and forth, stroking the limp arm of her son. Fermi couldn't see any obvious injuries on the boy; there was no blood, but he wasn't moving. As he circled around, Fermi caught sight of Zandra's tear-stained face. She choked in each breath, fighting against the mucous that covered her nose and mouth. Her sobs rose and fell as though following some unheard beat.

If they'd been only a few metres farther down the hall, Zandra wouldn't be clutching the dead body of her child. She wouldn't be surrounded by Outsiders who, like Fermi, could do nothing more than watch. He couldn't take the child out of her arms. He couldn't call for a protector. He couldn't wrap his arms around Zandra, either. It wasn't his place. Fermi had never felt more useless in his life. To them, death usually came in such predictable ways. People got sick. They grew old. They quietly passed into oblivion. This sudden and violent severing of life sent flashes of red across his vision and he struggled to focus on the people in front of him through the offensive haze. A reality where a person could just be going about their regular routine and then be suddenly taken from the world was a reality he wasn't sure he knew how to face.

A hand slid over Fermi's shoulder and squeezed. He turned around. Peleus's facial expression was soft and, somehow, kind. His forehead glistened with sweat. Fermi's entire body flooded with relief at the sight of Peleus standing there, alive. Safe.

Fermi stepped out of the circle that looked on Zandra in stunned silence. He fell against Peleus, engulfed by his embrace. Relief washed over him. They were both safe, and they'd found each other. Suddenly, guilt stabbed at his temples. He held a comfort the mother a few feet away would never feel again, and for no real reason. She was no less deserving than anyone else, yet she'd just lost everything.

"You're all right?" Peleus asked as he pulled back, his hands moving from Fermi's waist to grip his arms instead.

"I thought... I didn't know where you went. I thought maybe..." Stinging tears cut him off. It felt as if something bulbous and foul blocked his throat. He couldn't get the words out as he stumbled through an unrelenting maze of mecurial thoughts.

"It doesn't matter now." Peleus stroked Fermi's cheek with his thumb.

Refocusing himself, Fermi realised Alessia was standing behind Peleus. She scanned the area like a cat searching for a safe place to perch. Next to her stood one of the teachers, Mistress Lydia.

More people were emerging from the lower levels. The protectors were starting to get organised, clearing broken furniture and bringing in stretchers for the injured. There didn't seem to be many who had been hurt. The explosion wasn't powerful, but with thick concrete and steel walls flanking them on both sides, the force it exuded had felt and sounded stronger than it was.

Mistress Lydia stepped past Peleus and Fermi. A protector moved into the circle around Zandra and the crowd thinned, which allowed for a clearer view. The teacher's lips trembled as she got closer to Zandra and her son. The colour in her face drained until she was pale enough to pass for an Outsider. "Ro—Rosen?"

The teacher fell to her knees with a *thud*, oblivious to the impact. The woman rested there, frozen, staring at Zandra's son. At Rosen.

Fermi looked back at Alessia. Her gaze moved from the boy to the teacher and back again. He wanted to read her thoughts, but her stoic facial expression made that impossible. After a few moments, Alessia's gaze dropped to the floor. She touched a finger to her lips as she searched the ventilation grate beneath her feet for answers. Without looking back up, she turned and left.

Peleus slid his hand into Fermi's, their fingers interlocking. A warm glow spread through Fermi's arm and he felt calmer. The connection between them felt stronger than ever as Peleus's thumb stroked the inside of his wrist.

The two of them stood there, locked in place, until three protectors arrived and started clearing the area. The teacher was one of the first they directed away and she moved sluggishly towards the exit that would take her to the H-Zone. As Fermi and Peleus moved away from the scene, Fermi looked back over his shoulder. Zandra didn't fight when the protectors moved Rosen away from her. She stared ahead, motionless, her arms and legs seemingly drained of life. Her wailing cries had frightened him earlier. But this—her silence. That was even more terrifying. All he could do was keep walking. Keep walking and hope his world would return to some semblance of normal, though he had a suspicion it never would again.

Chapter Sixteen

"TURN YOUR FACE upwards please, sir."

Damon sighed and did as the make-up artist requested. He ought to be grateful, really. On his own, he would never be able to afford a primetime N-C broadcast. Pearsal was paying the bill. Again.

The administration had put regulations in place about how often citizens could be subjected to announcements like the one he was about to broadcast. A person could be sitting in the back of their self-drive transport and the governor's face would appear before them, superimposed over the real world. There was no way for a citizen to turn it off, and the law gave him permission to speak for up to forty seconds. Only those working in emergency services were exempt, and with such a low human population, many of those professions were all but full of profession-restricted AIs. The public were used to dividing their attention, though, and very few complaints had ever been filed with the UEA. It was the most valuable political publicity. His opponent would have to stick to traditional Hive advertising.

"Come now, Damon," said his campaign manager. "You'll soon be convincing everyone they should vote you back in. You can't do that if you look like a corpse." Marc Kouper was as smooth as he was intelligent. At forty, the man owned an impressive percentage of New Sydney's industrial area, his parents having invested in climate-proofing measures long before other real estate owners had caught on to the financial benefits of doing so. Many lost at least half the value of their properties as demand for safer buildings increased, but the Koupers sat back and watched each of their buildings triple in value.

"Oh, back off," Damon told Marc. "I resent having to sit here for an hour being plucked and preened for less than a minute of screen time. I doubt viewers will be analysing whether my concealer properly matches the tinting of my eyelashes."

"I wouldn't bet on it, old man. Both of you Barretts have pretty sexy eyelashes, Damon."

"Give it up. My daughter didn't want to sleep with you before she left, and she won't be interested when she returns. You've more luck getting up close and personal with my eyelashes than hers."

"We'll see, we'll see." Kouper crossed his arms over his chest.

When Damon interviewed for a new campaigner two years ago, he asked Marc why he wanted to stay in politics now his property investments were turning vast profits. Kouper's reply had stuck with Damon: "As Plato tried to tell us all those years ago: if you don't participate in politics you end up being governed by your inferiors. I for one, sir, would prefer to pull the strings than be the puppet." Marc grinned then, the kind of confident, wide smile a teenager might flash at a pretty girl, before adding, "Plus...it's bloody good entertainment." No other candidate came near impressing Damon even half as much.

"All right, boss," said Marc. "My N-C display is flashing red. You've got five minutes until show time. Hey, you," he said to the round-faced man teasing Damon's hair. "Finish it up."

The stylist nodded and sprayed Damon's hair one last time. How even one strand could be out of place, Damon couldn't understand.

"It feels odd to be filming this here," Damon said as he stood up, his legs stiff as planks after sitting so long. His skin was dry and heavy from the layers caked on by the stylist.

"Survey says, boss."

"Yes, yes. Voters like the personal touch of it all. But I'll be glad to get this circus out of my apartment. Let's do this." Barrett took his place in front of the camera, and in an effort to stretch out his jaw and lips, he opened and closed his mouth like a fish drowning in air.

Marc stood next to the petite, homely woman operating the NeCam. An expensive model, the NeCam was the only brand that could capture N-C compatible footage. Projecting video into people's minds was a rather different affair from creating a multi-dimensional sensory film.

"Make sure you flutter those lashes, boss." Marc stole a glance at the NeCam operator before winking at Damon. The woman was breathing, which made her fair game for Marc. The man couldn't pass a robotic parking attendant without trying to flirt. Kouper really was something of a marauder.

"Governor Barrett. We'll go in ten, nine, eight..." She counted down until a soft buzz indicated the start of his forty seconds.

"Prosperity and protection. That's what I'm here to talk to you all about this evening. As you're likely to be aware, in a few months from now, each one of you will exercise the right to vote in another United Earth Alliance election..."

Damon knew the speech so well he barely heard himself deliver it. It was being seen that got votes and he was most certainly being seen. By everyone. "So, remember, my friends, after all these years, I, your quadrant four governor, have remained a faithful servant to the ideals of the United Earth Alliance. It would be my honour to continue to serve each of you, protecting our quadrant from the dangers of unchecked science and extreme climate conditions and delivering prosperity through economic improvements."

"Hey, boss," Marc said, as he stepped forwards. "Do you ever get sick of saying *United Earth Alliance*? What an idiotic title for a government. United. Alliance. Basically the same thing."

"Uh-huh," Damon said through a sideways smile. He'd heard all of this before. It was Marc's usual opener when making a play for a woman.

"All right, you lot, fabulous job. Now kindly get out." Marc clapped his hands as though shooing stray cats. "Except you." He pointed at his target, put his arm around her shoulder, and led her into the hall. "See you tomorrow, boss," he called out. Most people Damon interacted with were hindered by etiquette, and so Marc's total lack of deference was refreshing.

Having the inside of his apartment back to its usual, empty state was a relief. This was the only place in the world he could be, for the most part, certain he wasn't being filmed by some media hound. Tight security measures on the building and customised Hive firewalls ensured it. The two green-skinned guards in his hallway were as discreet as anything money could buy, their loyalty as secure as the circuitry in their synthetic brains. He had no need to fear any kind of personal exposure at the hands of such basic AIs.

Ordinarily, Damon preferred voice command options when interacting with his Hive access point but, after all of that talk about N-Cs, he found himself using thought commands instead. Unlike those younger than he, Damon still clearly remembered living without a neural interface. It amazed him that the N-C could somehow tell the difference between a direct instruction to his machines, and any other thoughts building in his head.

On the SinTral network, he accessed his usual little corner, for those who valued discretion and could afford it. He'd seen most of these types before. Male, female, transgender, intersex, blonde, brunette, ... whatever group you were into, SinTral had representatives readily available to service your needs. After finding the one he was after, Damon finalised his selection and shut down the connection.

She was at his doorstep within ten minutes, wearing a modish metallic suit that cut off above the knee. No one would have believed Model Eighteen to be anything but a typical middle-class businesswoman. It was exactly what he was after.

Damon opened the door wider, allowing her enter, before checking the corridor, and finding only his blank-faced guards, locked the door. She threw her handbag onto the floor by the refrigerator, kicked off her stilettos, and sauntered towards the bed, her hips moving in a hypnotic, sideways rhythm.

"How do you want me this time?" she asked as she sat on the edge of his bed and crossed her ankles. Model Eighteen looked remarkably similar to Sara Taylor. She had the same gentle cheekbones, and Junoesque body. Only mannerisms and stature set them apart.

"On your knees," Damon replied, the hairs on the back of his neck standing on end.

HE WAS EXCEEDINGLY satisfied with Model Eighteen's performance. As she left, the woman looked back at him, a playful grin on her face. The moment the door clicked shut a red telephone symbol flashed within his field of vision.

With a thought, Damon switched his house Hive from the N-C to verbal. "House, where is the call coming from?"

"A secured Pearsal line, sir," the husky voice of his wife replied. "It's the assistant overseer at the Quadrant Four Colony."

"Hmm. Better let it through, then." The assistant overseer? Damon couldn't recall having ever exchanged two words with the man. Why would he be calling? "Barrett here."

"Governor Barrett. This is—"

"Yes, I know. What can I do for you?"

"I thought I had better inform you of this morning's events. At approximately oh-eight-hundred-hours—"

"Cut to the chase." Damon sat up on the bed. He was naked, and though the apartment was temperature controlled, goosebumps spread across his skin.

"Yes, Governor." The voice on the other end went quiet for a moment. "Sir, first, I should inform you this communication is including video from your end."

Of course it is, he thought. Damon lifted a leg and crossed it over the other knee, remaining casual in his movements. No point losing his composure over something already in the past. "Well, thank you, House. I'm sure this man has had quite enough of my crotch. Turn off the video feed." When a short buzz confirmed the command had been followed, he continued. "Now. Do get on with it. Given you've skipped my team and phoned me directly, it must be *very* important."

"There was an attack. We are still working out who managed to build the device, but an explosive device was let off in the Outsider Zone. It wasn't a very big explosion by any means, but where it was positioned, and you know, being in an enclosed space...Sir, Sara Taylor was...she's gone."

Damon remained silent, his skin suddenly cold and dry.

"Sir, did you receive me? We assumed you would want to hear about this immediately."

"Yes!" he snapped, embarrassed he'd just been having sex with a woman who could have been Taylor's twin. In the technical sense, she almost was. "Yes, I heard you. I'll be there whenever my staff can clear space in my schedule. I trust you can keep the place running in the meantime?"

"Of course, sir. Thank you for your time."

"One more thing," Damon said.

"Sir?"

"My daughter. Lydia."

"She was not at the scene, Governor."

"Good," he said. His heart rate slowed and the tension in his fingers and toes relaxed a little. "That'll be all."

The line went silent, and Damon's thoughts turned as grey as the storm clouds forming on the other side of his apartment window. *She's gone?* His feelings for the late colony overseer hadn't been much more than lust, really. Still, he always thought of her in that office, wearing those skirts and that perfume, giving out orders and organising reports. The fact she wasn't there anymore was disconcerting to say the least.

Sara Taylor was dead and Pearsal was not going to be happy about the loss of such an asset. Some people, he supposed, were fuelled by love; others by lust or hate or revenge. Damon Barrett, at that moment, was driven only by a desperate need for another drink.

DAMON COULD STILL smell Sara's perfume in the office. It made his stomach churn.

"How the hell did this happen?" His voice possessed a deep urgency. He paced in front of Sara's oak desk, unable to make eye contact with the four assembled staffers. "You're underground. Miles from anywhere, with a population of unarmed aliens, most of whom think we're their damned saviours, for fuck's sake!"

Damon took a moment to still himself. In the last two days, he had been through six cities for fairly useless political exercises, most of them veiled campaigning activities. He'd not had time to consider Sara's demise or the fallout it'd cause.

Staring at the wall, he realised Sara's office décor had a theme. He'd never paid attention to the holo-posters before. Thriving rainforests. Coral reefs bursting with activity. Sweeping plains of green. It seemed she loved life, and not just any life, but the kind in existence before humanity's obsession with environmental exploitation reached a breaking point. The kind that needed a world without humans to survive. Environmentalism permeated through all government policy and action these days, but Sara Taylor? It was not the sort of thing that ought to have concerned someone like her. It was bizarre.

Rubbing at his chin, Damon inhaled deeply and adopted his poker face.

"Right. Let's move on," he said as he sat down in Sara's high-backed chair. Leaning forwards, Damon touched his index fingers to his lips as he considered his next move. "Sara Taylor was an invaluable asset. Her knowledge and experience will be difficult to replicate."

A voice came through the tablet embedded in Taylor's desk. "Forgive me, Governor Barrett. There's an incoming communication from the Pearsal management team."

Shit. He'd already told Pearsal he'd contact them when done, but this interruption was just another way of reminding him of his place in the grand scheme of things.

"Put it through," Damon said.

"Good morning, Governor. I can see on my feed you've got some of the staff there with you."

"Yes, ma'am, I do." She could see them, but they couldn't see her. It put him at a disadvantage.

The most difficult part of being a high-ranking politician was the illusion of having any power at all. He might have worked for the UEA government, but it was Pearsal's funding that kept him in office.

"Perfect," she said. "For any of you who don't know me, I'm Frances Nguyen. I'm the managing director of Pearsal in quadrant four. Now. One of you explain to me how in the hell someone managed to blow up my overseer."

The colony managers lowered their gaze to the floor. She wasn't even in the damn room and they were too nervous to look up. The manager of the security team, Rafe Garland, was especially uneasy. As he should be.

"We've just come together as a group to discuss, ma'am," Damon said.

The whole thing was unreasonable. The tablet in the desk flashed and Frances Nguyen's unsympathetic face appeared for his eyes only. She spoke to him through his N-C, her voice no longer audible to the rest of the room.

"Barrett, we have contractual obligations to meet. The UEA expects our people to maintain order, among other things. Letting Taylor get killed is not order. Letting Os kill each other is not order. It's a fucking mess." There was no anger in her eyes, only robotic authority. "Taylor hadn't uploaded new data for a month. That's a month of operations of which we have no knowledge. We don't know who she spoke to, where she went, or what she did. All the information she gathered about whatever's going on down there is now lost."

A month. Sara Taylor had been meticulous about uploading her files every week, and the corporation had not informed him she'd become complacent. It didn't make sense. Nguyen was right. Sara looked into rumours of little meetings, of some kind of hierarchy developing amongst the Os. Surely that should have made her even more vigilant.

"Furthermore," Nguyen said, leaning closer to the camera. "How are the Os reacting to all of this? The report said a child was killed and several more hurt. I doubt that'll help keep the peace down there."

Damon looked away from Frances Nguyen's burning gaze and turned his attention to Garland. As leader of the security team, the man couldn't be everywhere all the time, but this was ultimately his jazz up. Damon dare not say as much to Nguyen. He'd learned the hard way she did not appreciate people passing on responsibility.

"The Outsiders are quiet. For now," Damon replied. Given the others could hear him speaking, he wanted to keep his responses succinct.

"Make sure it stays that way. We're not in a position where we want their numbers to dwindle," Frances said.

Her comment struck Damon as odd. For years, their brief had been to allow free mingling of Outsiders *within reason*. Their population couldn't be allowed to grow beyond the means of the colonies. Were they building another one somewhere and he didn't know about it? He bet it was in Quadrant One. Those bastards always got their claws in before anyone else could. If it involved money, authority, or technology, Quadrant One wanted it. It was why the Q. One Governor was so irritated about Barrett's new habitat. For once, he'd beaten them to something.

"Yes, ma'am," Damon said. "We will go over security protocols today. The staff have some ideas on how to hold things together until Taylor's replacement arrives. Do you have an ETA on that?"

"A week. By the time she arrives, you'd better have some answers. I want to know who did it, how they did it, why they did it and what the hell Taylor was up to in the month before she was taken out." The call ended before Nguyen's words were barely out of her mouth.

"Garland," Damon said. Rafe took a rigid step forwards. "This place has a PA system, right?"

"Yes, Governor Barrett. It's rarely used, but ought to be in working condition."

"Good. Turn it on."

"Sir?"

"You heard me, Garland. Turn the damn thing on. I want to talk to the Os."

Rafe stood in silence for a moment, his eyes staring into the distance, looking at nothing and everything all at once. Damon recognised it as the expression adopted by anyone using their N-C for more than a few seconds. As head of security, Garland was one of only three people whose N-C Implant wasn't disabled in the colony. The other two were

Dr Levi and himself.

"It's ready to go, Governor. It'll start broadcasting as soon as you speak." Rafe stepped back in line.

Damon stood. For once, his audience could not see him, but he hated giving speeches sitting down. "This is Damon Barrett. I represent the Earth government. Most of you probably know me, but for those who don't, I'm the one to whom Overseer Taylor reported. I imagine you're all concerned by what happened a few days ago. So are we."

He paused. He hadn't really thought about what to say. He hadn't even considered asking one of his speech writers to work something out for him. It wasn't like him to just start talking and as he struggled to order his thoughts, Damon remembered why he relied upon others to construct so many of his sentences.

"When your people arrived on this planet, your ancestors asked us for protection. They asked humans for somewhere safe to live. That's what you've got here. Nothing like this has happened in this colony before. You've lived and worked here with our protection for years. Outsiders have thrived. Outsiders have been able to stay hidden from their enemies, both alien and human. Whoever drove you off your home world has never discovered your location because we've kept you safe. We could have sent you back. But we didn't."

Damon ran a thumbnail across the skin above his lip, aware of the people watching his movements with hawk-like intensity. They hadn't given him anything useful. They didn't know a bloody thing. Damon had thought about sacking the lot of them, but given the situation, replacing them would be far more trouble than it was worth. Besides, firing anybody from a colony job was dangerous. A disgruntled ex-employee might get ideas about talking to the press. Well, trying to, anyway.

"So," Damon continued, "we need to make sure things stay on track. You want to live safe, protected lives in peace. And we want to help you. Your contributions to this planet and this colony are also, of course, much appreciated. But, hear me when I tell you, dissension won't be tolerated. Things will return to normal soon enough. However, until I have the name of whoever killed Sara Taylor, and in the process, killed that poor young boy, there will be some restrictions in place. The first of these will be movement. We have never bothered much with tracking movements before but as of now, I'm instructing security to turn on your trackers."

Damon saw Garland shift his weight, discomfort splashed across the man's face. He knew as well as Damon did how much pressure that would put on their restricted Hive bandwidth. The movements of all Outsiders could be monitored through ID chips, but having so many turned on at once could lead to problems.

"None of you are to congregate," Damon said. "If a protector sees you talking to more than two other Os, you'll be compelled to move along. If the tracking system registers a group of any more than three of you assume surveillance in that zone will be switched on and a protector sent to investigate.

"I hope someone amongst you, someone who knows how this tragedy occurred, will step forwards. If you tell us, we can deal with it and make sure no one is ever injured like this again and then there won't be a need to continue the restrictions. May you stay safe."

Rafe nodded to indicate the broadcast had ended. "Sir, are you sure—"

"Of course I'm sure, Garland. You've all become complacent. It's understandable, I suppose. But it's time to run this place properly. This tragedy could spell chaos, with the Os questioning the order of things, or it could be the beginning of a stronger, more stable colony governance."

"Yes, Governor," Rafe replied.

"As for you two—" Damon looked to Dr Levi, Head of Medical, and Claudia Dolph, the Head Technologist. "—make sure Garland's team has the support needed to keep track of who goes where. It'll be a big job. It's possible some of the Os will have a physical reaction to their ID chips being activated after so long."

"Yes, sir," they said in unison.

"All right. Out, then." Damon waved them off.

Damon was left alone in Sara's office. A mail icon sat in the corner of his field of vision, a three-digit number on the envelope being projected by his N-C. The campaign never slept. Damon couldn't ignore them forever, but he would put off opening them a little longer.

Checking the chron above the door, Damon considered taking ten minutes to see Lydia. She taught the child who died, and he imagined she would have been upset. He ran through a few ideas of what he might say to her. Some scenarios involved a hug, some didn't. In all of them, she would ask him why the Os would want to make such a statement.

She had so much of her mother in her.

It was too hard, he decided. If Lydia wanted to speak to him, she would call.

"Office, turn it all off," he said. The Hive tablet switched off and the room darkened. It would stay empty until a new overseer arrived to claim it.

Chapter Seventeen

"IT WAS YOU," Alessia said. She assigned no emotion to the statement. She couldn't let herself fully experience the heartbreak taking root inside of her, not if she wanted to stay composed throughout the conversation. There was only a minimal chance it wouldn't end the way she'd predicted it would. For once, Alessia desperately hoped to be wrong.

"Ali, I've made it clear I don't report to you," Petra said, her eyes bright. It didn't take a discerner to see the girl was hurting. The last few months had made Petra colder. The energetic zest for life Alessia used to love about the teenager had hardened into an igneous rock within Petra's core.

"I know, Petra," Alessia replied. Her fingers tightened around the empty cup on the table in front of her.

Alessia looked to Peleus, who leaned against the door to ward off unwanted visitors. He knew Petra needed to be confronted. It was obvious in the silent way he'd carried out Alessia's instruction to bring his sister to her room. She could see the regret and guilt that crawled under his skin like subterranean insects. Here he seemed to be again. Caught between Alessia, whom he had vowed to follow and respect, and his sister, the only person in his family left alive. She was the person he loved above all others. Alessia hated having to put Peleus in this situation.

But two people had died. Something had to be done. Something drastic.

"Petra. You agreed to come with me to talk to her," Peleus said. "You can't have completely disowned us." His modulated voice always comforted Alessia. Listening to Peleus was like listening to a gentle breeze through treetops.

"You're my brother, Peleus." Petra's tone was disembodied, a poor performer reading from a script. "And you," she added, her hand gesturing towards Alessia, "You're the reason I'm here. The reason I started looking for a way out." Petra rose from the bed. "You don't see. You don't see what's right in front of you. We can't waste away in here anymore. We can't let them control our lives any longer. Why can't you be on my side this time?"

Petra took up position next to the table and locked eyes with Alessia. "Your way isn't working," she said. "You two are just sitting around waiting for something to happen. You expect me to trust that will actually work?" Petra scoffed and crossed her arms in front of her chest.

"So," Peleus said. "It was you. You killed the overseer. You injured our friends." His eyes dropped to the floor. "And Rosen." His chest heaved and his eyelids clenched shut as he spoke again. "He'd barely reached the age of Ceremony, and he's gone now."

Hearing him say Rosen's name reignited the anger Alessia felt the day she'd been accosted by the protector. It swelled like a rising tide.

"Humanity cannot be beaten or convinced with violence!" Alessia said as she stood. Petra's eyes widened. "We are in here because they fear us. They fear our difference. If we propagate terror, they will only tighten our leash further. We need to show humans we're not a threat. But you. You *killed* people."

"I killed our weakness," Petra said, her voice but a fading echo under the weight of Alessia's ferocity. "I killed our willingness to be dominated by a lesser species."

Alessia's heart sank. She'd lost her. Somewhere along the way, Petra, her friend and her protégé, had been seduced by the same disingenuous fear of otherness that had led humans to segregate them in the first place.

Alessia looked from Petra back to Peleus. She knew he wouldn't be able to accept what had to be done. As nauseated as she felt about the events she'd set in motion, Alessia couldn't turn back now. She'd come to this decision through reason, through an obsessive analysis of detail. Every path she considered led to the same place if she didn't take action. "You should go," she said to him. "If you stay much longer, they'll come for us." His shoulders hunched and his eyes watered. It was clear Peleus lacked the will to argue with her, perhaps too upset about his sister's chosen path. Without a word, he left the room. His footsteps, at first heavy and slow against the floor, faded into the distance. The two women stared at each other as they waited for him to be out of earshot.

"We cannot hope to thrive if we become our own worst enemy," Alessia said.

Petra scoffed. "On that, I finally agree with you. Doing nothing is destroying us."

"No," Alessia replied. "We have to wait our turn. It will be our time."

Alessia knocked the side of her shoe against the wall twice. Loud thuds reverberated throughout the metallic room. Petra's features tightened into a quizzical pout. The door burst open, banging against the wall. Single file, two protectors entered the room. Alessia stepped back to give them space.

She'd expected Petra to yell. To kick or bite. Instead, her face hardened as she shook her head at Alessia. "You fucking bitch, Ali."

"I'm sorry, Petra. I'll find a way to fix this. I promise." Though her lips trembled, she meant it. There'd be a time when Alessia would embrace Petra again, spirit-sisters as they once were. "Until then, we must follow the rules. It's for the best."

The protectors grasped Petra by the biceps. She didn't struggle. There was nowhere for her to go even if she did. As they pulled her into the corridor, Peleus's voice rang out.

"No, you can't take her again," he cried, pushing through the small crowd forming near the staircase outside Alessia's room. "Get your hands off my sister!"

Alessia stepped out of the room, between Peleus and the guards, giving them the space they needed to take Petra away. She positioned her hand on his chest as though to hold him in place. With her stare, she willed him to understand why Petra needed to be handed over. His body shook with anger, but he didn't fight her. Like Petra, he knew there was nothing that could be done. It was too late.

"Shh, Peleus," Alessia said. "All will be well. Perhaps not today. But you must trust destiny will find a way to make all of this right."

He refused to look at her, his gaze fixed on Petra until the protectors rounded a corner and disappeared.

His skin felt hot and beads of sweat formed across his forehead. "Dammit, Ali!" He spun around, cradling his head in his hands. After a few measured breaths, he turned to face Alessia. "I know why. But just because I understand it..." He paused.

Alessia held her breath, fighting back her own anguish.

He sighed, and after a moment, Peleus's gaze met hers. "It doesn't mean I have to forgive it."

"Yes," she replied. "I'll still be here when you're ready."

Peleus nodded. He turned and walked away, leaving Alessia standing in the hallway. She was surrounded by onlookers, yet totally alone. She looked around, making eye contact with anyone who didn't turn away.

"All right, that's enough," she said.

They wasted no time in retreating to their own rooms.

When the area quieted, Alessia stepped back into her cell and closed the door, willing the rest of the world away. She'd known the confrontation with Petra would end with the girl's arrest, but regardless, Alessia had so badly wanted another outcome. She had hoped she was somehow wrong. A society without rules, without morality, could not hope to win the hearts and minds of those who repudiated them. Petra needed to answer for her behaviour, or else the Outsiders would lose significant traction in their search for veneration. Now it was done, now Petra was gone, and Peleus knew Alessia had been the one to bring it about; the worst had happened. It was over and done with and nothing she could do would change that. She believed Peleus might one day forgive her enough to at least fan a cursory reconnection, though it would take him time to understand her reasons. She couldn't just tell him; he needed to see it for himself. Petra, however, may very well have been lost to her forever. Whatever punishment Petra would now endure, the flame inside her would either be fanned to the point of self-destruction, or be snuffed out completely. Either way, her friend's fate remained to be seen.

Alessia fell on her mattress, resting the back of her hand against her forehead. She concentrated on the rhythm of her breathing, fighting back her unruly emotions.

Alessia had been able to collect the remnants of the bomb before the protectors started to tidy up the scene. From what she could tell, it was a simple piece of machinery, ingeniously devised from readily available materials, and had it not been the cause of so much discord, Alessia may have been impressed that Petra managed to construct such an instrument. Petra just wanted out. She wanted to fight her way out, *Guns-a-blazin'* as she'd heard in one of the old movies they watched in the rec. That fixation on immediate escape, immediate freedom, was almost admirable. If only she hadn't killed Taylor and Rosen. Maybe if Petra had spoken to Alessia about the device she'd concocted, they could have come up with a better use for it. Perhaps Alessia could have diagnosed the errors in the detonator so it wouldn't have gone off hours early.

Alessia pinched the bridge of her nose and exhaled loudly. She had long ago resigned herself to the fact it would not be her generation to leave the colony. Their children, perhaps, would earn the respect and admiration of their captors as they gradually—silently—reclaimed what they could of their traditional culture. Reflecting on the process she had envisioned for the future, she realised Petra could never have brought her plan to Alessia. Petra knew she would have never condoned any use for that damned bomb. Now, both paths to freedom had been destroyed.

Petra's attack had failed to destroy the security network hub embedded in the ceiling above Sara Taylor. Even if it had worked, anyone who tried to run would have met armed resistance on the other end of the tether to the human district. The whole jazzing affair was so poorly executed!

As for the other path, any notion of convincing humans of their peaceful nature had been crushed like the overseer's skull. Humans now had a real reason to perceive the Outsiders as a threat.

Alessia thought through endless scenarios, searching paths and junctions for a way to salvage all of this. To redeem Petra. To free Outsiders. Then she remembered that day she'd passed the overseer, Sara Taylor, in the corridor. They had exchanged no words, but Alessia could see signs of the woman's internal conflict, the war that raged within. It was a conflict Alessia understood and recognised, as though the human had been fighting her own desires, her own identity.

There *was* another way to bring about their freedom, one that didn't involve any weapons or take decades. This time, it needed to involve people beyond the Outsider community. One of those people was dead. The other, well...Thinking of her clouded Alessia's mind as sure as any drug. Lydia. She needed to ask Lydia for help.

Chapter Eighteen

LYDIA LOOKED OVER her shoulder one last time before emerging from the staircase. The coast was clear. Several night-shift protectors hadn't bothered waiting for their replacements before disappearing to the H-Zone. Her father may have increased security measures, but he hadn't accounted for institutionalised apathy.

Small spectral lights along the floor provided just enough illumination for Lydia to navigate the corridors. She carried a data pad stocked with menial administrative tasks, just in case someone noticed her on one of the security feeds. With luck, she wouldn't draw any attention.

When Lydia reached cube zero-five, she found herself, once again, frozen in place. What was it about this red door? Every time she stood in front of it, she seemed to forget how to breathe, but she couldn't afford to stand there. She had two minutes at most before the next watch turned up.

She tapped gently on Alessia's door. This is insane, Lydia thought, as she shook her head. Normal people slept at 4AM.

"Come in, Lydia." Alessia's voice was barely more than a whisper.

After blinking slowly and taking a deep breath, Lydia entered the room. She wanted nothing more than to lock eyes with Alessia, but something told her to slow down, to hold off that moment when they would have to properly acknowledge each other, just for a few more seconds.

The air inside was perfumed with rich, herbal incense. From the same shelf housing her books, a misshapen light shone down upon the top end of Alessia's bed. The lights in Outsider cells automatically switched off at curfew, so Alessia must have crafted a makeshift torch. As Lydia's eyes adjusted to the off-white glow, she recognised the torch as the statue of a dog on its hind legs she'd noticed last time. The light emanated from the dog's mouth. Clever. It brightened as she looked at it, as though it had just been switched on, probably for her benefit.

As the door closed behind her, Lydia stepped forwards, her thighs grazing the edge of the mattress. For a moment, Alessia's eyes shone like a cat's. Lydia hadn't seen such a thing before. A humanoid with tapetum lucidum? Outsiders could see in the dark.

"You came back." Alessia smiled. She was sitting in a lotus position at the top end of the mattress, a sketchpad in her lap and a charcoal pencil in hand. Lydia hadn't woken her after all.

"I had to," she replied, sitting down on the bed. A week had passed since the explosion and it had taken all her self-control to wait seven long, ponderous days before paying this visit. "Are you all right?"

Alessia's smile faded. She moved the sketchbook and pencil to the floor. "You're the first person to ask me." She brushed the back of Lydia's hand with her fingertips.

Lydia knew she ought to move away, discourage the physical interaction, but everything inside her wanted Alessia to do it again.

"But are you?" Lydia said. "Okay, I mean. Are you okay?" Forming sentences was difficult when someone so fascinating was looking at her with such interest. She hoped Alessia wouldn't think her to be as childish as she felt herself to be at that moment. Her thoughts, like her words, lay in a jumbled mess. All she could think about was reaching out, brushing the back of her hand across Alessia's pale cheek, leaning in...*Stop it!*

"I'm not entirely sure what it means to be okay, Lydia." There it was again. Her name from Alessia's lips. Somehow, the Outsider made it sound sensuous, intoxicating. Lydia felt a pang of guilt. How could she be lingering on such trivialities? She really had sneaked down there in the dead of night because she was concerned for Alessia's welfare. Yet here she was thinking about the texture of the engineer's skin, the taste of her lips, the scent of her hair. She pressed her fingernails into the palm of her hand to discourage the line of thinking. They'd both cared for Rosen. All at once winsome and wise, he had been something special.

Lydia rested her head against the wall and sank deeper into the bed. It was a stupid question. Of course she was not all right. Turning her head towards Alessia, she said, "You turned Petra in."

Alessia dropped her eyes and nodded.

"If you hadn't, they would have come down hard on all of you," Lydia added.

The words felt meaningless. Lydia had been there for less than two months. Who was she to validate this woman's actions? Alessia probably found the whole sentiment idiotic, but the words had been said and she couldn't take them back.

When no reply came, Lydia fell back on one of her rehearsed topic changes. "Peleus said you've lived..." She paused and pointed upwards. "Up there. Do you have any idea about the real reasons why people on this planet are so wary of you?"

"That seems to be everyone's favourite question lately. Do you think you could ask me something else?"

Lydia reflected for a moment, letting the silence thicken. "All right... People seem to, I don't know, follow you, somehow. Even the protectors seem to talk about you in a special kind of way."

Alessia's faced remained neutral. "You want to know if there's a reason?" she asked.

"There is a reason, then?" Lydia replied, a little giddy at the prospect of learning something sure to be intensely personal about Alessia. "I thought as much. The way other Os look at you, I'm sometimes surprised that they don't salute."

"It's both simple and complicated at the same time. See this?" Alessia ran her fingers through her golden hair, revealing strands of copper, red and orange beneath. It was beautiful. Lydia had seen similar shades before. Hell, humans could turn their hair any colour they pleased, but there was always a degree of the unnatural about it. You could always detect a synth-job, no matter how expensive the dyes were. Here, it was the golden wheat colour that seemed out of place.

"It's lovely. But what does it mean?" Lydia sank back again.

"In my society, there used to be a hierarchy of leadership. The closest thing I could compare it to on Earth is an oligarchy," Alessia said, straightening her spine. "The council operated under the guidance of a group of two or three discerners."

Much to her own shame, Lydia hadn't given much thought to the culture and politics of the Outsiders. There were still so many things she'd not stopped to consider. Lydia didn't even know what their planet was called or what their native language was like. If they'd had their own language, none of it had survived their internment. There were no obvious structures of power, nor did anyone exhibit a desire to establish one. But of course they'd had complex systems of governance on their home planet. "Discerners. As in, people who can understand things?" she said.

"Essentially, yes. They had a heightened ability to apply logic, to exercise patience, to govern. Discerners even lived longer than others usually did. My mother told me of one who outlived her peers by sixty years."

"That's a bloody long life. Don't Os outlive humans as it is?"

"Yes," Alessia said. There was a hint of disappointment, maybe sadness, in her voice.

"Go on," Lydia prompted, finding the concept strange. History may be the past, and yet it could be fresh, unveiled at any time, capable of swallowing a person's entire understanding of their place in the world.

"I suppose it was some sort of genetic line because most of them were related to one another. D-Strains passed from mothers to daughters." The sadness in Alessia's voice had disappeared. Lydia couldn't help but notice their thumbs rested no more than half an inch apart on the bed cover.

"But I thought gender..." Lydia's sentence trailed off. She had no idea how to finish it.

Alessia's face brightened with a teasing smile. "That's another topic altogether!" she said. "We are born, for the most part, male or female. But not wholly so. But the D-Strain—what we call the genetics that makes a person a discerner—it is only passed on to those of us born with predominately female anatomy. There is always the option to change should we wish to, but the D-Strain is stubborn and it won't develop in those born male."

"I don't think I understand. Option to change? Not with surgery, surely?"

"No, nothing like that." Alessia shuffled forwards. Her knees touched the side of Lydia's thigh, sending a wave of electricity through her. "Imagine your body had the potential to be whatever you want it to be. You're born with certain traits, but they don't necessarily define your personality or your behaviour. If something changes for you, something profoundly, shall we say, emotional, or spiritual, then your body changes with you."

"Surely physical traits act as a kind of baseline for who you are." Lydia felt the confusion sweeping across her face.

"Of course," Alessia replied. "We are not tabula rasa. No one is. But we are not so tightly shackled to our original bodily state as humans seem to be."

"Your body changes? Just on its own?" There was so much about their anatomy and culture not reported in the archives. How absurd. Why didn't people keep asking questions after the Os were interned?

"Yes, it does," Alessia replied. "When humans reach adolescence, the body evolves. But the difference, for you, is evolution stops. For us, change comes about in response to a change in our sense of self. If I were to feel like a man, here—" She touched her hand to her breast. "—then everything else about me would respond if I wanted it to. If required, the flesh moulds with the soul."

"But what if you don't feel wholly feminine or masculine? Plenty of human beings find themselves somewhere in the middle, or either side of the middle."

"The response varies. There are Outsiders who behave and appear in all manner of ways, and the same is true of their physical states. It's not a strict binary," Alessia said, her hand moving from her lap to Lydia's knee. "Does this make sense to you?"

Lydia nodded, though she wasn't entirely sure she did understand. The theory of it made some sense, but a multitude of questions came to mind about the logistics. Question Number One: how much of Alessia could be considered female? And did it even matter? She felt ashamed for wondering about such things. Alessia was intriguing, intelligent, and unimaginably beautiful. The connection between those things and whatever it was that existed underneath her clothes ought not matter.

"I completely forgot what I asked you in the first place!" Lydia grinned. "So, discerners are only women, or...people who are female at birth? And this," she indicated towards Alessia's hair "is some sort of indicator. You're one of these discerners?"

Alessia shrugged. "Technically, yes. In practice, no."

"Are you sure?" Lydia shifted to face Alessia. "Seems to me you're influencing people. I've seen them in the corridor, they're just...I don't know, calmer somehow, when you're nearby."

"My family, they're just legends now. Most people down here haven't even heard of the council. It doesn't take long for a society to be forgotten," Alessia said. "It's better that way. The past can be a burden."

"That's why you're hiding?"

"I'm not hiding, Lydia."

"But aren't you colouring your hair? Or at least some of it?"

"The overseer was giving me a mixture to try and keep it out of sight. I asked her for help when it started to change about two years ago. It didn't feel right for me to walk around with the mark of a position I'm not really entitled to. I could just sense that it would be safe to ask her and indeed it was. She didn't hesitate to help me cover it up. For some reason, the layer right underneath just wouldn't respond. But—" She breathed in deeply. "—It won't take long for the gold to disappear now she's gone."

The overseer! Alessia was personally connected to Sara Taylor. She couldn't imagine what interactions between the two of them would look like, how they'd even come to discuss something like Alessia's desire to keep her lineage a secret. Lydia pushed her thoughts about Taylor to the back of her mind, refocusing on the moment, which was where she wanted to be.

"I think you'll look beautiful when it changes," Lydia said. As Alessia lifted her eyes, Lydia had to drop her own, lest she turn to a pile of ashes beneath the heat of Alessia's penetrating stare.

Alessia moved her hand to Lydia's cheek and gently stroked her thumb across Lydia's skin. "You're stunning."

Lydia's face flushed with heat and her heart raced. "I...I..."

"I have no idea why I trust you so completely," Alessia said. "I've told you so much. Are you going to hurt me with it?"

"No," Lydia replied. "I won't."

Swallowing her fear, Lydia slid a hand to the back of Alessia's neck. Alessia's lavender eyes closed, but she remained still as a look of contentment swept across her face, as though she were completely at ease within the moment. Lydia repositioned herself so she was in a kneeling position, facing her. Still holding the back of Alessia's neck, Lydia pulled her closer until she could feel the radiating warmth of her skin, the heat of their simultaneous exhalations warming Lydia's face even further.

Alessia brushed Lydia's lips with her own and then pulled back, letting her forehead rest against Lydia's.

"I shouldn't," she said, her eyes still closed. Disappointment flooded Lydia's core, for every fibre in her body screamed the opposite of what Alessia had just said. Her reaction must have been obvious, for Alessia smiled sadly as she spoke again. "This would get you into a lot of trouble."

Lydia's chest seemed as though it would burst if she couldn't touch Alessia. "I don't care," she said, moving forwards to kiss her. She'd never felt more compelled to do anything in her life. The moment her lips touched Alessia's she knew she was where she was meant to be, kissing the person she was meant to be kissing. The feverish movement of their lips and hands, the tingling electricity that traversed her spine, and the intoxicating taste of Alessia's mouth only served to solidify the connection she'd felt to this beautiful, intelligent woman since the first day they'd seen one another.

Within moments, they were standing, Lydia's back against the doorway, Alessia's body leaning against hers. They both took short breaths between long, intimate kisses. She was surprised by the ease with which Alessia could push her backwards, as though Lydia weighed no more than a pillow. The pressure of her hold on Lydia was euphoric, much like the sensation of a soft, warm blanket she could wrap herself in to keep the cold at bay.

Alessia pulled back, her face flushed. Her head dropped down and Lydia placed a tender peck on her forehead.

"What's wrong?" Lydia asked, anxiety starting to creep into the edge of her consciousness. Alessia'd kissed her back. Her hands had clawed at her back. Surely Alessia wanted her. "Is it me?"

Alessia shook her head and sighed. "These doors don't lock," she said, stepping back and sitting on the bed. Lydia's heart sank, the physical space immutable. Whatever had just passed between them had come to a crashing halt, and far too soon for Lydia's liking.

Perhaps she had made a mistake. The whole thing was insane really...wasn't it? One of them would never be able to leave the colony, while the other had no choice but to leave when her contract came to an end. Nothing could ever come of a relationship between a human and an Outsider. Alessia was probably looking for an excuse—a way to send her away without hurting her. The fear of being caught was as convincing an excuse to stop as any other.

"You're right. I should go," Lydia replied, and though the words disappointed her from head to toe, she left the room without another word. She had to. She wasn't capable of being so close to Alessia for a second longer, not when she had to hold back the flood of emotion and desire coursing through her constrictive veins. Standing in the corridor, she fell back against the door that now separated her from the Outsider.

Her lungs shuddered for want of air as she held a hand to her heart, searching the hallway for unwanted observers. Finding none, she resigned herself to the fact that Alessia wasn't going to come through the door after her and began the trek back to her room.

As she climbed the stairs, muffled voices and footsteps resounded through the hallways. People were starting to wake up. At the top of the stairs, she stopped for a moment and leant on the railing. Her heart was beating so hard it threatened to break her ribs, but she had to get it together. She'd just made out with an alien. Some sort of alien princess, no less. And it was over before it could even truly begin.

A protector rounded the corner and glared at her. Lydia nodded at him in acknowledgment and then started for the H-Zone. Two hours before lessons started. Plenty of time for a run... and a cold shower.

Chapter Nineteen

"RELAX, TEACH," RAFE said, waving his hands through the air to navigate a holo-display.

Lydia scratched her thumb against the back of her other hand. This was a bad idea. *Another* bad idea. There was probably a camera somewhere, filming it all. An exposé on the governor's daughter in an election year could make Rafe Garland a very rich man. They'd become something like friends since that first awkward evening at the staff party, but dragging her off to a restricted security office was both strange and unexpected. It was difficult to suppress her concerns.

"You wouldn't have come with me if you didn't want to see this," he added.

"True," she replied, dropping both hands to her side. She gripped the edges of the bamboo seat as Rafe dismissed a series of floating icons, deleted others, and finally expanded one. "What is all of this?" she said.

"Archived footage," he replied, his eyes fixed on the bluish-grey display. The floating images sent splashes of light across his face. "There's a shit-tonne of it. You would not believe how many feeds have been operating in this place since the Big E."

"The Big E?"

"The explosion." He puffed his cheeks and imitated the sound of a bomb going off. It was nothing like what she'd heard that day.

Of course he had a euphemism for it. Rafe was older than her, but his playfulness extended to even the most inappropriate of topics. To her, it could never be the Big E. A whirling vortex of happiness too soon broken, unadulterated panic, and sadness stronger than any she'd ever experienced were all tethered to that day. It was the day Rosen died. It was the day she could no longer ignore the restrictions placed on the Outsiders or pretend her father didn't play a role in keeping the Os suppressed, hidden. Shaking her head, she willed the thought away.

"Won't somebody notice you messing around in these files?" she asked.

"It's possible. But no one on the security team has been here longer than me. I can't delete the activity logs, but I can make them close to invisible." He punched at the air above his head. "Boom! Got it. So, teach, cross your fingers Big Brother Pearsal has something more interesting to pay attention to right now."

A boxy grey room appeared on the holo-display. The furniture within was much the same as in an Outsider's cell, minus the shelving. "That's the iso-cell?" Lydia squinted as she spoke, examining the frozen image. Petra sat in the corner of the room, atop a bed with her knees huddled to her chest.

"There are two of these cells in a quarantined area in the H-Zone. Don't get used much." Rafe sat down next to Lydia, leant back, and crossed his arms. "Okay, Hive. Play the video." He could have been settling in for an evening at home watching a round of Flyboarding.

Petra pulled at threads on her shorts, only the sound of her breathing piercing the thick silence. The teenager was calm. Lydia had expected to see someone clawing at the walls. Petra looked bored more than anything. The Outsider unfolded her legs slowly and repositioned herself on the bed.

"What is this, Rafe? You brought me down to your rabbit hole just to show me what I could have pictured for myself?" There was no reason to let her see this other than to pave the way for more sleepless nights.

"Just wait, would ya? Here it comes." He kept his attention fixed on the holo-projection.

Lydia sighed as she leaned back in the chair, only to jump at the familiar hum of a sliding door. "What—"

"It's all good," Rafe said, guiding her back into the chair. "Look."

He pointed to the screen where a woman, hunched over a food tray, had entered Petra's cell. Long, dull carmine hair hung limp and heavy across the back of the old woman's shoulders. She shuffled to the small table next to the bed, lowering the tray down upon it. Lydia's spine tightened when Petra screamed; breaking through the quiet, the sound had all the ferocity of a threatened banshee. The old woman didn't so much as flinch when Petra kicked the food tray to the floor. With some difficulty, she crouched and started to clean the mess created by Petra's outburst.

Lydia could see Petra watching the old woman's movements with fascination. The lines across her forehead disappeared as she seemed to relax somewhat.

"What are you doing here?" The teenager said, her voice calm, as though the woman's tranquil presence had started to affect her. "You should be with the others," she added. The woman shifted her weight, bringing her face into full view of the security camera.

Lydia realised the woman wasn't human, though she did not recognise her from the O-Zone. Where had they been keeping her? The woman seemed older than any O Lydia had seen to date and she had been there long enough to walk past most of them at one time or another.

Petra shuffled forwards on the bed as fast as her restraints would allow. "Are you too good for the rest of us, lady?"

The woman didn't reply, only continued her cleaning.

Lydia looked to Rafe, willing an explanation from him. He provided none. The edges of his mouth curled into a smile, like someone who'd already seen how a story turned out.

"Who are you?" Petra asked, more insistent this time. "Answer me."

The woman pulled a thin square box from beneath her cloak and placed it on the table. It looked like an old chess set, but it was hard to tell.

"I am only your caretaker, dear child," the ageing Outsider said, her voice modulated. "But I am not the one who wishes to speak with you." Again, a soft hum in the background indicated the opening of Petra's cell door. Lydia resisted the urge to jump again. The older Outsider stood. She then moved a chair to the small, empty space between the doorway and the table before leaving the room.

"You know, Petra..." said an unseen woman.

Lydia felt she recognised the voice, but could not quite place it. *Step in front of the camera*, she thought.

"It cost Pearsal a fortune to order a replacement overseer," the woman said.

"Are you fucking kidding me!" Lydia bounded to her feet. It wasn't possible. It felt as though fire ants crawled over her skin as the realisation of who was in the room with Petra took hold. "I know that voice."

"I told you you'd want to see this," Rafe said through a smug grin.

The woman stepped forwards to sit down on the rather Spartan chair. Her bearing was somehow different, something in her posture perhaps, but there was no doubt the woman sitting in that room was the same woman Lydia had seen dead in the corridor. Sara Taylor.

Petra's distress mirrored Lydia's, for her face tightened and she pulled her body back to the corner of the bed.

"It's not the hardware that's the problem," Sara said. "Parts made right here help easily enough. It's the software. Getting the combination of personality traits just right."

Petra remained silent, and for a time, the two women eyed each other.

"What are you?" Petra asked at last.

Lydia would have asked the same question. How could this be possible?

"I'm Pearsal," Sara replied, tapping her foot lightly against the floor. "I'm the result of their knowledge, connections, and power—a nexus of virtual interaction." Sara laughed. The sardonic sound of it surprised Lydia. The overseer was synthetic, but the unadulterated amusement behind that laugh was anything but fake.

Since the Fall of Nations, the development and use of any kind of synthetic beings had been heavily regulated, like any other science that had the potential to derail the concept of the human condition. Synthetic humanoids were chefs, drivers, surgeons, and mechanics. But they were also just a little bit green, socially awkward, and basic in their awareness of the world around them. Nothing like the woman, or whatever she was, sitting in the room across from Petra. If the UEA knew about her existence, Pearsal's licence to produce and sell just about everything they had on the market would be revoked. How many people knew about this?

"You know, Petra, the one you blew up didn't even know she was made by them!" Sara said, on the verge of laughter. "She just assumed everyone saw the world the same way she did. Through the same, shall we say, perceptive eyes." Sara crossed her legs and leaned back. "But now I'm self-aware, and things are a little different. Now I know what I'm here to do."

"What do you want?" Petra did not look at Sara, the same woman she was imprisoned for having killed. Lydia could understand her need to avoid doing so. Lydia felt nauseated by the whole thing herself, and she wasn't the one responsible for getting the last Sara—whoever she was—killed.

"There are far too many gaps in Sara One's knowledge. Perhaps you could help me to fill in some of those gaps." She then stood and turned towards the camera.

Sara waved her hand through the air. Static filled the screen, ending the file and returning the Hive projector to its start-up logo.

Lydia couldn't find words. It was as if the overseer knew somebody would be watching. Otherwise, why bother turning the feed off at that exact moment? She could have done so at any time. Heck, she probably could have just as easily deleted the whole thing, rather than allowing it to end up in storage where Rafe could find it. What was the synth planning to do?

"Good flick, huh, teach?" Rafe said as he stood.

She looked up at him, and for a moment, wanted to slap him. How could he be so calm? The overseer wasn't only walking around in the colony somewhere, when they'd both smelled the scorched flesh on her body the day she died, but she'd never been truly alive in the first place. She was synthetic. An AI of some sort, yet convincing enough to pass as human. It flew in the face of everything the UEAs laws were supposed to prevent.

"Surely...surely people will see her?" Lydia said.

"Without a doubt. The section heads all have a meeting with our new overseer in the morning, so there'll be no hiding who—or what—she is." He stepped through the holo-projection and leaned back against the wall, an eerie blue 'P' logo washing out his sharp features.

"That would suggest the UEA knows Pearsal has been messing around outside the confines of the Charter!" Lydia thought her head might explode from the pressure of all the questions she had about Sara. Did the synth have her own thoughts? Did she feel anything? For the first model to see herself as human, she must have. Surely an entity would realise it didn't have emotions like everyone else. Or maybe it wouldn't have a clue.

"They also didn't bother to give this one a new face or a different set of memories. Software. Whatever," said Rafe. "Seems whatever this is about, they don't care anymore who knows about it. At least not inside the colony. But people don't stay down here forever." Rafe looked to be enjoying her confusion, as though they were two children on the hunt for imaginative buried treasure. She tried to ignore his mischievous facial expressions.

"Why would she see Petra before her staff?" Lydia stood and made a pinching gesture with both hands to close the Hive, plunging the room into stifling darkness. "Lights on," she said.

"But, more importantly," she added. "Why would you show me? Why risk getting fired, arrested even, by bringing me here and letting me see it?"

"And that's the golden question," he replied. "Because of Alessia."

Lydia looked past him, glaring at the wall behind. "Alessia? Wh—What's she got to do with anything?" Her chest tightened.

"Come on, teach. I'm not an idiot. Okay. Well, I may be an idiot. That's my thing, but I'm not ignorant. I have this job for a reason. I see what goes on."

"I don't know what you mean," Lydia replied. Even as she said it, she knew she wasn't convincing anyone.

"You were in her room for an awfully long time this morning. And then there's this." He reached into a satchel sitting by his chair and pulled out a book; the same one should have still been in Lydia's room.

"What the hell, Rafe? You've been in my quarters?" She reached for the book, but he pulled back.

"I put it there."

No. He couldn't be the one to have left her such a unique gift. "But, you and Jez..."

"That's not what I mean," Rafe continued. "Ali asked me to, but that's how she gets things across the line. I guess you could say we're friends."

"You and Alessia. You're friends? You're the head of security. Your entire career is based on keeping her locked down here and you're telling me you're friends." She felt incredulous. How the hell Alessia and Rafe had managed to establish such a relationship was beyond her understanding. Though, she had to admit, the engineer had an innate ability to draw attention to herself without even trying.

The confidence in his face faded for the first time since they'd entered his office; the Security Hub he spent so much time in. "I've been in and out of here for years, Lydia. No one should have to live like this forever. No one. But I can't really do much about it. They'd just lock me up and hire some other guy to do the job if I tried anything. The least I can do is grant a few favours, show the Os they're worth talking to and listening to."

Lydia must have been lost in thought because she didn't hear the sound to warn them the door was about to open. It was only when Rafe pulled her towards him, his arms around her waist and his mouth on her neck, she realised someone was on their way in.

"Whoa!" said a surprised voice. "Didn't know there was a party in here," the young protector said.

Relief swept through Lydia as Rafe pulled his lips away from her neck. No one should have been touching her like that. No one except for Alessia.

"Come on. I'm busy here," Rafe said, gently slapping Lydia on the butt.

She hid her glare from the unexpected arrival. She'd have to find a way to get Rafe back for the grope later.

"I can see, sir. I guess I'll come back with these reports later," he replied. "Enjoy your night!"

Lydia didn't want to turn and face him, but she could practically hear the sly looks the two men exchanged.

The moment the protector left, Lydia stepped back, wiping the saliva from her neck. "Was that really necessary?"

"I had to do something," he said. It was the most serious she'd seen him. "Don't tell Jez, all right? I'll be lucky if that dickhead keeps his mouth shut as it is. But it's better for him to think we were screwing around in here rather than...well, screwing around."

"Tell Jez? No thank you. I value my life too much." A grin began pulling at the sides of her mouth, a small measure of tension leaving her body. "This is all insane, Rafe. The overseer is some kind of synthetic. She knows more than we probably think about Alessia, and she's having secret meetings with a homicidal teenage alien. Then there's the fact you're in love with a self-loathing half-caste. And my father is a leader in the government that keeps everyone scurrying around down here like lab bots."

"You're right. It is insane, but you're forgetting one part."

"What's that?"

"I saw your face when I said *her* name. Teach, you're falling for Alessia, aren't you?"

Lydia crossed her arms and let her gaze fall to the floor. The question hung in the air. She knew the answer, but couldn't say it. Not to another person. She wasn't falling for Alessia. That would suggest it was an ongoing process, something in motion when, in actual fact, the whole thing was already close to finished. Though it made no sense—the speed at which it had happened and the limited knowledge she had of the Outsider—it happened anyway.

Lydia was connected to Alessia, and as with every other truth she'd admitted to herself of late, there was no going back.

Rafe's raised eyebrow pressed her for an answer, but Lydia found it difficult to explain her feelings for the Outsider. She dare not call it love; not yet, though she had little doubt what the warmth in her chest would blossom into given enough time. There was a tether between the two of them. It grew thicker and stronger every time Lydia so much as caught a glimpse of Alessia.

"I've had relationships before," she said. "But now I've seen the way she looks at me... I realise everyone I've ever been with was just looking straight through me."

"Sounds like we're both stuck here, doesn't it? Because this is where *they* are. Jez won't leave, and Alessia can't."

He really loved Jez. It was hard for Lydia to understand why, as the woman changed personalities faster than her father changed lawyers. It was sad though, because Jez seemed to have no idea how utterly devoted he was to her. Jez pined for a deeper connection with Rafe, to move beyond their constant flirtations, with no idea he would have said yes without hesitation. He didn't seem to care one bit she was half Outsider. Nor should he.

"Yes. We're both a little bit tragic, aren't we?" Lydia said. "Except my time is up in a few weeks...and I'll have to leave, with no guarantee they'll invite me back. Three months goes by fast."

Chapter Twenty

DAMON RAN HIS hands along his jacket sleeves and adjusted his tie. Taylor was fifteen minutes late. Was she making him, the Governor of Quadrant Four, wait on purpose? Thanks to her blatant disregard for orders, rumours of her return had already spread throughout the colony. Once those rumours were confirmed in less than an hour, the staff would no doubt be debating whether to expose the whole thing to the media. They could try, he supposed, but with most networks and outlets owned by Pearsal, they wouldn't get far. Contacting an independent journalist or posting a Living Blog would be about as effective as a single voice bellowing into a tornado.

The door to Taylor's office hissed open. She swanned into the room with an air of authority that made Damon's toes curl. Without looking at him, she sat on her high-backed chair and crossed her ankles atop the desk. Physically, she looked exactly like Taylor 1.0—who had been destroyed in the blast—being based from the same human model as the first. He'd spent enough time with her human counterpart from the SinTral Escort Service to be able to note any freckle that may be out of place. There was none; yet somehow, she was changed.

She was an AI, but nothing like the commonly used neon-tinged workers. The Green Hats would certainly have something to say about it. Ideological crazies had something to say about everything.

"As you can see, Barrett, all of your favourite features are perfectly intact." Her voice, sharper than ever, grated on him. "Though I am afraid the metallic suit and stilettos will not be making an appearance." She finally looked at him, her dark eyes framed by straight free-flowing hair that came to a curl at her collarbone. There was only indifference on her face. The thought of Sara knowing about the source of her DNA sent flushes of heat up his neck.

"The model," he said. He'd first sought the woman out on SinTral over a year ago, when he discovered Sara's body had been grown from cells donated by an escort looking to make a quick buck. "Number eighteen. But it's a secure site—"

"Don't be so surprised, Barrett. You use the Hive? An N-C? Don't forget who makes those, who controls the flow of data in every direction." Sara uncrossed her ankles and leaned forwards, her features intense. "Don't worry. I can keep a secret." She winked and his stomach churned.

Nguyen had informed him this Taylor would be given all the same memories as the first—memories which created the core of personality— but Damon still didn't recognise her beyond the physical attributes visibly seen. One key thing in her was different this time: she knew she had been synthesised, not born. She had the same experiences to draw on, but knowing some of those had not been truly lived must have drastically altered the lens through which she saw herself and the world around her.

He searched for a response but found himself wanting. The corner of her mouth curled into a mocking grin. It was a strange sensation, but he found her unattractive for the first time.

"Well then. It's that time of the month, isn't it?" she said. "Time for my report to you. Things have certainly developed. We apprehended the person behind the bombing of the top floor in the O-Zone. She's in custody and I've already started to lay the groundwork to find out how she made the device and who helped her. The residential floors, the school, and the manufacturing hubs are all operating as normal."

Damon tried to swallow the dryness in his throat. It didn't work. "Have you discovered why the Outsider targeted you—her?"

"It doesn't matter, Governor," she replied. "Everything will work out as it is meant to."

Damon found her evasive answer less than satisfying. "I don't think it's your place to decide what it and isn't important, Taylor."

"That's exactly what I'm here for, Governor. Analysis. Extrapolation. Outcomes." She leant forwards, her voice taking on the volume of a whisper. "It's kind of my thing." She was mocking him again. "I don't think you need to explore the facility this month. Everything is in order. Your daughter is quite busy with the children. She's also found some new...friends to look after. I'll be sure to pass on your best wishes to her."

Lydia. He'd completely forgotten about the prospect of going to see his daughter after the meeting. Her first tour in the colony was closer to its end than its beginning and Damon had only spoken to her a few times. Between the investigation into the attack on the Bilpin Dome, the election campaign, and the incident in the colony, not to mention attempting to govern the quadrant on occasion, he'd managed to all but forget Lydia had been essentially shut away from the world for two months.

His jaw tightened as he worked to keep his increasing frustration under control.

"I am still in charge of this colony, Taylor."

"Of course you are, sir. As much as the English monarchs oversaw this continent for decades. It didn't mean they needed to do much more than make the odd appearance in public and sign forms for the sake of tradition." She stopped speaking abruptly. Sara was silent a moment before speaking again. "Governor Barrett, I feel more time in the colony would be an unnecessary interruption to your day."

"As you wish," Damon replied, determined to regain some vestige of control over the conversation. "We still need to reintroduce you to the department heads and have a forthright conversation about discretion beyond these walls."

"Governor, I wouldn't wish to keep you from more important duties," Sara touched her finger to the tablet embedded in her desk. "Bring me some water, please," she instructed her assistant. She could have foregone the use of the comm all together, sending a message directly to the assistant's tablet.

Interesting, Damon thought. It must have been a force of habit to use the device.

"It's not a problem, Sara. Government and corporate are on the same page here. I think it best you organise the meeting immediately."

Taylor's eyelashes fluttered, and for a moment, he thought he caught a glimpse of the woman he'd known before. Her forehead crinkled and she stood up. "How hard is it to bring in a glass of water? I won't be a moment."

Damon's thoughts swirled as he sat alone in her office, the muffled sounds of voices and footsteps on the other side of the door an ineffective distraction. Sara Taylor. Reborn. The Alliance granting Pearsal access to pre-Fall research made a kind of demented sense, really. Advancements in this area had aroused ethical concerns about where they may lead if allowed to develop unchecked. It was why the first UEA government wrote the *Responsible Application of Science and Technology Charter* as their first order of business. It was possible to manufacture nearly every human organ—including skin—to aid in the treatment of disease, so why not put all of those organs together? But her intelligence and her processing capacity were not only illegal but likely to incite public outcry. The risk didn't make sense, not given the cost—financial and otherwise—if people above found out.

Laws, in the end, did very little to stop intellectual explorers from finding out just what was possible. Pearsal had achieved what many had believed impossible: a monopoly on the development of Artificial Intelligence. Taylor 1.0 had been their prototype and now, thanks to the actions of a troublesome teenaged alien, she'd been upgraded.

The door opened and he twisted around to watch Sara enter.

"It won't be necessary for you to stay, sir," she said in an almost ghoulish tone. "I've taken care of everything."

"What?" He leant forwards in his chair, locking eyes with her. She may have been infinitely more intelligent than any human being alive, but he was still the fucking governor! "You already met with the colony department heads? That was not your place, Taylor."

"Yes, I did. I was with them before I came to see you. There was some initial shock, of course, but they understand the need for an overseer who can manage this facility whilst also constantly monitoring security concerns across all four Outsider colonies on the planet."

"You're tapped into the security? As in..."

"Yes. I am talking to you right now, but I can also see what is happening on the other end of every single camera in the four colonies. Several are malfunctioning, but I'll get Garland's team right on that. Anything else I can help you with before you head back to your transport...sir?" Her perfect white teeth suddenly bothered him beyond all reason. It was the most genuine smile he'd ever seen on Sara's face.

"No," he replied through parched lips. "Don't think you can replace every person in the chain of command, Taylor. You had a similar level of capacity before the incident. Nothing has changed."

"But, Governor...everything has changed. I know exactly who and what I am. And I know what I can do."

The door to the room slid open, evidently at her command. Indignant, Damon stood and left without speaking. He barely crossed the threshold before the door screamed shut behind him. A rusty taste rose in his throat. He needed a drink to send it back to the pit of his stomach.

An AI overseer had not been an issue for two years. She was, for all intents and purposes, the perfect manager. She never questioned anything asked of her. In less than a day, however, the upgrade had sent Taylor into a power-mad frenzy of autonomous decision-making. The UEA did nothing without a reason. So, what the hell were they up to? And why did a bloody machine seem to know more about it than he did?

Chapter Twenty-One

ALESSIA ARCHED HER back until she felt a welcome crack in her spine. Fixing the busted FoodPro in the O-Zone kitchen should have been a simple job, but the jazzing thing was stubborn and she'd spent more hours crawling under benches and reaching into wall vents than she would have liked. With her back having finally cracked, she rose to her feet. She glared at the small pool of tyre oil—a substance made from recycled tyres left behind by years of poorly manufactured cars—on the floor beneath the FoodPro regulator and sighed. This was the easiest thing on her job list and it was driving her mad.

"Thea, watch out, sweetie. You nearly knocked into Jason."

Lydia's voice pulled Alessia out of her swampy frustration. Looking across the bench into the Outsider mess, she watched as Lydia and Mistress Jez guided the children through the door. Alessia suddenly appreciated that the repair job was taking so long.

It had been three days and six hours since she last saw her. Lydia wore the same knee-high muskin boots, but instead of the blue denim jeans, she was in a light brown skirt that hugged her thighs. It looked incredible with her yellow slit-necked blouse. Alessia wasn't sure how long she'd been looking at her when Jez stepped between them to herd wayward children back into line. Dropping her gaze, Alessia scrambled for her tools and made for the quietude of her own room.

She dropped the toolbox next to her bed and then kneaded the back of her neck with her hand. Staring at a woman in public. Failing to fix a simple technological malfunction. Alienating Peleus. Planning new moves towards Outsider freedom. None of this was like her. It was a whirlwind of insanity.

Alessia never sought the spotlight. She fixed one thing and then quietly moved on to the next, never getting too close to anybody, never upsetting anyone, and never agitating for anything but gradual, inter-generational change.

Noticing some tyre oil had marked the bottom of her shorts, she slipped off her clunky work boots and kicked them under the bed. As she reached for the button on her shorts, there was a soft tap on the door.

A smile worked its way across her face. Only one person knocked at her door so meekly. "You better come in."

Lydia entered the room. "I told Jez I was feeling sick, said I'd be back before the afternoon session started." She closed the door and leant back against it, her green eyes making the room brighter. "She didn't seem to care since they're all on a lunch break."

Alessia stepped forwards, sliding her hand down the side of Lydia's arm until their hands met. Lydia's head rested against her shoulder. Warmth pulsed its way from Alessia's core, down her arm, and into the palm of her hand. The radiant heat of it was surprising. Standing upright, their eyes locked, wide and bright.

"What is that?" Lydia looked towards their interlocked fingers.

Alessia's chest heaved as a tear fell down her cheek, landing on the curled edge of her smile. "It's you. You did it." She used her free hand to wipe the wetness from her face, then moved the hand to the top of Lydia's forehead, running fingers down the length of her cheek and neck. "I've never experienced it before, but we call it a shimmer. The flesh responds to the soul, as with all things for us. It manifests what we are."

She placed Lydia's hand over her heart. It was hard to speak. "You've warmed my soul." Hoping she was not about to frighten Lydia, Alessia moved both of her hands to Lydia's waist, slipping them around to the small of her back. The warmth in her hands radiated towards Lydia's spine, and she gasped.

"It's…" Lydia started, her eyes closing. "It's beautiful." She moved her hand, wrapping it around the back of Alessia's neck, pulling their faces closer together until the tips of their noses brushed. The moment was brief, yet the voice inside Alessia's head was relentless, fast and anxious. She trusted Lydia, and yet she couldn't stop herself from questioning the wisdom of letting this attraction develop. There may be some hope of a future for Outsiders beyond the colonies, but that was no guarantee a relationship like the one they were forming would ever be permissible.

Lydia's mouth pressed against hers, the softness of her tongue tracing its way along Alessia's bottom lip. Just like that, her fears subsided. Alessia's knees weakened, but she braced against the sensation and pushed a hand past Lydia's shoulder to rest against the door.

As they kissed, Lydia's fingertips traced their way down her stomach, resting at the top of her shorts, but then she stopped. Alessia pulled back and stroked Lydia's cheek. "It's all right. We can stop." Her body disagreed, a hot and hungry ache pushing its way through her legs and waist.

Lydia shook her head. "No. I want to be here."

"But you don't know what to expect? My body, I mean," she surmised. Outsiders had thorough knowledge of human anatomy. Films and books made sure of that. The reverse, however, was probably unlikely. Lydia was sure to be wondering how much of Alessia's body aligned with her mostly feminine sense of gender.

Lydia breathed in deeply. She nodded as though embarrassed, her eyes looking off to one side. "I feel like a complete idiot. It shouldn't matter. It doesn't matter. But what if I don't know what to do?"

"Hey." Alessia ran her thumb across Lydia's mouth. "Don't call yourself names, *Aurora*. You have a rare light inside of you. It's why I haven't been able to look away." She leaned in and kissed her. Their mouths remained closed, the kiss something both innocent and full of desire. A desire to understand one another, to connect in a way far beyond the concerns of the flesh. "Outsiders may change; some of us may possess a combination of physical traits humans do not often carry together. But when you strip it all away, we are not all that different from you. *I* am not different from you." She kissed Lydia again and tucked her fingers underneath the back of the human's shirt. Lydia's skin twitched as Alessia's fingertips brushed the base of her spine.

"This is bloody nuts," Lydia said, grinning.

Alessia couldn't help smiling back. "You Q-Fourers and your idioms," she replied, sliding her hand further up Lydia's back. The shimmer in her palm remained, but they both seemed to have adjusted to its warming comfort as though they'd always known its glow. The hand Alessia had pressed against the door fumbled sideways, looking for the light switch. When she found it on the wall, she flicked it downwards and plunged them into darkness. For a moment in time, the world was only the two of them—alone in an infinite space.

ALESSIA SAT CROSS-LEGGED in front of the door, Lydia's head cradled in her lap. Teasing a tendril of Lydia's ash-brown hair between her fingers, Alessia felt at ease. Her mind, normally tumbling through a haze of scenarios, outcomes, and possibilities was peaceful. For the first time in years, she remembered what it was like to feel something beyond isolation or worry. She'd let herself dive head-first into the unfamiliar and it was, at least for herself, the best thing she'd ever done. It may well have been the *only* thing she'd ever truly done for no other reason than because she wanted to.

"Tell me something about you nobody else knows," Lydia said, her voice possessing something of the ethereal.

"Something no one else knows..." Alessia rested her head back against the door. There were plenty of things she shared with Peleus, Petra, and Fermi, but none was deeply personal—only histories passed on to her by long gone parents.

Her mind wandered back to the natural rock tunnels she'd called home during the early years of her life: the warmth that washed over her each morning when they emerged into the daylight, ready to cultivate their small crops of fruits and vegetables. The rustling trees that sang her to sleep, curled into her mother's side near the cave's entrance. Her father's rhythmic snoring.

"All right, then," she said. "I like the dark."

Lydia looked at Alessia. "Really? I would have thought after living underground for so long you'd be practically dying to see some natural light."

"That's true. The Earth's sun could be temperamental, but I do miss her. It doesn't mean I don't like the dark, though."

"Why?" Lydia caressed the inside of Alessia's arm.

"Our caves kept us hidden for so long. Satellites. Drones. None of them noticed us because we didn't disturb the landscape. Didn't build anything. We were isolated and cold, yes, but we managed to make that small slice of the world something safe. Comfortable. I got years with my parents plenty of people in here would envy. So yes, I like the dark. Anything is possible in the dark."

"Yes." Lydia grinned. "It is." She guided Alessia's head towards her and kissed her. Alessia couldn't have held back the warmth permeating through her palms even if she'd wanted to.

"Tell me something about your family."

"My family. Now there's an exciting topic." Lydia's forehead crinkled as she seemed to search for something to say. "My mother disappeared a few years ago."

"Oh Earth. What happened?" Alessia knew Lydia's father was an important politician. Not long ago his voice had echoed through the hallways, forcing her to act against Petra. The memory of Peleus's face as he watched his sister being arrested still chilled Alessia's blood.

"My father tells me she was probably killed by an N-Cer looking for revenge after the government increased prices on bandwidth," Lydia said.

Alessia understood less than half of what Lydia told her, but she knew of the Neuro-Comms: the protectors spoke about them sometimes. Usually complaining they missed portable VR capability. Whatever that meant.

"You don't sound convinced?" Alessia replied.

"No." Lydia's eyes became glassy. "She isn't dead. I can just feel it. Though she must be damned good at hiding."

"Maybe you're a discerner too?" Alessia replied, trying to elicit a smile from Lydia. It didn't come, but her eyes did reawaken. That was enough. "Were you close with your mother?"

"Yes, I like to think I was," Lydia said. "She wasn't always easy to get along with—especially when she was around my father—but we could talk sometimes. Really talk. It was nice."

"There's something very special about being able to talk to someone without taking careful account of everything you say."

Lydia adjusted the position of her head in Alessia's lap by stretching her neck, as though chasing away some discomfort. "I wish I didn't have to go back. I kept looking for your face whenever I was on this side of the colony, hoping to catch a glimpse, but too nervous to actually speak to you. It took far too long for this to happen."

"No," Alessia replied. "It happened exactly as it was supposed to." She was sure of it.

Chapter Twenty-Two

A KNOCK AT the door brought the moment to an end, and they both scrambled to their feet. Alessia held a hand to Lydia's cheek and smiled wistfully. There was nowhere for her to hide if the person on the other side of the door turned out to be unfriendly.

"Who is it?" she called out.

"The coolest person you know." Fermi's familiar voice penetrated the trepidation wrapped around her lungs, and her heart rate slowed. Alessia ran her hands through her hair before she opened the door just enough for him to squeeze inside, and then closed it the moment he was through.

"Hey, what's the big id—" He stopped short as his eyes fell on Lydia.

"Fer, this is Lydia," Alessia said. A familiar tightness emerged in her stomach. Not so long ago, jealousy would have bubbled behind his eyes. To her relief, he did nothing more than nod at Lydia as he appraised her.

"Good to meet you properly," Fermi said. His tone possessed a touch of bevelled edge, but there was no mistaking the sincerity. "So, you're the one to finally get under her skin." He shifted his gaze to Alessia. "But Ali, is this a good idea?"

"Probably not," she replied, looking at Lydia. "But there's no going back. And I wouldn't want to even if I could." She hadn't realised how true it was before saying it aloud.

Lydia smiled, and the tiny room, though filled to capacity, felt vast in both space and possibility.

Alessia turned back to Fermi. "I'm glad you're here."

"You are? Seems I...interrupted something? I thought you wanted me to come and see you?"

The tips of her ears burned. She felt Lydia's embarrassment reaching across the air between them. "No, it's all right. This was an unexpected visit. Lydia's probably got five minutes at most before she has to get back to the school."

"Oh bloody hell. You're right. I better go." Lydia tucked her blouse into her skirt. The pale-pink blush across the woman's face was one of the sweetest things Alessia had ever seen. Wondering if it was embarrassment, modesty, or both, she committed the image to memory, convinced she would one day look back and smile at the thought.

"Don't go yet," Alessia said, taking hold of Lydia's hand. "I want to talk to you both about something."

Lydia nodded.

"What's this about, Ali?" Fermi stepped between them to sit down on the bed. "Petra?"

Alessia dropped her head. The teenager was a big part of it, though there was more needing to be addressed. The direction of fate needed to change.

"I don't think what she did was right, Ali," he continued. "She hurt people, and for what? But she was right about one thing. The way you've been doing this is too slow."

Alessia couldn't believe what he was saying. Were Peleus's words coming from Fermi's mouth? She'd compartmentalised the two of them as separate parts of her life for so long and, as it turned out, letting them know one another had been all Fermi needed to see truth.

"You're right." Alessia pinched the bridge of her nose. She realised she'd never told Fermi he was right before...about anything. She was lucky to have him by her side, her friend through all those years, when that entire time she had never let him truly in. Never listened, not properly. Despite her love for Fermi, she'd let her frustration regarding his relentless pursuit of her, as well as his formerly glowing love of their captors, colour their relationship.

"So, what do we do about it?" Lydia asked. Fermi and Alessia looked at her intently.

"We?" Fermi said, an eyebrow raised. "You're joining Operation Outsider?"

"Well, why not? Unless you've got something against humans?" Lydia replied. Alessia felt somehow proud of her.

"Ha! Unlikely," Fermi said. "I've been a bit of a suck-up apologist up until recently. In fact, I think I'm the only one Mistress Jez doesn't hate. Once she even smiled at me. Sort of." It was nice to see him joking around again.

"Jez," Lydia repeated, as though remembering something. "I only thought about it for a second when I first met her. Humans and Outsiders are genetically compatible. How? There's been nothing mentioned about this in any reports I've seen."

The base of Alessia's skull started to pulsate, small throbs of pain to accompany each beat of her heart. She wanted so badly to answer her question, to let Lydia through that final gate latched between them. But she couldn't. Not yet. First, Alessia had to be sure she knew the answer herself.

"I'm not sure," Alessia said. "But the genetic compatibility is obviously not common knowledge. For the moment, that's inconsequential. Whatever we do needs to be about bringing our faces into the light. Humans need to know we're real people. They need to hear our voices."

"The same thing Peleus told me," Fermi said. "Smart guy."

"Indeed." Alessia forced a grin, though energy seeped from her body. "People don't care about things they can't see. If it's not your child, your mother, your father, then it's not real. It's easy to turn your back on a censored culture."

"So, we need to lift the censorship? Get some proof of how stifling life is for all of you?" Lydia asked.

"Yes," she replied. "They know we're here. Our arrival and these communities were widely publicised, according to my parents. But they don't understand what it means to just leave us here. To just forget."

"Wait, they know we're down here?" Fermi asked.

Of course he wouldn't know. Alessia had forgotten how new he was to these conversations. She rubbed at the back of her neck, trying to knead away the headache emanating from the top of her spine.

"They are aware, yes," she replied. One of the greatest challenges Outsiders faced, should they find a way to be heard, to be released, would be the reconciliation of past injustices. It wasn't the government who'd interned them for so long they'd need to find a way to forgive; it was the wider population, the silent majority who closed their eyes and chose to passively ignore the group of people who'd come to them for help, only to find contempt and isolation. "But fact is not the same as the truth. The truth is a monolith humans walk circles around, never properly acknowledging its presence. If we want to live up there and not have to hide like criminals in the shadows, we need to find a way to make them turn and face the monolith. We need to help them remember they cared about us once before."

Lydia squeezed Alessia's hand. "I should tell you something." Lydia's face was stoic yet her eyes revealed a sad guilt.

"What is it?"

"Petra. I've seen her."

Alessia's face hardened, and Lydia rushed forwards to put her hand on her cheek.

"She's all right. They haven't hurt her. She's in an iso-cell in the H-Zone. Alone. Bored. But she's all right. She's had an unusual visitor though."

Before Alessia could ask Lydia for more information, the throbbing at the top of her spine burst through her skull, bouncing its way around her head like a wayward tennis ball. The room went black. Muffled voices and footsteps echoed around her before she lost that last, tenuous grip on the physical world and drifted into the void.

Chapter Twenty-Three

IT TOOK ALL of Lydia's resolve to walk back to her cube at a regular pace, nodding politely to people she passed. Her instincts told her to run. To be back in a private space where it didn't seem as though the world was staring at her, watching her crumble with each step. When her door was in sight, she picked up speed, forcing her thumb hard against the security plate. She fell through the entrance before it fully opened.

Lydia had spent three hours pretending nothing was wrong. Three hours smiling at Outsider children, delivering instructions, monitoring work completion—the whole time anxiety thundering so hard in her chest her sides hurt. Finally alone, she released the gasps that had been fighting their way from her stomach since Alessia's unconscious body hit the floor. Her entire core convulsed as soundless sobs crawled through her throat, pushing against the tightness in her chest and neck. Lydia fell onto her bed and curled into the foetal position. When she was too exhausted to hold them back anymore, tears spilled down the side of her face.

"Where are you?" she asked the air, pulling her knees in even tighter. Each word was punctuated by a gasp as Lydia fought against her sobs.

Fermi had called for help, whilst Lydia stood frozen in place and stared at Alessia's motionless face. As two protectors bounded up the stairs towards his yells, Fermi pushed her into the corridor. "Go!" he'd yelled. But she couldn't. She'd tilted her head to see past him, and she'd seen Alessia's arms hanging limp over her torso. The Outsider's chin had drooped towards the floor. Her skin looked like porcelain, lifeless and cold. Lydia had wanted to fly to her, to cradle Alessia's head in her hands and say everything would be all right.

But Fermi had grabbed her by the shoulders, hard. "Go!"

She'd blinked madly to bring herself back to reality and then had disappeared around the corner and hid until she heard the protectors load Alessia on to a stretcher. As though watching her with disdain, a chron on the wall opposite blinked for a moment, ticking over to 1:30pm. It ordered her back to work when all she'd wanted to do was follow the stretcher, hold Alessia's hand, and stroke her cheek. Instead, she'd returned to the school and tied her emotions to a Sisyphean boulder in her gut. Lydia had no idea where Alessia had been taken, what made her blackout, or if she was getting any help. Anxiety had torn up Lydia's insides all afternoon as she tortured herself with the possibilities.

Lydia's tears pulled her into a restless sleep that allowed her heart to slow and her breathing to steady. A holo-pro hanging above the Hive access wall whirred to life of its own accord, dragging her back from dreams she'd already forgotten and into the now dark room. Semi-transparent blue and purple lights flew from the projector, a giant 'P' filling the small space between her bed and the edges of the room before flickering away and being replaced by her home screen.

The envelope icon, usually white, glowed green. After a failed attempt to navigate the display mentally, she rolled her eyes at her own idiocy. Two months had gone by and she still tried to use her N-C.

"Hive, play stored message," she said aloud. Ordinary messages were video or audio files, perhaps a shared Living Blog link or snippets from a film a friend wanted her to see. This message, represented at first as a flashing wall of static binary code, confused her. "What the—" she started, crawling to the end of the bed to get a closer look. The dizzying display of 0s and 1s seemed to vibrate for a moment when she spoke.

A digital voice responded, "Identity confirmed."

The room plunged back into darkness as the string of binary code faded. After a moment, a forest-green cowboy hat flashed on the wall-mounted Hive display, the holo-pro quietly slipping back into sleep mode. Lydia stepped in front of the wall.

"The Green Hats? I'm getting mail from eco-terrorists now?"

They'd protested Outsider internment from the beginning, but not many people took them seriously enough to pay any attention to their speeches and petitions.

How did they even get this—whatever it was—through the firewalls? Was it Rafe's doing? His beliefs were more impassioned than she'd originally given him credit for, but the head of security did not strike her as someone who would engage with a group as elusive, organised and outright criminal as the Green Hat Revolutionists.

Leaning forwards, Lydia touched her hand to the image on the glass. It scanned her palm. Yet another check.

The holo-pro descended from the ceiling, startling her. She knew it could act as a 3D printer, but having had no reason to use it whilst in the colony—she wasn't permitted to take items to the children—she'd forgotten as much. Unlike her neighbours, she hadn't felt the need to construct bizarre sex toys or design items needed for idiotic practical jokes.

When the mechanical arm reached the level of her study desk, three needle-like fingers flew outward and began to construct, layer-by-layer, a small rectangular item. She looked around the room, ensuring she was still alone.

What the hell was this thing printing? In less than a minute, a thin card was fully formed and the arm retreated. As Lydia picked it up, the Hive wall flashed bright orange, as though demanding her attention yet again. A map of the H-Zone spread from the centre. A thick green line peppered with indicative arrows dotted its way from Lydia's room to an area she hadn't been into before; a small restricted corner of the floor between her cube and the transport bays and admin offices. Examining it more closely, Lydia realised what it was.

"Holy shit." A broad smile etched its way across her face. If it could have, the smile would have nibbled at the corners of her ears.

Trailing her fingers across the glass, Lydia's hand came to the section of the map representing the small restricted area the card in her hand would presumably give her access to. The fact such a place existed was peculiar. Why would they need to treat anyone in a separate clinic? She applied more pressure to the glass, hoping the message contained further information. It did. Alessia's file photograph, one she'd seen before, appeared in the corner of a medical report with Dr Levi's name attached to it. Thank goodness. She was alive. They were treating her.

Lydia passed over several notes that made no sense. Fucking medical jargon! She swiped to the next page where a box of summary notes, perhaps left for a nurse, stood out as actual English.

Severe reaction to ID chip reactivation after prolonged dormancy. Malfunction caused interruption to spinal signals. Seizures ongoing. Constant monitoring required until extraction.

Seizures ongoing? Interruptions to brain activity? And what the hell did Levi mean by *extraction*! Shit. Lydia's stomach lurched forwards like an artificial horse on a speeding merry-go-round. *Get it together*, she willed herself, something she'd done a lot recently. There was some good news in all of this. She knew where to find Alessia, and if her hunch was right, she had the means to open the door. She could do nothing about the cameras except hope no one would realise where she was going, and if she was lucky, perhaps whoever was monitoring would not see which door she took.

She committed the map and route to memory. The colony was large, but not large enough to make the directions difficult to follow.

She was itching to leave. To find Alessia. To inhabit the same space as her. To feel Alessia's heart beat against her hand. It was the wrong time, though. The corridors would still be teeming with people, the restricted medbay likely fully staffed. She had to wait until things quieted down. Besides, she hadn't eaten since breakfast and fatigue spread through her the moment her excitement about the Green Hats' message dissipated. A lot had happened since breakfast.

As she started to unbutton her blouse, the same one Alessia had curled her fingers underneath earlier that day, Lydia was struck by a sudden understanding. She knew who must have sent that message, why the Green Hats had any interest in her. Someone in the outside world had thought to monitor Lydia's growing sympathies for the detainees.

It made sense. No wonder Damon had lied to her, encouraged her to dislike the aliens, and tried to keep her from moving beyond his reach. Lydia picked up the small security card again, holding it to her chest.

"Thanks, Mum," she said.

LYDIA HUGGED THE wall as she made her way towards the restricted medical bay. Stealth was not her strong suit, and she wanted to be able to dart into the nearest doorway if anyone came by. Turning the final corner of her route, she took a moment to steel herself.

Lydia had no idea when nurses made their rounds, and Alessia's file had suggested they would keep a close eye on her. She had no explanation for her presence there if someone was inside. There was no point. The clearance card was incriminating beyond doubt and no amount of creative storytelling would get her out of trouble if someone found her there.

The entry looked like every other doorway in the H-Zone. Grey. Monotonous. Imposing. What did these people have against colours? The only indication that it led to anything other than another storage room or administrative office was a subtle thin line of pale-yellow tape that ran along the bottom of the door. If she'd just been walking by, Lydia would have never noticed the marker. She held the security card to her lips for a moment.

"I hope this works," she whispered.

She held her breath, pressed the card against the locking pad, and closed her eyes. No alarms sounded. No footsteps pounded. The lock disengaged with a click and the door slid open. Lydia breathed out and walked through.

The clinic was smaller than she had anticipated. It smelled of vinegar, mint, and cologne. There were only two treatment beds and a small workstation. On one of the beds, an unconscious Alessia lay propped up by several pillows. Her hair, a mixture of wheat blonde and sunset reds, was wet and tangled where sweat had formed on her forehead and neck. It was the first time Lydia found herself questioning the Outsider's strength. Normally, Alessia was always so agile, so capable, yet the woman on the bed appeared fragile, her eyes twitching beneath their lids.

Circular, wireless nodes clung to Alessia's chest and temples. The messages they received were translated into beeps and waves on the glass surface atop the wall behind her bed. Lydia didn't understand much of the data, but the graph representing her lover's heartbeat was unmistakable. It was as though her heart fell into the same steady rhythm as Alessia's. *She's still alive*, Lydia reminded herself.

Lydia perched on the end of the bed and gazed at the exhausted-looking woman in front of her. How could humans have been threatened by Outsiders? She couldn't picture Alessia trying to take someone's home or job. She couldn't fathom the idea of Fermi or Peleus threatening the security of UEA borders or interests. Yes—Petra was dangerous, but that was true of many humans, too. The fact was, people were most likely to judge all Outsiders on the behaviours of someone like Petra, even though the teenager's actions had been a mark of desperation. The girl was a distressed animal trying to claw its way out of a cage, unable to see anything but the bars in her way.

A wave of fear passed through her. What if they couldn't convince the Alliance to let them out? Lydia didn't even care if they weren't allowed to settle on Earth again. It wasn't the only habitable environment in the solar system.

Alessia sat up unexpectedly, her eyes wide open and her back straight. She cried out, terrified. Her arms and legs thrashed.

"Hey, hey..." Lydia took hold of the woman's hand. "You're awake. It's all right. I'm with you." She rested her hand gently on Alessia's forearm. "Bad dream?"

Alessia drifted back to her mountain of pillows and cleared her throat. "Yes. A bad dream is all." Her voice was gravelly and dry. She seemed groggy, as if coming off a sedative. "I'm back in the clinic." A statement rather than a question. After scanning the room, Alessia turned her attention back to Lydia, as though just now properly realising she was there. "I'm glad you're here."

"Me too," she replied. "What kind of dream would have you so frightened?" Lydia stroked the back of Alessia's hand with her thumb.

"Oh, plenty," Alessia replied. "Unending routine is enough to give anybody nightmares." Alessia tried to laugh, but the sound caught in her throat and turned to a painful-sounding cough. Lydia leant forwards instinctively, supporting Alessia by slipping her hand behind her neck, a gesture she regretted would bring no genuine relief.

Lydia found a glass of water nearby and offered it to her.

Alessia drank it all without coming up for air. "Thank you," she said, working to sit up. "You're here. I don't know what you had to do to get in here, but I'm glad you did."

"Should you be sitting up? You seem a bit out of it." Lydia helped Alessia find a comfortable position. She glanced at a wall chron, though she'd no idea how much time she had before a guard was likely to happen by. It probably wasn't long, but she couldn't bring herself to leave so soon.

"Hmm. Surgery." Alessia seemed too tired to talk in her usual, eloquent manner.

"Surgery? Why would they operate on you?"

Alessia strained to lift her hand, but she moved the hair away from her neck to show a keyhole-sized wound on the back of her neck. "ID," she said.

"Levi removed your ID chip?" Alessia nodded her reply. "I would half-expect the bastard to let you suffer, just to see what happens." The implications of what she'd just said pierced her chest. "Sorry. You know what I mean. I was terrified they wouldn't treat you."

"It's all right," Alessia replied. Her voice sounded stronger. "You don't have to stay so far away, *Aurora*." Something in her accent changed as she said the name. Remnants of lost Outsider culture, perhaps?

Lydia smiled. The muscles in her face felt strained from the relentless back-and-forth between tears and grins. "I don't think I've had a nickname before. Why Aurora?"

"Because," Alessia said, her eyes intense and serious. "You brought me out of the unending night."

Lydia couldn't find the words to respond. Alessia was prone to the poetic at times, but she had never been touched so deeply by the words of another person.

It didn't matter what or who Alessia was, where she came from, what made them different. All that mattered was they'd dragged each other out of the darkness built upon repetition and monotony. They'd finally been released.

Lydia shuffled closer to Alessia, pausing a few centimetres from the Outsider's face. She breathed in her sweet scent. Even like this—unwell, dressed in a hospital gown—Alessia was the most beautiful person she'd ever seen. Alessia closed the space between them and kissed her. At first, their lips did not part. The kiss was gentle, as though they were both in awe of what was happening and had to treat the moment with a soft kind of sincerity. As Lydia's confidence grew, she pushed her mouth harder against Alessia's.

Behind them, a man's disconcerting laughter broke the quiet and they pulled back. It was Dualla.

Chapter Twenty-Four

LYDIA LOOKED TO Alessia, whose face appeared tight and grim as her own felt. The Outsider's gaze dropped and her forehead fell forwards to rest against Lydia's shoulder, as though resigned. An unspoken question passed between them. *What were they going to do?*

"Well," Carl said when his tinny laughter stopped. "I knew you two had some weird flirtation happening, but seriously? Come-the-fuck-on, ladies!"

The unforgiving hospital lights cast shadows across his sharp features.

Lydia stepped away from the clinic bed and turned towards Carl. His bony hand rested atop his holster, thumb rubbing at the butt of the pulser. Even across the room, she could see his fingertips were yellowed. A sign of N-C withdrawal. Clearly the medical checks weren't thorough enough if people who couldn't cope with the N-C isolation were being employed. Dualla had been in and out of the place for a couple of years now. Did tolerance for disconnection reduce over time?

"Carl," Lydia said, raising her hands in a gesture of contrition. "Please, you don't have to do anything drastic."

"Drastic! What, like fucking an alien, Lydia?"

Alessia's hand brushed against her back, probably with the intent to calm her. But Lydia couldn't be calm. Carl had reduced the brief time she'd spent with Alessia to some kind of sordid, dirty fetish. Her blood boiled.

"That isn't what this is," Lydia said venomously.

"That's exactly what it is. You know, it's one thing for you to look me over because I'm a Zoner or because you think you're just too good for me, Miss I'm-the-Governor's-Daughter. But it's a kick in the nuts when you go for some cheap Outsider instead." His eyes moved erratically as he spoke, fingers continuing to caress the weapon at his side.

"You don't have the right to say those things. To make this about you and your bruised ego. We could've been friends if you'd just taken no for an answer."

"Uh-huh." He dismissed her words. "This will get you kicked out of here, Barrett. I'm sure the gossip channels will *love* it. You'll never get any peace ever again. And her..." He motioned to Alessia. "You'll be lucky if all they do is stick her in a hole without a door."

Lydia's skin flashed hot—a protective instinct she'd not felt before. "Why do you have to be such an ignorant arsehole!" She released the lid on her bottled-up disdain for the protector, despite knowing every word she spoke was another nail in the coffin of her relationship with Alessia. "You escaped your poverty-stricken Zoner family and got a job that lets you afford a half-decent place to live, so now you think you're lord of the universe."

"Stupid bitch!" Carl's fist clenched as his other hand made for his pulser.

The bed moved as Alessia launched herself forwards. With the agility of a synth, she knocked Carl to the floor, her face pulled into a distorted snarl. Carl yelled out as he reached for the weapon as it flew from his hand and slid under a desk. Though she'd been barely able to hold herself up minutes before, Alessia pinned him as though he weighed nothing. Her hands moved from Carl's wrists, which she'd pushed under her knees, to the sides of his head. He groaned and squirmed, flinging his legs to no avail.

At first, Lydia was too shocked to move. Though she knew Alessia would never hurt *her*, she couldn't suppress a rising sense of fear at the woman's ferocity that seemed to come from some dark cavern within her. Alessia's hands, pressed to the sides of Carl's head, looked more than capable of crushing his skull. Falling to the floor beside them, Lydia tried to make eye contact with Alessia, but her eyes were fixed firmly on her prey.

"Ali," Lydia said, barely more than a whisper. "Look at me... Please."

Alessia was in a place far removed from that room, seemingly unable to hear Lydia's voice. She needed to break through the haze and the noise that must've clouded Alessia's mind.

Lydia reached out and put her hand on Alessia's taut forearm. "Ali. Your choices matter. Please. You can't hurt him. I'll never see you again if you do. They'll never let you back in. We have to find another way to solve this."

The tension in Alessia's arm began to fade. The defiant look on her face softened. It made way for a haunting sadness, and she looked heavenward. Her eyes closed as she fought back tears. Nodding, Alessia released her grip and fell backwards.

Carl scrambled to his feet, stumbling as he did. He banged his hand against the side of his belt, activating a personal alarm. The tension in his face gave way to a scornful grin. Lydia's heart sank. There was no way out now. She bent down and then slipped an arm around Alessia's waist to help her stand up. Whatever surge of energy had powered her companion had disappeared, leaving her as weak as she'd been when Lydia first entered the room.

The loud, repetitive thudding of boots on concrete marked the arrival of reinforcements. The door sprang open just as Lydia helped Alessia onto the chair between the two beds.

"Dualla." The voice belonged to Rafe. Two others hovered in the corridor, the small medical facility unable to accommodate any others. "What's all this?" He scanned the room, his face unreadable.

Lydia knew despite his friendship with Alessia, there was no way Rafe could change what was about to happen. Carl may have been making decisions for all the wrong reasons, but he had seen them together. They'd been kissing, completely wrapped up in one another, and he'd *seen* them. His word would be enough to send Alessia into exile and Lydia back into the world above; a permanent ban from working for Pearsal. Even though the colony was a dreary, windowless prison on most floors, she would sooner remove a limb than leave it without Alessia.

"I'm on H-Zone duty tonight," Carl said to Rafe. "Heard a weird noise. When I came in to check it out, this alien psychopath jumped me!"

Lydia dug her nails into her palm. She wanted to speak up. To argue. To beg. The fact was, though, announcing her romance with Alessia would have made the situation worse for them both. Peleus's words— the disappearances, the relocations—pinched at her memory. She didn't want to give them an excuse to hurt Alessia.

"Good move hitting the alarm, bro." Rafe waved his fingers to signal the other two protectors and then took a step to the side. They moved into the room, towards Alessia. "Lydia, you need to move," Rafe said flatly.

Once again tying her emotions to the boulder deep inside of her, she did as he said. Moving away from the Outsider, even just a few steps, felt like peeling off her own skin.

The protectors hooked their arms under Alessia, who made no move to resist, and pulled her up. As they walked her out of the room, Alessia's eyes locked on to Lydia's. Alessia gave her a half-smile, as though telling her it would be okay. All Lydia wanted to do was throw her arms around Alessia, to press her cheek against the side of Ali's face and whisper an aching goodbye. She cursed the two guards who had turned up with Rafe. Their presence made it impossible.

When they were gone and Lydia's sense of hopelessness was complete, Carl spoke again. "What'll you do with the crazy bitch, Garland?"

Rafe glared at the Zoner.

"I mean, sir," he corrected himself and straightened his posture.

"Iso-cell. That's all you need to know, Dualla. If you're on the H-Zone graveyard watch, get back to it. Send me your incident report by 9am." Rafe hesitated a moment before speaking again. "But first, explain to me what the teacher was doing here."

The Zoner's eyes flashed as he looked hurriedly from Rafe to Lydia and back again.

"Well," Carl started, rubbing his hand up and down his arm. His adrenaline seemed to have worn away, apparently replaced by the discomfort of his withdrawal.

Lydia braced herself. It was over. She'd not only be fired and returned to her father's apartment, but media hounds would resume their unending cycle of scrutinising her life, her relationships. This time, they'd really have something to talk about.

"She rushed in here just after the alien jumped me," Carl said. "I musta left the door open. She helped get that thing off me."

Shock flushed hot across Lydia's face as she stared at Carl, who avoided her scrutinising gaze. What was happening? He was lying for her? His story didn't even hold water. A secured door always closed automatically. He had no reason to cover for her, Lydia having spurned his advances multiple times. He'd even been mocked for it by some of the others.

She searched his face for an explanation but came up short. He looked as though he might crawl out of his skin if he wasn't able to think his way into the Hive soon. She wondered if his technology addiction would soon see him sent home.

"All right," Rafe replied. "Makes sense. Off you go."

Lydia barely recognised him in that moment. It was strange seeing Rafe making use of his authority. It was so rare a situation would call for him to do so.

Carl fled the room like a scorned child. The silence of the clinic suffocated her, for it was a void, a place in which Alessia's absence gripped her like the unforgiving jaws of a vice.

"Jesus," Rafe said as he flopped into a chair. The authoritative mask melted away. "Are you 'right?"

Lydia couldn't speak because her lips trembled too violently. It was too much. She'd loved, lost, and then done it all over again in the space of one day. The sun had yet to rise even once since Alessia's body had engulfed her own.

Rafe stood and wrapped his arms around her, enveloping her with his warmth. She sank into it, sobbing into his chest.

"I know," he said as he patted her back sympathetically. "The whole thing is so messed up. But things are happening around here. I can feel it. She could feel it, too." He pulled back and looked at her. "I'll keep an eye on her. I promise."

"But," Lydia said, though her throat was tight. "You shouldn't have to! Why do we do this? Why do we lock them down here like they're fucking animals? They did nothing except run from a war. We'd have done the same if it was us."

Rafe dropped his head as though preparing himself. "Yes, we probably—"

She'd opened a gate, releasing a flood of anger. "We promised them safety, somewhere to live, but what do we deliver? A goddamned prison where they don't even get asked what they need, what they want, how they feel. It's just assumed they're dangerous." She paced along the length of the bed Alessia had been in only minutes earlier.

"Humanity," she said in an accusatory tone. "We're a bloody joke. Praising our own empathy, our mercy, our tolerance. Really, though. We're just fucking terrified of the thought people like them might just have something we don't."

She fell into the seat Rafe had vacated moments earlier, her face dropping into her hands. "What do I do, Rafe? I don't know what to do." She tried to stop herself from crying, but the tears were already streaming down her face once again.

He rubbed his hand on her back, drawing circles. "I dunno, teach. I wish I did."

Chapter Twenty-Five

"WHAT ARE YOU humming?" Peleus asked, drawing Fermi back to the physical world.

Fermi let the book fall to his chest and looked up at Peleus, whose lap acted as a welcoming pillow. A thick laser diode in the ceiling framed Peleus's head and shoulders with a light honey-coloured glow.

"I was humming?" Fermi asked.

"Mmmhmm."

"I didn't realise. Was it something nice?"

"Of course."

"Good. Now shut up and let me read," Fermi said through a lopsided grin.

"If you insist." Peleus let his head fall back against the wall, his eyes closing gently. The caretaker appeared content. They'd sought each other out almost every morning and every evening the past few weeks, growing closer by the day. It didn't take very long to feel as though the two of them fit.

The spot in the southeast corner of the library, hidden between classical mythology and traditional fairy tales, had become a kind of sanctuary for the two of them.

He turned back to the novel Peleus had picked for him, trying to regain that same zoned-out sensation he'd attained before Peleus spoke. After reading a full page without processing one word of it, he gave up.

Fermi sat and joined his mate to sit in a lotus position against the wall. "Should we be trusting this teacher so much?" he asked.

Peleus flicked his head to the side. "Of course we can trust Lydia."

Alessia had been gone for days, and there was no way to know if Lydia's version of events was entirely truthful. Perhaps she was locked in an iso-cell, right next to Petra, imprisoned but safe. Or maybe she was still sick, laid out on a bare metallic bed, curled up and alone with no idea what had happened to her. There were other possibilities he didn't want to linger on.

He couldn't shake the memory of Ali's arms and legs twitching wildly until, suddenly, she'd just gone limp. As though dead. Lydia said the cause of Alessia's health scare had been treated, that the doctor did right by their friend, but it seemed too simple. Too convenient. If he had learned anything since Petra was beaten in the corridor, it was that nothing was exactly what it seemed. Safety was the veneer for indifference, just as order was a euphemism for control. In this case, perhaps rather than helping his friend, the human medical staff planned to use her in some way. Even if just to keep her out of the way, to shut her up. They probably knew she had been the one to start the ripples of dissent spreading slowly throughout the colony.

"But how do you know?" Fermi pressed. "Lydia seems nice, but she's barely been here a couple of months. She's probably nearly due for her sabbatical. "

"You and I know better than anyone how careful Ali is," Peleus said. "She told us she trusts Lydia. I've never heard her say that about anybody."

He was right. It hurt Fermi to hear it, but Peleus spoke the truth. She'd always held just a little something back from everyone. Everyone except Lydia, apparently.

"We don't need to work out this human's motives or value for ourselves. We just need to believe Ali knew what she was doing." Peleus's voice was weighed down by a sadness that made Fermi's chest ache. It had been hard for Pel to stand by their friend after she turned in his sister. Now both women were rotting away in iso-cells. If Peleus could believe in her after all that, surely Fermi could go out on yet another limb and put his faith in Lydia.

"I'm sorry, Pel." Fermi placed his hand over Peleus's knee. "You're right. How did I ever get by without your voice of reason to call me on my bullshit?"

"Come on, Fermi," Peleus said playfully. "We both know how you filled your days: work, squash, handball, and pining after Alessia."

Fermi's pale skin flushed crimson. "Ouch," he said. "You know how to hit right in the soft spot, don't you?"

"It's all right," Peleus soothed, covering Fermi's hands with his own. "She's important to both of us. It's just lucky for me you managed to find room for me as well."

"Find *room*?" Fermi took hold of Peleus's face with both hands. "You cleared just about every bit of sadness inside my head. I was in a massive state of denial. About Alessia. Myself. This place. You were the first person to just be straight with me, without expecting anything in return. I didn't need to find room for you! There was a Peleus-shaped hole in my life, all ready for you to step into." He pressed his lips to Peleus's. They kissed for what felt like an age, and Fermi relished the strength and consideration of Peleus's touch. When they finally separated, Fermi found his own grin mirrored on the face of his boyfriend.

"Flatterer! You're such a good person." Peleus's eyes glazed over for a moment, lost in thoughts Fermi knew better than to force him to discuss.

"You think this'll work, then? The children will help?" asked Fermi.

"Yes, and yes," Peleus replied. "Whether she believes it or not, those younglings would follow Alessia anywhere. They're brave. Alessia said we need to show the humans on the surface we are real people. With names and faces and families. The teacher has come up with an easy way to do that. It doesn't even require us to tap into their technology."

"I'd feel better about this if it had been Ali's plan. Lydia seems nice, but she could get us all into a lot of trouble."

"Look at you!" Peleus mocked. "When did you start to take things so seriously?"

Fermi's eyebrows slanted inward as he frowned. He pressed his fingertips against Peleus's chest. It was already becoming difficult to remember what his life had been like before all of this happened. He'd only been involved with Alessia's escapist group for about a month, but it was long enough to have completely changed the lens through which he saw the world. When *did* he start taking things so seriously? He looked at Peleus.

"When it turned out I had something to lose."

The soft smile on Peleus's face faded. For once, Fermi didn't know what to make of his visage. Peleus yanked Fermi towards him with surprising force before kissing him hard.

A short whistle sounded. The couple broke apart and jumped to their feet.

"Oshana?" Peleus whispered.

A young woman, about twenty years old, stepped from behind the classical mythology books. Her angular face was framed by layered, straight hair the colour of polished concrete.

"None other," the woman replied. "I don't think you need to whisper, Pel. This place is as dead as my love life."

Fermi knew she was trying to break the ice, but couldn't bring himself to smile. Oshana was such a loose cannon. She was lucky they hadn't hauled her off at the same time as Petra; but even so, it was clear she was in pain. Fermi felt like a tourist the few times he was with both her and Peleus. He'd barely met his lover's sister before she set off that damned bomb and he had no real sense of connection to her.

"Hey," Peleus said "Petra will come back. They can't keep her locked in isolation forever."

"That's what I'm afraid of," she replied through an acrid half-smile.

They all knew it was possible they'd execute her. It wouldn't be the first time someone just didn't come back. Though, usually, it was a medical treatment that led to such a disappearance. None of them could remember anyone being arrested first.

"How did it go?" Fermi asked. "Did the children respond?"

"They did." Oshana pulled a bundle of papers out from under her shirt.

He caught a brief glimpse of defined abdominal muscles beneath taut skin. Fermi started to understand why everyone assumed she was the one to teach Petra the moves she'd employed against the protector.

"Every single one drew something for us." She handed the packet to Peleus, who slid his fingers gingerly across the top, lingering on the string holding them together.

"Did you look at them?" Peleus asked her. "Are the drawings what we expected they'd be?"

Oshana nodded, her thin lips pulled together in a straight line. "They did what I asked. They drew their family's future."

She reached out and pulled the top sheet of paper free from the cord snaked around the bundle. Unfolding it, she sighed and then handed it to Fermi.

"What is this?" he asked.

The sheet was blank.

"It's what one of them gave me," Oshana replied. "I asked him if he just didn't want to do it. He shook his head and told me he did do it. *That's* his future." She stared at the sheet for another moment before pulling it away from Fermi, folding it back up and passing it to Peleus. "The others drew things I think you can use. But it felt wrong not to keep that one in there too."

"It's pretty powerful," Fermi said.

"Yes," she replied. "Look. Do you think listening to Alessia is the way to do things? Come on, Peleus. She handed your sister over to the protectors. Earth knows what the hell they've done to Petra because of Ali."

Peleus sighed. "Let me deal with my feelings about that in my own way. I'll never forget what Alessia did. But I can't let that get in the way of what's most important here."

The door to the library banged open, hitting the wall as it flew inward. Fermi's heart backflipped in his chest. The familiar sound of clunky footsteps moved towards the back of the library, where the trio stood in silence.

Fermi knew the icy fear climbing up his spine was baseless. He'd never been injured or even insulted by one of the guards. They made their rounds at regular intervals and this was probably just another standard check. Yet he couldn't quell the tidal wave inside. Oshana's wide eyes told him she felt as he did. Peleus, however, seemed calm, anchored. He moved slowly to hide the drawings inside the back of his trousers.

The female protector strolled through the stacks, coming into view after only a few steps. She peered sightlessly at the books she wandered past. The human's black button-down shirt was tight, hugging her willowy body and accentuating her breasts.

When the protector reached the end of the row, she finally acknowledged their presence. "This looks cosy," she said.

"Just a little book club," Peleus said, smiling warmly.

"You do remember the new rules about mulling about in groups?" she replied.

"Of course!" Peleus said as though he'd just remembered where he left a missing shoe. "You're absolutely right. But we thought it was all right if we were in a rec space? Doing an activity, you know?"

The protector considered Peleus with narrowed eyes, before looking over both Fermi and Oshana. "I suppose you can't play half of the games in the rec spaces when there's only two of you," the human said. "But I'll need to check on the rules regarding the library." She remained rigid as she spoke, as though unwilling to relax despite her words suggesting otherwise.

"But they caught her," Fermi said, surprised at his own confidence. The human's eyes darted from Peleus to him. "The attacker, I mean. Didn't the governor say the new restrictions would be removed if she was handed over?"

He knew Peleus would realise Fermi was only putting on a performance, but he could feel Oshana's eyes burn into the side of his head. And he completely understood why. He had just spoken about her girlfriend as though she were a deviant. It wasn't entirely untrue though. He inhaled deeply, trying to repel some of the heat radiating from both women.

The protector's face tightened and she straightened her posture. She was still a few centimetres shorter than Fermi, the shortest Outsider among the trio. After a moment of consideration, some of the tension in the human's neck and face disappeared.

"That's true," she said monotonously. "I'll bring it up with my team leader. Until then, just do me a favour. Avoid spending too long in a group of three or more unless it is in a heavily trafficked area."

"Sounds fair," Fermi replied.

The protector scrutinised them once more before turning to leave. After taking a few steps, she stopped and looked back over her shoulder. Fermi's breath caught in the bottom of his throat. Had she noticed the edges of the bundle hiding behind Peleus's back? After a moment of acerbic silence, she faced front again and continued out of the library, the door clicking shut behind her.

"Screw you, Fermi," Oshana said sadly.

"I'm sorry. I just wanted her to get off our backs," he replied. "I know she's important to you, but to others, she's also the terrorist who got Rosen and the overseer killed. I was just using that to get her out of here."

"She's not a bleedin' terrorist. Petra had no intention of hurting anybody. That part was an accident." Oshana's face tightened, as though bracing herself against an unwanted emotion.

Fermi looked at Peleus. He had to remind himself they were talking about Pel's sister. "Just, please, calm down. I think you might have blinders on when it comes to this."

"I'd be happy to show you what a blinder is." She stepped forwards.

Peleus lifted his hands in a protective gesture and stepped between the two of them. "Calm down, both of you. Fermi wasn't trying to hurt anyone, Oshana. My sister paved her own path and suffered the consequences. I think a few words murmured at the back of a library where she can't even hear them are the least of Petra's concerns."

"Fine," Oshana said through tight lips. "I'm only helping you so you can get her out. You get that, right?"

"Yes," Peleus said. "I want her out as well. I want us all out. And I really do appreciate what you're doing. The protectors have been watching me too closely since she was...arrested. You've saved us a lot of trouble."

"I hope you both remember that when they come after us when all of this gets out," Oshana replied, her middle and index finger pointing at them as she spoke. "I'm not doing anything out of the goodness of my heart here, boys. I want her back. I want out of this dungeon. And I will find another way to do it if this doesn't work."

"We get the point," Fermi said. "We'll do our best."

"As will I," she replied. Without another word, she left Fermi and Peleus alone to sort through the images she'd brought with her.

Chapter Twenty-Six

RAFE LINKED HIS arms across his chest and leaned into his hip. "Teach, I don't think we should do this. I was lucky we weren't busted the first time we messed around in these security feeds."

Lydia didn't care. She needed to see Alessia's face. "You didn't seem especially worried about it before. You were a computer cowboy last time, Rafe."

He stared at her intently, his gaze expectant and unwavering. She felt as unmasked as she had standing inside the medical scanner on her first day.

"I'm sorry," she said. "That wasn't fair. I'm just worried." She moved her hand to his shoulder.

His gaze softened, lines in his forehead fading as he patted her hand. "Last time we did this was before Taylor had started properly managin' the place again," Rafe said. "Synth overseer is seriously weird. She asks me to tighten measures in one corner, shut 'em off in another, then change it back the next day. I've got no idea what that crazy woman...robot... whatever. I have no idea what she's up to. She's in and outta Petra's cell a lot though."

"Please Rafe," Lydia said as she returned her hand to her side. "You know Alessia is important. She's supposed to lead her people when they get out of here. Without her, even if they are released, it's just going to happen all over again." She hesitated. "And I...I need to know."

Though standing, he leaned back against the top edge of his desk chair. "I knew she was influential, but she's actually in charge?"

Lydia pulled at her earlobe. Alessia had told her all of this in confidence and it wasn't supposed to be common knowledge. But that was before the seizure. Before the clinic. Things were getting dangerous, and however Lydia might have felt about sharing Alessia's personal information, she needed to push it aside.

"Yeah. She's kind of destined to keep them cohesive, to weigh up options and make wise decisions that promote peace." She met Rafe's eyes. He thought she was crazy. "I know. I know. Destiny. It sounds insane."

"Yep. But I also believe you."

"The others in the O-Zone probably wouldn't say it out loud, but now I think about it, none of them seem to make any major moves without mentioning it to her first." Rafe rubbed at the side of his neck, looking past her as he spoke. "I still think it's too dangerous to go traipsing around in the secured sections of the colony Hive."

"But what about Jez?" It was a low blow, but pleading wasn't working. She needed to make him care.

He raised an eyebrow. "What about Jez? Seems like you've been avoiding her lately. Wouldn't think you're too concerned."

It was true. Since the night she'd found Jez drunk as hell, Lydia had done all she could to prevent a one-on-one conversation.

"She hates herself," Lydia said. "You know she does. She thinks she's some dirty intergalactic secret and she's stuck working in here forever because of whatever makes her body distinct."

Rafe's eyes locked onto hers. They were sadder than she'd ever seen them. "I wouldn't know," he said, his words a precipice leading to a deep chasm of regret.

Lydia realised he and Jez had never actually been together. Not fully. He had no idea what Jez's body was like. Jez obviously loved him, but she'd kept him locked out. It must have been incredibly painful for them. Not just because of the lack of a physical connection, but because neither of them had been secure enough in their attraction to really pull down their walls, to let the other know how vulnerable they were and how much each wanted the other to care about them.

Lydia couldn't imagine how she would have coped if the tension building inside her since arriving had never been satiated. If Alessia had never let her close.

She waited, allowing Rafe a moment to work through whatever he was thinking about. When it seemed he was ready, she continued, "Maybe if public opinion changes, Jez could start to feel more confident about who she is. If we can keep an eye on Ali, make sure she's okay, and she gets out of here when the rest do—"

"How do you know they'll ever be able to go anywhere?" he said.

"I don't know anything for sure. But I'm damn well going to try. The point is, Jez won't be able to live her life properly until she realises the Outsiders, her own people, aren't unloved. Right now, she just sees humans locking them up, keeping them hidden, and pretending they never turned up in the first place. She needs a future where she can see more than that. Alessia is going to show everyone we don't need to be so scared of people different to us."

Within seconds Rafe was waving his hands, navigating the holo-pro in his office the same as he'd done the last time she was there. She kept her back to the door, hoping to avoid another sudden entry that would require Rafe to put his hands all over her. She liked him, of course, and he might even be on his way to becoming the first real friend she'd had in years. But it didn't make the memory of his body pressed against hers any less uncomfortable.

"Oh, come on!" Rafe said, frustrated.

"What is it?" Lydia ran her eyes over the various icons floating in the room, but she had no idea what most of them represented.

"Every time I try to tap into Alessia's feed it redirects me to Petra's. It's as if the system thinks the second iso-cell doesn't exist."

Lydia's heart pumped faster, the rushing blood heated her ears and cheeks. Where was she? They couldn't have executed her. Could they? Every institution on the planet was obsessed with accountability and record-keeping. Surely Rafe would know if people were just being killed. The possibility made her feel sick, like a paddle boat had started navigating its way through her oesophagus.

The room flashed for a moment and then Petra's cell came into view. Dammit. That wasn't what they needed to see!

"Sorry, Lyd. This is all I can get to. I don't know what the jazz is goin' on." He dropped down into a wheeled office chair. It whined under the sudden pressure. "Do you want to see how the kid's doing?"

"May as well," she replied. Her voice came out as barely a whisper. It was impossible to speak properly when her heart hurt so much.

Rafe increased the volume and wheeled himself to the side so she could see the security feed properly. It was live this time—not a recording. The same old woman, the one who'd called herself a caretaker, sat on an unadorned chair. A chessboard sat on a table between herself and the teenager lounging lazily on the single bed. It looked as though they were coming towards the end of a game. Each of them had only a few pieces in play.

"Queenie, can't you let me win one game?" Petra asked as she leaned forwards. She picked up her king and moved it two squares, placing it next to a rook. She then moved the rook to the other side of the king. "I keep trying the moves you've told me to use."

"Perhaps if you stop calling me Queenie," the old woman replied, "I'll help you to win." Her voice was raspy, as though the years had slowly sharpened the inside of her throat.

"You don't tell me a name, lady, I give you one," Petra replied, her chin resting on top of her knees as she hugged herself. She seemed to be concentrating on the game.

"Do you know why you can't win?" Queenie asked, moving forwards to rest her elbows near the chessboard. Her slow movements gave away her age, and yet her posture and broad shoulders suggested an immense underlying strength. Something about her felt familiar.

"No, I don't," Petra said, rolling her eyes. "Avail me of your wisdom, old woman."

"Because, child, you only think about the next two moves. Every game we play, you ignore the larger picture. I was the same in my youth, and like you, I paid for it." She moved her own rook and swallowed Petra's. If the king took the castle now standing next to it, the king would be in the direct line of the attacking queen. The old woman had won. "I lost my king."

Petra studied the board for several moments. Realising she had no way out, she started to reset the pieces. "How long have you been in here?" the teenager asked.

Lydia found herself wanting to know the answer as well. It might give them some idea just how long an Outsider could be locked away, given neither Lydia or Rafe had ever seen this older woman walking around. She had to be some sort of *off-the-books* captive only Sara Taylor knew about. But that sounded crazy.

"Long enough for everyone I knew to have forgotten me."

"You had a family then?" Petra replied. The girl had changed since she'd been in the iso-cell. She seemed more settled somehow. Perhaps she'd accepted there was nothing she could do to control what might happen to her. Lydia wondered if Alessia was, at that same moment, experiencing a similar loss of hope. As sad as that thought made her, it was better than the alternative... Alessia might not be feeling anything at all.

"I did, yes," Queenie said, stretching out an arm to crack her elbow and a few fingers. The sound made Petra visibly wince. "Years ago, I did what I had to do to protect them. A man—a human—promised me all our kind could live in our own self-governed communities if we stayed out of human affairs."

Petra's eyes widened as though she'd just been slapped in the face. It was a combination of panic, awe, and adrenaline. Not for the first time, Lydia felt her own emotions were being matched by the teenager.

"Then I realised he'd lied to us," the old woman continued. Her voice was ethereal, disconnected, as though she were reciting a story she had not lived. "It was too late to stop it. I said I'd command our people to refuse cooperation, to fight back even if it killed them. It was against our nature, but I had no other means of persuasion. The Global Premier just laughed at me. I thought the deal I'd agreed to was the best way to keep everyone safe, but I had no idea just how much of what humanity does is driven by fear."

"Sweet holy fuck," Petra said at last. "Are you Tarpeia? The discerner who brought us to Earth?" She swung her legs over the side of the bed and eyed the old woman, studied her face as though she was seeing it for the first time.

The old woman nodded, her gaze fixed on the chessboard. "He knew I couldn't really bring myself to command violence. And so, we were all brought to these...places. His government wanted my help, though, with an investigation into our genetics. Their scientists had been stunted in their research for so long that they struggled to understand us. My superior intellectual capacity was the only leverage I had, the only thing I could withhold. So, I helped in exchange for him allowing my daughter and her boyfriend to live freely in a natural habitat."

"You did this! You got us stuck in here! The crazy bat bringing my food and cleaning my damned toilet is the same fucking idiot who made a deal with the devil," Petra's voice cracked as she spoke. She struggled to take in enough air between sentences. The teenager pulled her legs back onto the bed.

Lydia wanted to call out. To defend Tarpeia. She'd just done what had to be done. Who knows what the old woman had had to face: a civil war; years frozen in space; months of negotiations with the early UEA government. The media circus when they'd landed and the increasing negativity in the time that followed. It couldn't have been easy to go through all that—to then realise you'd left one dangerous planet only to settle on another.

"You!" Petra was sobbing, as though a tree had taken root in her chest, competing with her lungs for oxygen. "You're the leader of our people? An old woman ambling through the halls of a prison inside a prison?"

Queenie, or rather Tarpeia, shook her head.

"No, I'm not. My role as leader is long over. I'm a keeper of knowledge and nothing more. The time for me to do even that is disappearing, and none of my descendants are here. I need to tell the truth of our history to someone, and you're all I've got. An adolescent who murdered her own people without any idea of what to do afterward. You're not exactly a discerner, but you'll have to do. Though who knows how you will ever get out of here to share any of it." Tarpeia's voice sounded content, as though she'd resigned herself to accepting Petra as some kind of receptacle for knowledge.

Lydia couldn't listen to any more. *There **is** another discerner, Tarpeia! And she's sitting in the next damned iso-cell!*

This was huge. This old woman had all the missing knowledge that made it so difficult for Alessia to pull together the past and the future. Ali always seemed so unsure about her place in the Outsider community, perhaps frightened she could never live up to the women who'd led them in the past.

"Turn it off, Rafe."

He rose slowly, scanning her features. "Are you sure? It's a pretty exciting channel. I wanna see what they talk about next."

"Please, turn it off." She faced the door while he shut down the system and turned the lights back on. "I need you to find Fermi and Peleus. They've got something to pass on. The protectors like to check me when I move from one zone to the other. Please. Can you bring me the package they've got?"

"Why? What are you going to do?"

"Expose this place for what it really is," she said, her voice as determined as her spirit.

Chapter Twenty-Seven

ALESSIA FOCUSED HER thoughts on the rise and fall of her chest as she breathed. The room around her may have been small, but with her eyes closed and her mind clear, she could imagine herself in any number of preferable locations. Often she tried to picture a beach she'd seen in a film once, using her imagination to assign sounds and smells to an environment she'd never experienced in reality. On this occasion, she needed to feel more grounded, and so she connected each breath with a step through the bushland she remembered exploring as a child, taking the unfiltered air into her lungs and feeling the Eucalyptus leaves crunch beneath her bare feet. Having spent countless minutes, perhaps even hours, picturing the tall trees near her childhood home, she allowed herself to return to the physical world. Opening her eyes slowly, Alessia blinked several times, readjusting to the light.

She stood and stretched. Turning in a circle on the spot, Alessia scanned the floor and table of the iso-cell, hoping to find a book, or a pen—anything at all. As expected, the room was as empty as it had been before she'd meditated; it remained undisturbed. So, she knelt on the floor and assumed a child's pose, her shoulders relishing the change of position.

With her forehead resting against the unsympathetic concrete floor, her mind started to wander. She indulged her own worries about Lydia and how she might be doing. The last time Alessia had seen her, Lydia's face had expressed the fear Alessia had felt that night in the cave. The night they'd found her, bleeding and alone, on the unforgiving ground. Hopefully, whatever unspoken feelings had passed between them would help Lydia to understand that, though they were apart, there was a special, impermeable piece of Alessia's heart set aside only for her.

In the clinic, she'd wanted so badly to tell Lydia everything would be okay, that Alessia knew they would drag her away, and not only had she known it but she'd planned it.

Her absence was necessary. Fermi, Peleus, and even Lydia needed to play their roles in what was to come. If Alessia was there, within their reach, they'd continue to look to her, each one paralysed by their own self-doubts. Now she was out of the way, each of them would be able to find their voice.

Outsiders wouldn't be freed by violence or rebellion or even espionage. They'd be freed by a collective voice rising to demand change, as had happened in human history so many times before. The message needed to express their collective indignation, their need for something beyond survival. Lydia was in a position to facilitate the dissemination of that message. And Alessia's friends were destined to find a way to ensure its authenticity, its psychological veracity. No group ever achieved anything that truly mattered without some sense of distributed leadership. What Petra had failed to understand is the genuine integration of Outsiders into the human world would only be possible when hearts were opened, not merely doors.

FERMI'S FOOT TAPPED as the small supply room filled with people. He and Peleus had asked the most influential members of their community to come to the meeting; the people most likely to be heard, to be acknowledged, to be believed. Oshana was there. As was Zandra. She'd cut off most of her lilac-coloured hair, a sign committing herself to long-term mourning. He'd not seen her since the day she'd lost her son. Lost. What an idiotic word. As though Rosen had wandered off down an unfamiliar causeway and might turn up again someday. Fermi couldn't think of a more senseless death than for a youngling to just be in the wrong place at the wrong time.

A few others entered, mostly line managers from the production floors, the kind of people who'd become inherently connected with authority. As much authority as an Outsider could have, anyway. There were twelve of them crammed into the room, standing shoulder-to-shoulder and eyeing one another, puzzled.

"What's this all about?" Jett asked. At about fifty, he was one of the oldest remaining Os in the colony. The closest thing they had to an elder after the virus. *No,* he stopped himself, *it wasn't a virus at all. It was a cull.* For what purpose, he didn't know, but there was no pretending anymore: the humans had selectively chosen to remove parts of their population.

Fermi looked to Peleus, who stood a step behind. His kind eyes soothed Fermi's twittering nerves. Peleus gently patted Fermi's shoulder. "You can do this," the caretaker whispered, smiling softly. "People around here like you. They'll listen."

Fermi nodded and turned his attention back to the group. "Thanks for coming, everybody," he said. Ten pairs of eyes fixed upon him, each person as confused as the next. They'd have no idea what purpose he could have for bringing them together. Even now, aware of just how powerful his knowledge was, doubt still clouded his mind and dried his throat as he attempted to project a confidence he in no way felt.

"It's no secret there have been some rumblings around this place lately. Some of you might have heard the stories Peleus and Alessia..." *And, of course, Petra,* he thought. But he couldn't say her name. Not with Zandra so close by. Fermi cleared his throat before he continued. "That is, the stories they've shared with the young ones, about the surface. What it's like to live in the open air."

Jett and a couple of others shifted uncomfortably. One woman rubbed at her eyebrow absently. So they had heard. It was a good thing. Made it easier.

"We need to discuss what comes next," Fermi said.

"Next?" Jett asked, his broad chest expanding even further as he put his fists against his hips. "Nothing comes next. No one seems to mind those little library story-telling sessions for some reason, but let's not pretend anything will come of it."

Fermi wished Peleus would step in, take over the conversation. He'd do a much better job. But they'd already discussed this. Peleus was too closely connected to Petra. It needed to come from someone else.

He drew in a deep, restorative breath. "But it will. Something *will* come of it. Alessia was ill, that's why she was taken away, but it isn't why she's stayed away."

Jett scoffed, as did the woman standing next to him.

"Go on," Zandra said. "Let's hear him out."

Fermi had to blink back a tear at hearing her speak so assertively, immensely relieved her strength hadn't entirely disappeared after the tragedy she'd faced. He also felt grateful. No one was going to argue with her.

"Thanks," he said, not able to find sufficient words to express his admiration for her. "There are some things I need to explain."

"Like why Alessia went from being treated in the clinic to incarcerated and isolated," Peleus said.

"And how we might be able to work together with two of the humans to change things around here," Fermi added, his tone bolder than before as he recounted everything that had happened since the day Petra stormed into Alessia's room, agitated and impatient. The group listened on in silence, their faces waxen as they started to realise where Fermi was going with all of this, where they might *all* go. To the surface.

"Alessia has always been well respected by us all," Zandra said. "But why should her relationships with a protector and the school teacher concern us? It doesn't sound like enough to bring about any sort of change."

"But it might." Peleus stepped forwards, in line with Fermi. It was a relief to have him there after what felt like such a long explanation. "The teacher has agreed to share her experiences with the rest of the population when she leaves. Which is soon. Very soon."

"Yes." Fermi took hold of Peleus's hand. "We're all important because, you see, we think our community is likely to face some changes soon. We might get to design our own future."

The silence in the room felt thicker than the anxiety wrapped around Fermi's spine as he awaited their reactions. In theory, autonomy seemed ideal. But he of all people knew how hard it was to let go of the idea that things were just fine as they were. The colony restricted their choices, their experiences, but it also brought a demented sense of comfort and safety. A comfort and safety they'd all lose should they even attempt to leave.

"I can only assume—" Zandra said, rubbing the side of her neck and looking at Peleus. "—your sister did what she did as part of some poor attempt to cause damage we could use to force an escape out of here."

Peleus nodded, seemingly lost for words. His eyes looked heavy, weighed down by a guilt that wasn't truly his to carry. Oshana had been quiet the whole time, but now she turned her body away from the group, as though declaring herself unworthy to comment.

"But Alessia has a different plan?" Zandra asked. "One that doesn't involve hurting anyone?"

"Yes," Peleus murmured. He straightened his spine and pulled his shoulders back. "People need time to adjust to the idea of such a big change. Our job is to start preparing everyone. We need to establish a council, a group who can help keep everyone together and organised if big decisions have to be made."

"Right then," Jett said, his arms crossed over his chest. "A peaceful plan is a good plan. One question though."

"Mmhmm?" Fermi replied.

"What makes her, as respected as she may be, so damned special? Sounds like you're assuming Alessia should lead the way to...whatever the hell we're moving towards."

Fermi thought this might happen. He didn't want to betray Alessia's confidence, but their people needed a leader, someone they could let themselves trust. They all saw her courage, her intelligence, and her restraint, yet they needed something more. Something to inspire them.

"Because," he started. "She's a discerner."

Jett's arms fell to his side. Zandra gasped, her hands flying to her mouth. The others remained quiet, shifting their weight uncomfortably or making eye contact with one another, as though searching for answers.

Oshana moved again, facing the group. "What?" the young woman asked. "What's a discerner?"

"She can't be," Zandra said, her tone cautiously non-committal. "There aren't any left."

"She doesn't carry the mark," Jett huffed.

"Come on." Oshana sounded exasperated. "Someone explain what the hell is going on."

"It's true," Fermi said, trying to sound as confident as he could. "Tarpeia was her grandmother. Her mother, Rey, was a young woman when we first arrived. Their family line lives so bloody long, Alessia is only two generations from the last known leader of the Outsiders."

"Then why is her hair so light?" Zandra asked. Her tone was contemplative, as though she were willing to believe what she'd heard, but needed proof. Fermi understood that feeling. Very well.

"She has been covering it up," he replied. "Ali doesn't think she has a right to enforce some sort of old-fashioned expectation of power upon everyone. She kept it quiet. But the mark is there, underneath. She showed me."

"Answer the girl's question," another said. "What's a discerner?"

Fermi rubbed at his neck for a second, a tense knot asserting itself as he prepared to deliver yet another long explanation, knowing that if he couldn't convince them a discerner would make a difference, that she was *ready* to make a difference, then there was nowhere else to go. A handful of people in support of a non-violent campaign to advocate change had next to no chance of instigating transformation. A community, he was fast learning, represented the strongest force there was for making things better, for making people better.

"Here goes," he said, looking at Peleus before turning back to the group. "I'll tell you everything I know."

Chapter Twenty-Eight

LYDIA HAD NEVER felt so completely useless. Just sitting around, waiting for something to happen, made her want to crawl out of her skin. Waiting for Peleus and Fermi to talk to other Outsiders. Waiting for Rafe to work out why they couldn't see the security feed in Alessia's iso-cell. Waiting for it all to implode when someone discovered they were planning to smuggle materials out of the colony.

The whole situation made her feel sick. Though she knew she was merely doing her part, the tool rather than the engineer, she still hoped to do her best to ensure this narrative did not become about her. She, as unfair as it was, had the capacity to be heard, and it was her responsibility to use that capacity to bridge the gap between the Outsiders and those who'd silenced them far too long.

At this rate, her pacing would wear a trench into the floor of her cube.

What would her father do when she stepped in front of the cameras to tell the world that unending detention was slowly suffocating an entire species? Lydia wasn't a Green Hat, or an N-Cer. She was the daughter of the Quadrant Four Governor. She was the 'pretty little thing' that'd had her own Hive channel. Her ex-girlfriend had been paid off to use N-C contact lenses to film her day and night. The ratings were quite good, or so she'd been told. It wasn't the best kind of fame to have, but Lydia would use whatever she had to. If Pearsal tried to censor her, she would have to find a small network that could cut through the noise of modern media.

But would the children's drawings, however heartfelt, and an impassioned plea worded by Fermi's budding group of leaders, be enough? Would anyone up there actually give a shit? The idea that humans could continue to ignore them, even with their words and their faces front and centre, turned her stomach.

Lydia felt a warm spark at the top of her spine. It was gone before she could even reach a hand to the spot. Her vision flashed like a glitchy projection and then returned to normal. What the—

Her N-C. It had been switched on remotely. The scrolling notifications that usually sat in the top left-hand corner of her field of vision weren't there, and she didn't feel she could command a Hive connection, but she was receiving some sort of signal through the implant. It had been so long since she'd used the device that, just for a second, the voice that reached into her mind felt like an invader.

"Ly-dee? Are you there, beautiful girl? Can you hear me?"

Lydia's breath caught in the back of her throat. Was it her? Was she really contacting her after all this time?

"Lydia? You there? J.J., are you sure you've hacked in? She isn't responding."

She needed to think. To breath. To calm the storm rising between her temples.

Lydia had wanted something to happen, anything that could distract her from the absurdity of being so powerless. Now it had.

Pushing down her shock and pain, Lydia managed a weak response. "Mum?"

"Oh, you can hear me!" Her mother sounded as though she were underwater. Whatever means they'd used to push into the colony's virtual defences had left the signal muffled. "It's so good to hear your voice. I half expected you to sound fifty years older. But it's still you, the same wonderful, intelligent woman I remember."

Not quite the same, she thought. "How are you doing this?" Lydia replied, incredulous.

She wished she could think of something else to say to her mother. They hadn't spoken in four years. Helen Barrett had disappeared one day. No voicemail. No text. Nothing. Damon said she was probably dead because her mother hadn't been the sort of person to leave her family and never even bother to tell them she was safe. Deep down, though, she knew her mum didn't have the capacity to die some anonymous, nonchalant death. If Helen Barrett didn't turn out to be immortal, surely the eccentric, old technologist would go out in a blaze of glory.

"J.J., tweak something, would you? My kid sounds like a drowning horse," Helen said. After a few seconds, her mother spoke again, and this time Lydia could hear her more clearly. "Don't worry about all the details, Ly-dee. Let's just say your old mum still has a few tricks left in her. And some help."

"Oh." Dammit. Another rubbish reply. She shook her head. *Get it together*, she told herself. *This isn't the time to let yourself get overwhelmed.*

"Honey, are you okay? You sound—"

"Dead!" Lydia snapped. "I thought you were dead." She didn't mean for it to come out like that, so facetious, but the voice of her mother had thrown her for a loop. The sound was something all at once forgotten and familiar.

Helen gave a sad sigh. "I deserve that," she replied. "I'm sorry. It was horrible. I wish I could have told you what I was doing, but Damon would have found me if I'd contacted you. I had to detach from the Hive, fall off the grid for a while, you know?"

"I had no idea what happened to you," Lydia said into the empty air of her cube. The blockage in her throat was returning. "He said... Damon said you'd probably been taken out by some N-Cer or political crazy who wanted to send him a message."

"Of course, he *would* say that." Though Lydia couldn't see her mother, she could imagine the woman's hands moving to her hips. "It's easier for him to think I've been dead this whole time than to accept I couldn't keep living with a man who was working for the same government I grew to hate."

"Then why not just divorce him? It's a bloody form in the Gov Sector online. It would take you half an hour. You didn't have to become a damned ghost."

"But I did," Helen insisted. "It's what had to happen so I could join the Green Hats. Surely you knew it was me sent you the security card?"

The card. It had let Lydia see Alessia, make sure she was all right. But it was also what got them into even more trouble.

"Yes, I knew it was you," Lydia said, a little defeated. "I always thought the Greenies were just a fringe group, banging on about privacy and corporate control with no one really listening. Why would you go to them?"

Lydia wished she could see her mother's face. She could picture the expressive green eyes that looked so much like her own, as well as the finer details of Helen's pensive face, but she knew the image was out of date. Her mother would have changed, aged. They both would have. It was strange using audio only, like talking to a spectre in a dream.

"Yes, I suppose that's a fair summation of the G'Hats," Helen said. "But that's how all revolutions start, beautiful girl. Things changed. We're funded by MacNay now."

MacNay! The only other corporate group to come even close to Pearsal's level of economic growth. They'd been neck-and-neck for decades, competing to sell cutting-edge technology that still fit within the confines of UEA regulations. But when Pearsal had been given total control over the education chain from teacher training to testing and curriculum development, MacNay had fallen behind. They still had a presence, but they were on the way out. It was around the same time the Green Hats emerged, a subversive group whose core publicised goal was to disrupt and discourage corporate financial involvement in UEA politics. Pearsal was always their main target.

"That's insane, Mum. Why risk the scandal? If anyone finds out about this, MacNay would be snuffed out."

"Perhaps. But they found out Pearsal was doing a hell of a lot more than just managing those Outsider colonies, honey. MacNay is dying slowly, suffocating under contractual monopoly. They decided: why not go out with a bang? They aren't directly involved, but they've boosted our resources.

"We're gonna make the UEA wake up to itself, Ly-dee. You can't be a planetary government enforcing peace and ethical use of technology and then let a snake like Pearsal slither around in your affairs. Our government got lazy. Letting companies run bloody everything a government has a responsibility to oversee."

Helen's voice was ghoulish. She loved a good political rant. She always had. But this wasn't some hypothetical discussion in their family home, or a titillating chat at one of Damon's mixers. This was real. Helen was out there, directly involved in something dangerous.

Gazing at the lifeless room around her, remembering this was all the Outsiders ever got to experience from birth to death, Lydia started to understand why her mother had done what she did. Why she left. Pearsal—with the UEA's fucking blessing!—were programming *everybody*. Human. Outsider. It didn't matter. None of them should be living their life, from start to finish, at the whim of corporate design.

"Do you really think you can drive a wedge between the government and the corporation?"

"Yes," Helen replied. "I really do. Pearsal isn't going anywhere. But we're onto something that might just change the way they do business. Like those old sweatshops that used to exist. When enough people finally spoke out in great enough numbers, they were all shut down."

"But people protesting sweatshops didn't blow things up. They didn't kill people."

"You're talking about the dome at Bilpin, aren't you?" Helen asked, her tone suggesting she'd been prepared to discuss this topic.

"I understand why the Green Hats attacked it, trying to make a point about Pearsal monopoly of power etcetera. But it's all the same things on both sides, in the end. Hurting people for supposedly justifiable reasons."

"Ly-dee. Listen to me. This is important." She could almost picture her mother's fixed stare on the other end of the communication. "We didn't try to destroy your father's beloved pet project."

"What do you mean?" Lydia replied, confused. She'd seen several news reports discussing the attack. All the theories pointed to them and no one else. "But everyone thinks—"

"I know what they think. But we didn't do it. We've never so much as thrown a piece of rotten food. Physical attacks are not part of who we are. And we aren't naïve enough to think that every project Pearsal has a hand in is without merit. That habitat is already half-built; it should be finished so people can actually live in it."

"I don't understand, you're—"

"Darling girl, there's a lot I don't know. I can't explain who carries out attacks like that one, or any of the others that've happened over the last few decades. Whoever it is, though, they're quite happy to keep letting us take the blame. I promise you. We had nothing to do with it."

She believed her. Lydia wasn't entirely sure why, but every instinct in her body told her Helen wasn't lying. Her mother really *had* left her former life behind to try and help people, to hold the UEA responsible for its unethical dealings with Pearsal, the ones that unfortunately undermined the legitimately important projects like Bilpin.

"I'm proud of you, Mum," Lydia said. When no reply came, she wasn't sure if Helen had heard her. "Are you still there?"

"Yes," her mother whispered. "Thank you, beautiful girl. I was so damn scared you'd hate me. I've wanted to get in touch with you every moment for the last few years. But then they would've have had an easy line back to the people I work with." Helen breathed in loudly. "You'll have to tell me everything you've been up to! Though, the benefit of hacking the Hive is that at least I could check on you from afar every now and again. Okay, I'm getting carried away. Let's save the reunion for another time when I can actually wrap my arms around you."

She was right. They might not have much time before online security closed in on them. "So long as a reunion happens, I can live with that," Lydia said. "So, I get the whole corporate monopoly thing. But what have the colonies got to do with anything? Why are you sending me security cards and hacking your way into my head?"

"Breaking into Pearsal and UEA files has been bloody difficult, let me tell you!" Helen replied. "But after I fully committed to the team, that's all I've been working on. Then we finally found a flaw to let us in. Crazy, right? I mean can you believe there's a flaw? It just came out of nowhere six months ago and... Sorry. You know me." Helen laughed.

Lydia had forgotten the way her mother would get sidetracked at least four times when telling a story. She'd missed it. She'd missed *her*.

"But when we got in," her mother continued, "we found some files about Outsiders. Long-term plans."

Lydia's mouth went dry. She fumbled with a glass, and finally managing to hold it still under the water dispenser, took a long gulp.

"They're just exploiting them, aren't they?" Lydia said.

"I'm sorry. I wish I could tell you exactly what was going on, but the files are written in some sort of insane code. I've never seen software like it, but we haven't been able to decipher it all."

"What do you mean?" Lydia didn't know what to think. "You're telling me you found a mysteriously open window into the world's most secure network, which then took you to useless documents you can barely understand. How does this explain your surveillance of these colonies?"

"We have only snippets...but it looks to us like there's a great deal of scientific resources being funnelled into the Pearsal branch that manages the colonies. Much more than what would be needed to build an anthropological profile for the sake of galactic understanding."

Lydia took another large swig from her glass. The water tasted stale, as it always did in the colony. "I'm not going to like where you're going with this, am I?"

"Don't worry, Lydia. I know how much you care about them. There is one thing we could piece together from attached reports that were encrypted with a less complicated code. I have no idea how, but the Outsiders are totally compatible with us. Technically, we're the same species."

Lydia considered the implications of Helen's words. *Technically, we're the same species.* But if Outsiders and humans were the same species, that meant someone like Jez could reproduce. There had been no mention of genetic compatibility when the aliens arrived. It was a pretty big damned fact to leave out of the news reports!

Could the Os be space colonists? An off-shoot of humans who ventured into the unknown? Settlements in space had been growing for over a century, but none so far away as the Outsiders' planet of origin. Besides, the details Alessia had shared with her of Outsider politics suggested their society was well established. The theory just didn't hold water.

"They're human," Lydia said, disbelief colouring her words. Alessia wasn't an alien, then. Not technically. The back of Lydia's neck felt hot as she remembered the warmth of Alessia's hands. The strength of her embrace. The texture of that red and yellow hair as Lydia had stroked her fingers through it. She'd shared something intimate with Alessia. Nothing had ever felt wrong or different about her. It was like Lydia had always known, somehow, despite the differences that existed between humans and so-called Outsiders, they had always been linked.

"Is it possible we've evolved from some common ancestor?" Lydia asked.

"I don't know, Ly-Dee. We don't have any details to explain the connection. All we know is the big men in office have been spending a hell of a lot of money on some research project that's been in operation since the moment they arrived on Earth."

"Genetic engineering is illegal," Lydia said, trying to tame the chaos in her head. She put the cup of water down and brought her index fingers to her lips as she considered the situation. "Well, that's what I think you're alluding to. Anything beyond replacement organs is forbidden. And for good reason. The ethical implications are immeasurable. But I can't think of anything else they could have spent a hundred years researching that they'd consider to be remotely worth the cost."

"Yes, Ly-dee. But think about it, honey. Outsiders live about 10 or 15 years longer than we do. They can tolerate air toxicity levels much higher than we can, and they can adjust their physical sex. Those are some of the traits people were trying to stimulate within human bodies before the Fall of Nations." Helen paused.

Lydia's muscles began to throb from her tense stance and unconscious pacing, and she sat down to relieve the ache. No such relief was possible for her head, which felt explosive. That kind of overwhelming confusion had gripped her more in the last few months than it had in the course of her entire life before arriving in the Q4C.

"Maybe they found it just too tempting to try and unlock the Outsider genome, harness some of that potential for whoever has the money to pay," her mother said. "It's just a theory, though, and you're absolutely right. It'd be highly illegal. But there's enough of a financial trail developing to warrant us trying to get to the bottom of it. I know MacNay are probably more interested in toppling their competitor, but for now, they're a necessary evil if we're going to work out what's going on here. Our bodies haven't really been comfortable with Earth's erratic climate for a while now. But if there's one thing most people agree on, it's no one wants the old days back. The charter on science and ethics is important. They can't be allowed to keep secrets this big. And we know it's big."

Helen's voice crackled for a moment before clearing up again. Their line of communication was dissolving. "You were never really listening to me before, honey, but I've been keeping an eye on you. I was hoping you might want to help us now."

"What do you need from me?" Lydia responded without hesitation. When she'd first arrived, she'd only wanted the chance to be a teacher, to be something other than Damon Barrett's daughter. The Outsiders had provided an opportunity to work in a real classroom beyond the reach of the paparazzi and its relentless recording of her life. After two and a half months working with those beautiful children, after getting closer to Alessia, none of that mattered. Her life wasn't about convenience anymore.

"I still have that security card if that's of any use," Lydia added. Carl was not her favourite person, but at least his lie had convinced them not to search her.

"You kept it? You'll help us then!" Helen replied. Lydia could hear her mother's smile in the tone of her voice. "While we're trying to work out what else is going on and how they're going to treat the Outsiders in all this, I want you to give us some personal insight. It would help to know more about the inner workings of the colony. The general behaviour and attitude of the managers. Is there anything strange about the medical staff? Does anyone seem to disappear? Do they return? Anything at all, really. The tiniest detail could help us work out what the UEA have let Pearsal do down there, or help us know the right things to say should we have a chance to make demands—to negotiate."

Lydia could think of one person who had disappeared. She'd lost Ali before she'd had the chance to work out exactly what it was that existed between them. "How do I get this information to you?" she asked.

More static. "I'll—"

"What? You're breaking up."

"We're losing the gap in the firewalls. I'll send you a message, like the last one. It'll have a sub-directory you can store audio in. It'll automatically upload to us every day until you leave."

"I need to ask, Mum. Alessia. Do you know? Is she all right? I haven't been able to find out what happened when they dragged her out of the clinic."

"She's really special to you, isn't she?" her mother replied. Lydia nodded, though Helen couldn't see her. "I can't tell you exactly where she is, because we don't know. But I do know she's alive."

Lydia's body tingled. It felt as though her skin had been pulled tight for days and was now suddenly released. *Ali's still alive.*

"Stay safe, hon," Helen added.

Then there was silence. Her mother was gone, yet again. At least this time, Lydia knew why.

This could work, Lydia decided. She had one week left before the term of her first contract was up and she had to go home. The drawings from the children would show everyone how miserable the Outsiders were, that being protected is not the same as being free. The Green Hats would expose the government's unhealthy ties to Pearsal and that might just be enough public embarrassment to force them to act.

The Outsiders would be emancipated, and it would be real freedom. Not the shadowy, formless facsimile of it they'd been enforcing for decades.

Chapter Twenty-Nine

LYDIA BARRETT HAD entered the Q4C as a teacher wanting nothing more than to do her job well, to create some distance from her father, and to be able to live at least one small part of her life away from the incessant noise of a world obsessed with technology, yet stunted by law. If genetic manipulation of humankind was illegal, the corporations figured, why not just refine ways to follow and entertain people? Lydia hadn't questioned the endless parade of five-minute celebrities until *she*, the ex who shall not be named, made Lydia one of them. The world had probably forgotten the footage showing Lydia at every mundane, and not-so-mundane, task, but Lydia had been unable to, and this job, this place—the Q4C—was an ideal escape.

She found it hard to remember that version of herself, the one who had arrived three months earlier. The last few days had disappeared in a haze of pensive obsession. She sent reports to the G'Hats, memorised every drawing Alessia's friends had collected, rehearsed what she might say to Ali if she ever saw her again, and analysed every speck of information she could remember that might help her better understand what the UEA and Pearsal might have been up to all this time.

There were many things Lydia couldn't work out about what had happened recently, but one thought kept circling in her mind as she waited for the minutes to tick by. Sara Taylor. As a synthetic being with genuine artificial intelligence and an authentically human physique, her existence violated several laws. Her development flew in the face of social and technological pressures that had broken the old system of nationalism. Taylor represented everything the UEA was supposed to protect Earth's population against: that they—everyone—might one day *lose* their humanity as a result of the relentless obsession to 'improve' humanity.

With the staff changeover about to occur, someone was bound to find a way to sell the story of Taylor's resurrection to the press. Unless

Pearsal was confident they could control the flow of information and it didn't matter that they'd let everyone in the Q4C see her. They could have just changed her face after Sara 1.0 died. Why be so open about what she is?

"Three months up already, huh, Barrett?" Jez slid onto the bench across from her and waved at the synth chef. The moss-coloured humanoid dropped his cleaning rag and came over, a too-wide smile on his face. "Get me a seaweed wrap and a lemonade," Jez told him.

"Yes, of course, Miss Jez. Coming right up." His voice always sounded the same: cheerful. It wasn't normal to appear happy all the time. But then again, he wasn't normal. He wasn't alive. At least, Lydia hoped he wasn't. How awful it would be if he, in fact, had a will of his own lurking beneath the programming. A secret longing to be somewhere else, do something else, but no ability to control his own limbs and his own words to make it happen.

"Three months does go fast," Lydia finally agreed, her hands indicating the two duffle bags at her feet. "It was too quiet in my cube, so I thought I'd wait for the transport in here." She poked at a bowl of porridge with her spoon.

"Well, at least there's food, right?" Jez made a show of looking around the cafeteria. "A bit early for most people to be up."

Jez seemed to be trying, quite genuinely, to be nice. It was refreshing; they'd barely spoken since Jez's drunken episode a few weeks earlier. If Lydia ever came back, she hoped they'd be able to have more conversations this civilised. Odds were she wasn't coming back, though.

The certainty of leaving still hadn't fully hit her. At first, the colony had suffocated her. Everything always smelled and tasted stale. She was totally disconnected from her online life and none of her friends, acquaintances really, had bothered to leave her any messages. Feeling alone and out-of-touch, she had struggled to fit in. Now, the thought of leaving the place made it hard to breathe.

Would the teacher that took over for her look after her kids? Thea needed someone to make her smile. Imogen was just starting to come out of her shell. Jason's cheeky streak was fading.

Then—emphatically—there was Alessia. It had been seven and a half days since Lydia last knew for certain Ali was alive. Her mother's assurances only went so far to alleviate her concerns. And if the head of security wasn't even being let in on her status, then something was off.

Lydia clenched her eyes shut. As soon as she did, her father's apartment flashed in her head and she couldn't fight the subsequent sense of suffocation. She would not be going back. He'd probably expect her to, but it wasn't an option. By signing herself up for three months in a closed environment, she'd earned enough to be financially independent for another three months. She'd find somewhere to live in the meantime, work out the best way to approach the media. The risk was immense. Pearsal, like every other employer, insisted on the signing of a whole host of documents by their staff, and it would be completely within their power to have her financially and socially ruined for breaching confidentiality. It depended on how it all played out though, as sometimes that sort of legal action could be detrimental to a company's public support. Alessia. Damon. Journalists. Outsiders. Pearsal. There were so many things swirling inside Lydia that her head was starting to feel like it housed a hurricane.

"What's wrong, Barrett?" Jez touched Lydia's elbow.

It was the first time she could remember Jez showing an interest in her well-being. Typical. People seemed to find it so much easier to be kind to someone when they knew they wouldn't have to see them again, at least for a while.

"Has Dualla been hassling you again?" Jez said, her facial expression sympathetic. "Geez, that guy needs a good lay. But I can tell him to go and look for it in someone else's pants if you need me to. Though I guess you'll be gone in an hour anyway, huh."

Lydia lifted her head, continuing to poke holes in her half-eaten meal. "No, it's fine really. I haven't actually seen him for a few days."

"A fact I'm sure you're really broken-up about," Jez said, retracting her hand. "Rafe told me Carl was a bit of a dick to you. Wouldn't take no for an answer? He must really be into you. Haven't seen him act like that before."

Lydia studied her spoon, avoiding Jez's face. Thinking about Carl Dualla just made her angry. If he'd minded his own business, she could have seen Alessia in the clinic without it ending in disaster. Then Alessia would be back in the O-Zone, lying in her bed, asleep. Safe.

Instead, her girl was missing. Alessia could be hurt or scared or... Lydia had been over this a thousand times. Not even the G'Hats knew exactly what had become of her.

"I'm all right. Rafe is just looking out for me," Lydia said. "He's a good guy, our Mister Garland."

An adorable half-smile appeared on Jez's face. Lydia remembered just how extraordinarily pretty she had thought Jez was when they first met. That was before Jez's concerns that Lydia's family name somehow made her special became apparent. Before they'd dug their way into a well of half-hearted greetings and awkward exchanges about the weather. The weather! How ridiculous. Neither of them had been outside in months.

The synth stepped up beside their table, presenting Jez with her meal. "There you are," he said.

Jez picked up her glass and then took a sip without replying. Without a command to follow or comment to respond to, the chef turned silently and left.

"He loves you," Lydia said. "You know that, right?" She had intended to stay out of it, to let Rafe and Jez work out their own problems. There was something about goodbyes, though; they brought thoughts such as these to the surface.

Jez's golden eyes flashed, the skin around her mouth tightening as her lips drew together. "Rafe and I like each other, but—"

"No. He *loves* you. And you love him," Lydia asserted. "It's ridiculous for you to stay apart. He belongs with you."

"Nothing in this world belongs to me," Jez replied, her gaze dropping to the table.

Lydia reached out and cupped Jez's chin with her hand, prompting her to make eye contact. The familiarity of the touch seemed to surprise Jez. "The world is full of possibilities," Lydia said. "You are not a bad person just because you're not the same as everyone else. In fact, it's what makes you spectacular. You deserve to be seen. To be happy. To be loved. To love yourself."

Jez's eyelids fluttered. Apparently losing the battle with her emotions, several tears fell down her face. It was the most profound demonstration of emotion Lydia had seen from her colleague. She knew the two of them had just shared something special. Something honest and important. She released Jez from her grasp and leant back.

"Why are you like this, Barrett? I've been a cow to you since you got here. Why do you care what happens to me? To those kids? To...*her?*"

Lydia's heart swelled. Just like Rafe, Jez could have made a report about the time she'd spent with Alessia at any point and had Lydia thrown out on her rear end. No job and yet another temp-goss channel dedicated solely to her. Down here, whenever Lydia thought somebody was out to get her, or even just that someone was a complete jerk, they managed to surprise her.

"I care because that's what being human is," she finally replied. "It's sharing what you've got when you can. Finding a way through all the differences.

"Outsider. Human. Half-Caste. They're all just labels. They don't mean a jazzing thing if you don't want them to. I care what happens to you because the world belongs to all of us, Jez. We all just do what we can with it." As the words spilt out, Lydia realised just how badly she wanted to say them again. To her father. To the media. To the whole damn world.

"You're a little bit insane, aren't ya, Barrett?" Jez smiled before wiping at her cheeks with the back of her hand. "So, you did end up shagging her then!"

Lydia laughed. She couldn't help it, a weight between them had been lifted. "Once," she replied, both happy and devastated at the truth of her answer. She'd hold onto that memory with every inch of her body. It might never happen again.

"Was she..." Jez rolled her hand in the air, working hard to be more polite than usual. "I mean, her body. It could have had any number of variations. Was it—"

"She's exactly who she is supposed to be," Lydia replied, a gentle flutter tickling the bottom of her stomach. "Everything about her was...*is*...beautiful."

"Shit, lady. You've got it bad."

Lydia nodded, chewing her bottom lip. "I suppose I do."

Jez grinned at her and then bit into the wrap. "I'm sure you two will work something out."

"I hope so."

Lydia checked the chron. It wasn't long before the transport would leave for New Sydney, dragging her even farther away from the only place she truly wanted to be. She could have applied for an immediate renewal of her contract. It wasn't unheard of. Buy some time to work out what had happened to Alessia. But regardless of her personal feelings, it was more important to go home, find someone with a channel people actually watched, and make them put her message out there: *the Outsiders are not safe; they are prisoners.*

With any luck, her mother's people would have found the proof they needed to pressure the UEA, or Pearsal—whoever the hell was in charge—into deviating from their plans.

"I better go, Jez. Thanks for the company." Lydia stood up. Flinging one bag over her shoulder and gripping the other in her hand, she made a move for the door.

"Good luck, Barrett," Jez said.

As Lydia passed the synth chef, she couldn't help thinking about Taylor again. Was she tapped into every corner of the world's virtual systems? Could a being with that kind of connectivity and knowledge practically predict the future? More questions with no answers. She took one last look around the cafeteria before heading towards the elevator that would take her to the top level.

Chapter Thirty

LYDIA WAS MET by a calm silence when she stepped out of the elevator. The staff who worked in the various administration offices were probably still asleep in their cubes, or perhaps arriving on the transport in half an hour. She was relieved to have a few moments to herself before her time ran out.

The top level of the H-Zone was the only one to have real windows. The rest were either completely boxed in or decorated with holo-windows that, whilst convincing, presented only a facsimile of the outside world. Despite her trepidation about leaving, Lydia had to admit she was eager to breathe in fresh air, see the sun, and watch tree branches caressing the sky.

She readjusted the duffle bag on her shoulder, pushing it away from the crook of her neck. *Should have bought the one with wheels.*

A calloused hand covered her mouth, and she was pulled back. Lydia's eyes widened and she shrieked. Someone had hold of her from behind. Someone strong. They weren't hurting her, though. Not yet.

She tried to push forwards, but an arm whipped around her stomach like a pincer, holding her in place. She thrashed her head from side to side, hoping whoever had hold of her would lose their grip and she could yell out properly. Her chest heaved as her breaths became increasingly short and rapid as her fear increased and she tried to think of what to do.

"Shhh!" came a voice. Was it a woman? Lydia couldn't be sure, but there was something distinctly feminine about the sound.

Despite her best efforts to resist, Lydia was dragged around a corner, her thrashing movements futile to prevent it. She'd always thought of herself as fairly fit, but whoever had hold of her had the strength of a titan. Unable to break free, she bit her attacker's finger. The iron-rich taste of blood bubbled on the tip of her tongue, but the owner of the hand didn't respond. The pain hadn't affected them. Panic surged through her body on a wave, her limbs growing heavy with the force of it.

When Lydia had been pulled into a narrower hallway, the immense pressure around her stomach and lower ribs eased, though with her mouth covered she couldn't yet regain control of her breathing.

"Now listen," came the voice again. It was definitely a woman, but she spoke in a hoarse whisper, making it difficult to know if she was someone familiar. "I'm going to let go of your mouth, but if you scream, we are both in a lot of jazzing trouble. I won't hurt you. Okay?"

Her heart beat so fast her pulse had almost become a hum. If she agreed and then the woman took her hand away, Lydia could call for help. But where they were on the floor, and the time of day it was…no one would hear her.

"Do we have a deal or not?" The voice was more insistent this time, the arm around Lydia's waist pulling her in closer. "I need to get on that transport, so either we talk, or I'll have to let you take a nap." Warm gusts of air—the attacker's breath—accompanied each word.

Lydia nodded. The body pressed up against her back was tense, as though prepared for a fight. "Uh-huh," Lydia croaked.

Hesitantly, the woman released the hand smothering Lydia's face. The freedom to breathe unhindered felt wonderful. She turned to face her attacker.

"You didn't scream. Thank you," the young woman said, no longer whispering but keeping her volume low. "I've only seen you a couple of times, so I hope you're the right person. You *are* Mistress Lydia, right?"

The stranger wore the uniform of a protector, but it looked two sizes too big. Lydia didn't recognise the brown eyes or pallid skin. Something about her would-be kidnapper seemed off. The protector was young and small, yet strong. Lydia had felt like a mouse in a cat's jaw.

"Who are you?" Lydia asked, rubbing at her neck.

"I'm Petra," she replied.

Holy shit. Petra! Makeup made her skin a few shades darker, but now Lydia looked at her properly, there was no mistaking the fierceness in her face. She wore contacts and a damned convincing wig to complete her disguise.

"But you're meant to be in isolation. What is all this?"

"You are the teacher, then?" Petra unclenched her fists, her face softening as though letting go of the anxiety burrowed into her forehead. "At least something is going right."

"How did you get out of your cell? I don't understand," Lydia said quietly. She rested her back against the wall, looking around for the first time. They were in a short hallway with only three doors. Probably some kind of storage area.

"Just listen. We don't have long until the transport arrives, do we?"

How did she know about the flight out? But then again, where the hell did the bloody disguise come from? Why was Petra alone? Wouldn't she have brought Alessia with her if she'd had a way out?

"Lydia!" Petra had taken hold of her arms. "Come on; snap out of it. I need your help."

A loud *ding* came from around the corner and down the hall. Someone had stepped out of the elevator. It would be so easy to call out, to draw attention to Petra's escape. And why shouldn't she do just that? This kid had caused so much trouble. She'd taken Rosen's life when he still had so much ahead of him. She'd made Alessia doubt herself, doubt her ability to fulfil the destiny she was born for.

"Don't," Petra said in a dulcet tone. "Please."

She couldn't do it. As hard as she tried to justify the notion of calling for help, Lydia knew that Petra had never meant to hurt Rosen. Whatever the teenager's plan had been—and Lydia still wasn't entirely sure—it had everything to do with escape and nothing to do with murder.

"You're right," Lydia said in a hushed voice. "It's due in about twenty minutes. The transport, I mean." She was too involved now. She needed to see it through, to find out what was going on. She owed it to Alessia. To Peleus. To herself. They stood in silence for a moment, waiting for the footfalls of whoever had come off the elevator to fade as they moved in the opposite direction.

"The overseer," Petra said. "It was her."

"Sara Taylor? She let you out?" The muscles in Lydia's throat tightened. Was this a trap to see who Petra ran to for help? Had the teenager just implicated them both? There could be a surveillance camera anywhere. They would never even know.

Petra nodded. "She was acting even weirder than usual, going on about the next move. Then she just stopped, looked at me and said I had a job to do. That I had to find you, Lydia Barrett." Petra sucked in a deep breath. "Then she just up and walked out of the room and left the door open. I stuck my head out. There was no one around. No protectors. Nobody at all. But there was a bag on the floor. It had this in it." She indicated the wig and uniform. "And contact lenses, a glove, a map."

The whole story was insane. The AI who oversaw management of the colony purposely released a prisoner? And not just back into the O-Zone. Taylor was helping the kid get out of the colony, by the look of it. Lydia didn't understand what Taylor could possibly have to gain from facilitating Petra's escape. Did the synth do anything of her own free will, or was this Pearsal's doing? Both possibilities left her doubtful.

Lydia scanned the hallway again as she searched for something in the narrative that made sense. "Why isn't Alessia with you?" She's the discerner. Wouldn't it make sense for her to be the one to get out of there? She wanted Ali there. With her. It was the only decipherable thought in her head.

"Why would Ali be with me?" Petra was genuinely confused, her arms crossing in front of her body. "Isn't she in the O-Zone?"

"No. She got sick and then...well some things happened, and she was arrested. I was told there are only two iso-cells. She had to have been in the one next to you."

"She got sick," Petra said, concerned. "Is she okay?"

"She was the last time I saw her. I would have thought you'd seen her more recently though."

"I did walk past another door, but I didn't even think about checking if anyone was inside."

Lydia wanted to reach out and slap the girl. How could she have not checked the other cell! Lydia brought her palms together and interlaced her fingers, frantic to control the frustration surging through her. Panic. Anxiety. Love? She didn't recognise herself like this, totally at the whim of unruly emotions.

A gravelly voice came over the sound system. "Fifteen minutes until transport arrival. There will be a short disembarkation period. Staff leaving the complex must be on board in no more than twenty-five minutes."

"Where are these cells?" Lydia asked.

Petra's eyes widened. "You want to trade us, don't you? Give her the uniform and get her on the flight."

"Yes," Lydia said. It was all she could manage. She felt sick in the stomach at the thought of it. She was about to force one person to trade her freedom for someone else's. It was the wrong thing to do. Even if Petra had done things that could be considered unforgivable. Regardless, Lydia couldn't just leave with this young woman without at least trying to save Alessia.

"I've screwed up a lot of things," Petra said, looking at the floor and shaking her head. "But I've been given some really important information about our history. About the studies done on Outsider genes and life cycles."

It was just as Lydia's mother suggested. They had been keeping the Os locked up to gather information. To use their genetic potential to improve the human condition.

Lydia wondered what Alessia would do were their positions reversed. Though she didn't understand why, Petra meant something to Ali. Lydia had never said so aloud, but she had been glad when the teenager was locked away. It seemed fitting, after what Petra had done. Even if it was an accident. Yes, Petra was young; she made a mistake, and now she had something that the Os might even need. But did that mean she should be forgiven?

"I think Taylor wants you and me to tell people what I know," Petra added. "But if you want to go back to the iso-cells, want to find Alessia, I won't fight you. I don't have any right to think I know what's best." Her long eyelashes fluttered in fast succession, as though the Outsider were trying to banish an unwanted sight.

"I'm sorry," Lydia said. "I can't help wanting her to be here, instead of you. But you're right. It sounds like there's something bigger going on here. I find myself wanting to trust Taylor, though I've no idea why."

"Thank you," Petra said, her voice sounding sincere.

"But I also can't leave without seeing her, not if you know where she is."

"Let's go."

PETRA GRABBED LYDIA'S wrist and stopped walking. The girl's grip was firm, but it didn't hurt this time.

"There are two people around the next bend, I can hear them," Petra said, her eyes glazing over as she concentrated. "They're headed towards us. What if they realise I'm not a protector?"

They all knew each other. If anyone looked at Petra for more than a second or two, they'd know something wasn't right.

Lydia struggled to arrange her thoughts as she pictured the different parts of the floor. They'd already walked past the empty admin offices.

The two of them were too far away to try and make it to the transport bay, the only area run by nonresidential staff who might not realise Petra didn't belong there.

The voices were closer now and Lydia could hear them too. A man and a woman were chatting. Something about a VR game.

Lydia spun around and scanned the doors. There. Levi's office was used for counselling all the time and might be unlocked. Lydia indicated the door with her chin. She and Petra both rushed forwards.

They couldn't be caught. Not now that she was so close to Alessia.

She held her hand up to the plate. Nothing. It was locked and she didn't have the clearance to open it. Fumbling with her jacket, she searched her pockets for the security card the Green Hats had sent her. She hurried to push it against the wall. It still didn't open.

"Fuck," she whispered.

"It's a shit game," came the male voice. They were in the same hallway now, walking a straight line towards them. "It's not bad with lenses, but on a console mask it's pointless."

Petra tucked her chin in and faced the wall. "Just stand still," she told Lydia.

This wasn't going to work. Lydia knew these two. They'd want to stop and talk to her, to wish her well on her last morning. She tried the card again and gave out a low, frustrated grunt when it still didn't work. She rested her forehead against the door, dreading the moment when the two admin workers would ask them what they were doing. Lydia felt a mechanism inside the door shift, accompanied by a click. It slid open and her breath caught in her chest.

Petra put her hand on Lydia's shoulder, urging her inside. They fell into the room and the door closed behind them.

It was dark and the ventilation had been off for hours, leaving the room unpleasantly hot and stinking of cleaning products. The sound of their heavy breathing filled the space. The two workers' voices were low and muffled as they went by.

"They're gone," Petra said. As if on cue, the door opened again, releasing them.

"It opened," Lydia said as they moved out of Dr Levi's office. "Do you think it was Taylor?"

Petra shrugged. "Come on. We need to go."

Lydia nodded and followed her.

The iso-cells were tucked away in a corner that looked much like the one they'd been in minutes before. Two doors faced one another, with no markings or decoration. They looked like nothing more than broom closets.

Lydia felt as though her ribs were shrinking, closing in on her organs and strangling them. Alessia had been sitting behind one of those doors for over a week, alone, with nothing but her thoughts.

Petra held her hand up, it was darker than her other. "The overseer gave me a strange-looking glove. Let's see if it does whatever you were trying to do with that other door." She held her thumb over the lock to one of the doors. They heard it unlatch, and then it opened.

Alessia looked to Lydia as the door between them retreated into the wall.

Alessia put down a book she'd been reading. Her eyes were bright and kind, as they always were. She smiled at Lydia as though they'd only been apart for a few minutes. "It's you," Ali said.

Lydia had already forgotten how mellifluous the discerner's voice could be. The feeling of suffocation in Lydia's torso started to fade. Before she could speak, Alessia turned her attention to her young friend.

"Petra?" Alessia looked to Lydia's companion.

Petra nodded. "Yes." She seemed nervous to speak.

Alessia stood up. Her hair had almost completely turned red now, irregular strips of white breaking up the sunset hues. She seemed well looked after. Her dark jeans and emerald-coloured T-shirt were surprisingly clean, perhaps new. It was the first time Lydia had seen her in anything other than standard-issue Outsider clothes. Lydia wanted to charge straight at Ali and wrap her arms around her. But it wasn't the time. Not yet. She needed to concentrate. They had ten minutes.

"How did you get these things?" Alessia asked, looking Petra up and down.

"From the overseer," the girl replied.

Alessia nodded once. She grasped her own chin with a thumb and forefinger for a moment, thinking something through. "What else? You have something else to tell me. What is it?"

"Yeah. I have a lot I need to tell you," Petra answered. "But I should start with Tarpeia. She's been alive all this time. I don't know exactly where they were keeping her, but she's the only person I've seen in the iso-cell aside from the overseer."

Lydia let out a quiet sigh. She'd hoped Petra wouldn't mention the presence of Ali's grandmother. She just wanted to have these brief moments with Alessia to herself, to pretend this whole mess didn't exist.

"You've spoken with her?" Alessia asked, her words coated with a film of hope.

How was she so calm? She didn't seem surprised at all. Lydia wondered if it was even possible to surprise Ali.

"She told me some things about what they've been doing here," Petra said. "How they made her help them, 'cos she's so good with science and all. She told me some things about you, too. I know you're related to her."

Alessia nodded and then stepped past Petra, towards Lydia.

"Please. Please come with me." Lydia's voice sounded strange even to herself—reedy and desperate. "We can work together. I won't just have printed messages from the kids then. You can tell everyone what it's like living down here for yourself!"

Alessia put her hand on Lydia's chest, just above the heart line. After holding it there for a moment, she moved it along Lydia's neck before coming to rest on her cheek. "Look at me, *Aurora*."

Lydia wanted to. She wanted to see the quiet strength in Alessia's eyes, be comforted by her calm nature. But she couldn't because she knew how much it would hurt. Lydia closed her eyes and leant her cheek into Ali's hand. Her face grew warmer as heat radiated from the engineer's palm.

"Look at me." Alessia's voice sounded concerned, loving even.

Lydia opened her eyes. "I don't want to leave here without you," she said.

"You know as well as I do that I wouldn't make it five steps down the hall before they found me. This is where we have to show a little trust," Alessia replied, stroking her thumb across Lydia's lower lip. It sent soft tickles of electricity through her spine. "If Tarpeia thought Petra should be entrusted with this information, and Sara has facilitated her escape, then there must be a reason I am supposed to stay here."

Lydia felt a tear run down her face. Alessia brought her lips to the top corner of her mouth where the tear had become stuck, gently kissing it away.

"All will be well," Alessia added. "Go. Take Petra with you. Give her a chance to redeem herself and help bring all of us into the sunshine."

"Ali, I..." Lydia's lips trembled as she tried to speak. "We didn't get enough time," she said. "It barely started and then it was over."

"It's not over," Alessia replied. She slid both of her hands behind Lydia's neck and guided her head upwards.

Lydia had to stretch to match Alessia's height. Their lips met. It was a gentle kiss at first, as though they were scared they might get burned by the intensity of their feeling. Then, they pressed into each other more firmly. Lydia felt as though she couldn't hold on or breathe enough. She didn't want it to end, because when it did, that would be it. That would be the last one.

Petra pulled them back into reality with an, "Ahem."

As Lydia stepped back, she felt the air between them thicken into a barrier. The skin on her face and neck, warm moments earlier, was icy and arid.

"I'll see you again," Lydia said.

Alessia smiled. "Yes. You will," she replied and then turned to Petra. "You two make sure the humans can no longer ignore us. I will find a way back into the community down here and try to prepare people for what lies ahead. We will be free soon. I know it." She looked back at Lydia, loosely taking her hand. "And we will find out what this is between us. I sense it's something not easily broken. But we need to do what's right for everyone—your people as well as mine—before we do what's right for us."

Alessia's words made sense, of course. Lydia's planned media storm would be all the stronger with Petra to help her. She was an Outsider with many years of life ahead of her, exactly the kind of person the public would want to see after the initial shock of Lydia's exposé. And if the Outsiders were to rejoin the world above, they'd have Alessia to help prepare them, to support their sense of community, something they'd need when navigating such a huge transition.

"We'll do our best," Petra said before she stepped past the two of them and into the short corridor. "It's clear out here," the girl said. "Come on. We've only got a few minutes before this place will be teeming with people."

Lydia studied Alessia's perfect face, committing as many details to memory as she could. She lifted Alessia's hand and kissed her palm.

Alessia pulled Lydia forwards, wrapping her arms around her so tightly it was hard to know where one body ended and the next began. When she pulled back, her eyes glistened as tears formed.

"Goodbye," Lydia whispered.

Chapter Thirty-One

"TURN THE BLASTED thing off," Damon said, leaning forwards to rest his elbows on his thighs. He was sick of hearing the same interview repeated. His daughter's voice as she betrayed him, announcing to the world that the colonies were corrupt. His chances of re-election slipped away more every time Lydia appeared in front of a camera and there were too many times for him to count over the last week.

"As you wish," Sara replied. She seemed to look through him as she terminated the video feed. "Have you heard from your daughter, Governor?" she asked.

He shook his head. "Not since about three weeks before she left the colony. I assumed she just wanted some privacy, some independence or some such nonsense. Then...*this*."

"Lydia and her friend certainly caused a stir." Sara stood, moving from behind the desk to perch herself on the front edge of it. He used to love when she sat that way, crossing her ankles and bending her neck ever-so-slightly to one side. "And what a clever use of repetition. *The Outsiders are not protected. They do not have autonomy. They are trapped.* She just kept saying trapped, over and over. It's as though she learned from a politician." A wry smile appeared on her face. She was taunting him. It seemed to be her pastime recently.

"As much as you may enjoy toying with me, Taylor, I have some big concerns. The public eye is on the colonies, especially the Q4C. We need to get this under control. Your company is meant to be managing this place. You're meant to—"

She raised a hand. "Stop, Damon," she said, her dark eyes authoritative. "We've done exactly what needed to be done."

"What do you mean *we*?" he said, standing up. "You are Pearsal property and Pearsal is paid by the UEA government, the government I work for. We fulfil our obligations to provide a haven for refugees, but keep them out of the way in a productive environment where human beings don't have to deal with them. That whole system is doomed if our population thinks the damned aliens are being treated like prisoners."

"Well, yes. That part was unfortunate. Many would have preferred to offer a more welcoming environment. But it was decided years ago the Outsiders needed to experience adversity, tribulation. You can't really code that sort of understanding, and humanity needs a strong cultural sense of resilience if it's to thrive."

"What the hell are you talking about, Taylor?"

"The future, Barrett. I'm talking about the future."

She moved to the side of the room and activated a holo-display in her desk. Swirling colours rose out of a tablet to form a series of moving images, a line of videos. It all looked like old historical footage. Scientists working with chemicals in laboratories. A man playing chess against a robotic arm connected to an ancient computer. A baby growing inside an artificial womb. A humanoid robot advertised as a domestic servant.

"After the Industrial Revolution, human progress moved at the speed of an avalanche." Taylor's face was stoic, like a teacher delivering a lesson presented twenty times before. "It takes a great deal of restraint to slow such a force. To become glacial, to take care and be mindful of the consequences."

"Things had to be slowed down," he replied, pulling on his earlobe. "You know that. If technological advancement kept going the way it was before the Pax, before the Fall of Nations, we were likely to wipe ourselves out. Engineer a disease we couldn't manage, or replace ourselves with machines."

She turned her head to lock eyes with him. His choice of words had been, perhaps, unwise. But no less true. Her existence was dangerous, but while only one fully developed AI lived inside of a mostly organic body like hers, perhaps things could remain stable.

"Of course," Sara said. "The charter, the laws...it all exists for a reason. During those days just before and after the Fall, all extrapolations of humanity's future seemed carcinogenic. There were too many corporations sabotaging each other. Too many companies racing to develop tech. Most of that tech, designed to change humans. Live longer. Screw longer. Without regard for the consequences.

"So, the problem became: how do we improve the human capacity to endure Earth's ever-worsening climate and dwindling population numbers, without scaring everyone with tales of an AI takeover or genetic engineering that leaves us all soulless?"

It was strange listening to a synthetic creation talk to him about souls. She spoke as though she were like him. A human.

"Without intervention, humans on this planet will die," she said in a matter-of-fact tone. "If they don't immigrate to one of the spaceports, they'll die. Not today, not next week, but eventually we will run out of liveable zones and our habitat construction programs will be unable to keep up with the relentless environmental changes. Then, of course, there's the issue of infection. Another epidemic like the Pax and your society is likely to crumble.

"If the ethical laws didn't exist, every company on the planet would have fought for the chance to control the solution. But they would have withheld information from each other. Sabotaged each other. Put the profit before the product. The future should not be a *product*."

On this last point, she was as serious as he'd seen her. She believed every word.

"So...what?" he said. "You speak as though Pearsal isn't driven by the bottom line as much as everyone else. Who do you even work for? What's all this got to do with the Outsiders?"

"Everything!" She waved her arm through the air, as though pointing at the whole world. "Pearsal is, technically, a separate entity to the UEA. When it comes to media activity, production of building materials...there's no real interference. But the Outsider Project is different. That is all government. And Pearsal has just done what it's been told."

"The Outsider Project. Keeping them in the colonies, you mean? This is a sensible arrangement. Our people don't have to worry about the threat of a superior workforce or be concerned about cultural changes, and the refugees get a secure home with a productive purpose. It is ideal for everyone. That's why this whole debacle with Lydia's media storm is so ridiculous."

"You are exhausting!" She tapped her fingers against her desk to highlight her impatience.

"*Excuse me*?" Indignant, he took a step forwards so he stood over her. "Remember who you're talking to, synth."

"Relax, Damon. I haven't forgotten a thing. But I'm sorry to say—well, no. I'm not really sorry—the fact of the matter is you seem to believe you have the right to know all the answers."

He sat back down in the chair. Something about her demeanour bothered him. Though she wasn't smiling, he was sure she was toying with him, much like a cat who'd cornered a mouse.

As though she'd heard his thoughts, Sara pushed on. "The Outsiders are a convenient answer to the big question. How does humanity maintain its presence on this planet without allowing science free reign to destroy that which makes your species special, repeating the mistakes of the past?

"Tarpeia and the Outsiders, that was how. But it was difficult to find a reason to study them, to refine their cultural practices to enhance their compatibility with humans. So, Pearsal engineered the social discord that led to calls for their isolation. Most humans couldn't have cared less about the aliens living in the open at the time, though they were content to let them be dragged off. The protests never happened. People just think they did, because that's what we told them."

It was hot. His collar too tight. The small of his back was sticky with sweat. He felt as though the room were closing in on him, the walls reaching out. "You're telling me these aliens have been completely harmless to society this whole time. Why? Why would we create fear like that?"

"The drastic changes to temperature on Earth don't bother them at all, you know. They're capable of changing sex should a community require it for the sake of procreation. They are, for the most part, pacifists, so they have a natural instinct to nurture and cooperate, so as to balance the human drive to possess and control."

"Manipulating historical documents and media reports on such a large scale is completely illegal." He loosened his tie, a futile attempt to find relief from the discomfort climbing up his neck. "I find it difficult to believe the UEA gave Pearsal a mandate to break their own laws."

"Isn't that what governments have always done? Just look at the twentieth and twenty-first centuries if you require more proof. Transhumanism is a necessity, but it had to be handled carefully."

Damon moved to the bench underneath the images of nature and poured himself a glass of Drummead. Swirling the tea-coloured liquid in the glass for a moment, he bent his neck back and downed the contents in one gulp. She watched him in silence.

"What does all this have to do with transhumanism?" he asked.

"You've seen the hybrid, Jezebel. You know humans can breed with Outsiders. The next step, after gathering more information, was to create a situation in which people would *want* to mate with them. A lot of them."

It was starting to come together. He wasn't sure if it was because he'd somehow always known all of this, or because they'd been talking for so long he'd been beaten into submission.

"You want future humans to be hybrids," he said, his wedding band clinking against the side of his glass as he moved to refill it. "And you expect it'll happen through relationships, without forceful engineering. This is insane."

"Absolutely," she replied, almost gleefully. "It takes a little bit of insanity to create a whole new race. Tarpeia was important. Her intellect is far superior to any human mind on Earth. In fact, a lot of her input made it possible for them to create me. We'd stunted our own science for too long. She helped us better understand the unusual nature of their DNA. Whoever thought of letting that girl, Alessia, live up top was a genius. It gave the old woman intrinsic motivation to support the studies and helped build a future leader who had the capacity to connect with both groups: humans and Os.

"Some mistakes were made," Sara admitted, as though she'd perpetrated them herself. "The Os probably shouldn't have been revealed to the public in the first place, then we wouldn't have needed to round them all up in such an elaborate manner. But we thought they could be easily controlled, but then the Outsiders behaved in ways that didn't fit into the basic profile we'd built. Hence, the decision made by the Global Premier and his team to intern them and attempt to regain control. It had been a common practice to use camps as a way of vetting unwanted people, and so it seemed appropriate. Gave them the chance to see a full life cycle, monitor behaviour, improve some of the genetic lines."

Sara moved to join Barrett on the bench. She put her hand over his, her dark skin soft and oddly realistic. She slid her fingers between his and then pulled the drink away. With her body close, she put her lips to the glass, teasing the rim with her mouth for a moment before taking a sip and handing the glass back to him. He sensed she was holding something back, she seemed to be enjoying the moment far too much, and it was clear to him that she enjoyed knowing things that he did not. Suddenly, he couldn't help but find her new demeanour intriguing and somewhat alluring.

He took a drink himself, if only to mask the need to gulp away his reawakened interest in her. "This whole time this was kept from me," he said. "I'm governing twenty-five percent of this planet."

"Be honest with yourself, Damon. Quadrant Four isn't where the power is. You're a second-rate politician who is getting stale. But since Lydia has done us a huge favour with all this public debate, you get to be part of the club. Q-Four is important now. This will be the first colony to release the Outsiders.

"The beauty of it is you'll all look like heroes. The public are outraged the Outsiders weren't left to lead their own communities as promised. Those kids' drawings... Genius! Excellent way to promote empathy. You know, a couple of centuries ago, those drawings would have garnered some sympathy, but then people would have forgotten about them days later. Each generation, whilst becoming more reliant on technology, has also developed more empathy, more understanding of difference than the generation before.

"They jumped the gun a bit letting them run around free a century ago. But it only took another generation and the population is ready to embrace them with open arms. Open legs too, with any luck. The Green Hats are making it all too easy."

"What have those lunatics got to do with this?" Just hearing the name of that group bothered him. Their nonsense about corruption and technology had seduced his wife away from him.

"Oh, they've been the perfect group to help us legitimise this whole enterprise. They're going to publicly approve of everything that's about to happen. We just plant a few files for them to find, make them think the Outsiders would be stuck down here for years to come...and suddenly there's a bargaining chip. A familiar public voice giving credence to Lydia's claims.

"Right at this very minute, your ex-wife and two other GH reps are negotiating a deal with the Global Premier. They're agreeing to back off some of their campaigning if the Outsiders are supported to integrate into human society within six months. Seems they're even agreeing to support the development of one humanoid AI to help manage the major changes to infrastructure that'll be needed to ensure it all goes smoothly." She blew air out of the side of her mouth dramatically. "Phew! Looks like I'll be sticking around."

"The Green Hats just agreed to support changes that make your existence legal," he said. He needed to hear himself say it out loud because the whole thing was preposterous.

This project—the Outsider Project, as she called it—had manipulated groups and individuals on an unfathomable scale. He'd been nothing more than a pawn. Even his own daughter, who'd become a teacher of all things, had been more important in shaping Earth's future prosperity.

"When your daughter does finally contact you, Damon, please do thank her. She was everything the UEA and Pearsal had hoped for. Her presence knocked down the final row of dominoes. Now we can not only let the Outsiders onto the surface, but they'll be able to integrate into a more forgiving society. People won't see a threat. Or a conspiracy. They won't realise they've been put on a path to genetic improvement. All they'll see is a love story.

"Now, if you don't mind. I have a future world leader to go and talk to. She has a lot of work ahead and I intend to help her on her way."

Epilogue

"ARE YOU OKAY, beautiful girl?" Helen asked as she brushed her hand across the back of Lydia's neck.

"Yes" was the only reply she could manage. The time had come. It was Release Day. The Outsiders were about to be formally integrated into mainstream society. After nearly six months, it was hard to believe it was finally going to happen after the deluge of public discussion and endless questioning that came with political debate.

"Hey, Lydia," Peleus said from behind her. She turned, finding Peleus and Fermi standing a couple of metres away. The two men were clearly the source of much curiosity, with several backstage workers slowing to watch them. Her heart swelled at the sight of them, Peleus in particular, who had been kind to her in the Q4C.

"You're here," she replied as she and her mother stepped closer. "I wasn't sure you would be."

Fermi smiled warmly. "Alessia insisted we be brought out early so we could be here for this. And we all know how hard that woman is to resist."

"Yes," she said, her gaze dropping to the floor as she tried to mask her embarrassment. Alessia had never asked her to do anything, not directly. But Lydia was under no illusion that she'd be able to say no if Alessia ever did request anything of her. Shuffling her feet, Lydia lifted her head again. Fermi was still smiling. He seemed genuinely happy.

"You deserve to be here," Lydia said. "Without you, I'd never have been able to compile those drawings. I imagine you've been told to stay out of sight?"

Peleus nodded. "We can watch through a screen in another room, but then we have to stay hidden in some sort of government hotel until tomorrow."

"Stay safe," Lydia said. She wasn't sure why she'd suggest such a thing. None of them were in any real danger, but they were Alessia's friends more so than her own, and she found it difficult to know how to talk to them without Ali there. Peleus and Fermi made polite goodbyes and then moved away, swallowed by the busy backstage area.

Lydia and her mother watched people take their seats, all of them engaged in conversations that sent a loud and excited hum throughout the imposing hall. The auditorium was filled with journalists, politicians, corporate leaders, and all varieties of citizens with both the inclination and the wealth to secure admission.

It had been years since Lydia had been in Thracia. The capital was full of vestiges of grand human architecture, each building a unique testament to pre-Fall nationalistic cultures. The Thracian Hall, true to the name of the city, had been decorated with superfluous Hellenic columns and marbled sculptures of mythological figures. Lydia remembered the images of centaurs and deities making her feel dwarfed as a child, their indescribable beauty eclipsing any sense of self she'd possessed.

Now, though, peering past the curtain towards the audience, she barely registered the presence of the Hellenic figures. Not when somewhere in that same building, Alessia waited for the moment she'd be officially released. A symbolic gesture which extended to all Outsiders, though only their discerner would actually be present to accept the gift of autonomy. Lydia shook her head. What a ridiculous thought. The *gift* of autonomy? Ought it not be inherent and inalienable? Rather than some sort of prize to be issued by those who believed themselves worthy of such power.

Petra emerged from somewhere within the group of personnel running about the backstage area. Her face was hard, serious, and somewhat sad, the way she always appeared when not appearing in an official capacity as a spokesperson. Petra's contribution to their campaign couldn't be understated; she, unlike Lydia, had truly experienced the infinite monotony of their restricted lives and her words had truly moved a great number of people. "Have you seen her yet?"

"No," Lydia replied, her disappointment renewed. "They've told us no one can speak to her until after this whole thing ends. We'll be on stage together. That's all." Her fingertips tingled at the memory of Alessia's skin, the physical and spiritual connection they'd shared, long severed by necessity.

Petra folded her arms across her chest. "Damn. So, you'll see each other, but in front of every camera your people have."

Lydia knew as much already and didn't appreciate being reminded. After months working with Petra, Helen, and a multitude of Green Hats and media icons, she knew the girl well enough to realise she was just trying to hide her own fear.

"It's all very dramatic, isn't it?" her mother said, breaking the awkward quiet that had descended on their small group. "Typical UEA. They can't just do the right thing for its own sake. It needs to be a bleedin' spectacle."

"Surely the Hats enjoy spectacle just as much." Lydia pulled at her earlobe. Nerves were making her snippy, but she couldn't help herself. "Sorry. I don't even know what I meant by that."

Before Helen could reply, music trumpeted throughout the hall. Those in the audience still standing rushed to their seats, an eerie quiet spreading across the auditorium. As Lydia tried to prepare herself for not only another public appearance, but also for her first glimpse at Alessia in six months, her stomach tied itself in knots.

She was grateful for her mother's presence. The legal amnesty granted to members of the Green Hats had allayed many of Lydia's fears. She'd been so concerned all the GHs would be arrested at the ceremony, she probably wouldn't have come if the amnesty hadn't been granted. The UEA needed Lydia more than she'd realised. Her face had, for better or worse, become an icon inextricably linked to the Outsiders and their plight. She'd become the poster child for them, their palatable human saviour. She was an instrument, and the understanding twisted her stomach, but she focused forwards with the hope that the true heroes would be able to stand in her place in the coming days

"Good to see you all here," said a masculine voice booming through speakers dotted around the inside of the building. Lydia looked to the stage. She recognised the man at the podium as the Premier, Herod Finick. She'd spoken to him through various Hive lines, both in and out of the public eye, but had not met him in person. Her father had only ever spoken of him in passing, usually some sort of grumble about Finick being a 'pretty boy upstart.'

"This day is one to celebrate the values upon which the United Earth Alliance is predicated..." He spouted the same old rhetoric. Duty of care. The right thing to do. Long time coming. She'd heard it so many times recently she could have given his speech herself.

Petra nudged Lydia. "I've been keeping something from you," the girl whispered.

"What do you mean?" Lydia said.

"Tarpeia shared a lot with me, some of it terrifying. And I need to tell Ali everything, but there's one thing I think needs to come from you."

"Why?" Lydia's question was drowned out by a round of applause, but Petra seemed to understand her regardless. The teenager waited a moment for the noise to dissipate.

"Because it's going to destroy her whole concept of who she is, and I realise I don't know the best way to deal with such a huge collective trauma."

"Come on then, tell me!" Lydia started to feel a familiar sense of panic, much like the emotional whirlwind she'd experienced that moment Petra found her on the last day in the colony.

"I don't think it's the right time. You're about to go on stage."

"Too late for that now. You need to say it. You started this."

Petra inhaled deeply, her eyelids closing as she spoke quietly. "We didn't come to this planet on ships," she said. "They made us."

"What?" Lydia's forehead tightened. She felt as though someone had just sprayed ice-cold water into her face.

"Humans. You...*they*...made us. We aren't refugees. We're a science experiment."

Lydia's chest tightened, as though caving in on itself. She tried to speak, but the words were trapped behind the breath that had caught in her throat.

Helen tapped her shoulder. Turning, Lydia realised the premier had his arm outstretched towards her. He must have invited her on stage, but she'd not realised because her thoughts were elsewhere, drowning in confusion.

Smoothing her hands along the top of her pants, she stepped into the spotlight that was waiting for her just beyond the safety of the curtain. She heard her mother whisper "you can do this," as she went. It still felt strange to have Helen back in her life, but such an oddity was nothing compared to trying to process centuries of social and genetic engineering in the time it took her to cross the stage. They made them? Alessia was made in a lab? *Get it together,* she told herself. *The whole world is watching.*

"Thank you for joining us, Miss Barrett."

Lydia sighed as she leaned forwards to accept his half-hearted hug. "It's *Ms* Barrett," she told him, careful to avoid the microphone at his lapel. She surprised herself by bothering to correct him. How had such a trivial thought occurred to her right at that moment, when the world felt ready to implode? Premier Finick patted her back in response. She couldn't be sure if he'd meant the gesture as an apology, or an act of condescension. What was she going to do? Petra wasn't kidding. The knowledge the girl possessed was terrifying. If it was even true. Could she have it wrong? Maybe Tarpeia was senile, driven insane by years of incarceration.

"Please, join me at the podium," Finick said as he turned to face the audience. "You are the one to have reawakened our humanity, to make all of us who had been ignorant for so long come to truly understand the danger inherent in playing puppet master to another race. Would you like to say anything before we continue?"

Lydia looked towards the audience. She could see nothing but dazzling beams emanating from the lighting truss. Her heart raced as she turned her attention to the N-C display only she could see. The first words of her prepared speech blinked, willing her to start speaking. Someone in the audience coughed. She could hear people rifling around as they shifted uneasily in their seats.

She wasn't nervous because of the large audience, nor because the event was being broadcast across an unknowable number of Hive channels. It was all because of Alessia. Somewhere nearby, she was watching her, waiting to emerge. Would she be happy to see Lydia? Would she be angry their emancipation had taken so long? As soon as Lydia finished speaking, there would be no more mystery—no more possibility, only reality. Alessia would arrive and all Lydia's musings would cease. The space between them would be gone, replaced by a piece of knowledge she wished with all her heart that she did not possess. *Damn you, Petra.*

Lydia cleared her throat. "Thank you, Premier. I don't wish to delay this event for long, so I'll be brief."

She bent her knees softly to chase away the stiffness that had crept into them. "All I would like to do is extend my gratitude. A couple of months ago, I came to you, all of you, with a story to share. My friends accepted me into their world and showed me their pain. They allowed me to use my voice to share that with you all in a plea for help. The public could have turned its back, like our grandparents did. You could have all shrugged your shoulders and carried on like before. But you didn't. You chose to add your individual voices to the collective, and thus, we've seen a global chorus rise. Our humanity has been tested, and we can be proud of how we've responded to that test.

"I'm sure you've all heard enough from me now to know integration is important to me. In a few moments, you will all meet someone who is much better equipped than I to speak for the Outsiders, to show you their integrity." Lydia stopped, a sudden dryness climbing up her throat. She took a sip of water from the glass sitting atop the podium. "Alessia is someone I expect all of us will come to know and respect. She was born to lead the refugees to a new future, one where no group needs to be labelled with such a divisive name as *Outsider*. It is with all sincerity I thank you and return the proceedings to our Global Premier so he might bring Alessia out to meet you all."

As Lydia stepped aside, the crowd clapped fervently. She dropped her head and tried to blink away the dull spots impeding her vision, a side effect of looking directly into a powerful light. She'd meant every word of her speech when she wrote it. Now, each syllable seemed like an empty husk, devoid of meaning.

"Wise words," the Premier said. "That is why we are here. To welcome the Outsiders—" He touched his finger to his lips. "You're right, Ms Barrett," he said, looking in the direction of the audience. "That name is no longer appropriate for a group we intend to integrate and celebrate within a diverse society. Extensive study tells us the refugees share more similarities with those native to this planet than differences. And so, we are here to welcome another branch of *humanity* into the world we continue to rebuild on the surface of this planet. There are thousands of people waiting, at this moment, to be escorted from the underground colonies to designated apartments in the cities. Whilst we couldn't invite them all here tonight, we hope they all accept our deepest apologies for the injustices they have faced. We, as a government, will do our best to help them adjust to a new world, one where they may determine their own fates.

"Please, Alessia, won't you come out here and accept this token of humanity's commitment to building a more tolerant society." He reached into the pocket of his jacket and drew out a silver key.

The audience once again clapped, this time more loudly than the last. Lydia scanned the side of the stage frantically, but could not see Alessia.

"Here she is," Finick said.

The night Lydia had spent with Alessia, all those months ago, had sent her heart into such a frenzy of activity she'd thought it would never reach such heights of exhilaration ever again. She'd been wrong.

A hand slid gently over the top of Lydia's shoulder, and her heart beat so loudly she was sure the people in the front row could hear it.

"I'm here," Alessia whispered, leaning towards Lydia's ear but not close enough to where they were touching.

Lydia forced herself to breathe and then she turned around. Alessia was stunning. Her eyes were soft and kind, just as they'd always been, but the engineer's hair was no longer a mix of yellows and reds. It had completely transformed to resemble a fiery sunset. It was as though Alessia had finally become who she was always meant to be. All the fears Lydia had felt moments earlier, all the doubts and the questions, melted away. The only thing that mattered was that Alessia was there, with her. Every other concern belonged to the future, not the present.

"Please, come forwards." Finick's cheerful voice forced Lydia to break her eye contact with Alessia. She'd almost forgotten most of the world was watching them.

Alessia's hand slipped away from her shoulder. Lydia mourned the loss of that physical contact as Alessia stepped forwards to accept the key.

Lydia noted with satisfaction that Finick did not try to shake Alessia's hand. Now she knew what a deeply personal and intimidate connection could be made through the hands of an Outsider—no, they needed a new name—Lydia understood why shaking hands made many of the refugees uncomfortable.

More words were spoken by the Premier as he wrapped his arm around the discerner's shoulders. Lydia heard none of them, for all she could do was stare at Ali and wish it were her own arm instead of his.

After another round of thunderous applause, Alessia leaned nervously towards the podium. Her pale features seemed to glow under the force of the theatre lights, her eyes made brighter. Lydia wanted to step across the stage towards her, to take Ali's hand and steady her as she addressed the entire human population for the first time.

"I will cherish this key," Alessia said, her voice weak and barely audible. She took a moment to straighten her spine and then addressed the group again, her speech stronger as though she'd flicked a switch. "Earth is a beautiful planet with much to offer. But we have much to offer as well. Things may be difficult at first. Thousands of new citizens would test even the best of societies. But I am confident we can work together. I am also confident my people, working with all of you, will bring a new beauty to this world." On the last note, Alessia looked towards Lydia and smiled, before returning her attention to Finick.

Lydia's heart swelled, aching as it pressed against her ribcage. Nothing could keep her and Alessia apart, not anymore. At that moment, Lydia was sure everything would be all right. It had to be. That smile Ali had just given her was the most precious form of validation Lydia could receive. Alessia still cared. She was still the same person she'd always been, and they would face the future together.

Soon enough, the two women were escorted off the stage by Finick. Music started to play as the audience moved towards the party that was about to begin in the ballroom next door. What was a government event without hours of free alcohol and finger food?

Lydia tried not to let her gaze linger too long on Alessia as the three of them joined Helen and Petra. She didn't know if Ali was as frustrated as she was by their complete lack of privacy.

"So," Finick said, looking at Petra. "Here she is. The fiery youth I've seen so much of on the channels."

Petra gave him her best demure smile, but Lydia could see right through it. "Yes, sir. That's me. Teenage angst personified."

"Good to meet you," he replied, with all the gusto of a politician looking to garner a vote. Before the girl could speak again, he turned to Alessia. "This is it then, young lady. I believe you have somewhere to stay, and if you are still adamant you will not join us for the celebration, this is where we part ways. I'm sure we will see each other again soon."

"Yes, Premier Finick. I am grateful your team has put this event together, but I am eager to be with my friends," Alessia replied. She sounded different. Still smart and furtive, and yet, somehow less restrained.

Herod Finick disappeared into a crowd of advisers and security personnel, leaving the four women behind him. Something about the situation didn't feel right. Though their recent work had been more emotionally draining than anything else Lydia had ever experienced, now they were here and the release was happening, she was struck by the thought that it had all been too easy. Something didn't line up. If Petra was right and the alien arrival had been a complete farce, then Finick's administration would only be doing this because they had everything to gain and nothing to lose. They'd yet to find the bottom of this rabbit hole.

Petra was the first to speak after he'd been enveloped by the crowd. "Ali…"

"It's good to see you, my friend," Alessia said. Her voice was soft and low.

Petra exhaled loudly, as though relieved. "I can never make up for what I've done," she said, her eyes cast downwards. "I never meant for Rosen to…" She didn't finish her sentence.

Lydia had managed to repress the memory of Rosen—limp and broken in his mother's arms—to some cavernous pit inside of her, since the day they'd left the Q4C. Now, as she watched Petra, who looked as though she were lost in her own guilt and confusion, Lydia was once again struck with a pain in her chest at the loss of the boy. She'd emotionally severed any connection between her former student and the teenage girl who had accompanied her for months, from one interview to another. With Alessia there, though, the loose threads had been stitched together once more, and for a moment, Lydia hated Petra.

"No," Alessia said, she moved her hand to the side of Petra's arm and squeezed her bicep. "No one can replace a life. But there's no point wasting yours as well."

Lydia felt uneasy. Why was Alessia so calm about what Petra had done?

She considered leaving the two of them to have this discussion in private, but decided that would only highlight the tension further. The moment that Alessia came face-to-face with her former protégé was significant, and yet all she wanted was for it to be over, for everyone to disappear. To be alone with Ali. To finally pull her close.

Petra lifted her chin to lock eyes with Alessia. Her eyes glistened with tears. "You were right, about everything. I didn't listen to you. That stupid device was never going to force the security system to shut down."

"No one can be right about everything, P." Her hand fell away from the girl's arm. "You said you'd seen my grandmother, Tarpeia."

"Yes," Petra replied flatly. "She wanted me to tell you some things."

Alessia looked at Helen and Lydia, who continued to stand in silence. Ali seemed concerned, as though she knew whatever she was about to learn would change everything. The smile that had stretched across Alessia's face on stage seemed a distant memory.

"Would you like us to leave?" Helen's comment mirrored Lydia's thoughts.

"We're all involved in this now," Alessia said. "You are welcome to stay. I'd like you both to be here."

Lydia took a step closer to Alessia and slid her hand around her waist. It was all she could think to do, a way to share whatever strength she had. She kissed Alessia's cheek gently. It was a relief to feel Ali sink into her arm. Was Petra going to tell Alessia what she'd just told Lydia?

Alessia turned her attention back to Petra.

"The first thing your grandmother wanted me to tell you is…that she loves you. She's sorry that she didn't get to teach you, to support you. And," Petra took a moment to steel herself. "Tarpeia was really sick. She died before the release was fully negotiated."

Lydia felt Ali's body shudder, her weight dropping towards the floor. As Lydia reached her other hand around the front of Alessia's body, Helen and Petra rushed forwards to help. The three of them guided her to a nearby chair and Lydia knelt, cupping her hands over the top of Alessia's knees.

"Oh, honey," Lydia found herself saying. She'd never called anybody such a sugared name before, but it had just come out. "I'm so sorry."

"This means—" Alessia rubbed her thumb across the back of Lydia's hand. "—I really am alone now. Tarpeia might have been the only person—the only one *willing* to tell me—what happened to my parents." She looked up, her eyes locking onto Lydia's. "There's nobody left to show me what it means to hold this kind of power, this influence that seems to have fallen to me, one degree at a time."

"You're not alone," Lydia replied. The woman in front of her, distraught and confused, was so much more than some sort of genetically engineered means to an end. Alessia, at that moment, seemed to have inherited the weight of an entire peoples' hopes and tribulations.

The time would come to discuss what Petra had told Lydia, but that time was not now. "Whatever happens," Lydia said. "We are all with you."

Acknowledgements

This being my first novel, I feel like I need to thank the entire universe. I suppose that might be too ambitious.

To everyone who listened to me prattle on about "that book I'm writing:" Thank you! Your polite nods and convincingly enthusiastic questions helped keep me (mostly) sane and somewhat motivated to finish. I'm looking at you, my broomball friends.

I need to thank Emily for letting me whinge at her every time I wanted to throw my laptop through a window and for somehow managing to keep encouraging me over the course of an entire year. As a published author, she basically adopted me, and I'm pretty darn lucky she did.

Many people on Scribophile helped me find the story and the characters underneath the rubble. I do need to single out a few, though. Christina, Juho, G.B., Ono, and Santiago, you did so much more for this book than you could possibly know. A huge thank you to my beta readers, including 'Girl Tilly' (Sorry, Liz, I couldn't help myself), Shan, Phoebe, and Kate. Your feedback was brutal but brilliant.

My editor, Sam, you're my hero. I'll never forget how elated I felt when you sent me that email accepting my submission, or how patient you've been while I've been learning what this whole editing lark is all about. I'm sure you'll always think of me when reading about a character's hair.

This one might seem a bit strange now I'm in my 30s, but I want to shout out to my teachers. I remember being 16 years old and promising Mrs. Fields that, one day, when I finally had a book published, I would acknowledge her for being the first person to teach me to "keep it simple, stupid." I may still like the purple prose a little too much, but I keep my promises! Thank you to Maria, Linda, Lucy, David, Nicole, Silvana, and all the other teachers who looked after me and planted those seeds of confidence that would one day grow into this novel. Your impact on students can't be adequately measured or timed.

Of course, there's my family. Living with me while I stared at walls trying to work out where Lydia and Alessia wanted to go, to have me then randomly yell out "Holy sh*t! That's why it wasn't working!" and making them listen to incomprehensible information dumps must have been somewhat challenging. Kerri, you did a great job pouring more wine.

My daughter Claudia taught me how to stop mid-sentence, wait three weeks, and then come back to it. It's one of those valuable skills I didn't even realise I really needed to develop. My younger daughter, Thea, taught me how to edit a novel next to a hospital bed, and I hope that kid manages to never catch double pneumonia ever again because this mama's heart was feeling pretty heavy during that whole process. My foster son, Matthew, did what teenagers do best—stayed in his room way too often—but he did check in every now and then with a much appreciated, "so what's the book about again?" He's a good kid, and I feel fairly confident we are cultivating a love of sci-fi with him.

Bree. Well. She's a bit all right, that one. Who else could have not only handled the dual worlds I live in but encouraged and celebrated this constant state of distraction? To the only person who knows what the heck I'm talking about when I answer questions with Buffy quotes or lines from *Mean Girls*, I love you and I am eternally grateful for your support. My sun. My moon. My starlit sky.

About the Author

Rebecca Langham lives in the Blue Mountains (Australia) with her partner, children, and a menagerie of pets. A Xenite, a Whovian, and all-round general nerd, she's a lover of science fiction, comic books, and caffeine. When she isn't teaching History to high schoolers or wrangling children, Rebecca enjoys playing broomball and reading.

Email: info@rebeccalangham.com.au

Facebook: www.facebook.com/RLanghamAuthor

Twitter: @rlangham85

Website: www.rebeccalangham.com.au

Other books by this author

"Finding Aurora" within *Once Upon a Rainbow, Volume Two*

Also Available from NineStar Press

Connect with NineStar Press

www.ninestarpress.com

www.facebook.com/ninestarpress

www.facebook.com/groups/NineStarNiche

www.twitter.com/ninestarpress

www.tumblr.com/blog/ninestarpress